DREAMS
SO FLEETING

Sylvia
HALLIDAY

DIVERSIONBOOKS

Also by Sylvia Halliday

My Lady Gloriana
Summer Darkness, Winter Light
Gold as the Morning Sun
The Ring

The French Maiden Series
Marielle
Lysette
Delphine

Diversion Books
A Division of Diversion Publishing Corp.
443 Park Avenue South, Suite 1008
New York, New York 10016
www.DiversionBooks.com

For more information, email info@diversionbooks.com

First Diversion Books edition January 2015.
Print ISBN: 978-1-68230-215-6
eBook ISBN: 978-1-62681-541-4

To my former husband and dearest friend, Sid, who encouraged and supported me, and never once complained when I dragged him to see just one more "old French church"; and to our wonderful children, Doug, Fred, Rog, and Julia, who launched their own futures with such confidence and independence that "Mother" was able to become "Writer."

"…a company of strolling players…rather disreputable, slightly noisy, full of swaggering triumphs and ignominious flights, of kisses and brawls and boastings and jealousies and loves and feuds…all enhanced by dramatic art;…the actor hardly knows if he is acting or not."

Molière, The Comic Mask
by D. B. Wyndham Lewis

Prologue
1670

"'...and the handsome prince lifted the princess to his saddle and carried her away with him to the beautiful château that overlooked the wide river.'"

The little girl smiled in wonder, her blue eyes shining. "Oh, *Maman!* I liked that one the best of all! The prince was so noble and fine. I thought of *Papa* as you told it. Did you not think of *Papa?*"

"I did indeed, my sweet." Ninon closed the book and stood up, smoothing the pale green satin of her skirt. There was no need to summon a servant; her few movements alerted a young girl who stood politely under an elm tree, at some distance from the stone bench upon which Ninon had been sitting. Ninon handed her the book. "*Merci*, Charlotte," she said. "Would you tell Girard I wish a table for supper to be set out here in the garden? It is such a pleasant evening. The children and I should enjoy it for a little longer. God willing, Monsieur my husband is finding the weather in Paris as delightful as it is for us here."

As the maid curtsied and withdrew to the château, Ninon smiled down at the little girl. "Come, Rachel, let us walk down to the fountain where the boys are playing." The child nodded her head, deep red curls bobbing vigorously. Ninon stroked her downy cheek, seeing in the eleven-year-old face the first contours, the first hints of the woman she would become. Hand in hand, they strolled the length of the garden, chatting about the stories they had read together, passing beds of nodding spring tulips and crystal ponds sparkling with brightly colored fish.

The two boys, sleeves rolled up, were deeply engrossed in a game they had devised, setting paper boats on the top tier of the fountain and watching as the flow of the water swept their fragile craft over the rim and into the next brimming basin.

"Ha!" crowed the elder, a lad of about ten. "*My* ships have taken much more buffeting than yours and still are at the top!"

The other boy, perhaps two years younger, thrust out a belligerent chin. "I spit on your boats! You cheated!"

"Arnaud! For shame," cried Ninon. "To speak so to your brother!"

"Well, he *did* cheat, *Maman*. He put his wax seal on his ships—they don't fall as easily as mine."

"Then put a seal on your own ships to give them weight."

The younger boy pouted. "He said only a vicomte may use a seal."

"*Nom de Dieu!* Pierre-Augustin, did you tell your brother such a thing?" Pierre-Augustin blushed guiltily.

"It isn't fair that he should have a title," grumbled Arnaud.

"Hush," Ninon chided. "Your father gave him the title of Vicomte de Bovier on his tenth birthday as an honor. It is his birthright. The eldest son in the family has always held that title. It was your own father's, while *his* father was alive."

"Shall I have a title someday?" asked Arnaud, still sulky, "or must I be only 'Chevalier,' with no proper title or seal?"

"There is no shame in being called 'Chevalier' with your father's honorable name appended. But I think, in time, *Papa* will give you one of his titles—and the lands to go with it. In the meantime 'Vicomte'..." she turned to Pierre-Augustin, frowning, "if you use your title to cheat at your games, or carry your brother with a high hand, I myself shall lay a switch to your lordship's backside that will make your tutor's thrashings seem mild by comparison!"

"*I* shall be a princess someday," piped up Rachel, by way of bragging to her brothers. "A woman is so much more fortunate. She can pick and choose. I shall marry into a fine title, as you did, *Maman*."

Ninon laughed gently. "And love, Rachel? Is there no place for love in your dreams?"

"Oh, *Maman!* I shall love him at once—like the stories. And he will be a handsome prince."

Ninon gathered her children to her. "Come," she said. "I see that supper is prepared. Let's enjoy our good fortune and the beauty of the evening. Never forget, while you are quarreling over titles, that you are God's favored few in this land. There are far too many Frenchmen who would sell a title—if they had it—for a crust of bread. Come along."

They supped quietly on river trout and squab, a fine bouillon, and *pain de rive*, a golden crusty roll baked gently at the edge of the oven. The wine they drank, watered down and sweetened with honey for the children, was from their own vineyards. Filled with peace and contentment, Ninon leaned back in her chair and breathed deeply of the sweet night, watching the first star appear in the sky.

"Do you dream of your lover, madame?" The voice was rich and musical and faintly tinged with mockery.

"*Papa!*" Rachel shrieked in delight, rushing from her chair to embrace the tall man who strode toward them in the twilight.

Ninon stood and turned, feeling her heart catch in her throat, the thrill she always felt at the sight of him. As his wife, she had shared his bed for twelve years, and still she found herself speechless, her heart too overloaded with love for words. She waited until he had greeted the children, then she smiled shyly and held out her hands. He bent and kissed her fingertips, then frowned and kissed them again, his tongue flicking across the soft flesh.

"Hm!" he said, straightening and smacking his lips. "Too much mustard in the fish sauce."

She found her voice at last. "Buffoon!" She laughed. "But I had not expected you for another three days!"

"Alas! Must I return to Versailles? Of course, there was that charming Madame de Grignot, and a sweet comtesse, and…"

"Enough! You may stay." She kissed him primly on the cheek. "But tell me, how did you find the king?"

"Louis is well. And deep in his plans for the improvements at Versailles. I saw the pavilion he is building at Trianon for Madame de Montespan—he calls it a charming little cottage, but I found it a palace." His eyes glittered wickedly. "But then a mistress, at least, is worth the expense!"

"*That* insult will cost you dear, my sweet husband!"

Like a magician performing a trick, he snapped his fingers and rummaged in a pocket of his coat, producing a diamond-and-sapphire brooch. When Ninon would have reached for it, he shook his head, his hungry eyes sweeping her body. "In payment," he said, his mouth twitching, and replaced the brooch. "By the by, while I was in Paris to register the leases on the new property, I took the occasion to see Molière and his latest play. Very amusing."

Ninon smiled. "He is truly a brilliant man, a genius. Next to him, the rest are hacks."

"All of them?" he challenged.

Evading a reply, she asked, "Have you eaten supper?"

"No." He shook his head, his eyes smoldering. "But not now. I have other hungers."

Ninon felt her cheeks turn pink, and cleared her throat nervously, conscious of the children, who were listening intently. "Charlotte," she said to the hovering maid, "take the children to their *apartements*. It is late and they have had a long day." Despite complaints and protests, good-nights were said and the children were bustled off to their rooms. She turned to him, her eyes warm with love. "Welcome home, my husband," she whispered.

He pulled her into his embrace, his mouth crushing hers, his arms tight and possessive about her lissome waist. She slid her arms around his neck and pressed against him, abandoning herself to the sweet warmth that had begun to pulse in her loins. He kissed her until she was breathless, then stepped back and bowed elaborately, his face a mask of propriety. "Madame," he said grandly, "would you care to accompany me to the château for some...negotiations? There is the matter of a brooch, I believe..."

She giggled. "This?" And held up the bauble.

"Pickpocket! Thief!" He lunged, but she was swifter than he. She pocketed the brooch and lifted her skirts, fleeing toward the château. He nearly caught her in the ground-floor vestibule, and again as she sped up the broad marble staircase, but his sheathed sword, banging against his leg as he ran, slowed his progress. As she reached the first floor, he overtook her and swept her into his arms, ignoring her squeals of protest as he carried her to the door of his *apartement*. The servants in the passageway discreetly averted their eyes—it was none of their concern if the master and his lady chose to behave like children!

He kicked open the door with his booted foot and carried her inside, nodding curtly to his *valet de chambre*, who had sprung forward to be of assistance as soon as the door opened. "I shall not need you tonight, Achille," he said, his voice rumbling with dignity, as though he were not carrying a squirming woman in his arms. "Be so good as to open the door to my bedchamber, then close it behind me. And set out a cold supper here in my antechamber before you retire."

"Yes, Monsieur le Comte."

"Oh. And one more thing." There was laughter behind his serious tone. "Dismiss madame's maid. She...has found another for the night!"

Achille nodded and left them alone.

"*Dieu du ciel!*" laughed Ninon, as her husband tossed her unceremoniously on the large bed. "What must they think of us?"

"What *can* they think," he said, dropping down beside her and stroking the delicate line of her chin, "but that I love you very much?" He kissed her gently, then reached up and untied the lace kerchief about her shoulders. "Now...I told Achille I would be your maid, and so I shall!" Strong fingers unhooked her stiffened and boned bodice, and pulled it open to reveal the white silk chemise beneath. He stroked her breasts through the fabric, feeling her nipples harden at his gentle touch. "*Mon Dieu*," he breathed, "why do you women keep your bosoms caged?"

She sat up and shrugged out of the green satin bodice, pulling free the tabs that were tucked into her skirts at the back. "'Tis a sweet cage," she said, "filled with remembrance. Look you. I have had my *busc* carved especially." Her fingers probed the lining of the bodice until she found the open seam, and withdrew the *busc*, the long piece of whalebone, some three inches wide, that ran down the front of the bodice from the low-cut neckline to below the waist. The *busc* was carved, in the current fashion, with flowers and birds; turning it over, Ninon showed him what was written on the other side.

"'Take not the roses from my days...'" he began, reading aloud, then stopped, his eyes warm with love. "You remembered the verse."

She dimpled prettily. "My cruel master would scold me in the old days if I forgot! He was always a tyrant."

He stood up. "Your master has better things to do now," he said, taking her about the waist and swinging her off the bed to stand before him. "Turn around." When she complied, he began to unhook the skirt fastenings at the small of her back. "By all that's holy, 'tis worse than peeling an onion!" He loosed the long trailing overskirt of green, the pale yellow underskirt, and the lace-trimmed petticoat. He untied her padded hip roll and finally reached a plain linen petticoat, tugging impatiently at it so that the drawstring snapped and the fabric fell about her knees.

"Sweet Madonna, what a clumsy maid," she said, stepping away from her skirts to smile wickedly at him. She was clad now only in her full-sleeved chemise, which reached to her thighs, and her shoes and stockings.

"Sit down, wench!" he growled, pushing her onto the bed.

"And insolent besides!"

Ignoring the challenge, he knelt before her where she sat, and removed her high-heeled shoes, then unfastened the ribbon garters at her knees and pulled off her stockings. Anticipating the final assault on her chemise, Ninon untied the ribbons that held the billowing sleeves tightly to her wrists, then gasped in surprise. He had buried his face between her bare thighs, and now his lips moved slowly upward, a tantalizing journey to the quivering core of her. She moaned softly and fell back against the pillows, while his mouth and hands teased and tormented her, and her insides turned to liquid fire.

At last he raised himself and smiled down at her, seeing how she trembled and sighed, how she opened for him in hungry anticipation. "My God," he said. "How I love to love you!" Quickly he tossed aside his sword and shed his garments, then returned to her and ravaged her mouth with his burning kisses, while his hands slid under her chemise to caress her heaving breasts. Remembering his last duty as her *femme de chambre*, he pulled off the chemise over her head; then, aroused beyond endurance by the sight of her pale body lying beneath him, he entered her. She cried aloud in exquisite joy, feeling the silken slide of his hard shaft, stroking slowly and rhythmically until she thought she would go mad with the sensation. Almost imperceptibly his movements quickened until his thrusts were hard and strong, and his hands on her buttocks pressed her ever closer to his pulsing loins. She clung to him, her hips moving with his rhythm, her senses spinning out of control. They climaxed together, a wrenching spasm that left them drained and limp, and gloriously fulfilled.

After a little he stretched and yawned, and rolled lazily out of bed, bending over to kiss Ninon once again before padding, barefoot and naked, into his antechamber to fetch the food and wine that had been left for him. He carried the tray back to the bed and lay, like a contented sybarite, while Ninon stripped bits of cold squab from the bones and fed them to him.

"For such a homecoming," he laughed, "I should journey to Paris more often!"

"No," she said, suddenly serious. "My heart yearns for you too much while you are away. I cannot manage the household, I cannot talk to the children, without thinking of you, seeing you everywhere."

"The children do not suffer, I think. They seem well and happy."

"Yes." She smiled, her eyes misty and faraway, as though she paraded the children before her mind's eye. "Rachel especially brings me joy at this age. I was telling her the old stories today, the *contes* and romances." A soft laugh. "She asked me if dreams come true."

"And what did you tell her?"

"To keep her dreams, for they will nurture and protect her through the years."

He sat up and poured himself another cup of wine. "How strange for you to say that!"

"Why strange?"

He smiled a wry smile, his eyes almost sad. "*Your* dreams did not come true!"

She put a hand to her mouth, her blue eyes filling with tears. "Oh, my dearest love! Here am I, safe in your arms, my heart bursting with joy and tenderness...How can you say such a thing?"

"But..."

"The truth is not that my dreams did not come true. Rather, I clung to the wrong dream for such a very long time. I did not know when I had found my Prince Charming!"

"Ninon," he murmured, "dearest, dearest Ninon..." He took her in his arms and kissed her tenderly, stroking back the copper curls from her forehead.

She sighed, snuggling against his broad chest. "Let Rachel have her dreams. Life will show her the sweetness of reality."

Chapter One

1654

"Ninon!"

Jacques Baugin's harsh voice cut through the spring twilight, routing the startled doves from their perches beneath the thatched eaves of the old inn.

"Ninon! Devil take that lazy girl! By the spires of Reims Cathedral, I'll have the brat's skin when I find her!"

Crouched among the high grasses that covered the hill behind the inn, Ninon Guillemot cursed under her breath. She would have to hurry now. Surely her stepfather would want to know where she had been. Thanks be to *le bon Dieu*, she had had time this morning to gather a small bundle of kindling and put it aside; it would give her a plausible excuse for her disappearance.

Staying low so that she could not be seen from the innyard, she moved toward the crest of the hill and the ruined shack. Something hidden among the tall grasses caught her eye and she nearly cried aloud for joy: a spring dandelion, its one blossom withered, but with three bright leaves, spike-edged and succulent. Carefully, so as not to uproot the plant, she plucked the leaves and wiped them with the corner of her apron, then nibbled daintily at them, savoring each bite as though she were a princess at a banquet. They barely touched the hole in her empty belly, but she smiled in pleasure, knowing them a harbinger of spring and—God willing—of future secret feasts. She removed the seeds from the dandelion flower and strewed them among the grasses, saying a prayer for a speedy harvest as she pressed them into the soft soil.

"Ninon! Where is that slut?"

This time the voice was high and shrill. Blanche, *la Bique*. The Hag, as Ninon called her in her conversations with herself. Her stepfather's wife. Ninon closed her eyes, fighting back the tears, remembering the sweetness of her own mother's voice. No! She would not cry! They would not break her spirit!

"I spit on you, Hag," she whispered, then laughed bitterly. She should be grateful to *la Bique*. Her mother had been scarcely cold in her grave before Baugin had taken that whore Blanche to wed. He was a ruttish man, full of ugly lusts and foul ways, cursing the many months of celibacy he'd endured while Ninon's sweet mother lay dying of the cancer that grew in her body. At least Blanche had kept him busy this last year (to judge by the animal sounds that came from their small chamber off the common room), and he had seemed not to notice or care as Ninon's body grew and developed. Still, she was glad that, at fifteen, her breasts were still small, and that the Hag shrieked with jealousy each time a passing farmer's wife caught Baugin's eye.

She reached the crumbling shack at the top of the hill. "Are you there, my sweet?" she whispered, and was greeted at once by a soft mew. Stepping over the barricade of rotting planks she had placed across the open doorway, she reached down and picked up a small bundle of warm fur. Sitting on the dirt floor, she cuddled the kitten tightly against her shoulder. "See what I have brought you! It was all I could save, my precious." While the kitten purred and snuggled against her neck, she pulled a crust of bread from her apron pocket and broke it into little pieces, dropping the bits into the jagged shard of an old crock she had managed to scavenge as a water dish. When the dry crust had sopped up enough of the water to be soft, she set the little cat before its supper, stroking the animal as it ate hungrily. Several large crumbs had clung to the rough linen of her apron; with shaking fingers she plucked them off and popped them into her mouth, then stopped, shamefaced. The poor creature was as hungry as she was, and at least she could look forward to a thin soup tonight. She ferreted out the last of the crumbs from her apron, carefully adding them to the cat's meal. When the kitten had licked the last corner of the dish, it looked up at her with soft eyes and meowed loudly.

"Hush, my dearest! They must not hear you! He thinks he killed you all. That pig. That villain! Do you know what I shall do someday, my love? I shall put *him* in a sack, and throw him in the stream, and laugh… the way he laughed…" She stopped and took a deep breath, willing away the tears. She must harden her heart. Tears were for weaklings, for cowards. If she was to survive in this evil world, she must be cold and hard, giving back hatred for hatred until she was strong enough to leave, to be revenged for all the pain and grief she had suffered.

A sudden breeze blew through the open doorway, ruffling the kerchief tied about her copper-colored hair, caressing her cheek, tantalizing her nostrils with the sweet odors of new grass and apple blossoms. She stood and went to the door, and watched the swallows take their last dizzying flight into the pink dusk before settling in for the night. She had almost forgotten how beautiful April could be. The château of Bellefleur had always seemed more beautiful in spring, with the blossoms of the fruit trees casting lacy shadows across the old stones.

"*Papa*," she would say, "will you lift me on your shoulders? I want the flowers from the top of the trees. I want the prettiest flowers!"

Laughing, her father would hoist her in his strong arms, tossing her up until she squealed in fear and joy; then he would set her firmly on his shoulders so that she might fill her arms with fragrant blossoms. Afterward, she would sit on his lap. "My little Ninon will always have the prettiest flowers," he would say tenderly, stroking her cheek while she broke off small bunches of the blossoms and twined them in his golden hair. And they would laugh together because he looked like a god of the woods with his crown of flowers: Oberon, king of the forest creatures.

It did not matter to her that her mother did not bear his name or his noble title; of all his children, she was the most beloved. His aristocratic wife, the haughty Madame la Marquise de Bellefleur, chafed at the mistress and the illegitimate daughter who lived in *her* home and supped at *her* table, enjoying the privileges that were *hers* by right and law. It was not uncommon, of course. Unless they were lecherous villains, most noblemen kept their mistresses openly, acknowledged their bastard children—educating and raising them as the equals of their legitimate offspring—and bequeathed lands and sometimes even titles to them. But the marquise could not forgive Ninon and her mother for being first in her husband's affections.

Ninon's father had died when she was twelve. She had never quite understood how the marquise had managed to cheat her and her mother of their inheritance. But her mother had been a humble seamstress on the estate when she had caught the eye of the Marquis de Bellefleur. With her scant education, she was scarcely a match for the widow's lawyers. Ninon and her mother had managed to survive for more than a year in a small village near Reims, eking out a living with needlework; but the uprisings of the nobles against the young King Louis XIV and his Cardinal Mazarin, a movement known as the Fronde, had plunged the region into ferment and war, and the nobility into worsening poverty. There were fewer commissions for the fine embroidery and beadwork at which her mother excelled, and in which she had already begun to instruct Ninon.

Ninon sighed, looking at her ravaged hands, raw and chapped, scratched and callused. She could scarcely hold a needle with *these* hands anymore. Her mother must have known she was dying when she married Baugin. Else why would she have yoked herself to such a coarse man? He had seemed kind enough at first, and the trade from the inn kept them well fed, but he was far beneath Ninon's mother; the poor woman must have thought she was protecting her daughter's future by such a marriage. How could she have known that it was the strength of her will alone that kept his true nature in check?

Ninon closed her eyes and rubbed her hands across her face, wincing as her fingers touched her jaw where he had struck her this morning. "Oh, *Maman*," she moaned softly, "I would that I had died with you."

No! She opened her eyes and shook her head, thrusting out a defiant chin. She would live, and grow strong, in spite of them! She would leave someday soon. If she grew to be beautiful, she would become a great courtesan; if she did not, she would live by her wits. After all, she was not an ignorant peasant, a helpless lump of common clay! *They* could not even read! *She* had copied her first Latin vocabulary at nine, and translated from the Greek at eleven. She smiled wistfully. How she missed her books. Even now, their memory sustained her. On the days when her back stung from the willow switch laid across her bare flesh, or her belly twisted in hungry pain because they had fed her supper to the pigs in punishment for some disobedience or oversight, she had only to remember her books and she was revived. She would recall the legends, the epic tales, conjuring up visions of fierce dragons and serpents; she would picture them gouging out her stepfather's eyes, devouring the Hag down to the last greasy curl on her head.

And often, when despair tugged at her heart, she remembered the *romans* and *lais*, the beautiful stories of courtly love and brave heroes that she had read time and again. She would play them out in her mind, or invent new ones, creating endless variations on the same themes. And always she was the heroine, living imprisoned in a dungeon, or a hostile country, or a desert island. Waiting to be rescued by the noble prince. In the tales she had read, he had always been dark, but she knew with unshakable certainty that *her* prince would be blond. Blond like her father. He would take her away, and they would live happily forevermore.

"Ho! Innkeeper! You! Innkeeper!"

Ninon started at the voice, and craned her neck to see the mounted figure who had just ridden into the innyard below. Sweet Mother of God! Could this be the man, the prince of her dreams, come to save her? He was tall, his long yellow curls spilling out from beneath his broad-brimmed hat. She could not see his face, but she knew he must be handsome. He was clad in a long military coat that reached to his mid-thigh, and full breeches gartered below the knee to accommodate the high boots he wore. His garments were travel-stained and worn, but it was apparent from the broad silk sash about his waist, the diagonal leather baldric slung across one shoulder and cradling a fine rapier, and the gleaming spurs, that he was a man of property and nobility. Ninon's heart leaped in her breast. He *must* be the man who would rescue her!

Ah, *Dieu*. It was a foolish child's dream, and she was a fool to cling to it. She tried to be reasonable, to think of practical reasons for her gladness at his coming—there would be additional food on the table tonight and she would not go to bed hungry for a change—but her foolish heart sang as she hurried to the large oak tree where she had hidden the kindling this morning. By the time she had reached the clearing in front of the inn, he had gone inside and Baugin was leading his horse to the stable. She shifted her armload of kindling, and was about to enter the inn when *la Bique*, her hair flying, came hurtling out of the door.

"Where the devil have you been?" she shrieked at Ninon. "We have a guest!"

For answer, Ninon held up her armload of wood, her mouth tight-clamped in defiance. She seldom spoke to them: they were hardly worth the effort. Besides, she knew how her silence maddened them, as if they guessed the words she spoke only to herself.

"Stupid brat," said the Hag. "Does it take you forever to gather a bit of wood? Are you as useless as your mother was?" She smiled in malicious pleasure at the sudden flash of anger in Ninon's eyes, knowing she had drawn blood. She reached out a coarse hand and savagely twisted Ninon's ear. "You lower those bold eyes, my girl," she hissed, "or I'll take a stick to you! Now go inside and stir up the fire and sweep the hearth. Monsieur will have soup as soon as it is hot. And a roasted pigeon if Baugin will wring its neck for me."

Ninon lowered her defiant gaze and nodded obediently, but her rebel's heart seethed. Mayhap he will wring your neck as well, Hag! she thought, pushing past Blanche to enter the common room and deposit her kindling in the basket next to the stone fireplace. She turned to look at their visitor. He was sitting at the table in the center of the room, his shoulders slumped forward, his strong hands playing absently with the pewter mug of wine that Blanche had given him. He had taken off his large plumed hat and set it on the table before him, and now Ninon could see his face clearly. She had never seen anyone so handsome in all her life. He had a neat mustache and a small pointed beard as golden as the curls on his head, and the indifferent eyes that he flicked in her direction were gray-green and beautiful. And dark with unhappiness. She smiled shyly and fussed self-consciously with the wisps of red curls that leaped clear of her kerchief to cling to her forehead and cheeks. Surely he would find her charming and take her away with him! But he sighed and took a long draft of his wine and turned about to stare morosely out the open door.

I curse you, stranger, she thought, knowing herself a fool and a dreamer. Why should he be any different, any better than any other creature in this godforsaken world? Than any other betraying man? Savagely she threw a large log on the fire and stirred up the coals, then swept the hearth free of the ashes with such vigor that clouds of dust rose up and sifted into the large iron pot of soup that hung on its hook over the center of the fireplace.

For the next hour or so she worked ceaselessly, feeding the swine, plucking the pigeon that Baugin had killed, chopping wood in the innyard, dragging heavy buckets of water from the stream alongside the inn. Her stomach rumbled in protest, for Baugin had decreed that she was not to eat supper until their guest was fed and ushered to his room. The smell of the roasting pigeon nearly drove her mad as she bustled about the room, ladling out more soup for their visitor, fetching another loaf of bread from the *panetière*, the large carved breadbox that the Hag was careful to keep locked during the day. Baugin and his Blanche fussed over the great monsieur, bowing and smirking in oily pleasure as they inquired of his needs, asked his destination, and drew out his name and his pedigree with smiling obsequiousness.

He was a great comte, Philippe de Froissart by name, on his way home to his château near Dijon. He had been fighting the Spaniards in the Netherlands in those intermittent battles that seemed still to be raging, even though the Peace of Westphalia had been signed six years ago, in 1648. Hurrying to fetch another bucket of water, Ninon frowned to herself. If he was a great lord, and had come from the battlefield, why was he alone? No retainers, no lieutenants? And if he was on his way home, why did he seem so filled with despair? She began to regret her earlier anger at him—perhaps he was as tired and unhappy as she.

Even the heroes in the *lais* grew weary of being heroes sometimes. In the morning he would be rested. His heart would reach out to save her. In the morning.

When she returned to the inn with her bucket of water, Blanche and Baugin were leading Monsieur le Comte up the stairs to his bedchamber, bearing a fresh jug of wine and the roasted pigeon, which Froissart had decided to eat in the solitude of his own room. Ninon hurried to the table. The pot of soup had grown quite cold—a thin coating of congealed fat lay on its surface—and there was very little left. The fine gentleman had eaten a great deal of it, and Baugin and his wife had nearly finished the rest, but Ninon gulped it down ravenously, spooning it into her mouth with the large serving spoon, then running her finger around the rim of the pot to get the last few drops. She ate most of the bread they had left for her, saving out a small piece for her kitten's breakfast, then rinsed the bowls and spoons and pot. She filled the pot with fresh water and set it on its hook, but away from the heat of the fire, so that all should be in readiness when Blanche wished to make the morning gruel.

She swept the hearth once more and finished the last of her chores, ignoring the Baugins, who had come downstairs again and were sitting together at the table, whispering to each other. She unrolled her small, straw-filled pallet and laid it on the floor before the fire, kneeling for a moment, hands clasped together, to say her silent prayers. She untied the knot of her kerchief at the nape of her neck and shook her hair free, running her fingers through the dense copper curls. When she kicked off her wooden and leather mules, she noticed that one of the straps had begun to rub against her stocking, making a small hole that would have to be mended. No. Not tonight. She was too weary. Her shoulders ached and her head was throbbing from hunger. Curling up on the straw pallet, she was soon fast asleep.

A sharp kick in the ribs jolted her awake, and she rose to her knees, snarling. Her stepfather was glaring down at her; beside him the Hag grinned in pleasure.

"Pull in your claws, you hellion," growled Baugin, "and listen to me. There is a task I would have you do. The *seigneur* seemed unhappy. I thought to cheer him up." He smiled suddenly, holding up a gold coin in his fingers. "His good cheer has earned me an extra crown. At first he was reluctant, but I told him it was not good for a man to sleep without a wench beside him!"

Ninon jumped to her feet, shaking her head vigorously, fear and anger burning in her blue eyes. "No! No!"

"Go to his lordship!" rasped Baugin. "He craves a woman tonight!"

"No," she whispered, backing away, horror clutching at her. He could not be like other men, her golden hero, filled with lust and animal hunger! She had always known it would happen someday: that a man would look at her and see the budding woman, and violate the purity that was one of the few gifts she had to give. But not him, sweet Madonna! Not him! To be used like a whore by the man her heart still dreamed of as her deliverer…

"No," she said again.

"Dare to defy me, you slut? Do you still hold yourself above me?" Baugin snarled and reached for the sapling switch that rested against the mantel. Instinctively Ninon dropped to the floor, curling herself into a tight ball as the twig whistled in the air and snapped sharply across her shoulder blades. She could feel the sting of the blows through her thin chemise, and she wrapped her arms about her head to protect her face from his anger. Let him kill me, she thought bitterly, then cried aloud as a particularly savage blow caught her on the shoulder.

"Name of God, Baugin," hissed Blanche, "will you draw blood? And still the stubborn fool will tell you nay! Let me speak to her."

"How can your words avail? The bitch only understands a beating!"

The Hag laughed softly. "Watch." She dropped to her knees beside Ninon, tugging at the girl's hair to bring the young face close to her own lined visage. "Listen to me, whore," she whispered. "I am not a fool. I know where you go. Unless you do as you are told, I will lead Baugin to that shack you guard so carefully up on the hill. He will drown your little cat as he drowned all the rest. Do you want that?" Ninon gasped in terror and shook her head. "Then get you to Monsieur le Comte and do all that he asks of you. It is a small price to pay for your little friend, *n'est-ce pas?* You see, my dear," she said to Baugin, as Ninon rose unhappily to her feet. "Sometimes a few gentle words will move the most stubborn of children. Take Ninon to our guest. And question him well in the morning. If he is pleased with the wench, mayhap it is not too soon to begin to let her earn a few extra sous each time we have a well-to-do visitor."

Sick at heart, Ninon allowed her stepfather to pull her up the stairs to the comte's bedchamber. What does it matter? she thought. Perhaps it was always God's will that she should be a harlot. And the comte would be kind to her. He *seemed* kind. Sweet Madonna, let him be kind!

The room was dim when they entered it: one candle on a small table, a second on the mantelpiece. The fire had been allowed to die down;

the night was warm. Besides, Baugin was not about to waste fuel and tallow, even on a noble guest. It was enough that he had not watered the wine—as was his custom—and had scarcely asked for more money than the food and lodging were worth.

Froissart was sprawled in a large armchair next to the table, a mug of wine in his hand. He had removed his spurs and his rapier, his sash, and his coat with its wide lace collar and cuffs. His voluminous shirt was thrown open at the neck, exposing a triangle of tanned flesh, and he spun his plumed hat aimlessly on one finger as he sipped at his wine.

"Well?" he said to Baugin, tossing his hat carelessly across the room to lie beneath the foot of the large bed.

Baugin bowed politely. "Monsieur le Comte. I have brought you the wench. She will please you, I'm sure. But…" he smiled a conspirator's smile and indicated the basket of kindling next to the fireplace, "you must not hesitate to take a stick to her if the lass proves troublesome." He bowed again, tugging politely on the sparse curl at his forehead, and left the room, closing the door softly behind him.

Froissart took another swallow of wine and stood up to look at the girl. He had scarcely paid her any notice all evening. Silent, sullen, grunting her compliance with every command given to her—she had not spoken even once! Now, his eyes slightly unfocused from the effects of the wine, he studied her more carefully. It was difficult to see her clearly in the dim light, but her whole pose, the attitude of her body, seemed defiant and angry—scarcely the willing bed partner he wanted and needed tonight. Damn! Why had he let the landlord talk him into this situation? He hadn't really been that interested in a woman at first. Now, having paid for her, anticipated her, encouraged his sluggish body to spring to life in preparation for her, he saw that the wench stood there like an animal poised for flight, her darting eyes hostile and suspicious.

"Well? What are you waiting for?" he said, annoyed, impatient now.

Ninon took a step backward. She had been prepared to be passive, trusting him to be gentle with her; but seeing him like this, swaying slightly from too much wine, his eyes lustful and almost cruel, made her stomach turn. As he put down his wine and reached for her, she cringed away from him.

"Damn you, girl," he growled, "I want what I paid for!" His hands clamped about her shoulders to pull her to him, but she raised her fists defensively and pushed against his chest, whimpering softly as she felt herself drawn ever more tightly into the circle of his strong arms. His fingers were tight and cruel on her flesh; there was no gentleness, no pity in him. He would take what he wanted, crudely, selfishly, with no thought to her pain or grief. With a desperate cry she tore one arm free from his grasp, and turned to pull away from him; his clutching hand caught at her chemise, ripping it away from her shoulder and back.

"Name of God!" he cursed, seeing the ugly welts on her flesh. He grabbed both her hands in one of his and dragged her, unresisting, to the table. As he lifted the candle and played the light across the scars of beatings, old and new, she hung her head as though she feared he would not think worthy a girl who merited such punishment. "Look at me!" he commanded, holding the candle before her face. Reluctantly she lifted her head. "*Merde!*" he swore. "How old are you?"

A timid whisper. "Fifteen."

"*Mon Dieu!* I wanted a woman! Not a child who had to be beaten into obedience!" He laughed ruefully and released her hands, throwing himself back into the armchair and lifting his wine cup to his lips. "It seems I am fated to be unfortunate in love!" He took a long drink of wine and leaned his head back, closing his eyes wearily. He sighed. "Go away. I shall not need you tonight."

Ninon adjusted her torn chemise so that it covered her shoulders, and watched him with tender eyes, seeing the pain on his face, the handsome mouth that drooped in misery.

Froissart opened his eyes. "What? Not gone yet? I said you may go, child." Ninon shook her head stubbornly. Froissart laughed. "What is it, my silent bird? Do you want to stay?" She nodded. "In my bed?" he said more sharply; then, "I thought not," at the sudden look of panic in her eyes. "Is it that he will beat you if he thinks I sent you away in displeasure?"

She nodded.

Froissart shrugged. "Stay, then. And you might as well be useful. Pour me some more wine and help me off with my boots. If you are quiet…" his eyes glinted mockingly, "I shall tell you the story of my lost love."

Ninon refilled his cup and knelt at his feet, tugging at the high boots, pulling off the decorative lace-edged boot hose that covered his fine silk stockings. As she ministered to him, he rambled on, his words hardly meant for her; the wine had loosened his tongue, and the tale he told was only to ease the pain in his heart.

He had loved his Rosamunde for many years, he said. She had teased and tormented him each time they met, at the Louvre Palace or Fontainebleau, unwilling to surrender to him until they should be wed.

But each time he tried to hasten a betrothal, she demurred. She was too young, it was too soon, she had not tasted all the sweet freedom of maidenhood. But soon, she would tell him. Soon. He had volunteered for the latest campaign against Spain, releasing his frustrated passion in the heat of battle. And then a letter had arrived from her: she was anxious to see him at her château. Like a panting swain he had rushed to her side, leaving his troops, his lieutenants to make their way home without him. He had rushed to her side…to be greeted by her husband.

He had tried to reproach her for her fickleness, but she had pouted angrily. He had not come soon enough to her: her husband had swept her off her feet. He should be pleased for her; it was an advantageous marriage. And besides, she said, she had begun to find him tiresome these last few years.

Froissart held out his mug for Ninon to refill it. His voice was thick now, the words heavy and slurred. "I almost threw her down and raped her on the spot. The lying bitch…scarcely worth my life…" He looked up at Ninon bending over him to hold the mug steady until she had poured in fresh wine, and smiled wryly. "Little bird…silent bird…do you understand? Do you care?" His eyes were beginning to close, but he lifted his finger and ran it along the edge of Ninon's thin face. "Poor little bird. So thin. Do they starve you as well? You must have my supper… there…my supper…for you, little bird…" His head dropped forward and the mug tipped in his hand, spilling the wine on his shirt front before Ninon could catch it.

She pulled the cup from his lax fingers and set it down, then struggled to pull his shirt off over his head while he grunted and mumbled, nearly insensible from the wine. She managed at last to get him to his feet, supporting him with one arm about his bare waist, while he leaned heavily against her and clung to her shoulders. Even as they stumbled together to the bed, she was conscious of the feel of his bare flesh against her. She had never been so close to a man's body before; it was frightening and wonderful.

It was difficult to get him stretched out in the right direction on the large bed; more difficult still to pull the downy coverlet from beneath his body and tuck it around his shoulders, legs, and feet. He had surrendered to the wine, and now clutched the pillow for comfort as he allowed himself to drift off into a drunken sleep. The wretched man, thought Ninon tenderly, brushing a wayward curl from his forehead. That wicked Rosamunde, to break his heart so! He was so beautiful, his face so strong and noble. A man in the full flower of his youth and manhood—she judged him to be somewhere in his mid-twenties—how could Rosamunde have chosen another?

She sighed and roused herself. She could not spend all night watching him sleep! Pouring out a little water from the pitcher into the washbasin, she rinsed the wine from his shirt, scrubbing at the stains until she was satisfied; then she draped the shirt across the back of the armchair and pulled the chair in front of the fire. She threw another log on the fire and poked the embers until she had a cheery blaze going again. By morning the shirt should be dry, though Baugin might scream at the waste of firewood. With loving hands she retrieved his garments scattered about the room, and smoothed them and folded them neatly before laying them across a small bench against the wall. She polished his dusty boots with her petticoat and set them near the bed, that they might be close at hand when he awoke.

She picked up his wine mug and put it on the table, then hesitated, her fingers poised above the half-eaten pigeon. He had offered it to her, but still...Foolish Ninon! She laughed softly. Great heroes were always noble and generous, and maidens never questioned their kindness! Sitting cross-legged on the floor, the dish of food on her lap, she stripped the pigeon bones clean with her teeth, savoring the sweet meat, then licked her fingers for the last morsels of flavor. She even washed it down with a bit of wine (I defy you, Baugin!). Sighing with contentment, she rinsed her fingers in the water she had left in the basin. She blew out the candle on the mantel, and carried the other from the table to the bed, that she might look at him once more as he slept, filling her eyes, her smitten heart, with the sight of him, before snuffing the candle and setting it on the floor. Like a loyal puppy, she curled up at his feet on the bottom of the bed, feeling honored to be near him as he slept. She lifted her skirt so that it covered her arms and shoulders like a cape, and tucked her legs under her linen petticoat, then smiled happily and closed her eyes.

The room was chilly and lit with the first streaks of daylight when Philippe de Froissart awoke. He shivered and sat up, rubbing his bare arms and shoulders, and ran his tongue around his parched lips. He scratched at his neat beard, absently smoothing it with his fingers. Where the devil was his shirt? The wine. He'd spilled his wine on it. That was it. And the little bird...had she stripped it off him? He closed his eyes tightly. It was too hard to think. Damn the teasing bitch Rosamunde! She was scarcely worth getting so drunk for. He opened his eyes again and glanced about the dawn-lit room. There was his shirt, on the chair near the fireplace. Easing out of bed, he made for the chair, stopping at the washstand to slake his thirst from the pitcher of water and splash a few drops on his sleep-stiff face.

The shirt was clean and dry, he noticed as he slipped it over his head and tucked it into the low waistband of his breeches. He was used to such courtesies in his own château, or when he traveled with his own servants, but alone on the road, subject to crude and chancy amenities, it was a pleasant surprise. He shook his head. That strange little bird. Why would anyone want to beat the girl so? Every child was raised by the rod, of course (he himself had had many a sore rump in his boisterous youth), and—it was pleasant to contemplate—had he married Rosamunde, he would probably have lifted her skirts as often to lay his hand across her bare bottom as to make love to her. It was a man's duty to discipline those in his care. But the little bird...she had been beaten savagely, cruelly. And not just that once. It made his blood boil, wondering what kind of animal the innkeeper could be, to treat the girl so.

When he crossed back to the bed to retrieve his boots, he saw her asleep there, curled up on her side, her face hidden by her hair. Gently he sat beside her. She sighed and stirred, turning in her sleep so the curtain of her hair parted to reveal her face. He nearly gasped aloud. By the clear light of morning, with her features relaxed in peaceful slumber, she was achingly beautiful. Her skin was very pale, clear and almost translucent, the bones beneath fragile and delicate. The hair that swirled about her head in tight curls and ringlets was a soft coppery red, almost pink where the frizzled wisps caught the light. Her sooty lashes lay beguilingly on the sweet curve of her cheeks; Philippe found himself wishing he could see what color were her eyes. But it was her mouth that drove him mad. Pouty, full-lipped, deep crimson—it lay like a bruise on the pale blossom of her face, waiting to be soothed, to be tasted, to be ravished. Enchanted, he stroked her parted lips with his fingertip, feeling the warmth of her breath on his hand. She started, and opened her eyes. Blue eyes. Clear and pale. They focused on him in recognition and remembrance and she relaxed, smiling gently so he could see the edge of her white teeth, the pink tip of her tongue. He felt the juices begin to stir within him. What a lovely child! Bending down, he kissed her gently, then deepened his kiss to taste the full sweetness of her honeyed lips. Her mouth, soft and ripe, was not a child's mouth. He kissed her until he had no breath left; then, panting raggedly, he lifted his head to see her gazing up at him, her blue eyes shining in adoration.

"If you want me, I'll not fight against you," she whispered.

"Sweet bird!" he breathed, and gathered her into his embrace, clutching her tightly to his heaving chest while his hands roamed her back and shoulders, and his searching tongue probed her yielding mouth. Impatiently he tugged at her chemise, his burning fingers aching to touch her cool flesh, to feel her stretched out beneath him. He cursed as his hand caressed her naked shoulder and she flinched in pain. The feel of her tormented skin, the long welts under his fingertips, jolted him back to reality. *Mon Dieu!* What was he thinking of? She was just a child! It was Rosamunde he wanted. Rosamunde…who would never be his.

He jumped up from the bed, and paced the room to hide his guilt and shame, breathing deeply while his passions cooled and his throbbing loins returned to a semblance of normalcy. "The day grows apace, child," he growled. "Have you no chores before that villain of an innkeeper decides to thrash you again?"

She sat up and readjusted her chemise, hurt and mystified by his sudden rebuff, by the sharpness in his voice. Without a word she rose from the bed and straightened her skirt and petticoat, then—the humble servant once more—shuffled to the table and picked up the tray with the remains of his supper.

He frowned. "Think you it is six of the clock yet, girl?"

She nodded in answer but said nothing.

Damn! He had not meant to be so abrupt. She must think his anger was on her account. How could she know he was cursing his own lewd appetites that would ravish a sweet and trusting child? "What do they call you, girl?" he said more kindly.

"Ninon."

"Well, Ninon. You were a good *valet de chambre* last night. Will you help me dress this morning? Will you tie my sash for me?"

She smiled in gratitude and put down the tray, bustling about to fetch his clothing, to fold the lace edge of his boot hose over the tops of his high boots, to button his military coat, and, standing on tiptoe, to brush the shoulders free of dust and lint. As she stood before him, head bent, adjusting the loops of the taffeta sash that she had wrapped twice about his waist and tied over one hip, he idly stroked the line of her collar bone, scowling down at the red marks on her pale flesh.

"Why do you stay, child?"

She stepped back and looked at him, her clear eyes and measured words showing an intelligence he had not suspected until now. "Where shall I go, monsieur? Every day, I see them pass on the road, the wanderers who have left their villages, their ruined farms, in search of food. Shall I join their number? I go to bed hungry, true enough. But my bones do not stick out from my flesh, like those of the men and women who pass by. Sometimes Baugin chases them off with an ax handle when they try to steal a pigeon, and sometimes we find them just down the road, their souls flown to God's heaven, their bodies stripped bare of every rag by the other unfortunates who have passed them by. Shall I be one of them?" She sighed and turned away from him. "And then…we are bound together by God's laws and the laws of man, he and I."

"*Mon Dieu!* Is he your father?"

"No. My stepfather."

"And she? Your mother, then?"

Ninon sneered. "Sweet Madonna! *La Bique?* No!" She turned back to him, her eyes suddenly soft. "My mother is dead. But…she *was* his wife."

"And so you stay."

Ninon shrugged. "For now."

"Do you wish to leave?"

"God knows I must! And soon. Else if I stay…" she broke off, the thought unfinished.

"If you stay…?" he urged.

"I shall most likely kill him one day."

Froissart stared, surprised again by the stubborn pride, the sharp intelligence behind those frightened, guarded eyes.

"I have chores," she said. Picking up the tray, she left the room.

By the time he descended the stairs into the common room, she was outside in the bright sunshine, her glorious hair bound into its kerchief, her shoulders curved into their usual posture of servility as she shuffled about in the yard to tend the pigs and fetch the morning's wood. Filled with anger, Froissart watched her for a moment through the open door, then scowled as Baugin hurried toward him, smiling and fawning.

"Good morrow, Monsieur le Comte! One hopes you had a pleasant night. Will you take breakfast now?"

Froissart nodded coldly and seated himself at the table, while Baugin and his wife set before him gruel and sausages and sweetened wine. Well watered, he noted with contempt, adding that fact to the long list of outrages that he had already catalogued against the innkeeper. When Ninon returned to the room, Blanche gave her a sharp command, and accompanied it with a rap to the girl's ear. Ninon glanced quickly at Froissart, her face crimsoning with shame, and fled into the yard. His eyes followed her out the door; then, scarcely able to hold his tongue a moment longer, he turned to Baugin.

The innkeeper smiled, blind to the rage that boiled behind Froissart's frozen countenance. "I see you cannot keep your eyes from the girl this morning, monsieur! She pleased you, then?" He continued smoothly, as Philippe choked on his words, unable to speak, "A pretty little thing, is she not? A trifle stubborn perhaps…but a nice piece of goods to warm a man's bed, eh? I broke her in myself, I did! As good as her mother she was," he laughed, low and ugly, "though not nearly so willing!"

Froissart stared, incredulous. "You took your own wife's daughter?"

Baugin looked hurt, hearing for the first time the note of disapproval in the comte's voice. "What was I to do?" he said, suddenly defensive. "Useless wife…lying in that bed, puking and dying…all those months… no good to a man! And that pretty little brat of hers, prancing about, high and mighty—like she was better than me! Just because she was some marquis's bastard! I didn't grow up in some fancy château, and drink sweet cream and eat strawberries, but my mother and father had a priest to say the words over *them!* Treating me like a common peasant the way she did. The little slut! She should have been grateful I married her mother when the marquis died and his family threw them out. So I took the brat! She wasn't so fancy then, I can tell you, crying and hollering…" He stopped, seeing the look of horror on Froissart's face. "Well," he stammered, "I…I didn't really rape her. I…took pity on her at the last minute, and changed my mind. It was just to teach her a lesson, you understand. And then her mother died, and I haven't touched her since." He was clearly pleased with his own pious restraint.

"And so you content yourself with beating the girl and pandering for her?"

"Only if the price is right, monsieur! There's no point in wasting such a tender morsel on a man who can't pay the price! I wouldn't want her to bring any bastards of her own into the world if I can help it!"

Philippe rose from his chair, his fists tight-clenched, his mouth a hard line. He had not thought such villainy could exist. Small wonder the girl was frightened and suspicious, trapped by circumstances and the misfortune of the times into a life of cruelty and horror. "How much do you want for her?" he rasped.

"What? For the night, monsieur? Again?"

"For all time! To be taken away from here!"

Baugin's face crumpled, his voice a pitiful whine. "For all time? How can that be? We love her as our own flesh!"

Froissart sneered his contempt. "Yes, I know. How much?"

Baugin frowned, thinking about it. The girl was growing into a woman. Sooner or later she'd get herself into trouble with a passing farmer, or run off with one of the inn's guests. Even now she could be carrying the comte's seed. Why not make the most of it, before he lost the girl without a sou of profit? "Thirty crowns," he said boldly.

"Ten!" said Froissart, his eyes burning, and put his hand on his rapier.

Baugin shrugged. Good riddance to the brat.

Ninon was brushing down the comte's horse in the courtyard when he strode out to her, his handsome features still taut with anger. "Gather your things," he growled. "You are to come with me!"

She turned, her blue eyes wide with surprise. "When shall I return here?" she asked.

"Never, by God. Never!"

She gave a cry of joy and put her hands to her mouth, her eyes sparkling with sudden tears. It must be a dream! Her noble hero…and he was taking her away. He was truly taking her away! She giggled and sniffled in turn, wiping at her eyes with the back of her hand.

"Come," he said gently. "I would be quit of this evil place."

"Wait…monsieur…" she murmured, shy and flustered all at once. "I have a kitten…I cannot leave…do you suppose…?"

"If it can endure the ride, bring it along in a sack."

It took only a few moments for her to collect her belongings: a quilted jacket, a tattered shawl, a spare apron. An ivory comb her father had given her, a bit of lace her mother had painstakingly reembroidered. Her kitten, its tiny head poking out of a small sack, fastened securely in her skirt pocket. She sat behind Froissart on the horse, her arms tightly about his waist, and never looked back as the inn disappeared from view.

They rode in silence for most of the morning. Ninon could scarcely drink in every sight, every copse and stream and lush meadow as they passed. The world was newborn to her dazzled eyes, gilded with the aura of freedom, sweetened by the love that filled her heart.

They stopped at length in a leafy glade hard by a small brook. Froissart unpacked a loaf of bread and some dried beef from his saddlebag, taking a portion for himself before handing the rest to Ninon. When he had eaten his fill, he leaned back against a tree and watched while she fed her kitten.

"What is your surname, Ninon?" he asked suddenly, remembering what Baugin had told him of the girl's past.

"Guillemot."

"Your father?"

"No. My mother."

"And who was your father? Baugin said he was a marquis."

"Yes."

"His name…?"

She shook her head. "No, monsieur, if you please. I do not wish to say. He was a good man. I would not have you think ill of him. He loved us very much."

An angry growl. "And did not provide for you?"

Her blue eyes flashed. "He gave us his affection! It was enough."

"*Mon Dieu!* His affection…Pah!"

"Please, Monsieur de Froissart…" She looked as though she would cry, the little bird retreating once again to her nest.

He frowned, suddenly abashed. Who was he to judge a man he had not known? And hurt the girl in the bargain. "Will you call me Philippe?" he asked.

She blushed furiously and cast down her eyes.

He smiled at such innocence. "Will you?" he teased.

"Yes."

"Yes…what?"

"Yes…Philippe."

"Rosamunde could not have said it more sweetly," he said, and watched her blush again. His face darkened with a sudden thought. "Your stepfather…How old were you when he…" He cleared his throat. "He said he tried to rape you. How old were you?"

She looked stricken. "Only just fourteen," she whispered.

He cursed himself for a fool. He had gone too far again. Filled with remorse, he watched her silently, seeing the distant look in her eyes as she cradled the kitten in her lap.

Only just fourteen. It had been the day of her fourteenth birthday. She had tiptoed about the inn all morning. Her mother had had a bad night, weeping in pain, tossing and turning in agony on the bed that her husband had long since ceased to share.

Baugin had begun to drink at dawn. By the time he caught Ninon in the barn, his eyes were glassy from the ale, and his frustrated passion was evident by the bulge of his breeches at his groin. She had struggled against him, kicking and screaming; he had thrown her down to the straw-covered ground and fumbled impatiently with the fastening of his garment. Then he had cried aloud and cursed sharply. Through her tears, Ninon had seen the wet stain spreading on the front of his breeches, his seed spilled prematurely in his anxiety to have the girl, to tame her bold spirit once and for all. Sprawled beneath him, she had begun to laugh hysterically, her fear making her all the more shrill and giddy. Enraged, he had slapped her face again and again.

Then her mother was there, leaning against the doorframe, gasping, her eyes black with horror in their hollow sockets. She had cursed him, called down on his head all the saints. "If you stain my child's virtue," she had croaked, "my phantom will return to haunt you!" Ninon had caught the flash of superstitious fear in Baugin's eyes as she scrambled to her feet and ran to her mother. "Sweet Ninon," her mother had whispered, and crumpled to the ground.

Ninon stirred herself and lifted the kitten in her arms, stroking its soft fur against her cheek. It still echoed in her brain from that terrible morning—the sound of her own heartbroken sobbing. She looked up. Philippe was watching her with pity in his eyes.

"Poor little bird," he murmured, "you need never fear again."

They rode all afternoon, heading south toward Dijon and his château. When Ninon began to droop tiredly, Froissart insisted that she ride sideways before him, that she might lean against his chest and sleep, if she were so minded.

"We shall stop for supper by and by," he said. "Near Troyes. But I fear we shall lose the light ere we arrive. Sleep for now. I shall wake you."

She snuggled against his chest, feeling secure, protected. There was a smell about him, compounded of sweat and leather and masculinity, that was more heady than the sweetest perfume she had ever breathed. She closed her eyes, listening to the rhythm of his heartbeat, feeling her own pulse quicken. She supposed he might want to make love to her tonight. She smiled to herself. Was it only last night that she had been afraid of his touch? And then he had kissed her this morning. Her first kiss, intoxicating, thrilling, his mouth parting her lips, his tantalizing tongue possessing her mouth, invading that warm recess in sweet imitation of the very act of love itself. Whatever he asked of her she would do, without fear. With her whole heart. Sighing softly, she drifted off to sleep, knowing she would love him till the end of her days.

"Come, Ninon. Here we are."

It was dark. By the light of the early-rising moon, Ninon could see that they were before a large gate set into a wall that seemed to run on for some distance in either direction. Philippe dismounted and helped Ninon from the horse. Still groggy, she soothed the kitten, who had begun to mew softly. There was a large bell to one side of the gate. Froissart tugged at it and waited, smiling down at Ninon.

"Are you hungry?"

She nodded. "Indeed, yes."

"They will feed us well. Ah, here is someone!" A light appeared on the other side of the gate, illuminating their faces.

"Monsieur de Froissart! We had not expected you!" A woman's voice, sweet and low.

"Am I not welcome, Sister?" His voice was gently teasing.

The gate swung open. "You are always welcome, Monsieur le Comte. I shall fetch the reverend mother." A slender nun stood before them, holding a torch, her linen wimple bright in the light.

"I have brought a young girl, Sister Solange. Think you there will be food enough for both of us? Or will you do without, to oblige me?"

"*Le bon Dieu* will provide, monsieur." She smiled, and a dimple appeared in her cheek. "Does He not give me patience each time you tease me?"

He laughed. "But only think how it strengthens your nature to deal with such a wicked man as I! If one is exalted by adversity, Sister, then surely you should be the abbess ere long!"

Sister Solange shook her head in mock dismay. The man was hopeless. Her eyes lit on Ninon, drooping beside him. "The poor child looks exhausted. Let me fetch the reverend mother."

As she hurried off to a low building set against the wall, Ninon turned questioning eyes to Froissart. "The reverend mother?"

"She is the abbess here. This is a monastery of the Visitandines, Sisters of the Order of the Visitation. The abbess is my cousin."

There was a stir at the door of the building. Several torches and half a dozen dark-robed figures appeared, moving across the clearing. A large and imposing woman sailed majestically toward them, her hands held out in greeting.

"Philippe! *Cher cousin.* We did not think to see you again this year. After the Netherlands, one would have thought you would be in Paris wooing your Rosamunde once more."

A heavy sigh. "No. I am returning to my château of Marival, and a life of contemplation."

"There is much to tell, I think. I have never known you to forgo your pleasures for contemplation! But who have you brought me?" The abbess cupped Ninon's face in her hand, smiling kindly at her. "Sweet. And very tired and hungry, *n'est-ce pas?* Put your horse in the stable, Philippe. We will talk after this child has been fed and bedded."

In a sleepy mist, Ninon allowed herself to be led by gentle hands to a dining room in the guest quarters, where she sat, head nodding forward, and tried to eat the food put in front of her. From there she was taken to a small cell in the dormitory. Her eyes saw only the narrow bed that beckoned. Her own bed. She had not slept on a bed of her own since her mother died. She curled up on the soft mattress, the kitten snuggled against her breast. She had dreamed of the joy of sleeping with her little cat, but it was a luxury, a freedom, she had not ever thought to enjoy.

And all because of him. Her golden hero. How many days before we reach his château? she thought. And drifted off to sleep.

A gentle hand was shaking her awake. She opened bleary eyes to the sunny morning to find Sister Solange smiling above her.

"Hurry, child. He is leaving."

"What?" Ninon blinked and shook her head. Sweet Madonna! She was scarcely ready to go.

"Monsieur le Comte. He is leaving, and wishes to say good-bye to you."

Ninon leaped from her bed, her eyes wide with shock and disbelief. "Where?"

"In the courtyard. Come. Let me take you to him." She laughed gently. "You need not run, child. He is a devil, but he will not go before making his farewells."

Philippe was already mounted on his horse, his plumed hat set rakishly on his head, when Ninon hurried to him. He leaned down from the saddle, stroking the side of her cheek with his gauntleted finger. "I leave you in the care of the good sisters, little bird. Grow into womanhood and be happy. You will be safe here until you can find your own way in the world." He smiled warmly, his hazel eyes twinkling with mischief. "Name your cat 'Philippe' in remembrance of me. Will you?" he urged, as she still said nothing.

She nodded and cast down her eyes, that he might not see the pain, the beginnings of tears.

"*Adieu*, little bird," he said. Urging his horse forward, he went out through the gate. He looked much as he had looked two days before, when he had ridden into her life. Jaunty, carefree, noble in his boots and spurs and plumes.

But she was no longer the same. Her body was free, released from the rigors and torments that Baugin had imposed. But hope and trust, newly awakened in her soul, lay in chains. She should have guessed he would betray her heart. Had life taught her any differently? Had any man ever done aught but break his promises? Her father, who had sworn to keep her and cherish her—how could he die? How could he leave them penniless? And Baugin—how could he seem kind at first, then prove to be a monster bent on her destruction? And now Philippe was gone. She would never trust a man again.

Never.

But he *had* rescued her, her golden paladin, her noble hero. For that, at least—despite the anguish in her heart—for that she knew she would love him forever.

Chapter Two

1657

"Sister Solange, has the post not come from the village yet?"

"It is still early, Reverend Mother. And Monsieur Moillon's horse was limping when he brought last week's letters. He might be late today."

"I pray *le bon Dieu* all is well with him." The abbess looked about the high-walled garden, seating herself on a low bench and smiling at the sunny morning. "How warm it is for March! I confess I thought we should not see spring this year."

"Yes. After the snows in February…" Sister Solange shook her head. "Do you remember last month, the terrible blizzard on Ninon's eighteenth birthday? What a storm that was!"

The abbess glanced across the gardens to where Ninon was already hard at work, spading the soft earth and raking it into smooth furrows to receive the first seeds of spring, cabbage and onions and peas. "There have been many storms in that young life, I'll warrant." She sighed. "But for all her silent heart that she guards so well, she has become a fine young woman. I would I could persuade her to stay with us and take the vows. There is warmth and sympathy in her. I have often been moved at the wonder of God's mercies when I see her with the widows, broken in spirit and body, who come seeking sanctuary. Ninon ministers to them with a sweetness that would make the angels envious. And what a joy to watch her with the children from the village—an infinitely patient teacher."

"And yet she is not a good Christian in her observances, Reverend Mother. She is often late for vespers, and comes to matins seldom."

"I know. In some ways she has scarcely changed from the rebellious, guarded child that my cousin Monsieur de Froissart brought to us three years ago."

Sister Solange laughed softly. "I confess that I have always been surprised at Monsieur le Comte's generosity of spirit at that time! He is a charming man, of course—a good man, I hasten to assure you—but hardly a man to notice the wickedness of the world...nor to care! Forgive me, he is your cousin..."

"No. You are quite right. I suspect that Philippe himself was astonished at his own impulsive rescue of the girl from her stepfather. But for our convent, and the haven it provided Ninon, Philippe would in all likelihood have soon regretted his hasty action. *Eh bien*, I have not regretted it. I shall be sorry to see her leave someday. She possesses many talents that will make her life easier. Her fine intelligence, of course, and her musical skills. But her domestic training was not neglected; that is apparent. I am minded of the lace and whitework collar she fashioned for *Monseigneur l'évêque*, my lord bishop, upon his last visit."

"Still, there is a strangeness about her that is difficult to fathom. Do you remember her fierce possessiveness with that cat of hers—how she would not even let others feed it? And yet when the Vignot family sought refuge here from the plague last year—leaving Monsieur Vignot dead in the stricken village—Ninon gave her cat to the fatherless children, without a moment's hesitation." Sister Solange frowned in bewilderment.

The abbess nodded. "There is a goodness in her she fears to show, a goodness she hides behind her silence and her reticent ways. I would she had been willing to tell me more of herself. She has been hurt by life, poor child. *We* have earned her trust, thanks be to God, but..." The abbess looked up, hearing the sudden creak of harness and tackle. "Ah! Is that not the sound of Monsieur Moillon's wagon? Mayhap there is a letter from my cousin today. He is an indifferent correspondent, despite my many letters to him. But I am surprised that he takes so little notice of my accounts of Ninon's progress as scholar and teacher. More especially as her deliverance was due to his own efforts."

"Oh, Reverend Mother. Perhaps he does not wish to be accused of the sins of pride and vanity in God's eyes."

The abbess laughed dryly. "Philippe has never worn humility well! I would think rather that he is far too concerned with his own secular pleasures to give much thought to the girl. But let us wish Monsieur Moillon a good morrow."

Ninon straightened up from the furrow she had been smoothing and rubbed the small of her back. *Le bon Dieu* knew she worked as hard as ever she had for Baugin and *la Bique*—tending the garden, making butter and cheese and soap, dipping tallow for candles—but the aches and pains at the end of the day scarcely bothered her. Perhaps it was the joy of being repaid with kindness instead of blows, the goodness of the sisters, the delight in teaching the children. She had found a serenity here she had not thought possible, a pleasure in giving of herself to those who needed her.

And she had the joy of books again. Even music. She had found an old lute and a guitar that a long-ago traveler had donated to the convent in grateful payment for the sisters' care. She had spent many a quiet afternoon reacquainting her fingers with the chords, smiling to remember the eccentric music teacher at her father's château of Bellefleur.

And of course she had her dreams. The fantasies of her younger days had become full-blown scenarios of love and romance, with Philippe as the heart and core of each one. She acted them out when she went to bed at night, kissing her pillow, whispering words of love in the dark as though he were truly there to hear them. As she went about her chores, she would pretend that he was with her, and imagine what he would say, how he would praise her work. And when a passing traveler would stop at the convent and tell of the latest news from the world outside, she would use that knowledge to construct elaborate dialogues with the imaginary Philippe, discoursing on philosophy and politics to dazzle him with her intelligence.

And she had his very own words. Hidden in a little tablet that she kept under her straw mattress. He had written seldom to the abbess in the last three years, and had told almost nothing of his life, if one was to credit the reverend mother. She could only guess that he was happy without his Rosamunde. But he sometimes included in his letters a line or two about Ninon; smiling gently, the abbess would read them aloud to the girl. She would hurry back to her small cell and copy them into her tablet before she forgot the words; and there they sat, ready at hand when she needed them, to read over and over, to commit to memory as though they were a love sonnet. "I send to Ninon my best regards." "I am pleased to hear that Ninon progresses so well in her studies." "Give Ninon my fond wishes for a happy Christmas."

She had never stopped loving him. Indeed, she loved him all the more because he was a sweet dream. He could not break her heart again if he were just a fantasy.

• • •

The coach jolted along the bumpy road, its leather-strap springs creaking loudly. From far away came the rumblings of thunder, blending with the coachman's tuneless whistle to play a noisy concerto to the gloomy afternoon. Alas, thought Ninon, smoothing the skirts of her new gown, it will surely rain before I arrive!

No matter. The pony cart would meet her at the signpost and hurry her to Marival before the rain could do its worst. Would Philippe be in the cart? she wondered. No. He would prefer to greet her at the gates of his château, greet her as an honored guest. Well, perhaps not honored guest; rather a long-ago friend, someone who was dear to him. His letter to the reverend mother had been very vague. "Monsieur my cousin wants you in his service at Château Marival," the abbess had said. She did not seem to know why, and Ninon did not care to ask. After all, he could hardly have told the reverend mother that he was summoning Ninon to be his mistress, his lover! But Ninon had no doubt of it. Why else would he have sent for her? Why else send money for this public coach, and the splendid new clothes?

Ninon smiled down at her garments. She had not worn anything so fine since her days at Bellefleur. To be sure, she had dressed as an aristocrat, as the bastard of a great noble at Bellefleur; now she was clad as a bourgeoise woman. Still, after her years of rags and hand-me-downs at the convent, she felt as elegant as a queen. The gray fustian jacket, braid-edged, with its large white linen collar and cuffs—she had not had time to frost them with her own embroidery. And *two* skirts over her petticoat, the blue underskirt banded at the hem with bright yellow stripes, the split overskirt—of the same gray twilled cotton and wool as the jacket—tucked up into large poufs over her hips. She had a large cape and a separate black hood—called a *chaperone*—that tied under her chin with a profusion of ribbons, and her shoes were square-toed and tied high over the instep with leather thongs. In a small straw hamper she carried the rest of the clothes that she had been able to buy with Philippe's generous allowance: a fitted bodice, cut low across the bosom, in blue like her underskirt, an extra petticoat, and two more linen chemises, one with lace to peep out above her bodice for formal occasions, the other simple and unadorned, to be worn with a sleeveless laced jerkin for everyday wear. There were several pairs of knitted stockings, one in red silk, and a crisp white apron. And the sisters, led by a smiling Solange, had presented her with a delicate lace fichu to drape across her shoulders. It was almost like having a trousseau.

Leaning back in the carriage, Ninon allowed herself to daydream once again. She was beautiful in her new clothes; she knew it with a certainty. Would Philippe be pleased? Would Philippe be dazzled? Would he kiss her at their first meeting? She prayed so. Her lips had been tasting his—remembering his kiss at the inn—for so long that she could scarcely recall a time when she did not love him. In spite of her resolve to guard her heart, she found herself filled with hope, certain that this time her dreams would come true. There might even be a marriage at the end of this journey, God willing!

It was nearly evening when the coach reached the signpost; the rain had been falling steadily for over an hour. There was no pony cart in sight, but the coachman was unwilling to linger, while Ninon stayed warm and dry within. He had passengers waiting in Dijon, to the south, and a charming doxy he had not seen in two months; besides, perched on his box, *he* had had no shelter from the rain. Why should he pity the mademoiselle? Pulling her light cape more closely about her shoulders, and clutching her hamper to her, Ninon stepped reluctantly out of the carriage. There was no protection from the driving storm among the still-bare trees, and the muddy road sucked at her new shoes and soiled her hems. By the time the cart appeared, and the gnarled old driver had apologized for the delay, she was soaked through, and cursing her own shortsightedness in not having bought a heavy cloak with the money from Philippe. But she had done without for so many years, she had not thought it necessary. Well, Philippe would remedy that.

Clambering into the cart, Ninon huddled miserably on the seat. It was not as she had imagined her arrival would be, jouncing through the darkening night, wet and cold. She could not even see Château Marival clearly; it was just a dim shape against the black sky. As the cart passed through the main gate to the wall-enclosed courtyard with its side wings of stables and workshops, she looked up to see lights twinkling here and there in the *corps-de-logis*—the central living quarters—of Marival. A side door opened; silhouetted in the sudden light was a heavyset woman who beckoned to her. As soon as the cart stopped, Ninon jumped down and hurried to the door.

"Mademoiselle Guillemot?" asked the woman, closing the door to the stormy night. Ninon nodded. "What a dreadful night to be out! You must be chilled through. Come along, my child." The woman stopped. "Ah! Forgive me! My manners. I am Agathe, and I welcome you to Marival." She smiled benignly. She was a robust woman, small but amply padded, with gray hair peeping from beneath her snowy, close-fitting cap, and ruddy cheeks like little apples. By her air of authority and the large ring of keys hanging at her waist, Ninon guessed she must be the housekeeper of Marival.

And Philippe nowhere about. Ninon began to shiver. She was cold, she was disappointed, and she was weary from the journey.

"By all the saints, you'll catch the ague if you stand there!" Agathe said briskly. "Come along. Come along!"

She ushered Ninon up two flights of stairs and into a room just off the corridor. It was sparsely furnished and small, with a single dormer window, but it had a large bed hung with straight draperies, and a broad fireplace that radiated a welcome warmth.

Still shivering uncontrollably, Ninon allowed Agathe and a young chambermaid to strip the drenched garments from her, to bathe her muddy feet in a basin of warm water, and to towel dry her copper curls, making them more frizzed than usual, so that her head glowed with a pink-gold halo in the firelight. Wrapped at last in a heavy blanket, she sat on a stool before the fire, sipping a mug of warm cider that the maid had brought, while Agathe went in search of a nightdress, horrified that Ninon would wish to sleep in her chemise. ("We are scarcely uncivilized here at Marival, mademoiselle!")

The door opened. The chambermaid, who had been draping Ninon's wet clothing across a chair near the fire, stopped and curtsied. "Madame," she murmured humbly. Ninon looked up.

The woman who had come into the room was tall and elegant, her lithe form clothed in a rich gown of pale peach satin, her ebony hair twisted up in the back and hanging loose in front with spiral curls that fell to her shoulders. She might have been twenty-six or -seven. She sailed majestically toward Ninon, her thin lips held in a tight smile.

"You are Ninon." Her voice was low and cultured. "If you please, stand up." It was not quite an imperious command, nor was it a simple request—clearly, the lady was a woman who expected to be heeded.

"Yes…madame," murmured Ninon, putting down her cider and rising to her feet. The woman made her uneasy, though she could not begin to understand why.

Pale gray eyes searched Ninon's face; then, without warning, the woman reached out and pulled the blanket from Ninon's body. This time the eyes held open hostility as they raked Ninon's bare flesh, the full young breasts, the dense patch of copper between her rounded thighs. "But you're not a child, are you?"

Ninon bristled, feeling her soul stripped as bare as her body. "No, madame," she said quietly, though her eyes darted blue flame.

"He said you were a child." The gray eyes lingered on Ninon's groin, then came to rest on her face once again. "Are you a *woman?*" There was no mistaking her meaning.

Despite herself, Ninon felt the hot flush wash across her face. "No, madame," she answered, wondering by what right the woman dared to ask such a question.

A honeyed smile parted the thin lips. "Good. It is wise to guard your virtue, to protect your virginity from the soft blandishments of men." She handed back the blanket, frowning in thought as Ninon covered herself once again. "Something must be done about that hair, however. It is ungoverned and wild, and the riotous color is an affront to every decent sensibility. We shall cut you a fringe across the forehead, I think, and bind the rest in a cap."

"But…I should prefer…" stammered Ninon.

"Nonsense! Do you wish to appear a slut? Every stableboy and carpenter at Marival will have his hand under your skirts if you flaunt those wild curls! Would you lose your virginity to a coarse finger? Tell Agathe you are to have a cap!" With a swirl of satin she was gone.

Ninon was still standing in shocked surprise when Agathe returned, bearing a soft nightdress. "I see you have met Madame la Comtesse. A charming lady. Now, here is your nightdress. Put it on, and get you into bed. Adèle here will bring you some supper."

Passively Ninon allowed herself to be dressed in her nightclothes and led to the bed; she sat up against the pillows while a tray of food was brought and a single candle was left at the bedside table. Adèle curtsied politely and Agathe bade her a good night. She was alone. The fire still burned brightly on the hearth, but her heart had begun to grow cold. Madame la Comtesse. His sister, perhaps. A cousin, surely, widowed and come to live at Marival to be his hostess, to be the chatelaine. A bachelor could not be expected to manage the complexities of a large household! Still…

She put aside the tray of food, barely touched, her soul filled with a dire foreboding. Madame la Comtesse.

The room was dim, cozy, and warm, but she could not sleep. She sat for a long time listening to the rain outside the casement, the thumping of her heart. There was a sudden light tap on her door. At her bidding, the door opened.

She saw the candle first, then Philippe behind it. "I am glad that you are yet awake, Ninon!" he announced delightedly, striding across the room to perch on the edge of her bed. "I did not wish to wait until the morning to greet you!" He set his candle next to hers on the table and grinned at her. "I see the sisters have fed you well. You were naught save bones when last we met! Well, are you still the silent bird, that you cannot greet me?"

She gulped, feeling too overwhelmed to speak. He was more beautiful even than she had remembered him. A little older, perhaps, a little more mature, the lines of his jaw stronger and more angular, the small beard and mustache more carefully manicured. But his shoulders, beneath his billowing silk shirt, were as broad as she had imagined them in her fantasies, and his golden hair still set her to recalling her father. "I...I am pleased to see you again...Philippe," she stammered at last.

"What a devil of a night for you to arrive! But I promise you fairer weather here at Marival. Have you met the boys?" She shook her head, mystified. He laughed. "*Mon Dieu*, then you must wonder what I'm talking about. Well then...Madame la Comtesse has been unhappy of late with the tutors for her sons. And every letter I receive from my cousin the abbess is filled with glowing accounts of your intelligence and skill as a teacher." He frowned. "By the by, have you taught lads?"

"Yes. There were boys from the village."

"Good! You shall not find these lads a burden, I'll wager. Jean-Claude is ten and Robert nearly eight. A little untamed, as is natural, but good-hearted. Do you think you are equal to the task?" At Ninon's silent nod he smiled. "And so I thought. As I said to Madame la Comtesse, let me but send for the clever child, the object of the reverend mother's unceasing praise. You shall not regret it." He smiled again, his eyes crinkling warmly. "And *I* shall not, I think."

She *must* be his widowed sister or cousin, thought Ninon. It would be natural for her, left alone with small children, to seek a home with her kinfolk. More natural still for Philippe to take an interest in their education.

"A hundred gold louis for the year, and room and board," he said. "That will be agreeable to you, will it not?"

"No. You gave money to Baugin for me. And the coins for my new clothes. Fifty louis will content me."

"Fifty? I shall not hear of it! I pay my grooms more! One hundred. And not another word, lest I change my mind."

"But...but...Philippe...the clothes and the coach..."

His mouth twisted in a wry smile. "As to that, child—Madame my wife is closefisted. I should prefer she not know of those expenses. And you had best not call me Philippe, little bird. You understand, of course. An unseemly familiarity, and one that my stepsons could scarcely fathom. *Eh bien*, it grows late. In the morning we shall discuss a course of study for the boys." He patted her gently on the head like a fond father, picked up his candle, and went to the door. "Welcome to Marival," he said, and left the room.

Ninon blew out her candle and lay down, pulling the warm coverlet about her shoulders. Her eyes were dry. Her heart had turned to ice.

Ninon stood at the window of the long *galerie* of Marival, looking out on the wide stretch of lawn, the formal gardens. Beyond, clothed in the soft green of April, was a wooded park, with artfully planted groves of trees, the studied casualness of massed rocks and boulders, and the unexpected whimsy of a small summerhouse—built to look like a woodcutter's cottage—in the midst of this charming but wholly artificial setting. She sighed heavily, filled with that mingled joy and sadness that always came with spring.

Directly below her on the terrace, Philippe was instructing Jean-Claude and Robert in the handling of a musket, helping them to load and unload the charge, to carry the weapon about, to march with it in the manner of well-trained soldiers. Most days, just before lunch, Philippe saw to some aspect of their military training: riding, drill with arms large and small, exercises with the pike, fencing with the rapier. Ninon taught them for most of the morning, and again for a large part of the afternoon, instructing them in writing and grammar, reading in French and Latin. Thanks to her own training, she was able to teach them the sciences as well—mathematics and ciphering—and guitar. After nearly a month, the routine had become steady, and she found that she could set them a full day's instruction and still have a great deal of freedom for herself. In the morning she particularly liked to give the boys lessons to copy for half an hour or so, while she sat in the common room next to the large kitchen, having a leisurely breakfast with Agathe and the staff and servants of Marival. She seldom spoke to them, preferring her own counsel, but it made her life a little less empty.

She sighed again. The boys were agreeable enough to teach: not especially winning, but not very difficult either. And although Madame la Comtesse was always unpleasant to her, she contrived to avoid the woman as often as she could. The matter of her hair had been resolved somewhat amicably. To please madame, she wore a starched linen cap that covered most of her curls, but she balked at cutting a fringe across her forehead, preferring instead to part her hair in the middle and sweep the pieces back under the cap. It was a pleasant life. She should have been happy. But...

She looked at Philippe laughing below with the boys. So blind to her, so oblivious to the pain in her heart. Still seeing her as a child. *Ah Dieu!* How was it possible to hate and love someone at the same time? Her eyes softened as she watched him, his lithe grace, his noble bearing.

"He is a fine figure of a man, *n'est-ce pas?*"

Ninon whirled to see the Comtesse de Froissart smiling at her silkily. "Yes, madame, he is," she said quietly, turning back to the window to look again at Philippe.

"'Tis a pity you never saw my first husband," the comtesse purred. "Extraordinarily handsome. And devoted to me and our sons. But perhaps not as wise as he might have been. He took part in the Fronde uprising in fifty-one and joined the Prince of Condé and the other nobles the following year when they occupied Paris and Cardinal Mazarin and the king were forced to flee. But when the king returned to power that year, and Condé became a traitor to France and allied himself with the king of Spain, my husband would not heed my advice. While most of the nobles were reconciling themselves with Louis and swearing allegiance to the crown once again, my husband was in secret correspondence with Condé in Spain. He was found out, tried, sentenced to death. And of course his lands were forfeit, leaving me and the children destitute."

"That is a sad tale, madame." Ninon turned to the comtesse in genuine sympathy, but the gray eyes that stared at her were cold.

Madame de Froissart smiled, a tight grimace that held more malice than if she had frowned. "Now I shall tell you a happy tale. I could not show my face in Paris, of course. And my sons, who had borne their father's name proudly, were spat upon by their fellows. I went to stay for a time with a cousin in Dijon. And there I met Philippe, home from the Netherlands, nursing a broken heart. You understand. We women have a sense of the precise moment when a man is…shall we say…ripe for the picking? Philippe was most anxious to prove himself a man, after his… Rosamunde—I think that was her name—spurned him." She laughed softly. "Come, come, girl! Look not so astonished. You are hardly a fool. You see the world with eyes that are scarcely deceived, I think. Why should my words shock you?"

Ninon looked down, trying to hide the anger in her eyes. "Have I your leave to go, madame?"

"No. I have not finished the tale. There is more to come, and a moral besides. As I have indicated, it was singularly easy to catch Philippe. Holding him has proven a little more difficult. But he has adopted my children so they no longer bear the name of a traitor. Common sense, and my boys' future, would dictate that I keep Philippe as a husband. And there is my tale."

"And the moral, madame?" said Ninon tightly.

The gray eyes had become hard as steel. "The moral is, perhaps, a warning as well. Desperate circumstances breed desperate acts. I shall use whatever I must to keep him by my side. Always!" She glanced down at Philippe in the garden, then stared again at Ninon. "You see, I too view the world with unclouded eyes. *He* is blind, as yet, to what I see. It would be best for you if he remains so. There is too much at stake for me to be generous. Do you understand?"

Afraid that she would cry, feeling helpless and trapped, Ninon turned away.

The comtesse put a gentle hand on her shoulder. "Ninon, my dear," she said, her voice dripping with honey, "I have only your best interests at heart. Surely you know that. You are lonely and ofttimes sad. It grieves me to see you thus. It is time for you perhaps to take a husband. And I am pleased to bring you happy news. Mathieu Couteau—I think you know him—the carpenter, has already asked me for your hand. I told him I would speak to you first. But he is a fine young man. You would be foolish to refuse. Come," she said, turning Ninon about to face her, and cupping the delicate chin in her hand. "What say you? I will, of course, provide a fine dowry. What say you?"

Sweet Madonna, thought Ninon miserably, *am* I a fool? She could spend a lifetime mooning about Philippe and never win his heart. Nor even his notice! Mathieu was a hard worker and a good man—there would be a comfortable life and strong children if she married him. Wasn't it time to put aside her childish fancies of a noble hero? "If you please, madame," she said softly, "I should like to think on it for a week or two. I shall give you my answer then."

The smiled faded from the Comtesse de Froissart's face. "Take care that you make the right choice," she said harshly. "Remember my tale… and its moral!"

Philippe de Froissart stared down at his wife. In the dim bedchamber, lit only by a single candle, Henriette's flesh seemed pale, almost gray, like that of the corpses that littered every battlefield. In truth, she lay like a corpse, her eyes closed, her arms stretched languidly above her head; when he stroked her breasts, she scarcely moved. He wondered why he even bothered anymore—it was always the same. The endless days of feeling the juices begin to rise in him, the stirring of his senses, the hunger in his body that cried out to be eased. And the dismal realization, each time he climbed into bed with her, that he could relieve himself as effortlessly, as mindlessly, with a whore from the village as with Henriette. Not that he really cared. Life was boring. Henriette was boring, at least in bed. But she catered to his craving for novelty in other ways, planning surprises, trips to Paris and Versailles, parties and fêtes.

Just now she was in the midst of planning a whole week of festivities. Several dozen of the local nobility were coming to Marival to stay as guests, while Henriette regaled them with dances and elegant suppers. She had even contracted with a traveling theatrical troupe to entertain them for several days. And she was clever. Several of the invited guests were notorious gossips in court circles. Philippe could afford the expense of the fête, of course, but it would not hurt if word got back to the eighteen-year-old, pleasure-loving King Louis of the gaiety at Château Marival. There might be a royal pension of a few thousand livres, an important post, if Philippe were to join the ranks of Louis's favorites.

Philippe himself was looking forward to the festivities for other reasons. He had arranged a hunt where his guests, comfortably ensconced on the side of a hill, would shoot at several dozen deer that he had had his woodsmen trap. When the animals were released, it would make excellent sport, and he was eager to try out his new musket. In addition, he had sent for a tailor from Paris to deck him out in the latest fashion; after several fittings he had become quite used to the new style. His guests, in their conservative clothes, would seem like provincial bumpkins next to him. The thought gave him great satisfaction—he would certainly set the fashion in the Dijon region for the next five years!

He began to feel an uncomfortable pressure at his groin. It was time. Even Henriette's lifeless body, numb to his caresses, roused him sooner or later. He parted her thighs with his hands and took his place between her legs. Her cousin from Dijon was invited to the fête. Philippe was not quite sure, but he thought they might be lovers. There was a brief time, in the first few months of their marriage, when he might have been jealous, but now...

He thrust into her with more force than usual, feeling an unexpected residual anger at her, at himself, at how the whole business had turned out.

"Oh!" she cried, petulant. "Mind you don't hurt me, Philippe!"

He mumbled an apology, then resumed his labors, pumping mechanically for his body's sake while his thoughts were elsewhere. He was looking forward to the party. The Marquis d'Enfant was bringing his new wife. A beauty, they said, and very accommodating. He hoped so. He hadn't had an interesting bed partner since that charming Lucie-Anne, and then it was the thrill of the chase that had made her so intriguing. After his initial conquest, he had found her less charming.

Yes, he thought. It was most assuredly the chase, the seduction that excited him. It was what had made Rosamunde so desirable—her maddening refusal. But once he was married to Henriette he had lost interest in Rosamunde. Infuriated at his rebuff, she had practically thrown herself at him. To satisfy his curiosity, and nothing more, he had taken Rosamunde to bed. He had found it difficult to keep awake.

Henriette now stirred beneath him. "*Nom de Dieu*, Philippe! Have done!" With a little effort, he brought himself to climax and collapsed against her. Grunting in annoyance, she pushed him off her and sat up, straightening her hair. "I shall need more money this week," she said. "Two hundred ecus, I think. There is the roof over the east pavilion, and…"

He held up his hand for silence. "It can be arranged," he said indifferently. "Spare me the particulars." He rolled out of bed and reached for his dressing gown, shrugged into it, and helped himself to a cup of wine from a small table.

"And if all goes well," she continued, "I shall need another fifty crowns next week."

"What do you mean?"

"I…have been concerned about Ninon of late."

"How so? She is a fine tutor for the boys, and she seems content."

"She is…too pretty, mayhap, with a face that could do the devil's work. A girl like that can make mischief. I have seen it happen before. Quarrels among the men, the wanton giving of her favors…The sooner she is married, the better. Let her husband fill her belly with children and beat her to keep her from other beds."

"*Dieu du ciel!* God in heaven, Henriette, she's still a child!" There was an edge of annoyance in his voice.

"Yes. Yes, of course," she soothed, "but not too young to marry. I married at sixteen. Besides, Mathieu Couteau has already spoken for her."

"That coarse oaf? The girl has noble blood, an education, fine breeding…"

Henriette sneered. "And is yet a bastard, *n'est-ce pas?* And a penniless servant. Would you want one of our noble friends to marry her?"

He frowned. "No. Certainly not."

"Then speak not to me of her birth! What matters is what she is now. Better she marry Couteau and not try to rise above her station."

"What does she say to the marriage?"

"She wishes to think it over. A shy flower. But I know she will agree. It's all for the best. I think she understands that. Thus, I shall need the fifty crowns. For a dowry."

"Do as you see fit," he growled, putting down his wine cup and striding to the door. "I shall sleep in my own chamber tonight." He closed the door on her passionless "good night," wondering why he suddenly felt so disquieted.

Ninon climbed the stairs from the kitchen, hurrying back to the children and their studies. She was glad to be out of the common room this morning. Madame de Froissart must have spoken to Mathieu Couteau, giving him to believe his suit would be successful. The carpenter had scarcely left her side all during breakfast, sliding his hand onto her lap under the table, grinning slyly, whispering coarse promises of what he would do to her once they were married. The thought of being yoked to him made her stomach turn, yet she feared madame's reaction if she refused. She sighed. Perhaps the marriage would work out, despite her uneasiness.

A door opened onto the passage and Philippe stepped out. "I would speak with you, Ninon," he said. "Please to come into my *cabinet*." Dutifully she followed him. His *cabinet* was a small chamber, one of several rooms that made up his *apartement*. Designed for reading and contemplation and quiet retreat, it was decorated with frescoed panels on walls and ceiling—depicting various gods and goddesses in myth and legend—and furnished with a few well-padded chairs. Philippe indicated one to Ninon, and seated himself on another, facing her.

"Is it true?" he said at last. "Are you to marry Couteau?"

"I have not agreed to it as yet, but…"

"You have given him cause to hope?"

Ninon's lip twitched in a wry smile as she remembered Mathieu's bold words. "He has hopes. Yes."

"But why?"

She said nothing, merely shrugging in reply.

"You're an intelligent girl, Ninon. Surely you can do better than Couteau," he said, like a reasonable parent trying to persuade a child.

Silent, she looked down at her folded hands.

"How can you be such a fool?" The tone was a little less reasonable now. "Would you waste yourself on him?"

Still she said nothing. What could she tell him?

"You're still a child!" he snapped angrily, reason flying out the window. "There will be time enough to find you a suitable husband. Until then, I will not have you throwing yourself at Couteau…or any other lout in the stableyard! Unless…" his eyes darted to her face, as a sudden thought struck him, "unless you are forced to marry him. Is that it? Have you succumbed to Couteau already?"

Her eyes flashing in fury, she jumped up from her chair and made for the door. He caught her there, grabbing savagely at her arm and swinging her around to face him. "Damn you! I will not have your silence when I speak to you! You are not the little bird any longer. Answer my questions!" It was a moment's wild impulse, but suddenly his mouth was upon hers, crushing her lips in a fierce kiss. She went limp in his arms, and when at last he released her, he was stunned to see that she was trembling violently, and her blue eyes, brimming with tears, were filled with anguish.

"My God," he breathed. "What have I done to you?"

She turned away, clutching her arms in misery.

"You love me." He put his hands on her shoulders and turned her back to face him, seeing with dismay the flush of humiliation that swept across her cheeks. "Since I rescued you from Baugin? Since then?" She nodded, weeping softly. "*Mon Dieu!*" he burst out, running his fingers absently through his hair. Then, "Why did you come when I sent for you?"

"How can you ask that?" she whispered.

"But…Henriette…?"

She buried her face in her hands.

He groaned. "You did not know."

She shook her head, her body still quivering, her grief beyond containing.

"Ninon," he said, his voice warm with pity. "You poor child…"

It was more than she could endure. Rushing past him, she fled up the stairs to her room.

Bewildered, confused, he sank into his chair, leaning back and staring at the cherubs kissing on the ceiling. The unhappy child, he thought. Then sat up, frowning, remembering the yielding warmth of her in his arms.

But she was no longer a child. Indeed, no. What a fool he had been. What a blind fool.

She was a woman.

Chapter Three

Philippe sat carelessly in his chair in the long *galerie*, facing the temporary stage that had been set up across one short end of the room. The players had worked diligently, transforming the bare boards into a playhouse, with a curtain on a brass rod that closed off the front of the stage, and small candles set along the edge, their glare shielded from the audience by semicircles of tin.

He was slightly tipsy from the wine, and hoping to be more so; a snap of his fingers brought a footman with a jug to refill his empty glass. Thanks be to God his guests were going home in a day or two—he had long since wearied of playing the gracious host. There had been a few brief triumphs, of course. His costume, for one. He had worn the new fashion his tailor called Rhinegraves: exceedingly wide and short breeches in a deep gold, gathered at the waist like a skirt, and trimmed at knee-length hem and waist with yards and yards of cherry-red ribbon loops. With these petticoat breeches he wore a very full white silk shirt, the sleeves puffed and ribboned and frilled, and a waist-length gold jacket with short sleeves beribboned and slashed to the shoulders, and left unbuttoned so that his shirt front billowed out and bloused over the top of his breeches. His tailor had not stinted on the ribbon—250 yards, he had been able to boast to his admiring guests! Just below his knees were wide white frills of fabric, gathered to the tops of his blue stockings. Canons, they were called, and they added to the elegance of his outfit. His pale yellow shoes were tied over the instep with more ribbon loops, and the heels, several inches high, were of red cork. He had even managed to master the mincing walk that his tailor had said was de rigueur with the fashion.

The hunt had gone well, with enough excitement to win the praise of his guests, and the acting troupe, which had performed once already, was passably good. They had done a farce and a pastoral with singing last night; tonight they were to do a tragicomedy.

But he had had his fill of triumphs, and was feeling the old ennui creep up on him, the need for fresh interests. And he had not had a woman in more than a week. Henriette pleaded the cares of a hostess, and there was not a female among the guests who stirred his blood.

He took a swallow of wine and motioned his guests to benches beside him and along both narrow walls. He would go mad tonight. He had spent the better part of the last two weeks watching Ninon, aware for the first time of her womanly charms, aware how the wanting of her tormented him. Now there was to be more agony tonight. It was traditional at Marival to invite the servants to one performance by a visiting company, and Ninon had just come in with Mathieu Couteau. If he turned his head slightly to the left, and glanced over his shoulder, he could watch them behind him, sitting close together, Couteau's arm draped protectively around Ninon's shoulder, his limp hand hanging down just above her rounded bosom.

Philippe smiled falsely as Henriette took her place on his right. He found her more tiring than ever, though she had sparkled and fussed over her cousin the whole week long. He wondered idly if she had dared to cuckold him in his own home. Look at her! he thought. How artificial she seemed: the boned bodice of her gown creating curves that nature had never intended and hiding the natural sweep of her bosom, the full skirts with their padded hip roll worn under her petticoats, the corkscrew curls of her black hair, held out from her head by a hidden wire frame.

And Ninon. A beautiful face, a soft body that had bloomed and ripened since first he had met her as a child. So fresh and sweet and natural. No corsets, no tortured hair—though he could never understand why she covered her glorious mane with that damned cap! Warm and sensual…and aching with love for him. He would die if he could not have her. But it must be before that drooling Couteau could take her; he could not bear the thought of the carpenter slobbering over that milky skin. Mother of God, he would die tonight!

Ninon looked curiously about the *galerie* as an actor stepped before the curtain to light the candles, and the guests settled themselves comfortably for the start of the play. There was not another man in the room as elegantly dressed as Philippe. She understood it was the latest fashion. It suited him, of course, accenting the nobility of his stance, the graceful turn of his leg. Still…she wondered if it would betray her love if, in a small corner of her mind, she thought the outfit a trifle *précieux* and affected. She had not imagined him to be a prancing peacock until now; she found his artificial clothing and his heavy perfume a bit of a disappointment.

Mathieu slid closer to her on the bench. She had decided to accept his proposal in the morning, but he was already behaving as though the answer had been given. As the actors appeared onstage, their faces heavily painted with white paste, Mathieu squeezed her roughly against him and kissed her neck with fevered lips. She stared straight ahead, concentrating on the play, listening to the verses that the players recited, their resonant voices booming out over the length of the *galerie*. She did not want to make a scene by pushing Mathieu away, and, after all, what did it matter? She might as well get used to his attentions.

The play was rather good, and well presented, a trifling piece about unrequited love and broken hearts. Since it was a tragicomedy, it would all come right in the end, as the audience well knew; but the path to happiness was strewn with some suffering and many impassioned speeches. Well written, Ninon thought idly, and the verses were facile. She did not particularly care for the leading lady. The women, of course, wore no white makeup, but Ninon thought it might have improved the leading lady's sour expression if they had managed at least to paint on a smile! And she was dressed in an extremely unattractive gown. Very highwaisted, in a style that had not been worn for twenty years. It made her seem large and lumpish.

Ninon stirred uncomfortably. Mathieu withdrew his heavy arm from her shoulders and stretched. Thanks be to God the play was coming to an end; she could flee his possessive grasp, his hot mouth, and seek her room. She looked up. Philippe was watching her, his eyes boring into her with an expression that made her tremble. She turned away, determinedly concentrating on the players. He tried to catch her eye again, but she avoided his glance, feeling a thrill of fear and excitement clutch at her heart. The leading man had begun a long speech, declaring his love. Ninon closed her eyes. She would listen to the play. She would not look at Philippe.

> "*My heart, a singing lark, by Cupid's dart transfixed,*
> *Now flutters in love's cage, its songs of freedom stilled.*
> *A willing captive bound by bright eyes and soft lips,*
> *It beats in silent thrall, 'twixt tender pain and joy.*"

Ninon nearly gasped aloud, moved and frightened by the rightness of the speech for this very moment. She opened her eyes and shot a wild glance at Philippe. He too had understood the couplets, and now he stared at her, his eyes burning, as though the words had been spoken by his heart to hers.

The play was over. The guests had begun to file into the *grande salle* for supper. Frantically Ninon pushed Mathieu away from her as the servants prepared to take up their duties once again. Philippe was still watching her, ravishing her with his eyes. She could not think. She could not reason. She could only flee—down the long stairs, into the dark night, the safety of the wooded park.

But she had not escaped him. As she stopped to catch her breath, he was there, his arms holding her fast, his mouth seeking hers. "Please, Philippe," she panted, "let me go."

He frowned and glared at her, as he tried to slow his racing breath. "Tell me you don't want me to hold you, to kiss you!" he growled at last. "Tell me!"

How could she fight against her destiny? She sighed and melted into his arms, surrendering her lips, her heart. His kiss was sweet and wonderful—she felt warmed and protected by his love. It was the end of her search. Her dreams had come true.

He took her by the hand and led her through the moonlit night to the summerhouse, pulling her inside and enveloping her in his embrace. This time the hands that held her were not so gentle, and his kiss bruised her mouth. She felt the first stirrings of uneasiness; backing out of his arms, she was dismayed to see that his face, in the light that streamed through the door, was tense with desire, his soft eyes black and glittering. No. No! This was not how it was supposed to be! Her fantasies had always ended with tender kisses, and nothing more.

"Philippe, please. No…please…" she began softly.

"Name of God, Ninon! I have waited so long. I *must* have you!" He pulled her back into his arms, his lips grinding on hers, his tongue invading her mouth, his roving hands roughly stroking her back and kneading her buttocks as though he would overcome her resistance by the force of his passion.

"Sweet Madonna…no!" she gasped, pushing him away with all her might. It was too soon. Their love was still too fragile for such unbridled lust. She wanted to be loved by her Prince Charming, not taken like a common whore by a hot-eyed animal.

He stared at a patch of moonlight on the rush-strewn floor, his mouth set in a petulant line. "You said you loved me. Was it a lie?"

"No. *Ah Dieu,* no!"

"Yet you refuse me."

"Philippe…I…"

"You let Couteau touch you tonight," he growled angrily. "Do you love him as well, that he may claim you before all the world? Caress you? Kiss you?"

"Stop…please…" she choked.

"Do you know how I am suffering?" He reached out and grabbed her by the wrist, placing her open palm against the swollen bulge at his groin. "There! And only you, only you, my sweet Ninon, can restore me."

She pulled her hand away, the touch, the hardness of him bringing an edge of panic to her voice. "I cannot. Please, Philippe. I cannot. Forgive me."

He stared at her for a long time, seeing her tremble, remembering the frightened child she had been, the frightened child she could become again if he was clumsy in his wooing. "No. Forgive *me*," he said softly. "I shall scarcely force you against your will." He took her face in both his hands and smiled down at her. "Only let me kiss you for a little." He kissed her mouth tentatively, his lips closed, his gentle fingers stroking her cheeks, her soft earlobes, until he felt her begin to relax against him. "Why do you hide your beautiful hair?" He removed her cap and pulled out her hairpins, running his fingers through the loose curls, breathing the sweet fragrance of her tresses. "My sweet Ninon…pretty little bird…how dear you are to me. I thought I should die when he touched you."

"Oh, Philippe," she whispered. "I could not bear his mouth."

"Let my kisses cleanse your sweet flesh." He allowed his lips to stray from her face to her neck, and from there to the rounded swell of her bosom above the lace of her chemise. When she made no move to break away, he undid the first few hooks of her bodice and folded back the fabric, caressing her heaving breast through her thin chemise. She closed her eyes and let her head fall back, little moans of pleasure coming from her parted lips. Emboldened, he released the last hooks of her bodice and slid the garment off her shoulders to the floor. Before she could protest, he had put his arms around her and kissed her, his mouth softly ravishing hers until he knew she had relaxed her guard once more. Swiftly, with practiced hands, he unfastened the hooks of her skirt and petticoat and pushed them down over her hips. Her eyes flew open and she stared down at herself, clad now only in her brief chemise, which barely reached to her knees.

"Philippe!" she cried in alarm.

"No. Let me look at you, Ninon. Sweet, beautiful Ninon." His voice was caressing and commanding at the same time. "Show me your body, my beautiful love. Take off your chemise. For me, my love."

I must be mad, she thought, her shaking fingers plucking at the drawstring of her chemise. But how could she refuse him, when he melted her heart with his loving words?

He knelt before her naked body, his eyes worshipful, like a man at a holy shrine. Reaching up, he encircled her hips with his hands and pulled her down to her knees in front of him. "My little bird," he whispered. "How you fill my heart and my dreams. I think I have always loved you, all unknowing. From the moment I first kissed you at the inn. Do you remember?"

She smiled and put her arms around his neck. "I have never forgotten." She kissed him softly, letting her senses reel out of control, feeling his hands on her naked flesh, his heart beating close to her bosom. She was not quite aware how it happened, but suddenly she was on her back, stretched out on her discarded petticoat and skirt, and he was on top of her, his hands libertine in their haste, his mouth hot and hard on hers.

"Ninon...sweet love..." he panted, the words tumbling out of him, "dearest Ninon...I shall not hurt you...I promise...I shall not hurt you..." He spread her legs beneath him, then knelt between her inviting thighs, fumbling impatiently among the ribbons at the fly buttons of his breeches.

She began to tremble, torn between longing and dismay. Sweet Madonna! She had not meant for this to happen. He had said he would not force her. And he had not. Then why did she feel helpless, powerless, as though she had just lost a battle?

"Ho! Monsieur le Comte! Monsieur de Froissart!"

About to release his burning manhood from its beribboned prison, Philippe cursed and leaned back on his heels. "Damn! Henriette has set her dogs to look for me! The bitch!" He jumped to his feet, straightening his tousled garments, refastening his breeches. "If I stay here, they will find us both. Ninon, forgive me. Sweet Ninon. One more kiss." He knelt to her and found her mouth. Then he was gone.

Holy Mother, she thought. Look at me. Spread wide like a naked strumpet—on a straw-covered floor—sighing with thwarted passion because my lover lacked but a second to pierce my maidenhead and leave me bleeding, while he fled to his wife. It was so ugly, so sordid. Not at all like her dreams.

With a sob, she rolled over on her side and wept.

• • •

Ninon hurried down the marble staircase and into the morning sunshine. It was a warm day; she had put only a sleeveless jerkin over her linen chemise. It would suffice. She crossed the stableyard, passing the troupe of actors busy packing to leave, piling their large open wagon with rolls of scenery and stage furniture, musical instruments and boxes of costumes.

If she went out through the frontispiece—the decorative main gate—of Marival, she could walk in the sunshine undisturbed while she collected her thoughts. Philippe might seek her in the gardens and the wooded park at the rear of the château; he would not think to look for her beyond the walls.

She had set the boys at their lessons, then hesitated about going to breakfast. Mathieu would be in the common room waiting for her answer. And she could not stay in the château. She knew Philippe wished to see her as well; Agathe had already told her so. He would not confront her while she was with the children, of course, but—after last night— she was not ready to face him.

Not that she hadn't reached a decision. She had tossed and turned all night, hearing the unwelcome voice of reason. Best to remain a virgin, best not to start an affair that could bring her nothing save grief. What kind of love could they share? She had scant hope for marriage— Henriette would never give him up. It would be like last night, always hiding, seeking out dark corners and stolen moments. Better not to start.

"Adèle, have you seen Mademoiselle Guillemot this morning?"

Ninon gasped. It was Philippe's voice at a side door. She would never reach the frontispiece without being seen. Swiftly she ducked into a stable, cool and shadowy after the sunny courtyard. There were three stone rooms, connected by arched open doorways, unused at the moment while the roof was being repaired. The stone floor was strewn with large piles of straw and hay, and rusting tools hung from the rafters. Ninon hurried to the middle room and leaned against the wall, breathing deeply to stop the pounding of her heart.

"Ninon! Why do you run away from me this morning?" Philippe stood in the first doorway and smiled at her, his eyes warm with desire. "And after last night…? Come and kiss me, my sweet."

She trembled. "No. Last night was…the finish. No more."

"You cannot mean that." He came close to her, holding out his arms. "My sweet little bird, who is so dear to me. And you love me, *n'est-ce pas?*" She nodded. "Say it. Say 'I love you, Philippe.'"

"I love you, Philippe," she whispered. It was a cry of agony, torn from her heart.

"Then lie with me here. Now. Open for me, little bird. Give me your sweetness."

"*Dieu du ciel!* Not here."

"Then meet me tonight. In the same place. The summerhouse in the park."

"No!" she cried, clinging desperately to the last shred of reason and common sense, lest his sweet words sweep them away. "I shall marry Couteau."

"I'll kill him before I let him touch you. You are mine! You belong to me!"

She felt a surge of hope at the strength of his love. The Church granted annulments somewhat readily, and certainly to a wealthy nobleman. Perhaps…"And what of Henriette?" she asked softly.

"What does Henriette have to do with my love for you?" He reached out to her, folding her in his embrace. His voice dropped to a soft caress. "Dear little bird, fluttering in my arms. I shall not let you fly away."

"*Ah Dieu!* Why do you torment me, Philippe?"

"I long to hold your soft body again—to see your velvet skin glowing in the moonlight. Let me feel you trembling beneath me again. Please, Ninon. I shall die of love."

"No…ah, no…" she panted, feeling her resolve weakening.

"I shall kiss every inch of your sweet body tonight," he murmured. "Tonight, my dearest. At ten."

"No…please…"

He kissed her gently. "At ten." Smiling softly like a man who knows he has won, he left her alone.

She wrung her hands, staring up at the dusty rafters. "Sweet Madonna, what shall I do?" she cried aloud to the impersonal walls.

She heard a low laugh, sardonic and ugly. A devil's laugh. She whirled about in stunned surprise. In the doorway to the far room was a man, leaning against the doorframe, his arms folded across his bare chest. He held a towel in one hand, and his broad shoulders were still wet; she guessed he had been washing up in the next room. For a moment she almost thought he *was* the devil, appearing so suddenly to startle her. Perhaps that was why her heart was racing, and her stomach was tingling in a peculiar way.

And surely he looked like a devil. Straight black hair, swept back from his forehead and falling just to his shoulders, glittering eyes as black as his hair, a handsome mouth twisted in a mocking grin. No cloven hoof, but there was a deep cleft in his chin that made him appear all the more satanic. His tall body was thin-hipped and hard, the broad expanse of his chest covered with a thick mat of black hair that tapered over his stomach and vanished into a point at the top of his low-slung breeches, like an insolent arrow pointing to the source of his power.

Ninon felt her blood boil. How dare the man eavesdrop on her and Philippe, then flaunt himself before her? She had not seen him before at Marival—a retainer who had come with one of the guests, no doubt. Curse the man! She would see to it that Philippe had him severely reprimanded.

He laughed again, a low rumble in his throat, and nodded politely at her, though the gesture seemed more derisive than humble. "Your pardon...Ninon...isn't it? But you certainly don't *look* like a fool! I recognized Monsieur le Comte's voice, but my curiosity was piqued. I had to see the idiot who would listen to such words, let alone play the whore for a man like that."

She gasped in shock, her jaw dropping open, too astonished at the man's effrontery to say a word.

He threw down his towel and swaggered over to her, his eyes raking her from top to bottom until she quivered, feeling stripped of her chemise by that insulting glance. "For a body like that, a man would say anything!"

This time she found her voice. "Hold your tongue," she said indignantly, "or I shall see to it that your master thrashes you!"

He shrugged off the threat. "*Mon Dieu*," he sneered, "are you so hungry for love that you *believe* him? That you give him your body time and again?" His face darkened, the black eyes glittering with contempt. "I have seen sluts in my time, but never a one so wide-eyed and foolish."

Sweet Madonna, she thought, why was she standing here listening to this half-naked savage? "Get out of my way."

He swept an imaginary hat off his head and bowed low. "Of course...Ninon. Sweet, lovely Ninon. Little bird. Let me kiss you. Let me feel you trembling beneath me. Were those not his words?" His voice was sharp with mockery. "But that was scarcely what he meant, I think. Shall I tell you the words that *I* heard, while he beguiled you with his flattery? Gullible Ninon, let me put my hard prickle inside you, when I will, as I will—and call it Love!"

It was too much for her to swallow her anger, as was her wont; to pretend that his vicious words had not hurt her. With a shriek she leaped for him and slapped him hard across the face. His eyes narrowed angrily. His hand lashed out, the open palm catching her across her cheek so that she staggered back a step. She gasped in surprise, her fingers cradling her stinging face. "Say what you will," she breathed at last, "but Monsieur le Comte would never strike a woman!"

Again the mocking bow. "True enough. But *I*, mademoiselle, would not bed one woman while I was married to another!"

"He does not love her—nor she him," she said defensively. "What you call 'flattery' are words of love to me. He does me honor by holding my heart in such esteem!"

He threw back his head and laughed. "Honor?"

Why did the man disquiet her so, make her shiver with uneasiness, his black eyes boring into her soul? "How can you know? A man like you…I can scarce imagine that love has ever touched you!"

He blanched at that, his face turning so pale that the marks of her fingers glowed red upon his cheek. His nostrils flared in helpless fury, and a small muscle worked in his jaw. Ninon glared in triumph and turned, making for the door. In two strides he reached her and swung her around with rough hands, one arm going about her waist, the other encircling her shoulders. He pulled her hard against his chest and bent to her mouth, his lips hot on hers, pressing, insistent. She struggled against him for a moment, fighting desperately against his powerful grip, then surrendered and closed her eyes, feeling herself drained of will, her head spinning, her heart beating frantically in her bosom. Savagely his tongue plundered her mouth, until she quivered and felt as though her legs would give way beneath her. She had never been so overwhelmed by a kiss before; when at last he released her, she swayed back against his arm, her fingers pressed to her mouth, blue eyes wide with shock.

"My God," he said. "If a man wanted you, he could have you on the ground with your skirts up in five minutes." He pushed her away, a look that was almost hatred coming into his eyes. "If a man were *fool* enough to want you! A-a-ah! Why the devil should I care? Run after your Philippe. Spread your pretty legs for him!" He strode angrily to the door, then turned, his mouth twisted in an ugly grimace. "But what will you do with the brats he gives you?" He laughed scornfully at the sudden look of horror on her face. "Did it never occur to you, little fool, each time your loving gardener Philippe plants his hot spade in you, he is perhaps planting more than you bargained for?" He laughed again, seeming more like a devil than ever. Sweeping his towel off the floor, he disappeared into the room whence he had come.

Fighting back her tears, she fled to the courtyard, trembling against the sunny wall while she tried to wipe from her memory the feel of his mouth on hers. Foolish Ninon! It was just a kiss that had caught her unawares—that was all. He had done it to humiliate her. Best not to think about it—or about her weak-kneed submission. It was his words that should concern her. As insolent as was the man, as crude and ugly were his words, they rang in her brain like a warning bell. She had not even thought of children. Nor the life she would doom them to. A life like her own. She would merely be repeating her mother's folly, trusting her children's happiness and security to a legacy that could be stolen by a vengeful widow. She sighed unhappily. But what was she to do? Even if she married Mathieu, she would succumb to Philippe sooner or later; she could not withstand his words of love. And Mathieu, coarse and lustful Mathieu. Would he be as careless and cruel to a stepchild as Baugin had been? *Ah Dieu!* What was she to do?

No matter Philippe's feelings for her, he would never forfeit his comfortable life, the convenience of his marriage to Henriette. She had been a fool to let him know she loved him. Hadn't she learned by now not to trust a man with her heart? Now he would beguile her with his sweet words and—willy-nilly—she would warm his bed, bear his children, do his bidding, however humiliating and joyless, if she stayed.

If she stayed.

"By the forehead of Zeus, Colombe, you shall not displace my guitar!"

An outraged shriek. "You mincing *tapette!* I'll tell you what you may do with your guitar! But for the nonce, I shall ride!"

Startled out of her reverie, Ninon looked up. Two of the actors were quarreling. The leading lady of the night before was brandishing an ornate guitar, alternately threatening to smash it to the ground and gesturing obscenely with the neck of the instrument. An equally irate man, large and fleshy like a soft dumpling, was guarding what appeared to be the last open space on the overloaded and groaning wagon. Ninon saw now why the lady had worn the outmoded and high-waisted gown the night before: in a simple skirt and apron, her large belly, obviously in the later stages of pregnancy, bulged like an overripe melon.

"Fat whore!" hissed the man. "Would you break the back of the ox? You can walk like the rest of us! Pay for your wanton pleasures with the soles of your feet!"

Colombe shrieked again, her face purple with rage, and raised the guitar to smash it over his head.

"Colombe! *Nom de Dieu.* Hold your temper!" A third actor appeared between the two combatants, snatching the guitar from Colombe's hands and momentarily cowing her with his glance. He seemed to be well along in years, perhaps fifty, with a gray spade beard and close-cropped hair. His brown eyes flashed angrily as he turned to the younger man. "And you, Marc-Antoine! You see that Colombe can scarcely walk in her condition. Let her ride. We shall find a place for your guitar, else I shall carry it myself." Though he still scowled, his voice was conciliatory and commanding all at the same time.

Colombe smiled smugly and clambered aboard the wagon. "A pox on his old guitar, Gaston," she sniffed. "Marc-Antoine is merely sulking because he cannot possibly be the father of my child!"

"Oh! A poisoned arrow to my heart!" Marc-Antoine slapped his hand to his breast—a silly, melodramatic gesture, it seemed to Ninon—and grimaced in pain. "You see what I must endure from that bitch?"

"Have done, both of you," Gaston growled in exasperation. "I fail to see why you should take such offense, Marc-Antoine. You have hardly made a secret of your inclinations!"

Colombe clapped her hands in delight. "The two pageboys in Bourboule—do you remember, Gaston? When Marc-Antoine..."

"Enough! There is too much for me to do today without listening to your viper's tongue! Sit you there and be quiet—or I myself, Gaston Floresse, will toss you out of the wagon! If we are to make Grancey by nightfall, there is work to be done. *Mon ami*, my friend," he said, as a curly-haired young man joined them, "fasten a line across those chairs. Mind they don't rattle."

The young man swept off his plumed hat, dragging the feathers in the dust of the courtyard as he bowed low. "*Monsieur le roi!* My lord the king. You have but to command me..."

Grancey by nightfall, thought Ninon. They travel far—and fast. There was no safety on the road for a woman alone. But with a band of actors...? She had already collected two months of wages; she could pay them for their protection. It would leave her very little, of course, to start a new life, but it could not be helped. Or could it? Her eye lit on the guitar that Gaston still held. She was a skilled musician. Why not offer her services for the few weeks she would be with them, until she had found the path that her future was to take?

Timidly she approached Gaston. It was obvious he was the leader of the troupe. "Monsieur Floresse," she began, "have you a need for another player?"

"You, mademoiselle?" She nodded. "What can you do?"

"I can play the guitar. And the lute. And I can read."

"Can you sing?"

"A little."

He handed her the guitar. "Show me."

She plucked at the strings, familiarizing herself with the instrument. "It is well tuned," she said, smiling as she nodded to the fleshy young man. "Monsieur...Marc-Antoine, *n'est-ce pas?*"

He bowed to Ninon. "Marc-Antoine de Ville de La Motte. At your service." He sneered over his shoulder at Colombe. "*Here*, at least, is a lady of sensitivity!" He bowed once again to Ninon. "You honor me, *ma belle.*"

Ninon began to play. Her voice was not remarkable, but she trusted in the skill of her fingers to show her talents. After two country airs, she stopped and looked questioningly at Gaston. He pulled aside Marc-Antoine and the curly-haired young man. For some moments they conferred quietly, looking now to her, now to Colombe, who sat pouting in the wagon, excluded from their deliberations.

At last Gaston turned to her. "Can you act, mademoiselle?"

"What does it matter?" Marc-Antoine simpered wickedly. "Colombe cannot!"

"I...I have never done it," said Ninon.

"But you can read a part that is written down?"

"Of course."

"And commit it to memory?"

"Wherefore not? Is it so different from learning lessons? But why do you ask?"

Aware of his delicate role as diplomat, Gaston smiled warmly at Colombe in the wagon. "You see, mademoiselle, the...ah...difficult situation of our charming Madame Linard. She is a superb actress, you understand, but...it is impossible to play the part of a...maiden, when all the world can see..." He stopped and cleared his throat.

Marc-Antoine giggled and the curly-haired young man threw him a warning glance.

"As you can see," Gaston went on smoothly, "Madame Linard must of necessity restrict her appearances on the stage for the next few months. We will need another lady to play the first parts."

Better and better, thought Ninon. Just the few months she needed. "Then you will take me on, monsieur?" she asked, proffering the guitar to Gaston.

"No. Keep it to show your skill to Val."

"Val?"

"The head of our illustrious company."

"But…not you, Monsieur Floresse?"

"Not I. You must speak to Monsieur Sanscoeur."

Ninon laughed. "*Sanscoeur?* Heartless? What a name!"

The curly-haired young man stepped forward. Warm brown eyes, as rich mahogany as the curls that spilled over his linen collar, smiled at Ninon. "His full name is better. Valentin Sanscoeur."

"A wry name. A name of unpleasant irony."

"An apt name, as you will discover." He grinned. "And scarcely conferred at the baptismal font, you understand!"

She laughed, feeling welcomed and warmed at once by his open countenance. "And what is your name? *Réjouissance?* Merriment?"

"No. You see me in my modest morning guise, but they call me Chanteclair."

"The Crowing Rooster. And do you live up to the name?"

Smiling, he took her free hand. "Sometimes I crow, sometimes I strut about, and sometimes…" he kissed her hand with mock passion, "I assail every hen in the barnyard!"

She laughed in delight. "Well met, Chanteclair!"

His eyes twinkled merrily. "But I warn you, mademoiselle, I will… Ah! Valentin! We have found a replacement. And just as I thought we should have to paint Colombe with copper and present her as a kettle in our next play!" This remark sent Marc-Antoine into a frenzy of laughter, while Colombe sputtered in fury. "*Voilà!* A replacement."

Ninon turned to meet Monsieur Sanscoeur, and felt her heart thud in her breast. It could not be! The arrogant man from the stable. His lip curled in a mocking grin, enjoying her discomfiture. He finished buttoning the cuffs of his full shirt and tucked it into his breeches, making even that simple gesture seem an insult. "You have talents… beyond the obvious, mademoiselle?" he drawled at last.

"Indeed, yes!" crowed Gaston. "She plays the guitar exquisitely."

Sanscoeur took the guitar from Ninon and handed it to Floresse, but his eyes never left her face, and the insolent cock of his eyebrow made her tremble with fury. "Guitar?" he sneered. "Name of God!" One slim-fingered hand reached out and pulled the cap from her head, releasing the glory of her copper curls. There was a chorus of a-a-ahs from the men, while Colombe muttered under her breath, her face pinched with jealousy. Valentin stepped closer to Ninon. Swiftly he pulled down her chemise so it rested off her shoulders and bared the first rounded swell of her bosom. "*That* is what they will come for, *mes amis!*" He stared at

Ninon, his eyes black and filled with hatred. "The race of men rejoices in the allure of a tormenting woman." A bitter laugh. "Though, curse me, I cannot fathom why!"

Furious at the indignities visited upon her, Ninon almost slapped his face again. She could hardly understand her intemperate urge to strike him, to crack that sardonic mask. Always before she had hidden her anger, swallowing her pride, fearful of the storm of retaliation her open emotions might bring down upon her head. She took a deep breath, willing her rage to cool, and straightened the neckline of her revealing chemise. "If you will but allow me, Monsieur Sanscoeur," she said coldly, "you shall see I am skilled with the guitar."

He smirked. "No. No guitar. It would cover your bosom too much. An actor learns very soon that it is foolish to hide one's best assets!"

She smiled tightly, determined to throw the insult back in his teeth. "Indeed?" she purred. "Then, my lord Valentin, you may safely wear Spanish breeches, loose and billowing. And with no fear. For surely you have no nether assets worthy of display!"

"Touché!" exulted Chanteclair. Marc-Antoine and Gaston roared with laughter as Sanscoeur turned purple and strode away quickly, finding a loose rope on the far side of the wagon to draw his attention.

Ninon turned to Chanteclair, the smile fading from her face. "You said the name suited him," she said quietly, so the others could not hear. "It is so. The man is heartless. It is plain I cannot join your company. I scarce can fathom the why of his hatred, but I feel it to the quick."

"No. It isn't you. He does not particularly care for *any* woman. Unhappily for him, the ladies in the audience are eternally sighing and love-smitten."

"Not *any* woman? Is he…?" she stopped delicately, leaving the question unfinished, and glanced toward Marc-Antoine daintily brushing the dust from his doublet with a lace handkerchief.

"*Ma foi!* My faith! No!"

She frowned and hesitated, torn by indecision. "The man is insufferable," she said at last.

"Yes."

"Arrogant, rude, insulting…"

"Yes."

"Not a shred of human decency in him."

"Without a doubt." Chanteclair smiled, his gentle mouth twisting at the quizzical look on Ninon's face. "I would trust him with my life," he said softly.

SYLVIA HALLIDAY

She stared, blue eyes wide with surprise. How could anyone speak well of Sanscoeur?

With studied indifference, Valentin fastened one last rope on the wagon, then marched back to Ninon and planted himself before her, arms folded across his chest. "Well? Have you decided?"

"Have you?" she challenged. "Am I...acceptable to you?" This time the mockery was in *her* voice.

He shrugged. "Only because Colombe has grown so large. And Hortense has not the looks, nor Toinette the art to play her roles. When she is delivered of her child...Well, we shall see what we shall see." He gazed at Ninon's flat belly, as though he were seeing Philippe's seed already growing there. It hardly seemed worth it to her to disabuse him of the notion that she and Philippe had slept together—what did his opinion matter to her? Besides, it was none of his concern. She was growing quite used to his malice, even in so short a time. And so long as it was not directed exclusively to her, she could deal with the man.

"Then it is agreed?" she asked.

"'Tis a hard life."

"I have known worse."

"We travel from town to town. And we are ofttimes...unwelcome. We have no rich patron, so we must manage as best we may. We divide equally...after expenses. If you have a hundred livres to spend at the end of a month you will consider yourself fortunate." His eyes raked her body, almost seeming affronted by her lush curves. "Of course, you may earn a few extra crowns from time to time, as our sweet Colombe does, but that is entirely your own affair."

He thinks me a whore, she thought. So be it. Let him think so! She smiled smugly. "I have no doubt I shall...earn my way," she said, "and with a little more besides for trifles and indulgences. You need have no fear of that, monsieur!"

He nodded curtly. "Let me introduce you to the company. You have met Gaston Floresse, I think, and our 'nobleman,' Marc-Antoine de Ville de La Motte. This is Chanteclair..."

She shook his hand, feeling as though she already had a friend in the company. "And does the Rooster have another name?"

"My mother called me Jean," he said, shamefaced. "Far too ordinary a name."

She smiled with warmth. "Then I shall be happy to call you 'friend,' Chanteclair."

"*Mon Dieu*," growled Valentin. "Shall we be at this all morning?

66

Colombe Linard, our somewhat indisposed *prima donna*. Over there…" indicating a plain-looking woman, "Hortense Joubert, a most accomplished comedienne. And that little tart flirting with the stableboy yonder—Antoinette Vivoin, our soubrette, who plays the maidservant roles."

"Toinette, you little minx!" Marc-Antoine cried waspishly. "Come and meet the charming creature who will show our fat cow what it is to be a leading lady!"

"God's blood," Gaston muttered in exasperation, as Colombe screeched in outrage. "Do you never stop, the two of you?"

Valentin puffed with impatience and put his hands on his hips, black eyes glittering in annoyance. "The last of our company you will meet in a little. Joseph Pélerin, the youngest of our number, is filling the water pouches at the well. And Sébastien Duvet…"

"A pox on him!" This last from the plain-looking Hortense, who had joined them just in time to hear Sébastien's name. She frowned and made an obscene gesture with her finger. "You must be a fool, Valentin, to have sent him for our earnings from Madame la Comtesse! It will be gambled away before we see a livre of it!"

"I trust the man, Hortense," Sanscoeur said tiredly.

She snorted in derision. "You? Trust? I'll wager you bit your wet nurse's nipple to see if she was genuine!"

"Only because she was female," he growled. "In truth, Hortense, I promised Sébastien that I would show the company your fat backside if he hurried with the money!" He took a menacing step toward her, one eyebrow raised in mockery. "You had best pray he lingers along the way! Now, let me introduce our new player. Ninon…"

"Guillemot."

"Welcome to the Peerless Theatre Company, Ninon Guillemot. I trust you will not regret your decision." Valentin interrupted the handshakes and greetings that followed with an impatient clap of his hands. "We leave in half an hour's time."

"Wait!" said Ninon, struck by a sudden thought. "I…I do not wish them to know, in the château…when, and with whom…I have gone. I should prefer to leave in secret."

"I knew it!" cried Colombe. "The girl's a thief. I could tell it in an instant!"

"How so?" Chanteclair said angrily. "What nonsense!"

"It's true," said Toinette, shaking her blond curls, ready at once to agree with anything that was said. "Only a thief slips away in secret."

Colombe smiled like a cat. "You see, Val? You will simply have to do without a leading lady until my child is born. That creature would murder us in our beds if we took her along! You see the evil cast in her eye? It gives me the chills! Surely she will put a curse on my unborn babe!"

"Sweet Madonna," murmured Ninon, stricken.

"Shut your pernicious mouth, Colombe!" barked Valentin. He looked at Ninon, a spark of compassion—just for an instant—flickering in his dark eyes. "The girl has her reasons. None of which are your concern. Or mine." He laughed sharply, the mocking devil returning once again. "Did you ever know a woman who did not have her schemes? Now…you… Ninon. You wish to be an actress, *n'est-ce pas?* I give you the opportunity to play your first role. Professionally, of course. I have no doubt you have always been capable of pretense—it is a beautiful woman's birthright! Now: your part. You are to bid us farewell for all the world to see. Do not play it too broadly, with grief and wringing of hands. Your preoccupation last night with the pawing oaf and the panting peacock of a gentleman made it rather apparent that our endeavors onstage were wasted on you! Now to the plot: obvious farewell by heroine; exeunt traveling players. There is a crossroads—some two leagues from here, I would guess. We shall wait there for two hours. No more."

She nodded and hurried into the château. It would only take a moment to gather her belongings and her carefully hidden wages, and tuck her straw hamper under the back staircase near the door. She would wave good-bye to the company from the window, the children beside her; who would fail to notice the racket they made? She would return with them to their room and their studies. After a decent interval, she would praise their work and send them down to the kitchen for a treat from the cook, cautioning them to remain there until she came to fetch them.

Her scheme worked perfectly. In no time at all she was on the road, hidden from the château by dense trees, hurrying toward the crossroads. Farewell, Philippe. Farewell, folly. She gulped back her tears; she must learn to be hard again. She thought of Sanscoeur, so cruelly mocking, so hurtful and ugly—she was almost glad he was so disagreeable. It would be easier to remember what Philippe had managed to make her forget for a little—that a man was a betrayer, a heartbreaker, taking a girl's dreams and giving back ashes.

Drawing a deep breath, she began to trot toward the crossroads. Toward the unknown life that awaited her.

Ninon Guillemot. Actress and traveling player.

Chapter Four

"Valentin, you plaguey villain, if I wake with my bones aching, I shall deliver you such a kick as would render you impotent for a month!" Colombe smiled maliciously. "That is, if you had the inclination, sweetling."

Valentin shrugged and turned his back to her, warming his hands at the fire in the clearing. Beyond the dark trees, an owl hooted into the night air. Chanteclair and the young lad, Joseph, set down an old and battered settee that they had lifted from the wagon, placing it within the circle of firelight.

"Put a cheerful face on it, Colombe," Chanteclair said mildly. "You shall sleep elegantly, while the rest of us must be content with the hard ground and a few branches."

"Bah! But for that great looby, that pricklouse, that shittlebrain…"

"Fair lady." With an elaborate bow, Chanteclair knelt before Colombe, gazing worshipfully at her scowling face, her swollen belly. "If the world but knew, when it glories to see your queens and princesses upon the stage, that beneath the trappings of the noble lady lies the soul of…" Discretion getting the better of him, he smiled benignly, rose to his feet, and said no more. Behind him, Marc-Antoine smothered a laugh.

Colombe sniffed. "But for Valentin, that fool, we should all be sleeping soundly at The Red Bull in Grancey. Two hours at the crossroads!" She whirled to Ninon, sitting apart from the group, finishing the last of her supper bread. "*Two hours*, mademoiselle! Two hours in the hot sun, and a cold supper. And not a decent bed! And all on your account."

"Have done, Colombe," growled Valentin, turning from the fire. "You shall breakfast well at Grancey. We needed another actress. You know it as well as I."

"Ah, but this one…this one…" Colombe's eyes were like a cat's. "To put ourselves out for *this* one. Not a shred of talent, I'll wager. And indifferent looks. And yet we waited half the day!" She laughed, an ugly sound. "Can the great Sanscoeur be growing soft toward a woman? You had best guard yourself, my dearest Mademoiselle Ninon, unless you wish…" She patted her own expanding girth.

Valentin crossed his arms against his chest, his dark eyes sweeping Ninon with contempt. "I scarce think Mademoiselle Ninon needs *me* for that. Better a nobleman's brat than a stroller's bastard."

It was clearly meant as an insult to Philippe. Ninon leaped to her feet, bosom heaving in fury, fists tight-knotted at her sides. Only Gaston's gentle voice and his hand on her shoulder prevented her from springing at Valentin. "As to the matter of 'mademoiselle,' we must change it, of course. Surely you know, Ninon, you must be called 'madame' henceforth."

Chanteclair smiled at Ninon's puzzled frown. He folded his hands in prayer, his eyes rolling heavenward. "Alas! Despite our most *virtuous* behavior," a sly wink at Colombe, "the world at large thinks actors a scurvy lot. And so, to preserve the illusion of propriety, every lady in the company must be assumed to be married, and is thus called 'madam.'"

"And if you are religious, 'Madame' Guillemot," Gaston said kindly, "you must be prepared for the scorn of the Church. You will be held ipso facto excommunicate until you abandon this trade and seek absolution."

"And absolution comes dear," said Chanteclair, rubbing an imaginary coin between his fingers.

"Excommunicate!" murmured Ninon, her eyes wide with distress. "But…but a child must be baptized, *n'est-ce pas?* And what of burial in holy ground, and…marriage, and…?"

"What a great blubbering fool you are!" sneered Colombe. "There is not a church register in the whole of France that has not recorded a host of sacraments for so-called musicians and singers. 'Tis a simple matter to gull a country curé, so long as the fee is large enough!"

"*Mon Dieu!*"

"Have you not the stomach for it after all?" growled Valentin. "Will you return to Marival in the morning?" The words were cast down like a challenge.

Chanteclair threw him an angry look. "If you wish to hide your name," he said gently to Ninon, "take another…as Valentin has done."

"Take two, if you wish," said Gaston. "I remember the great Robert Guérin, who played in Paris when I was a boy. When he played comedy he was *Gros-Guillaume*, 'Fat William,' but on the days he essayed tragedy he called himself LaFleur."

"No," said Ninon, looking Valentin firmly in the eye. "I shall be Madame Guillemot. At least until I can find a name that suits me as well as others' suit them! I cannot imagine you ever had any other name save Heartless!"

"Valentin! *Nom de Dieu.* Can we not get on with the business of the itinerary before we lose half the company?" Marc-Antoine, his fleshy lips pursed in disapproval, indicated the edge of the clearing where two couples seemed about to vanish into the privacy of the dark forest. At Valentin's call, they reluctantly joined the rest of the players to sit around the fire, Joseph putting his head in Toinette's lap and smiling vapidly up at the girl, Sébastien with his hand under Hortense's skirts.

"Well then," said Valentin, "what say you all to Nevers, Moulins, Bourges, Auxerre? And a few towns in between, if profit beckons?"

"Montluçon before Bourges," said Gaston. "There is a fine tennis court there. And if we arrive before the eighth of June, Saint Médard's Fête, there should be a goodly number of folk willing to spend their money on a divertissement or two."

"I heard that there was plague at Auxerre. Perhaps we should avoid that town." This from Sébastien, who seemed more concerned with his hand under Hortense's petticoat than with the conversation.

"Plague be damned!" said Hortense, her eyes flashing. "You're afraid of the bailiff at Auxerre! The one you cheated at cards some years agone, and who swore to kill you if you gambled again in his town!"

"I never cheated the man!"

"Then why avoid Auxerre? Unless you intend to gamble again, damn your poxy soul!" Hortense and Sébastien glared at each other; there was a sudden movement of Sébastien's hand under the skirts and Hortense let out a great shriek, half-rising to her feet and subsiding again to the ground at some distance from Sébastien. "Sleep alone tonight, you dunghill!" she spat.

"If we are to be in Bourges," Marc-Antoine said petulantly, "I do not see why we cannot go on to Orléans or Tours."

"Because we are not good enough," said Valentin. "Their theaters and actors are the equal of Paris. How can we hope to vie with them?"

"That's what you always say! But how are we to know, unless we try? If you were agreeable, we could go in a tiltboat on the Loire from Nevers to Orléans. Sometimes I think you avoid the big cities intentionally."

"True enough," said Gaston. "I fail to see why, when we were so close to Dijon after our commission for Froissart, we could not have tried our luck in the city."

Colombe had been reclining like a queen on her settee; now, the conversation having touched a theme dear to her heart, she struggled to her knees and pointed an accusing finger at Valentin. "We could have stayed until the *Parlement* of Burgundy was in session and the great nobles were assembled! Do you think I never tire of being cosseted by a country lord, too poor to go to Paris or the big cities, his title too mean to be talked of more than five leagues from his château?"

Chanteclair snickered. "You never tire of being cosseted by anyone."

"The nobles who fill the public theaters in the big cities are rowdy and dangerous," growled Valentin. "And powerful. If you break one of *those* heads in a brawl, it will cost you your neck! I say 'no' to the cities, and let us have no more on it!"

"We will talk of it another time, I promise you," Colombe said ominously, settling back onto her couch.

Joseph yawned and sat up, giving Toinette a kiss on the cheek, so that she giggled. "Is there more that we must talk of tonight?"

"The matter of money," said Valentin. "We have saved out enough of Froissart's gold to pay our expenses until our next presentation, but who will lend expense money to Madame Ninon until she earns her first share? I, for one, shall not."

"Nor would I take a sou from you, Monsieur Sanscoeur!" Ninon reached into her pocket and withdrew a leather pouch, counting out a handful of coins and throwing them angrily at Valentin. "There! Twenty-five crowns! Half of what I own in the world. Sweet Madonna, I shall not be beholden to *you!*"

Valentin nodded silently and pocketed the coins. In a few moments, Toinette and Joseph, arms about each other, had disappeared into the woods. Colombe sighed and curled up on her settee, the men made themselves as comfortable as possible on the pine boughs they had gathered for their bedding, and Hortense, still sulking, sat with her back to the fire, gazing into the blackness of the night sky.

Ninon leaned against a tree trunk and covered her face with her hands, feeling the ache in her legs from the unaccustomed walk, the deeper ache in her soul. She envied Toinette and Joseph and their youthful love, her longing for Philippe almost more painful than she could endure. Ah *Dieu!* Had she made a mistake? Was she a coward to run away from Philippe and her destiny? And she could not even pray to *le bon Dieu* for guidance. Was she not an outcast now? As godless and scorned as these, her new comrades? She looked up to see Valentin staring at her from across the fire, his eyes black with hatred, a hatred she had not even earned. Have I traded Philippe's love for this? she thought, and closed her eyes again.

"What? Saucy wench, will you go to sleep without bidding me a good night?" The voice was high-pitched and quavering.

Ninon's eyes flew open. Leaning over her was Chanteclair, a pair of spectacles perched on his nose, a large white chambermaid's cap covering his mahogany curls, a dark shawl across his shoulders.

"Look!" cried Marc-Antoine, sitting up in delight. "'Tis Grandmère, the old hag!"

"Grandmère, you sweet lady, where have you been these past weeks?" laughed Sébastien. "Learning to speak like a *castrato?*"

"Mock me not, you naughty children, else I shall crown you with a piss pot!" simpered Chanteclair, limping into the firelight and giving Sébastien a sharp rap on the nose.

"Name of God, Chanteclair," muttered Valentin, "will you play your silly part at this hour of the night?"

"Pish-tush, you great sour face, Grandmère always comes to visit when she is needed. Now, Hortense, you goose—is it worth a cold sleep to show Sébastien how angry you are at the mere expectation of his gambling? Punish the sin, but not the contemplation of it—else we should all be damned in Hell! Come, come, Hortense, up with you, and go and give Sébastien your lips…" "Grandmère" leered wickedly, "and whatever else you wish to give."

Prodded by Chanteclair, Hortense arose and embraced Sébastien, who beamed in triumph and pulled her into the trees. "Grandmère" pranced about the clearing, tweaking Gaston's beard, whispering a bawdy remark to Marc-Antoine that brought a roar of laughter, thrusting out his belly and waddling in imitation of Colombe's clumsy gait. In a few moments everyone except Valentin was smiling and chuckling at his antics.

"Now," said Chanteclair, stopping before Ninon, "what can Grandmère do to bring you cheer? I cannot give you a prettier face, God knows!" Chanteclair cackled delightedly and pointed a quivering finger at Valentin. "Aha! I have it! I shall turn your tormentor into a frog."

Ninon giggled. "Leave him as he is. For is he not a wild creature already? A great grumpy bear?"

"Indeed he is!" said Chanteclair, his voice a high squeak. "Now give Grandmère a kiss goodnight, and let her go to see what the children are up to. I have no doubt Joseph, at least, is 'up,' though I cannot be sure about Sébastien."

"Grandmère, you are a devil," laughed Ninon, kissing Chanteclair on the cheek and watching in delight as he hobbled off into the woods.

She felt her life put into balance again by his warmth and humor. She moved closer to the fire and glanced up. Valentin was still staring at her, his broad forehead creased in a deep frown. "Do you never smile?" she asked.

"Why?"

"Are you so filled with bile that you find nothing to smile about?"

"What do you know?" he said bitterly. "Living your days as a pampered princess at Marival—your first disappointment to find you could not have Philippe all to yourself."

Ninon flashed him an angry look, but said nothing.

"What? Not a rejoinder? No tears to excite my pity, no waspish words to sting me for my insolence? None of the tricks of womankind?"

She sighed and turned away, suddenly too weary to bother.

He laughed cruelly. "Think your last thoughts of your lover, Ninon, and your easy life at Marival. Tomorrow you learn to work!"

They set out early the following morning, traveling westward from the mountains of Burgundy to Nivernais and the rolling green hills watered by the Loire River and its many tributaries. Colombe wolfed her breakfast at Grancey with ill humor, determined that Valentin and Ninon should know how she had suffered on their account. With an eye to Ninon, Chanteclair suggested they hire a few horses to take them to the next town, but there were none to be had in Grancey.

The day was fine, with a soft May breeze that ruffled Ninon's hair and cheered her spirits. Except for Valentin, the strollers appeared a pleasant enough lot, no better or worse than she had a right to expect. Chanteclair and Gaston were unfailingly kind to her, and even Marc-Antoine, for all his affectations and florid manners, seemed good-hearted, though he took great joy in insulting Colombe. Joseph was young, perhaps eighteen or nineteen, Ninon guessed, with all the brashness of his tender years, and the appetites to match. He walked along the dusty road behind Toinette, his eyes on her swaying hips, his desires plain on his face. Sébastien and Hortense spent the morning bickering with each other; it was hard to believe they had been lovers the night before. And Colombe, perched precariously on the swaying wagon, was sometimes agreeable, smiling and gracious—especially when Gaston nullified Marc-Antoine's sharp remarks with compliments. She was very beautiful, Ninon thought, though her raven hair, rich by firelight and candlelight, seemed an unnatural hue under the glare of the May sun; Ninon wondered if nature had been aided and abetted in the matter.

Ninon glanced at Valentin striding along beside her. Hard and lean, he moved with the suppleness and grace of an actor, forever poised for the sudden leap from a pasteboard balcony, the mock duel, the sham brawl. Even his words, cynical and cruel as they could be, or merely instructive, as they were now, were delivered in a voice that flowed in a musical rhythm, rich and resonant.

"We shall start with the improvised comedies, I think. We imitate the Italian manner. Are you familiar with it?"

"Indeed," said Ninon, smiling in remembrance of her days at Bellefleur with her father. "I had occasion once to see the great Scaramouche, Tiberio Fiorello."

Valentin snorted. "I scarcely thought Monsieur le Comte de Froissart had the taste—or the pocketbook—to engage the Comédie Italienne."

"Fiorello, the Scaramouche?" said Gaston, coming up beside them at the mention of the actor's name. "Did you know that once, when King Louis was still the Dauphin, and a child of three or four, he laughed so hard at Scaramouche, while being held by the great comedian, that he quite forgot his manners?"

"What happened?" asked Ninon.

"He wet the man thoroughly!"

Ninon giggled. "Truly?"

"They say the king tells of it even today, with great relish."

"He is a great comedian," said Valentin, his voice edged with impatience. "But Ninon will be no comedienne at all, if we cannot get on with the business at hand! Now, unless we acquire a written comedy newly brought from Paris, we work from a rough *soggetto*, as the Italians call it, merely an outline of the plot. You will be expected to improvise, but I think you have a ready enough wit for that. We play stock characters, though they may have different names. And each of us plays his own characters, and none other. Thus, Gaston is the Pantalone, the rich merchant, the deceived husband; Marc-Antoine the doctor or savant; Chanteclair, the Polichinelle, the clever servant, the intriguing Brighella, the knave. Joseph and Sébastien," he added dryly, "play the lovers—even onstage!"

"And you?" asked Ninon.

"I am the fool Arlequin, or Scaramouche, the bragging captain."

"Full of wind and fire, but no warmth?" asked Ninon, her eyes wide with feigned innocence.

"Touché. You must remember that line. I had thought to make you one of the lovers, as Colombe represents, but with that tongue you might do better as the soubrette, the comic maid. Toinette has always been indifferent in that role—with her limited wit more suited to the inamorata parts, but Colombe's vanity would never allow herself to be laughed at. When there was a maid to be played, it had to be Toinette."

"But what of Hortense?"

"Hortense, alas, is too plain to play aught save old gossips and confidantes. Yes. 'Tis a fine arrangement. Toinette will be pleased. She can play the lover roles that suit her, and you will be our soubrette." He stopped in the road, coolly appraising Ninon from top to toe. "You have a good enough shape. How are your legs?"

"Well suited to carry me, monsieur!" she snapped.

"*Morbleu!* Will you play the virtuous maiden still? After all that I overheard at Marival? I asked merely because the soubrette often disguises herself as a man. It is to your advantage if your legs are shapely in trunk hose. Now, as to your speeches. It is not such a difficult matter as you might suppose. Not all of your speeches must be *extempore*. They must only appear to be so. The *soggetto* will indicate entrances and exits, day, night, time, and place; where a bit of comic business is needed—such as falls, disguises, drunken stumbling, asides, mimicry. The Italians call these comic bits *lazzi*. And every player has a book of 'conceits,' set pieces writ down for any occasion—entrances, dialogues, reproaches, greetings, contemplation of a lover's virtue, grief at a lover's betrayal. He commits them to memory, and uses them at the proper moment in a play, adding more to his book as he invents them. 'Lament for a Lost Lover' might make an interesting conceit. Think you so?" His face betrayed no emotion, but his dark eyes studied Ninon carefully.

She smiled tightly. "But then, Marc-Antoine, as the pedant, must have a book filled with fatuous maxims, such as 'A crude oaf is not a gentleman.' Or even, 'A blind man sees nothing'!"

"And mayhap, 'A woman who pines for a lost love is a fool'!"

"'A simpleton speaks with the tongue of a simpleton'!" said Ninon, her eyes flashing. "Shall we fill a complete book with insults, or shall we proceed with my initiation into the mysteries of the farce?"

He smiled and bowed mockingly. "Your grief has not blunted your tongue. *Eh bien.* We have had some success with a play called *The Imaginary Cuckold*, or *Le Vicomte Jaloux*. I shall give you the *soggetto* to study, of course, and you may use Toinette's book of conceits, but the basis of the plot is the wife—you—who contemplates betraying her braggart of a husband—myself—because of his jealousy."

Ninon laughed. "Scarcely a part written to the life! A man who has no love for women has no jealousy either!"

His eyebrow twitched sardonically. "It is a triumph of my art. And then, of course, I get to beat you."

Ninon stopped in her tracks. "The devil you do! Gaston," she called to Floresse, who had walked on ahead, "in *The Jealous Vicomte*, am I to be beaten by this brute?"

At these words there was a chorus of laughter from the company. Chanteclair, who had been urging on the ox, halted the animal and turned grinning to Ninon. Only Toinette looked distressed.

"Is she to have my part, Val?"

He smiled reassuringly. "But only because I wish you to represent the lover Isabelle. That way, you may kiss Joseph on the stage as well as off. Does that please you?"

Toinette nodded her head, her pale blond curls bobbing vigorously. "I never liked the role of Fiamette."

Ninon stamped her foot. "Answer me, Gaston! Is he to beat me?"

Gaston nodded his head solemnly. "But you are to crash half a score of plates over his head."

"I always hated that part," said Toinette. "I could not do it aright."

"I shall have no such fears," muttered Ninon. "Beat me, indeed!"

"*Nom de Dieu*," growled Valentin. "Lest you think we are savages, let me assure you that we beat one another with slapsticks, and nothing more. Look!" He rummaged in the wagon and pulled out a broad bat that consisted of two wide strips of lath loosely bound into a handle at one end. Whirling, he clapped Chanteclair on the top of the head with the weapon. There was a loud crack as the top lath strip smacked down upon the lower. Chanteclair began to whistle. "As you see," said Valentin, "there is much sound, but no damage. Upon occasion, we will put a squib of powder between the two strips. The noise and the flash seem to enchant children—and provincial nobility, who have little to do except watch plays and commit adultery!"

Ninon ignored the gibe. "And the plates?" she asked.

Gaston made a face. "It is my chore to glue them back together again after each representation of *The Imaginary Cuckold*. They will break with the slightest tap upon Valentin's skull. And no harm done."

"What a pity," said Ninon.

They stayed that night in a little inn outside Epinac, taking three large rooms and a small one just off the kitchen, which was all that the innkeeper had to offer. They supped in the women's chamber, seated about a large trestle table that their host had put up; then spent the remainder of the evening at trictrac and storytelling, the women lolling on the two beds, the men at the table with the board and dice. Valentin gave Ninon the *soggetti* for *The Jealous Vicomte* and half a dozen other farces, as well as the written parts to several tragedies and pastorals that she was to commit to memory. Colombe, while making clear that no one could ever play tragedy as well as *she*, graciously offered to assist Ninon in the learning of her parts.

They retired at half-past twelve. Ninon shared one of the beds with Hortense; Colombe, used to having a bed to herself, grudgingly made room for Toinette. The largest room, with a bed and a small cot, was shared by Joseph, Sébastien, and Chanteclair. Despite the innkeeper's insistence that Monsieur Sanscoeur, as head of the company, should sleep alone in the small room, Valentin was adamant about not being alone, almost coming to blows with the man over the matter. In the end, it was decided that Gaston should sleep in the room next to the kitchen and Valentin and Marc-Antoine would share a bed in the fourth chamber. Ninon found Valentin's anger inexplicable, but she was too tired to care. She slept quite soundly, though she thought at some time during the night Hortense had left the bed.

In the morning, the innkeeper announced that there would be horses for rent to take them as far as Autun, if they would but wait another day. It seemed a sensible idea. There was a broad meadow and a stream hard by the inn, where the company could rehearse, and do their laundry, and take their leisure. While the women, stripped down to their chemises—the garment knotted high on one hip—knelt in the shallow water with armloads of petticoats and neck linen to be washed, the men, clad only in breeches, practiced their fencing with blunt swords, and perfected a tumble or a pratfall or other *lazzi*. Ninon was surprised at the ease with which they revealed their bodies to one another. Indeed, when Joseph decided to go for a swim, he stripped off his breeches and jumped naked into the stream; and Hortense, angry at something Sébastien had said, turned her back to him, lifted up her chemise, and waggled her bare backside. Ninon was scarcely prudish, but she was glad that she was busy with Gaston and Valentin, learning the techniques of acting. It would take getting used to, this dressing and undressing before her fellows. It didn't help that Valentin, sitting next to her on the grass with several books of plays, seemed aware of her discomfort and viewed it with amusement.

"Did I not tell you it was a hard life?" he smirked.

She flashed him an angry look and snatched a book from his hands. "The life is not difficult. Only some of the people! Now tell me of this play."

"As you can see," he said, "it came to us from the Théâtre du Marais in Paris. *Scévole*. Du Ryer wrote it some years ago, but had it published only last year. We cannot copy a play, however great its success, until it is published."

"Which is not to say," interrupted Gaston, "that we have not, upon occasion...hem...borrowed an idea or two!"

"It is in five acts, with Alexandrine verse. Remember that. If you forget a line (I trust you will not) and you must improvise, try to keep the rhythm, if not the rhyme, of the Alexandrine."

"You should not be concerned," reassured Gaston, seeing the look on Ninon's face. "Now that she can no longer appear upon the stage, Colombe will be the book-holder. Unless a sudden wind blows out her candle, she will quietly supply the verse you lack." Remembering Colombe's vanity and jealousy, Ninon wondered whether she ought to find Gaston's words comforting.

"How quickly can you learn the plays I gave you last evening?" asked Valentin.

"I shall do the best I can."

"You know," said Gaston, "you need not memorize the parts to the very word. Particularly those in prose." He held up a warning finger. "Except, of course, Val's plays. He has been known to rage at a misplaced 'if.' Is it not so, *mon ami?*"

Valentin grunted.

"I did not know you were a poet as well as an actor," said Ninon, with genuine warmth. "How splendid! Were any of them yours, the plays that you gave me last night to read?"

"Spare me your patronizing. Yes. Two of them were. *The Amours of Phocidon* and *The Spiteful Wife*."

"I might have guessed," she said sourly, stung by his rudeness toward what, surely, he knew was meant to be a compliment. "Your verses deal with the wickedness of the female sex, the evils of love. They suit you."

He laughed. "They suited Monsieur le Comte de Froissart as well. He was positively inflamed! Do you recall the verse? I made it up especial, on the spot."

"Curse you," she whispered, feeling her face flame red.

"Ah! Then you *did* hear the lines. I thought perhaps not. You seemed...otherwise engaged at the time. Tell me, who *was* the lout showing the world he owned you with his slavering kisses?"

Ninon turned to Gaston. "Are all women whores in his eyes?"

Floresse shrugged. "Pay him no mind. It is his nature."

Valentin leaned back on the grass, his eyes scanning Ninon insolently. "What did you do at Marival?" His mouth twitched in a mocking smile. "That is, what was your employ?"

"I was tutor to the children!" she snapped.

"Alas! Does that mean I cannot mock you in Latin, lest you divine my meaning?"

"Nor Greek! If they bothered to teach you the language in your misbegotten youth!"

"Come, come," said Gaston. "Let us have peace! There is so much to be learned. And little time for it."

Valentin glared angrily at Ninon from beneath his brows. "There is no point in bothering until she learns her parts."

Ninon returned his look, her chin set in a hard line. "No point at all!" She stood up and kicked off her shoes, then quickly removed her stockings and stripped off her clothes until she stood in her chemise before him. Defiantly she pulled it up above her thighs, seeing the flicker in his eyes at the sight of her bare legs. "No point at all!" She knotted the garment at her hips, turned on her heel, and splashed furiously into the stream.

They made music that night after supper, sitting comfortably on the beds and elbow chairs in the women's room. It was common to have interludes of music and dancing between the acts of a play, and many a dismal tragic performance had been saved by a sprightly roundelay or a well-turned step. Since Marc-Antoine could play both the guitar and the bass viol, he chose the larger instrument so that Ninon might use his guitar. Sébastien took up his theorbo, a kind of bass lute, and sang to his own accompaniment a mournful ballad. His voice was sweet and clear; Ninon thought it was quite the most beautiful voice she had heard, until Marc-Antoine began to sing in a high tenor and put the decision in doubt. And when they joined together for a duet, the room was filled with a sound the angels might envy.

They both were good teachers: in a while Ninon was able to join them in trios of sad and merry songs. Valentin, despite his scowls, grudgingly conceded Ninon's skills with the guitar, if not the fineness of her voice. Chanteclair put in a brief appearance as "Grandmère," sending them all to their beds in an aura of goodwill and camaraderie. Ninon sat up late, studying and memorizing her lines by candlelight until Colombe, petulant, implored her to blow out the candle that they all might sleep. Ninon was not certain, but it seemed as though Hortense was missing a good part of the night.

In the morning, well breakfasted and riding double on the horses they had rented, they set out for Autun. The days were pleasant, but busy ones for Ninon. The weather was hot and they stopped often at inns, or in cool woods, to refresh themselves, while Valentin gave Ninon instruction in his art. And while they traveled, there was always one of Ninon's comrades to hear her recite her lines. She soon had committed half a dozen plays to memory, as well as Toinette's book of conceits—scores of rhymes and poetic passages she could insert into the improvised comedies. Valentin was a strict taskmaster, rehearsing her over and over again in the playing of her parts. "You must speak loudly enough to be heard in the highest reaches of the *paradis*, the topmost gallery!" he would insist, stepping farther away from her into the woods. "Louder!" he would shout after her every recital of a line, and, "Again! Again! Again!" until she felt as though her voice were being torn from her throat. And when she had no voice left, he concentrated on her facial expressions and gestures. "If they cannot hear you," he said, "as is often the case in the old converted tennis courts, they must understand you by your grimaces and gestures. Enlarge every movement. Clutch at your breast if you are in love, spurn with your hands a faithless friend, stamp your foot in anger. Your 'tirades,' those long, impassioned speeches in the tragedies, must be carefully rehearsed with suitable gestures, and your comic maids must know how to toss a disdainful head, shrug up a shoulder in coquetry—though I scarce think any woman needs to be taught such tricks. It is in their natures."

"If you please," Ninon said through clenched teeth, "must you take the occasion of my instruction for one of your insults against the members of my sex? Let us agree, once for all, that you do not like me, nor I you, and get on with the business!"

The sharpness of her rebuke seemed to abate his venom somewhat, and he contrived to be a little less unpleasant for a time. And Ninon found herself less and less bothered as the days went on—in part because Valentin (though a good comrade to the men) was disagreeable in equal measure to all the women of the troupe. And because, as Gaston had said, it seemed to be his nature, and hardly worth her ire.

After a week or so, Valentin decided that Ninon was ready to rehearse with the full company. Now when they stopped in the heat of midday to rest the horses and seek the coolness of a shadowy grove, they took the occasion to play out whole scenes, indicating to Ninon where to move, on what line to stand, how many steps to take before she turned. And more than one traveler, seeing on a distant hill a man tearing at his hair, a woman pacing to and fro with a wringing of her hands, was sure that the country folk had gone mad.

At night, snug in some cozy inn, the whole company cheerfully criticized Ninon's delivery and movements, and lamented the failings of her wardrobe. Since most of the plays were costumed in current fashions, she was expected to supply her own, using her own gowns as necessary.

"Upon my word, Valentin," Hortense said good-naturedly, indicating Ninon's blue gown, "if Madame Ninon is to play the queen in *Herod*, she cannot do it looking like a meat merchant's wife! An audience expects to be dazzled."

"When was the last time *you* dazzled an audience, Madame Joubert?" Sébastien said to Hortense, his voice hard and mocking.

"The last time you were able to make an audience believe in your prowess as a lover, Monsieur Duvet," she responded coldly.

"But 'tis the best gown I own," said Ninon.

"And scarcely fit if you are to represent nobility," sneered Colombe.

"Wait," said Chanteclair, rummaging in a large trunk. "Have we not a bit of tinsel and copper lace to festoon the bodice? If you are skilled with a needle, *ma petite*." He proffered the glittering fabric to Ninon, and indicated his own plain suit of clothes: narrow breeches fastened at the knee, a simple, waist-length doublet, square-toed shoes, and unadorned linen at neck and wrists. "I myself have turned this humble garb into an emperor's raiment when necessity, and an empty purse, demanded it."

Valentin nodded in agreement. "True enough. It can be done. And we have enough glass 'diamonds' and 'rubies' to trick her out as royalty. Of course, if you are to play a character role, Ninon—a Turkish princess, a Roman slave—you may borrow a costume from the many we keep at hand for such parts. And could she not use your velvet gown, Colombe? You have quite outgrown it."

Colombe flounced on the bed, her eyes narrowing in jealous anger. "No! She should tear it at the seams. She is neither small enough nor dainty enough!"

"Nor are you, my sweet, nor are you!" simpered Marc-Antoine, holding a pillow against his belly and prancing about the room. He dropped the pillow and ducked as one of Colombe's shoes came flying past his head. He bowed low, then picked up the shoe and passed it under his nose, pretending to be overwhelmed by the odor. "Madame! A scented rosebud for my performance. You are too kind!"

"You unnatural man!" she shrilled. "Go and find a little boy to play with."

"Oh-h-h! You have killed me," he said. Swiftly he drew a dagger from his waist and plunged it into his heart. Ninon gasped in horror as he crumpled to the floor, clutching at his breast, and a crimson stain spread across his doublet.

"Name of God!" she cried, rushing to kneel at his side. "Valentin… Gaston…please! He cannot lie here! Are you all quite mad? Have you turned to statues? Will you not…" She stopped. The "corpse" had opened one eye and was now winking at her. As she stared, Marc-Antoine slowly uncurled the hand that still pressed against his bloody chest, revealing a small sponge. He squeezed the sponge and a red stream spurted forth. "You villain," she breathed, then glanced up at the laughing faces above her. "All of you!" She laughed in spite of herself, and thumped Marc-Antoine on the chest. "And the knife, you great lout! What of the knife?"

Marc-Antoine sat up and showed Ninon how the blade of the knife collapsed into the handle. "Was it not a masterful performance?" he asked, grinning.

"Indeed," she said, pretending anger. "You have cost me a year of my life." She looked up at Sanscoeur smiling above her. When he forgot to frown, he could be almost human. "Val," she said, "if ever I must kill this oaf on the stage, I wish to strangle him, not stab him. That way the job may be done aright!" She was delighted to see him laugh, as though the merriment had momentarily lifted a burden from him. She smiled back and held out her hands. "Will you help me up?"

He scowled and turned away. "If you are to make your gown fit for the stage, you had best begin! We shall be in Nevers in a day or two."

I curse you, wretched man, she thought, hating him for robbing the moment of its joy. She rose to her feet and crossed to the large trunk, pulling out the pieces of tinsel that Chanteclair had offered. Then she threw them back again, feeling too dispirited to begin her sewing tonight. Her despondency was intensified by the arrival of Joseph and Toinette, who had (so they said) gone for a walk in the moonlight. But Toinette's face was flushed, her bodice awry, and Joseph looked too self-satisfied for a man who had merely gazed at the moon.

Ninon sighed. Tonight she felt more at home with Sébastien and Hortense, who had bid each other a frosty "good night," than with those cooing lovers Toinette and Joseph. Tonight her heart was heavy with yearning and grief, her thoughts dwelling on the sweetness of Philippe, the cruelty of Valentin. The one had rescued her from a life of misery; the other could not even give her his hand for aid. When she crept into bed, she turned away from Hortense, that the woman might not see her weep.

At dawn, with the sky still gray and one star lingering like a solitary diamond, she sat up in bed, startled. Something had awakened her. In the other bed Colombe still snored, her rasping voice and bulging belly directed toward heaven. Next to her, Toinette stirred and sat up, scratching her neck. Ninon turned to the pillow beside her; Hortense was gone.

Toinette yawned and went back to sleep. Ninon remained sitting in her bed, listening. Yes. There it was again. The sound of voices. Indistinct, save for what seemed occasionally to be a female voice, its sharp pitch carrying through the stillness of the dawn. Quietly Ninon eased herself out of bed and tiptoed to the door; when she opened it to the passageway, a soft breeze bellowed her chemise. The oaken staircase was cold on her bare feet; she was beginning to feel like a fool, wandering about the inn at this hour—and half-naked.

Then a woman's shriek cut the stillness. It seemed to come from the courtyard of the inn, near the stable. She heard voices from behind, and Valentin pushed past her, tying the fastening of his breeches and hurriedly tucking in his shirt. Marc-Antoine and Chanteclair followed close at his heels, Marc-Antoine in a lace-trimmed nightgown and embroidered nightcap. Chanteclair had had time to put his shoes on his stockingless feet, but had left his room without his breeches; his shirt, which he had slept in, slapped around his bare legs as he ran.

The sight in the courtyard made Ninon shrink back, her hand pressed to her mouth. Sébastien, fully dressed, and holding a poniard, was lunging at a half-naked Gaston, while Hortense, her chemise torn from one shoulder, tried in vain to pull him back. At second look, Ninon wondered if they might merely be rehearsing a scene. It seemed too improbable for reality: the outraged lover Sébastien, the wailing Hortense, the elaborately carved dagger that surely collapsed harmlessly.

Then the men were among them, scuffling, restraining the combatants, kicking up a cloud of dust in the pale dawn. At last, breathing hard, Valentin broke from the group and leaned against a hay wagon in the yard, his arms folded tightly across his chest. "Let them fight," he growled. "Let them kill each other!"

"No," said Gaston, smoothing his gray beard with as much pride as he could salvage, considering his state of undress. "I have no quarrel with the man. Hortense had a right to do as she pleased." He turned to the inn door.

"The whore!" cried Sébastien, still struggling against Chanteclair.

"And you?" Hortense planted herself before him, her eyes blazing. "You sleep with every woman you can! Will Colombe's child have the Duvet eyes? The Duvet nose? The Duvet love of Dame Fortune? Do you think me a fool? You lost ten ecus in Autun playing piquet. Damn you!" She slapped his face as hard as she could and stormed into the inn.

In a moment the rest had followed, except for Valentin, who was still leaning against the cart with his arms crossed. Ninon was too shaken to return to her bed. Absently she crossed the courtyard to retrieve the carved dagger that had been dropped in the scuffle and now lay forgotten in the dust. She looked up.

"Sweet Madonna!" From between the fingers of Valentin's hand, held tightly to his upper arm, seeped droplets of blood. Ninon moved quickly to him, meaning to tend the wound, then stopped as the look in his eyes curdled her benevolence.

He laughed cruelly and lifted his hand to show he held no actor's sponge. "Yes," he said. "Real blood. And all for a woman, *nom de Dieu*. Hortense is plain. You had half the men of Marival pining for you. Think of the mischief *you* might have caused had you stayed!"

Chapter Five

The sun was well up before they were able to continue their journey to Nevers. Shamefaced, Hortense had mended the tear in Valentin's sleeve where the knife had gone through, and bound up the slight wound, but she could barely get a civil word from Gaston; and Sébastien, a large hat pulled well over his eyes, refused even to look at her. He took Toinette up behind him on his horse, turning his head to whisper to her from time to time, until she blushed and giggled by turns and pressed her face up against his back. To placate Joseph, Colombe pulled him into the wagon with her, where he was content to lean back, the morning sun on his face, and rest his head on her ample bosom.

Seated behind Chanteclair, Ninon waited impatiently for the rest of the men to mount their horses. Tonight they would be in Nevers, God willing, and in a day or two she would know if she was an actress or no. Hortense, who had returned to the inn for a last cup of breakfast ale, emerged into the innyard. She stopped for a moment before the mounted Gaston, then seemed to reconsider and moved on to Marc-Antoine, holding out her hand for a lift up onto the rump of his horse. His face set in a prim mask, he shook his head from side to side, and put his heel to the horse's flank, moving some paces beyond Hortense.

She smiled uneasily. "Gaston?"

He scratched at his beard, then shook his head. "I think not."

"Valentin, may I ride with you?"

Sanscoeur gazed down at her, his face twisted into a grimace.

"I always ride alone, Hortense."

She laughed nervously. "It is a jest, *n'est-ce pas?* Gaston…Chanteclair… Damn you all! Am I to walk?"

Valentin shrugged. "You lie by night—you walk by day."

"And what of that fat whore Colombe?" Hortense's voice rose to a shrill pitch. "She does everything save allow a man to bed her in front of the whole company!"

Marc-Antoine snickered. "And if there were applause…who knows?" he muttered under his breath. Ninon tried not to laugh.

"You're right, Hortense," said Valentin. "You should not have to walk. I have asked the innkeeper to prepare a steed, especial for you." He clapped his hands together. Immediately there appeared from the stable the sorriest-looking donkey that ever Ninon had seen, his swayed back weighted down with a shabby and lopsided saddle. Valentin indicated the animal with a dramatic sweep of his arm. "*Voilà*, Madame Joubert! You have a fondness, I think, for being ridden by asses. Now ride one yourself."

At this, Chanteclair laughed so hard that Ninon feared he would fall from his horse; Toinette and Marc-Antoine began to giggle, and even Gaston found it a cause for merriment. In a while the whole company was laughing uproariously at Valentin's jest—even Hortense, who allowed that it was a fitting revenge for her night's mischief, and swore she would ride the ass as far as Nevers though her rump be sore by evening.

The laughter had dissipated the ugly tensions of the morning, and they set out on their path with light hearts. Marc-Antoine recited a tirade from *Artaxerce* at the top of his voice, and even Valentin began to whistle softly as they moved through countryside bright with sunshine and spring flowers.

Ninon settled herself more comfortably behind Chanteclair and tapped him on the shoulder. "Are you fond of playing such tricks upon one another?"

"Indeed, yes," he said. "It is a hard life—we have no roots, we have no home. It is a calling we all enjoy, but sometimes…sometimes…if we did not laugh, we should go mad. Is it not so, Valentin?" he said to Sanscoeur, who rode beside them.

"It is the human condition, I think, to live on the edge of madness."

"Come!" said Ninon. "On such a lovely morning would you both lapse into gloom?"

Valentin smiled. "A fitting rebuke! 'Tis too fine a day for gloom. But I am minded…" he began to laugh, "do you remember…Chanteclair… the joke that…with the tinker…?"

"*Mon Dieu*, yes! The trick turned upon the tricksters!"

"Oh, tell!" said Ninon. "You must tell me."

"You tell it, Chanteclair. Humor comes more easily to your tongue."

"Well then," began Chanteclair, speaking over his shoulder at Ninon. "We had set out one evening with Joseph and Gaston, leaving the rest behind. We were to perform in…Vézelay, I think it was, and wished to get the lay of the land before the rest of the company should join us. The night was cool, with a wind that blew through the trees with a mournful sound, and the full moon danced among clouds that churned and turned. 'Twas a night, my old nurse would have said, the very spirits were abroad. Val and I began to tell stories of ghosts and demons, and creatures that haunt the night, souls that would not be laid to rest. We did not plan the jest—we did not speak of it. Did we?"

Valentin shook his head. "No. It was only that Joseph and Gaston were growing uneasy…the night, the stories…"

"And then, near Vézelay, we passed a dark grove where men had been hanged. Three dried corpses, I think, and one so old it had slipped its noose and fallen to the ground. And Val, meaning nothing by it, said that the poor creature wished to travel with us, and had only waited, propped against a tree, until we should come along and bid him join us. Joseph and Gaston trembled, and spurred their horses to get out of the wood."

Valentin laughed. "In that moment, I think, the jest was born. Chanteclair hung back on the edge of the forest. I turned about in my saddle and shouted as loudly as I could, 'Well, dead man, are you coming? Will you travel in our company? You! In the woods! Will you join us?' There was a moment's silence. I thought that Chanteclair was waiting until the moon should disappear again and plunge the road into darkness. And then there was a voice: 'Wait for me. I'm coming! I'm coming!' Gaston and Joseph put spur to horse and did not stop until they reached Vézelay. Chanteclair rode out of the woods and guided his horse to me."

"And I asked him," interrupted Chanteclair, "how he had managed to speak in a voice so different from his own! 'I did not speak,' says he. 'You did!' 'Not I,' says I! And out of the woods came running this great deformed creature, with a hunched back, and with a sound of rattling such as ghosts in torment are said to make with their chains."

Valentin threw back his head and roared with laughter. "And still it cried, 'I come! I come! Wait for me!'"

Chanteclair shook his head. "I like to have wet myself at that moment," he said. "It was all I could do to keep from following Gaston's example, and running for my very soul!"

"But what…or who…was it?" asked Ninon, wide-eyed.

"'Twas only a poor tinker, with his pack upon his back and his tin pots rattling, who thought we meant to have him as our companion. He had fallen asleep, and Valentin's shouts had wakened him."

"And gave us a fright we shall not soon forget," Valentin said ruefully.

"It serves you right!" said Ninon, giggling. "But how nice to see *you* laugh, Valentin. You see, Chanteclair, he is almost handsome when he smiles. Think you so?" She had meant it to twit him and nothing more, and was shocked to see how the smile froze on his face, how his eyes seemed to flicker with hatred. No. More than hatred. Fear. She remembered something that Colombe had said, mocking him for sleeping with Marc-Antoine. Useless *tapette*, she had called him. As unmanly as Marc-Antoine. Could that be why he hated and feared women? She laughed brightly to cover the sudden awkward moment. "Did you ever tell the others how the 'hanged man' had frightened you?"

Valentin relaxed. "We never had the courage."

Chanteclair shuddered, his face suddenly serious. "I should not care to spend eternity dancing in the wind."

"What a thought," breathed Ninon, and made the sign of the cross.

As they neared Nevers, night was falling. They made a strange caravan: Colombe, big-bellied, perched atop the wagon and surrounded by shabby furniture and rolled-up back curtains; Hortense on the hapless donkey; Marc-Antoine tricked up in his usual laces and furbelows, as though all of life were a performance to him. Several children, bringing the cows in from the fields at dusk, had followed them for half a league; now, as they reached the outskirts of Nevers, the children began to dance and sing around them, announcing to all who leaned from their windows that here were great actors come to entertain them. And more than one housewife, opening her casement at the noise, saw the handsome Valentin and blew kisses, calling to her neighbors to come and see a man who could surely steal a woman's heart.

By the time they drew up before an inn, Valentin was in a foul mood; it was not helped by the leering of the innkeeper, a frowsy woman who put her arm through his and invited the monsieur to come and see the room she had especially for him.

"No," he growled, "I do not sleep alone."

"Nor did I intend you to, monsieur," she smirked, her coquette's smile seeming out of place on a face that had known youth an age ago, and beauty never. For a moment Ninon thought that Valentin's rage would get the better of him, then Chanteclair put a calming hand on Sanscoeur's arm and turned to the woman.

"Your pardon, madame," he said smoothly. "My friend and I have much to discuss this night—the cares of managing a troupe of strollers, you understand. 'Tis best that we share a room."

Crestfallen, she allowed as how it mattered little to *her* where the monsieur slept, so long as he paid for his lodging. There was a certain amount of confusion until it was decided who should sleep where—and with whom, with a casual shifting of partners that surprised Ninon. Toinette paired off with Sébastien (Joseph having taken a fancy to a serving girl at the inn), and Colombe invited Gaston to see that her condition had not yet rendered her totally useless in bed. As usual, Ninon was to share a bed with Hortense, although the thought of sleeping anywhere in this place had begun to make her uneasy. Baugin and the Hag had been penny-pinching innkeepers, charging too much, skimping on food and candles and firewood, but at least their inn had been clean. Now, as a table was set up for supper, Ninon prowled the room, peering under benches, stripping back the bed she was expected to sleep in. *Mon Dieu!* The sheets seemed not to have been aired for a month! She looked about at the rest of the company, pouring wine, preparing to sit before the supper that was being laid. Were they so used to the mean conditions of the road that they had not the wit to demand what they were paying for? She felt infinitely wiser than they, for all their worldliness. It was clear that not a one of *them* had ever been poor!

"Madame," she said to the innkeeper, who was busy supervising the serving maids, "when the girls have quite finished laying out supper, you will kindly have them put fresh sheets on all the beds. And they might take a broom to the floor, while they're about it!"

The innkeeper drew in her breath sharply. "What? Saucy miss, will you take that tone with me?"

"I will take any tone I choose," said Ninon. "Have the linens changed!"

"My God, Ninon," Valentin said impatiently, throwing himself into a chair and taking a long drink of wine. "Let it be. We have had a long day, and a longer one to come tomorrow. Let it be! This is not Marival... not your fancy château...and, Sweet Jesu, you are no longer a pampered mistress to a comte!"

Ninon whirled on him. "I, for one, shall not share my rest with lice and bedbugs! This slattern is taking my coins—and yours!—for those beds. Let them be clean, or we might just as well sleep out-of-doors with the field mice!"

They glared at each other for a moment, then Chanteclair's voice broke the silence. "I'm for clean sheets," he said. "I have no wish to scratch in the morning." There were murmurs of agreement from the rest of the company. Finding herself defeated, the innkeeper grumbled but gave orders for the beds to be changed and aired.

Ninon sat down and poured herself a cup of wine, deliberately turning away from Valentin. Pampered mistress indeed! Seated next to her, Colombe began to dish up supper from the large pot that had been placed on the table, ladling out the stew into bowls. Joseph, hungry and impatient, picked up his spoon in anticipation and broke off a large chunk of bread from the loaf on the table.

"A moment," said Ninon, putting her hand on Colombe's arm. She called out to the innkeeper. "Madame. If you please."

Valentin groaned. "Now what? Is the food not to the great lady's liking?"

Ignoring him, Ninon looked sternly at their hostess and gestured toward the pot. "What is this?"

"Fricassee of pigeons."

"Fair enough, but where are the pigeons?"

"What?"

Taking the ladle from Colombe, Ninon stirred the pot, then indicated the bowls that had already been filled. "There are a great many turnips and onions—and half a garden's worth of cabbage—but I have counted only one wing, one breast, and two necks. For all ten of us. You have asked a deal of money for this meal. You will either give these hungry men more meat, or lower your price."

The innkeeper drew herself up. "How dare you! Will you insult my table? Kind sirs, will you allow this?"

Ninon stood up and faced the woman, her voice hard and controlled, though her eyes blazed blue fire. "I give you another choice, madame. I marked a dovecote in the courtyard as we rode up. With these hands, I myself shall wring the necks of half a dozen birds and throw them into the stewpot! Do you understand?" The innkeeper wavered, clasping and unclasping her hands, then curtsied politely and scurried from the room.

"Bravo!" cried Chanteclair.

"Well done!" said Gaston. "You played the scene like a queen."

Valentin poured himself another cup of wine. "Pah! That was merely the ranting of a spoiled child who is used to the best that life can offer."

"Oh!" Ninon restrained the urge to hurl her wine in his arrogant face. "Are you a fool, who lets himself be cheated? Do you hold money so cheaply that you can throw it away? *Mon Dieu!* Even the wine in this filthy place has been thinned with water. Did you not even notice?"

She was prevented from saying more by the appearance of the innkeeper, who bustled in bearing a large Westphalian ham on a platter, and begging madame's pardon. It was all she had tonight, but she promised madame that the company should breakfast on a *petit pâté* and a hare pie that even now was being set to bake.

When they had eaten their fill, Gaston put down his spoon and knife and leaned back in his chair. "I say that henceforth Ninon should make all our arrangements concerning lodgings and food."

"I agree," said Chanteclair. He looked pointedly at Valentin. "Must we put it to the vote?"

Sanscoeur shook his head. "No. I agree." He was strangely silent as the company bade their good-nights and went to seek their beds. Only when they had all gone did he rise from the table to stand before Ninon. His black eyes searched her delicate face, a bewildered frown creasing his brow. "Perhaps you are sturdier than I thought," he said at last.

She gave him a withering look. "Perhaps you are a fool."

In the morning, Valentin, Gaston, and Chanteclair visited the provost of Nevers to obtain a license to act in the town. He was a difficult man, seeming unwilling to make the effort on their account, grumbling about the bother of sending to the deputy governor of Nivernais for the necessary permissions. Valentin could scarcely keep his temper, but Chanteclair calmed his friend and pulled the provost aside. Did the provost know, he asked, that Valentin's cousin-german was married to the brother of the deputy governor? And that the aunt of Madame Ninon, one of their chief actresses, was *femme de chambre* to the governor's wife? Suitably impressed, the provost promised to make every effort to obtain the license as soon as possible. Chanteclair sweetened his task with a small purse of coins.

The next order of business was to find a hall, theater, or tennis court in which they might perform. After some inquiry, they found that there was a large tennis court near the center of town, and well suited to their needs.

Since the sixteenth century, when the Valois kings had enjoyed the sport of *jeu de paume*, the game of the palm, hundreds of tennis courts had been built throughout France. The game had fallen from favor in the last fifty years; it was still played, but not so frequently, and the proprietors were only too glad to rent out their premises to strolling players for a few extra coins.

A tennis court was ideally suited for conversion to a temporary theater: a long and narrow building, with a high-pitched roof and a row of windows that ran just under the line of the eaves. Next to the playing floor, on either long side (or sometimes both), ran a boxed-off gallery from which the spectators could watch the matches safely and comfortably.

Valentin was pleased to see, as they entered, that the *jeu de paume* of Nevers was large enough to have an upstairs gallery as well. The petty nobility of a small town was always delighted to pay a little more to enjoy the exclusivity of the upstairs boxes. Several gentlemen, clad in shirts and breeches, or breeches alone, had just finished playing a *partie;* calling for wine, they gave their short-handled racquets to a servant and trooped up the stairs, there to be rubbed and dried in a private room before changing into fresh shirts and donning doublets, capes, hats, and swords.

Valentin beckoned to the master of the tennis court and explained what they wished. Would there be any difficulty, he asked, for them to play in the afternoon? It was their custom, he explained, to give a performance at two, since it was hard to get the good bourgeoisie to come out-of-doors at night.

"Howbeit," said Chanteclair, always conciliatory, "if there are matches in the day, we shall be content with evening."

"No, good masters," said the proprietor, "you may have the afternoons."

It was agreed that they should have the *jeu de paume* for up to a week if the audiences of Nevers proved receptive. The master of the tennis court was given an advance fee of seventy-five livres, the balance of payments to be agreed upon according to the moneys collected by the doorkeeper, a chore (for honesty's sake) to be shared by Joseph and the proprietor's servant.

"Have you a decorator?" asked the master of the court.

Valentin indicated Gaston. "Monsieur Floresse has that function in our company. If you can direct him to a worthy joiner in Nevers, he will see that a temporary stage is built to our needs."

The proprietor frowned. "Can it be removed for morning tennis matches?"

"*Mais certainement!*" Valentin gestured with his arm to one end of the building. "There, Gaston? Will you put the shelf stage there?"

Gaston squinted up at the high windows. "No. By afternoon, the sun will be shining in that direction. Even with shutters or curtains...you *do* have something for the windows, *Monsieur le Propriétaire?*...it will be too bright. We would be better served with the stage at the other end."

"I leave it to you," said Valentin. "But one thing..." He pointed to the center line of the tennis court, just under the net. In the middle was a large drainpipe, used for eliminating rainwater and debris that might collect and covered now with a wide plank. "Put a new piece of wood there. Larger and stronger. That one does not look sturdy. I am minded of the time a musketeer from Périgord stamped in such anger at seeing Julius Caesar killed upon the stage that he broke the wood and fell into the drain."

Chanteclair laughed. "I remember! There was such a riot in the pit that we could not go on with the play. Poor Caesar was not avenged *that* day!"

Gaston rummaged in a pocket. "Here are two crowns for your candle-snuffer, monsieur. Enough to buy candles for a week—unless he steals more than he is expected to. In which case I shall take a stick to him."

Chanteclair found a printer to print up the handbills advertising their arrival, while Gaston set about his task.

In less than a day the stage had been constructed. The back-cloths, with their painted villages and palaces and gardens, were hung from bars against the back wall, and the free-standing wings—lengths of painted canvas that had traveled rolled up—were backed with fresh strips of wood so that they might stand upright. There were several different wings waiting at each side, and out of view of the audience by reason of the permanent set of wings—representing two Greek columns—at the front of the stage. As the locale of the play changed, the back-cloth would be changed and new wings would be pushed into position; since all these shifts took place in full view of the audience, Gaston had hired several men from the town as scenemen, to see that the changes were made quickly. A large front curtain was placed even with the front wings, but once it was drawn it would stay that way until the conclusion of the play. An elaborate chandelier was hung from the ceiling over the center of the stage, and—as the tennis court was well ventilated and there would be no problem with smoke—a line of candles rimmed the edge of the stage. Gaston, as *décorateur*, had done his job well.

Now, thought Ninon, pacing backstage, pray God *she* could do her job well tonight!

Toinette peeked out between the curtains, then turned back, her eyes shining. "So many people! I could not count all the filled boxes, though I saw many a plumed hat and jeweled sword. I did not know there was such quality in Nevers! And the *parterre*...by my faith, there is hardly room for another soul to stand there, the pit is so crowded! And oh! the handsome soldiers! There was one musketeer who caught my eye..." She clasped her hands together in rapture.

Sébastien was of a more practical bent. "If the house is nearly full," he said, counting on his fingers, "at forty sols for the *parterre*, double for the boxes and the *paradis*…"

"'Tis only more money for you to gamble away," snapped Hortense.

"If I wish, my love, if I wish."

"You'll wind up in a pauper's grave, and I shan't weep over you!"

Sébastien shrugged and turned away, appraising Ninon with his eyes. "You look charming, *ma chère*," he said, patting her on the cheek. "Are you afraid?"

"Only that I shall forget my lines."

"You must not be. We shall help you. And you see…there is Colombe…" He indicated where Colombe perched on a stool behind one of the permanent wings, a copy of the play in one hand, a candle in the other.

"If you forget the words," said Valentin sarcastically, coming up behind Sébastien, "we can arrange to cut some of the passages for you, to make it simpler."

There was a high-pitched cackle and Ninon whirled about to see Chanteclair hobbling toward them, "Grandmère's" spectacles on his nose. "The only thing that should be cut is your sharp tongue, villain!" he squeaked, frowning at Valentin and putting a comforting arm about Ninon. "You forget that 'Grandmère' saw *your* debut upon the stage. Shall I tell this charming child what a great bumbling oaf you were that day? Tripped over his own feet, he did, and…"

Valentin groaned. "'Grandmère,' you are like a fairy godmother in the old tales, but you sprinkle venom instead of moon dust. *Eh bien*. I grant you leave to cheer that trembling creature, but only if you hold your tongue."

"No better way to give cheer," said Chanteclair in his normal voice, and, sweeping Ninon into his arms, he kissed her resoundingly on the mouth. Lifting his lips from hers, he smiled down at her surprised face. "Have I restored your courage?"

It had been a kiss of warmth and friendship, not passion, and she was grateful. "You have restored my soul," she whispered.

"Name of God," growled Valentin impatiently. "It is well past two of the clock. Are we to wait till nightfall? Gaston…prologue…your place!"

Gaston cleared his throat and went through the curtains to address the audience. There was applause and the sound of stamping feet, then loud hisses and calls for silence, and at last a degree of quiet as the audience settled down. Gaston, in a loud voice, announced that they were to do a tragedy, *Rinaldo and Armida,* so it please the kind messieurs and their ladies, taking place in the fair city of Jerusalem. He begged his listeners to give the players due honor for their noble efforts with the benevolence of their silence, and pleaded their indulgence in the matter of an occasional lapse. He finished the prologue with an effusive tribute to Nevers and its citizens, bowed elaborately, pulled aside the front curtain, and withdrew.

Valentin made his entrance upon the stage, dressed as a tragic hero, with a short Roman tunic and brass breastplate. His long legs, in their flesh-colored hose, were muscular enough not to need the padding that many another actor employed. His helmet was bedecked with several large plumes, a sure sign to anyone familiar with the theater that a tragedy was being played. His appearance, so handsome and noble, caused a stir in the audience, not least among the women. From her place in the wings Ninon could see a flicker of disgust cross his face. Then he turned, lifted a dramatic arm to the painted sky, and began his "tirade." He really was a superb actor—she had to grant him that—despite his obvious failings as a man, and as a human being.

So fascinated was she by his performance that she almost forgot to make her first entrance. Only Toinette, giving her a little shove, brought her to herself. She took a deep breath and swept out to the center of the stage. In the light of the candles her tinseled gown and false jewels sparkled brightly, but her own beauty—the luminous, creamy flesh, the halo of pink-red hair—outshone the costume. There was a chorus of oohs and aahs and scattered applause: to most audiences, even sophisticated Parisians, appearance was as important as performance on the stage.

She opened her mouth to recite her first line. To her horror, her voice cracked; she coughed and gasped, finishing the Alexandrine verse in a whisper. There were several catcalls from the listeners. Valentin smoothly responded with his verse, but when a voice shouted from the audience that they had forgotten to wind up their mechanical doll, Ninon's mind went blank. She paced the length of the stage, hearing the boards creak loudly beneath her, praying that the verse would come back to her. Valentin still smiled, as required of his part, but his black eyes were like knives. She looked into the wings for help. On her stool Colombe flipped through the pages of the book that rested in her lap, making a gesture to indicate that she had lost the page, then looking helpless as the book slid off her lap to the floor and she was forced to maneuver candle and stool and ponderous belly to retrieve the book.

Ninon whirled away from her, vowing never again to trust the bitch, and tried to think while the panic rose in her throat. The afternoon was hot, even with the sunlight curtained out; she could smell the foul odors of the audience—sweat and stale perfume and the remains of yesterday's dinner on many a skirt and coat front.

She looked again into the wings. Colombe was still pretending to fumble with the book, but beyond her Chanteclair had put "Grandmère's" spectacles back on his nose and was nodding in reassurance. The sight heartened her. Smiling her thanks, she felt Armida's lines flooding back into her brain. She was the queen, she was the enchantress. She drew herself up and addressed Valentin, her voice strong and sure and regal.

The rest of the play went smoothly, and though she guessed that she was an indifferent tragedienne, there was some weeping in the audience when she died in the last scene.

The musical interlude came next. In spite of Valentin, Ninon had insisted on playing and singing a roundelay, which was poorly received, inasmuch as the lemonade sellers did a brisk business while she was performing. She hurried off the stage, ignoring Valentin's sardonic "I told you so," and went to change her costume while Sébastien and Marc-Antoine entertained with their songs.

In the changing room of the tennis court she surveyed her limited wardrobe. They were doing *The Jealous Vicomte* next, and it had been decided that she should wear her gray skirt and jacket, with a lacy chemise beneath. Now, looking down at herself, and the plainness of her garb, she was having second thoughts. Valentin had been right about her playing and singing; perhaps he was right about her assets as well. She stripped off her jacket and pulled the chemise to the edge of her shoulders, revealing a goodly show of bosom. She laced on her sleeveless jerkin, taking care that it rested under her breasts. Then she ran her fingers through her copper-colored hair and fluffed out the ringlets and curls. She nodded in satisfaction. If she was to play a saucy wench in the farce, why not look the part?

She found the playing of improvised comedy much easier than tragedy. Perhaps because she had a quick wit and a ready mind. And perhaps because she could be revenged upon Valentin for all his torments. She was never sure, when a particularly wicked jibe sprang to her lips, whether she was insulting the character or Valentin. The *soggetto* was nailed to the back of a wing piece, and there was a certain amount of frantic scurrying to and fro during the performance as one or another of the players forgot his *lazzi* or his next entrance and had to consult the outline.

Ninon and Valentin played beautifully together, tossing their lines back and forth with a crispness of delivery that had the audience howling with laughter. She even managed to catch Valentin by surprise. It was a silly bit of business. He was to ask for a box. She was to hand him a large box that, by a touch of a secret spring, was to explode before his eyes. He was to ask again, and again she would hand him an exploding box. On the third request, she was to hand him a small box, the contents of which were essential to the plot.

It went well at first. He asked for the box, leaped back when it exploded, and stumbled about dazedly. There were howls of glee from the audience. In a moment he had recovered himself. "Shameless hussy!" he roared, his eyes, behind his comic half-mask, raking her exposed bosom in disgust. "Give me the box!"

She turned and dimpled prettily at an overdressed nobleman who had been waving to her from the gallery. Damn Valentin and his accusing eyes! The actor in him expected her to exhibit her charms; the man resented it. "Shall I give him the box?" she asked slyly, making the audience conspirator to her plans. She turned back to Valentin. "Verily, I *shall* give you a box...a box about the ears!" She swung at him with all her might. His timing was perfect. He dropped to the floor, howling, just as her hand would have connected with his face. She bent over him, pretending to pummel him on the ground, while the audience roared with laughter.

Valentin was smiling up at her. "You minx," he whispered between howls of pain. "You might have warned me. But 'tis a good *lazzo*. We shall keep it in." He curled up like a dog, whimpering as she tweaked the false nose of his mask, then crawled away and stood up, his hands clasped in supplication. "Please, madame," he whined, "will you give me the box?"

Ninon made a great to-do, pretending indecision, asking the opinion of the audience, scratching her ear and then her rump, before finally handing him the box he wanted. The scene ended to much applause, and they went offstage grinning to each other. The rest of the play went well, particularly the scene in the "kitchen." Ninon, piling the table with plates and saucepans, heard a noise and went to the window, bending over to peek outside. Valentin, the jealous husband, thinking she was looking for her lover, tiptoed in with a slapstick and delivered a resounding whack to her bottom. She stood up and shrieked at him, calling him all manner of ridiculous names, and proceeded to break the plates over his head while he reeled about the room. They had rehearsed the movements down to the last steps, but the laughter and the approval of the audience had so buoyed Ninon and heightened her senses that she threw herself into the scene, playing with a zest she had not thought possible.

By the time the stagemen had closed the curtain on the bowing company, the audience was roaring its delight, stamping and whistling and calling for more. Breathless and exhausted, Ninon leaned up against a wing, a hand to her heaving breast, her eyes shining for joy. The voice of the audience had changed. Now it seemed to be chanting her name, over and over again. She looked up. Valentin, mask in hand, was grinning broadly.

"They call for Madame Guillemot," he said.

"What shall I do?" she asked, her eyes wide with fresh panic.

He laughed. "Do?" He picked up her hand and kissed her fingertips, the first kind gesture he had ever made toward her. "Do? My dear Ninon, you go out and take your bow. You have earned it!"

The whole company was treated to supper by two vicomtes and a marquis, who could not make enough of the enchanting Madame Guillemot, pouring her wine, offering lavish compliments, making overtures that she chose to ignore. It suddenly seemed a hollow triumph. She found herself thinking of Philippe. If he had seen her tonight, would he have forsworn Henriette to be with her forever? Dear Philippe. In the midst of the merriment she felt alone and lonely.

She looked at Valentin at the other end of the long supper table and nearly laughed aloud. She could not decide if he was more disgusted with the attentions paid to her or with the clutch of silly women—the vicomtesses and their friends—who giggled and fawned over him. And when the marquise remarked that she had a cast-off gown for Madame Ninon, and several of her husband's old suits, archly suggesting that Valentin himself could ride out to her château to receive them, Valentin looked as though he would make a scene. What a proud and haughty man, thought Ninon. Repelled by the woman's attraction to him, insulted by the thought of accepting cast-offs.

"Monsieur Sanscoeur, alas, is burdened by appointments, Madame la Marquise," Ninon said smoothly. "Mayhap you will accept Monsieur Chanteclair and myself as unworthy substitutes. Will tomorrow at eleven suit you?"

The matter was quickly concluded, Chanteclair being of as practical a mind as Ninon, and eager to acquire a new doublet and breeches by whatever means.

They returned to their inn at ten, to be greeted sourly by Colombe, who had chosen not to sup with the nobility, but had spent the evening eating alone, nursing her jealousy, and washing out her stockings. She straightened up from the washbasin as they came into the room, and dried her hands on her petticoat. "Did the great Madame Guillemot know how to greet her admirers without a book-holder to give her the lines?" she asked sarcastically.

Valentin's eyes narrowed. Marching across the room, he grabbed Colombe by the back of the head and pushed her face into the basin of water. She came up gasping and squealing and cursing, pouring forth a stream of oaths that might have shamed a soldier. She paused for breath and wiped her hand across her wet face. Toinette giggled nervously, then was silent.

In the stillness of the room, Valentin's voice rasped like a knife. "That was for your performance with the book today! Restrict your petty jealousies to your private life! You may claw Ninon's eyes out at your leisure, but when we are performing we are a company! Don't forget that again."

"Don't be an ass, Valentin," Ninon said mildly, unwilling to make an enemy of Colombe. "I cannot believe that Colombe would have done it deliberately." She turned to the other woman with a benevolent smile. "If the task of minding the book is too difficult for you, sweet Colombe, be so good as to tell me, that I may not rely on you anymore."

"Indeed," said Chanteclair. "If that's the best that you can do, Madame Linard, you will be as useless as a painted tree is to a dog!"

Marc-Antoine began to laugh, seeing the opportunity for a gibe. "But if the dog must piss…"

"*Tais-toi!* Hold your tongue, Marc-Antoine!" Ninon said sharply. The joke was going too far, and Colombe had been humiliated enough tonight. And after all, who could blame her, in a way? Her beauty temporarily eclipsed by the bloated body she carried about, her place on the stage supplanted by an upstart. Ninon neither liked her nor would depend on her again, but she could understand the jealousy. "Come," she said kindly. "You look tired, Colombe. Let me comb your hair for you before you retire."

The week in Nevers went well. Colombe, chastened, tended her book diligently. Each afternoon's performance was well received, and at night the company was treated like visiting royalty, their appearance a welcome interruption in the monotony of provincial life. The cast-offs from the marquise proved a boon—a sumptuous wine-velvet gown for Ninon, a black-velvet suit that fitted Gaston to a hair, and a bottle-green brocade that, with the help of a tailor, did quite nicely for Chanteclair.

On the last day the house was full, and Joseph, beaming, announced that they had already collected well over three hundred livres. They were doing a tragicomedy this afternoon, one they had done several days before; it had been greeted with such applause that they had not been allowed to leave the stage without promising another presentation of it before they departed Nevers. The men's faces were painted with white lead, which highlighted their exaggerated facial expressions in the light of the chandelier. Valentin, as the noble hero, endured all manner of catastrophes before winning his true love, and Ninon, magnificent in her new gown, was a fetching heroine. She made such a success of her role that the audience stamped and hooted after her final speech and would not let the play continue until she had recited it once again.

They celebrated by having a fine supper at a tavern just down the lane from their inn. The food was plentiful, the wine flowed. By midnight they were all a little tipsy and congratulating one another on the financial success of their stay in Nevers. Marc-Antoine announced that he would buy a new hat with a thousand feathers on it, and Toinette fancied herself in diamonds. Colombe rubbed her belly and allowed that she would give every crown she owned to be quit of her burden.

Ninon was feeling quite giddy, drunk from the wine, and her successes, and an odd contentment that surprised her. "What will you do with your money, Chanteclair?" she asked.

He shook his head. "I have all that I could wish for. I shall save my money and buy a little cottage someday. For a wife. And children."

"Too serious. Too serious…" mumbled Gaston, his voice a thick slur.

Ninon giggled. "I know what Valentin would wish for his money. A world *sans* women!" The whole company burst into laughter as Valentin drew his brows together and glared at Ninon. "Oh, oh, oh," she mocked, laughing. "Look how he glowers, the great sour-faced monsieur! Do you never laugh?"

He poured himself another glass of wine and turned away, ignoring her. "I shall buy the rights to a new play with my share," he said.

The wine had made Ninon reckless. "Don't shift the discourse," she said. "We are talking about why you do not laugh. Do you fear your beautiful face will crack?" She turned to Chanteclair. "Have you noted that, for a man who dislikes women, Val takes great pains to make himself handsome upon the stage? Tell me, Monsieur Heartless, do you hope that women may swoon for you, so that you may feel contempt for them and their weakness?"

"Damn your viper's tongue," Valentin said quietly.

Gaston drained his cup and poured another. His eyes were beginning to close. "Too serious…too serious…"

"Yes," pouted Toinette. "Too serious. I wish 'Grandmère' were here."

Chanteclair jumped up from his chair and did a handstand on the floor, then a backward flip. When he landed on his feet, the spectacles were on his nose. "*Voilà!*" His voice became a high soprano. "You need no cheering tonight, my children. I can see that!" He indicated the pitchers of wine, now nearly empty. "Dame Tipple has done my work for me. So, then. I grant you each a question."

Joseph stood up from his chair and crossed unsteadily to Chanteclair. "I have a question. Why do you dress like a man, Grandmère?" Gaston snickered drunkenly and nudged Sébastien.

Chanteclair sighed, a helpless squeak, and smiled demurely. "I am such a charming wench that I would soon find myself…set upon…by great stumbling oafs such as yourself," here he gave Joseph a shove that tumbled him to the floor, "if I did not disguise myself as a man!"

"Tell me, Grandmère," said Colombe, when the laughter had died down, "shall I be delivered of a boy or a girl?"

"I must ask *you* a question first, my pretty," lisped Chanteclair. He swept his arm about the room, indicating the company. "Tell me first who is the father, then I shall answer *your* question."

"*Mon Dieu*, Colombe," said Marc-Antoine, as the woman flamed red, "I did not think you could still blush."

"I can tell you who is *not* the father!" she shrilled. "That *tapette*…and his bedfellow, Valentin!"

"To my credit, madame," Marc-Antoine said through his teeth. "To my credit!"

"Come, come, children! Grandmère will brook no quarrels."

"I have a question, Grandmère," said Ninon. "Why is Valentin afraid to sleep alone?"

Chanteclair began to chuckle. Valentin threw him a murderous look. "Chanteclair, if you…"

"Come, Val. 'Tis a funny story."

"Nevertheless…"

"Yes, tell it," interrupted Sébastien. "I have always wondered myself."

"Sweet Jesu," muttered Valentin, throwing himself back in his chair and gazing up at the ceiling.

"It was when Ragotin was with the company. You remember, Marc-Antoine. Before Sébastien and Hortense joined us. We had gone to a town, the three of us, Val and Ragotin and I, and stayed the night at an inn. It was very full and we had to share rooms with the other guests. But, as luck would have it, there was a small room with a single cot bed, and, as luck would have it again, Val chose it for himself. The innkeeper's wife, finding him attractive, had done him little favors throughout the evening: an extra chop, the chair nearest the fire, the finest wine. In spite of this, I rather fancy she was a virtuous woman, though her husband seemed to burn with suspicion and jealousy. *Eh bien.* It happened that the woman, getting up in the middle of the night, had a need, as the poet Scarron would put it, to go 'where kings are forced to go themselves in person,' or so she said afterward. Her husband, awaking and finding her gone, and thinking she had a rendezvous with the handsome actor, tiptoed through the dark corridor to seek her out. Hearing a breathing on the stair, he attacked her in the dark, pulling her by the hair and calling her all manner of foul names at the top of his voice, which, needless to say, brought us all running, candles and weapons in hand. His adversary was not his wife, but the poor old family dog, too sick and weak to cry out when he was attacked. The woman, guessing what had been in her husband's mind, rapped him sharply on the top of the head and stormed back to her bed, leaving him to apologize to us all for disturbing our rest. And that is why Valentin no longer sleeps alone!"

Joseph and Sébastien roared with laughter, while Ninon rocked back and forth in her chair, chuckling softly. "Poor Valentin," she gasped at last. "The fair flower who entices all the honeybees!"

"Say what you will," he growled, "but there would have been the devil to pay had the man reached my room, whether his wife was there or no!"

"Then God bless the dog," said Ninon, struggling to keep from laughing.

Colombe smiled, but there was malice in her eyes.

"A *real* man would not avoid such a fate. At every inn, at every turn! A *real* man would not fear a woman's approach in the night."

"Go to the devil. All of you." Valentin strode to the door and stormed out. They could hear his footsteps crunching loudly on the gravel outside the tavern window as he headed back to the inn.

"*Ah Dieu,*" said Ninon, looking to Chanteclair. "It was my doing...I should not have..."

"I should not have told the story," he said with a sigh. "We have all drunk too much, I think."

"Too...serious...too..." Gaston put his arms on the table, laid his head upon them, and fell asleep.

"Yes. Too serious," said Ninon. Without another word she rose from her chair and went out into the night. It was only a short walk to the inn. She hurried up the stairs and found Valentin in his chamber, hanging his doublet over the back of a chair. He glared at her angrily.

"Go back to your cackling friends!"

"Val, please. I had not meant…We were all a little silly tonight." She held out her hand, smiling in conciliation. "But it was a funny story. Can you not allow that? Just a little bit?"

"I saw no humor in it then. I see no humor now."

"Oh, you try my patience! You can find nothing to laugh in that? And yet if it were played on a stage you would find it funny."

"Would I?" His lip curled in scorn. "Would *he* find it amusing? Your lover Philippe? All that sneaking about in the dark to find a lover's bed?"

Ninon whirled about and made for the door.

"Ah, ah!" he mocked. "So that's the way of it! When we speak of things that touch *you*, you can find naught to say. *Mon Dieu!* I could write a comedy on that!"

She swirled back to him, her blue eyes blazing. "And you? You humiliated Hortense with the donkey, and called it a joke. But you see no humor when your *own* pride is pricked! The great Sanscoeur. And such an overbearing pride it is!"

He grabbed her by the shoulders and slammed her up against the wall, pressing against her with his body so that she was immobilized and helpless. "Who are you to preach to me?" he bellowed.

She caught her breath, suddenly frightened by his strength and power, half-expecting him to beat her or put his hands around her throat. They stood thus for several minutes, locked together in silent rage, black eyes challenging blue ones. And then, incredibly, Ninon felt a hardness against her body, the unmistakable firmness of his member swelling within his breeches, impelled by an emotion that was far from anger. She saw the surprised look in his eyes; then he blushed, a deep red stain that crept up from his collar and swept across his face. She began to laugh. With a growl he pushed her aside and turned away, his shoulders stiff with the effort at self-control.

She laughed again. "How it must gall you to know that there are some things over which you have no control!"

"You bitch!" he said, and swung at her, his open palm striking the side of her face with such force that she staggered back and nearly fell to the floor. She panted hard for a moment, then wiped the back of her hand across her mouth, seeing the thin line of blood on her knuckles.

"Were you born with such hatred? Or did someone put it there? Did your mother spurn you in the cradle? Is that what robbed you of your joy? Or did she…"

"Enough!" he roared. "She was the only woman I ever knew who was good and honest! The rest are but lying, betraying whores!"

The venom in him made her recoil, her hand to her mouth. "How pitiful you are," she said softly. "Imprisoned within your own black heart." She went out the door, closing it gently behind her.

He stared at the paneling for a moment, then covered his eyes with one hand, his face twisted in agony and torment.

Chapter Six

In the morning, Valentin behaved as though nothing had happened. He was unpleasant, of course, but no more than usual. Ninon found it difficult to get used to: the way the company quarreled and reconciled so easily. Perhaps because they were actors they magnified even the smallest difficulties, making every dispute a war, every disappointment a tragedy, only to be forgotten in an instant, as though a curtain had dropped; perhaps, since they traveled together, depended on one another, they knew it was vital to keep peace.

They were able to rent fresh horses at Nevers for the journey to Moulins. Their ox, well fed and rested after a week in a comfortable stable, had to be prodded and pushed into his traces, but at last they set out. They stayed overnight at Dornes, and arrived at Moulins late the following afternoon, finding an ancient theater that would suit them nicely.

There was to be a marriage between two old and aristocratic families in the district. Moulins was bustling in preparation for the number of visitors who would arrive at the lord's château, and venture into town if there were attractions enough. Every shopkeeper dusted off his best goods and arrayed them temptingly, and the resident whores cast off their country lovers in anticipation of a noble bedding or two.

The Peerless Theatre Company anticipated a rich week, as profitable as the one they had enjoyed at Nevers, and in consequence rented the theater for at least eight days, half the fee payable in advance. The theater, its general layout the same as a tennis court, needed very little renovation, and the first afternoon's performance, a pastoral and a farce, went well.

That night, Marc-Antoine swept in to supper with a flourish, wearing a magnificent black beaver hat adorned with half a dozen white and pink plumes; behind him trailed a lad, perhaps fourteen, dressed in the costume of a pageboy out of some exotic court, his doublet heavy with gold braid, his petticoat breeches swagged with pink ribbons. "My servant," explained Marc-Antoine, ignoring Colombe's jeering laugh.

Toinette looked bewildered. "Why do you need a servant? To help you dress in the morning?"

"Don't be a silly goose, Toinette," said Colombe, her lips curved in a smile of malice. "Marc-Antoine needs the lad to help him *un*dress. And to get him up." There was no mistaking the lewd meaning of her words.

"Shut your mouth, Colombe," growled Valentin. "You have your ways, Marc-Antoine has his. Who is to say a whore is better than…"

"Than an unnatural man? That shittlebrain? That pretender to nobility? Marc-Antoine de Ville de La Motte? Ha!"

"What is your servant's name, Marc-Antoine?" Ninon asked quickly, hoping to still Colombe's poisonous tongue.

"Pierre."

Ninon turned to the lad and smiled. He was soft and baby-faced, almost pretty, his hair falling over his eyes. She guessed from the roughness of his hands, and the way he fidgeted in his new clothes and glanced uneasily about at the roomful of flamboyant actors, that Marc-Antoine's newfound *valet de chambre* had lately been a farmer or menial servant. "Have you supped, Pierre?" The boy shook his head. "Then sit you down, next to me," she said, ladling out a bowl of soup.

"Poor Valentin," cackled Colombe. "Where will you sleep now? You have been cast aside for a downy-faced child."

Sanscoeur's face twisted into a sardonic smile, reminding Ninon once again of the devil she had first thought him. "Whenever I begin to think I have judged the female sex too harshly, Colombe," he drawled, "you are there to show me I have not."

In the morning they rehearsed the play they were to present that afternoon, nearly coming to blows because Marc-Antoine stopped every few minutes so Pierre could hurry over and dab at his face with a silk handkerchief. And when they went to dine at twelve, Marc-Antoine fussed over the lad, heaping his plate with meat, pouring more wine, like a lover who could not do enough for his new *amour*. The boy still seemed dazzled—though delighted—with his new station in life.

As they dined, a messenger appeared with a letter for the whole company. Monsieur le Vicomte de Léris, whose daughter was getting married in a week, had heard only favorable reports of the Peerless Theatre Company. Accordingly, he now invited the strollers to perform at his château as part of the festivities honoring the bride and groom. On Saturday, five days hence, if it pleased the players. It would be his pleasure to pay them the lordly sum of five hundred livres. Gaston was ecstatic, and even Valentin beamed as he sent back a message agreeing to Monsieur de Léris's terms.

"Five hundred livres!" crowed Gaston. "We did not make that much on our best day in Nevers."

"Shall we do *Le Vicomte Jaloux?*" asked Chanteclair.

Valentin nodded. "And *Herod.* 'Tis a noble tragedy, and Ninon plays it well."

Gaston shook his head. "Not without a new throne. We cannot appear before nobility with the wretched piece we have now. I saw a chair in an upholsterer's shop yesterday. Larger than the one we now have, and with a little ornamentation and gold leaf quite suitable to our purposes."

"*Mon Dieu*," said Chanteclair. "Larger, you say? And thus heavier. The ox cannot bear the added burden. The creature suffers even now."

"Get another ox," said Valentin. "We could use a team."

"A new throne and an ox? We shall be woefully short of funds."

"But only until Saturday," said Valentin.

It was agreed that Gaston should, that very day, buy a companion to their beast of burden and arrange to have the upholsterer's chair converted to a suitable throne. They went off to the theater in good spirits.

The play had barely begun, however, when a great noise arose in the pit. Ninon would have stopped to notice, but Chanteclair, who was on the stage with her, continued his tirade as though nothing were amiss. She responded in her turn, but the noise had grown so loud that she could scarcely be heard above the shouting. It soon became clear that a young dandy—a nobleman, to judge by his sword and boots—was attempting to take a seat in the gallery without paying for it, and half the men in the pit had taken sides either for or against him, and were shouting at one another.

"God's blood!" bellowed the young man, his voice more than a little slurred by too much wine. "I have paid to get into the *parterre!* Why should I pay more to sit in the gallery?" This was greeted with a chorus of catcalls. "A pox on the lot of you! Show a little respect for your betters!"

Ninon looked in consternation at Chanteclair. They could scarcely continue with this disturbance. She knew it was a favorite pastime of the young blades to attempt to get into the theater without paying, to show that they were worthy. And once allowed in for nothing, or for only the price of the pit, they used the threat of future quarrels to keep from paying ever again. Still, something had to be done to silence this drunken coxcomb. She stepped to the front of the stage.

"Monsieur!" she called. "If you please!" And waited until the noise had died down a bit. She smiled down at the malcontent. "Kind sir, sit where you will. Only allow us to continue with our representation."

He looked up at her. "Upon my word, but you're a pretty wench! I should like to get under *your* skirts!"

"Sit down, monsieur." She was still smiling, but her voice was tight and controlled.

"With pleasure, fair one." He bowed elaborately, if unsteadily, and turned to the usher. "Fetch me a chair. I shall sit upon the stage."

The usher shook his head. "Only if you pay for it, monsieur."

"Plague take you, you pricklouse!" The young gentleman swung his fist with all his might, and the hapless usher went down, blood gushing from his nose.

It was too much for the spectators. With cries of "Throw the wretch out!" they bundled the dandy to the door—ignoring his threats to them, to the players, to the world at large—and pushed him out into the afternoon sunshine.

The company thought they had seen the last of him. But the next day, waiting backstage to begin the play, they were interrupted in their last-minute preparation by a distraught Joseph, who had been counting the house with the doorkeeper.

"He has come back," he announced. "And with his friends."

Valentin pounded a fist into his palm. "Damn! How many?"

"Half a score."

"Can they not be thrown out?"

"No. They have all paid. Some have paid double, for good measure. And bought every tallow end the candle-snuffer could sell them."

There was a murmur of unease among the players as they crowded around. Valentin and Chanteclair frowned at each other. Reaching into his pocket, Valentin threw Joseph a small purse. "We shall play *La Mort de Sénèque* to begin. You have no part in it. See how many horses you can rent, and have them waiting at the inn. And the wagon and oxen at the ready. Have Marc-Antoine's boy Pierre help you." He turned to Chanteclair. "We can save the back-cloths, but if need be we shall leave the wings behind."

"Better yet," said Chanteclair, "I'll have the scenemen remove the laths now, and roll up the wings; we can play without them."

Valentin nodded in agreement. Crossing to a large trunk at one side of the stage, he opened it and removed several rapiers, which he distributed to the other actors. Slipping the leather harness over one shoulder, he adjusted the rapier on his hip and glanced up to see Hortense and Toinette looking at him with worried eyes. He smiled gently in reassurance. "God willing, we'll not have to use them!"

Chanteclair had been peering through the closed curtains. Now he straightened up and turned to Valentin. "I thought I saw the lieutenant to the provost of Moulins in the audience. If he has brought his men with him, all will be well."

"Monsieur?" A stranger tapped Valentin on the shoulder.

Sanscoeur whirled, clutching the man by the shirtfront and lifting him off the ground. "Who let you in here?" he exclaimed, his eyes blazing. "What do you want?"

The man began to blubber. "I'm just a poor farmer, monsieur! Sent to look for Monsieur Sanscoeur."

"What do you want of him?"

"Please, monsieur, put me down. I only have a letter. I'm just a poor farmer from Nevers. I was asked to deliver a letter. No more. I've just come from Nevers with a cart full of squash…fine squash, monsieur. I mean you no harm. My squash mean you no harm. Please put me down!" The farmer was nearly in tears.

Valentin sighed in relief and lowered the man to the floor. "Well then, give it here. And a crown for your trouble," he added. The farmer snatched at the coin and scurried away. Valentin took the letter and turned it over in his hand. At sight of the handwriting on the covering, his face went white. "*Merde!*" he whispered, and tore the missive into a thousand pieces. He looked up. Ninon was watching him, a mystified look on her face. "Damn you," he growled, "have you nothing better to do than stare at me? We play *La Mort de Sénèque*, instead of *Miriamne*. Do you know your part?"

She nodded curtly and took her place in the center of the stage. "Whenever the prologue is ready."

The first quarter-hour of the play went well. The brash nobleman and his friends, crowded together in the front ranks of the pit, were content to clap loudly at the end of each speech. But then they began to pelt the actors with the candle ends they had bought, taking great delight in hearing Toinette squeak each time she was hit.

"Go on," hissed Chanteclair from the side of the stage. "They will soon tire of the game."

At last the supply of candle ends was exhausted, and Ninon breathed a sigh of relief. Perhaps now they would be content and let the play continue.

"You. Pretty little wench with the red hair. Will you let me touch your breast?" The rowdy from the day before had come close to the edge of the stage and now was leering up at Ninon.

His companion, a swaggering man in red velvet, nudged him. "This one with the yellow curls is for me! If she squeals at the prick of a candle end, what would she do for a full taper, stretched to its entire length?" He scratched at his groin and made an obscene gesture with a finger.

The dandy turned to his companions. "Will no one have the plain one?" he asked, indicating Hortense, who was standing to one side of the scene.

Another nobleman stepped forward. "I will." He shrugged. "All cats are gray in the dark!" This remark was greeted with raucous laughter.

"I wonder if the pretty doxy has red hair all over?" said the first one, and leaped upon the stage. Before Ninon could defend herself, he had her about the waist and was trying to kiss her, his slobbering mouth on her face and neck and bosom.

The man in red velvet followed suit, jumping up to grab Toinette, who screamed helplessly as he plunged his hand down the front of her gown. Gaston, standing next to her, tried to pull off the ruffian, receiving for his trouble a cuff on the ear that sent him flying over the edge of the stage into the pit, where he lay groaning and clutching his arm in pain. With a growl, Valentin leaped into the fray, swinging his fists like an avenging angel, taking on the noblemen as they scrambled onto the stage to help their companions. In a moment the stage was crowded with brawling bodies, flailing and striking in all directions. Ninon picked up a lath strip that had been left by the stageman as he pulled down the wings; she swung it at the first aristocratic head she could find, and was delighted to see the oaf go down crying.

There was now general fighting in the pit as well, the audience having decided that there was more joy in a good brawl than in a play; the spectators in the gallery, feeling deprived of the sport, had begun to pick up their benches and hurl them into the *parterre*. But on the stage the battle suddenly turned serious, as a sword was drawn, and then another. The nobleman in red velvet lunged at Sébastien before he could unsheath his sword, slashing him across his neck and forcing him backward so that he tripped and fell; then he stood over him with his blade against the actor's throat.

"Turn, you coward!" roared Valentin, and drew his rapier. He leaped at the man, his blade flashing, his weapon a graceful extension of his arm and hand. The skills of an indolent gentleman were no match for those of a trained actor who played the battling hero every day upon the stage. Valentin could have run him through at any moment, but he merely kept him at bay, playing with him, while he pondered how the company might extricate itself from this dilemma.

Above the noise in the theater there was the sharp report of a pistol. The place became suddenly, eerily quiet as the brawlers froze. The lieutenant to the provost of Moulins stood in the pit, a smoking weapon in his hands. "Put up your swords, messieurs," he said, "and go your ways in peace."

There was a general grumbling as the noblemen sheathed their blades and straightened their fancy doublets and capes. The spectators in the pit began to file out of the theater. Sébastien and Chanteclair jumped from the stage to help Gaston, who sat in a daze, supporting his injured arm. But the dandy in red velvet was still smarting from his humiliation at Valentin's hands. With a growl, he turned about and lunged at Sanscoeur's retreating back with the point of his rapier.

"Val!" Ninon's voice was shrill and urgent.

Valentin whirled, parrying the murderous thrust and leaping forward to pierce the red velvet doublet just beneath the man's ribs. With a look of surprise, the man clutched at his side and dropped to his knees.

"Damn!" said the lieutenant. "I had hoped it would not come to this." He turned to the rest of the noblemen. "Get Monsieur de Léris out of here!" Shamefaced, like a bunch of bullies whose game has gone too far, his companions picked up the wounded man and hurried him out of the theater.

"De Léris?" said Valentin. "Monsieur le Vicomte?"

"No. His son. The Chevalier de Léris."

Chanteclair groaned. "And brother to the bride, n'est-ce pas? I fear me that is one wedding we shall not attend!"

"Alas, no, good masters," said the lieutenant, not unkindly. "Although I can attest to your innocence in this affair—you were clearly provoked, all of you, and the Chevalier de Léris attacked you in most cowardly fashion, monsieur—still, Monsieur le Vicomte is a powerful noble in this parish. It will be best if you leave Moulins as fast as ever you can, before Léris sends half a hundred of his men to avenge his son's honor. The provost does not have enough men-at-arms to protect you. Get out of Moulins at once."

They packed as quickly as they could. While Hortense bound the cut on Sébastien's neck, Ninon brought Gaston to a surgeon to set his arm, which was clearly broken. Joseph had managed to rent only a few horses.

They left Moulins as the sun was setting, riding double and even triple on their mounts, and urging on their new team of oxen.

By ten o'clock Gaston was in too much pain to continue. They built a campfire back from the road and prepared to settle in for the night, trying to cheer one another for the loss of the day's receipts, the wedding commission they had been counting on, and the precarious state of their finances. But Marc-Antoine's little pageboy, Pierre, far less innocent than he appeared, had managed to steal a roasted leg of mutton and a large demijohn of wine from their innkeeper before they left. They sat around the fire eating and drinking, reliving—with much boasting and drunken laughter—the events of the afternoon.

Only Valentin stood apart from them, leaning against a tree on the edge of the clearing and gazing into the black night. At last Ninon rose from the ground and went to stand beside him.

"'Tis not such a terrible thing," she said gently. "We can sup on ale instead of wine, cheese instead of meat. And there is always the next town."

He seemed to look at her from a great distance, frowning in bewilderment. "What?"

"The money," she said. "I only came to tell you…"

"Little fool, what makes you think I want to be disturbed? Go away!" The voice was harsh and ugly.

How strange, she thought, seeing the handsome face distorted with hatred. A month ago she would have cringed at his tone, or answered him in anger. She had thought his venom, his hatred, a weapon, a sharp sword with which he attacked the world; she was beginning to see it in a new way—as his shield. "I only came to cheer you," she said, "because you are worried about our means."

He laughed, a low, guttural laugh of derision. "Our means? My God! We have known harder times than this and survived! Do you think I worry about that?"

"Yet you are downcast tonight."

"God's blood!" he burst out. "Leave me be. It is my nature. Go and be cheerful with poor Gaston, who truly suffers this night."

"What was the letter?" she asked softly.

He knotted his hands into tight fists and pounded them against the trunk of the tree, drawing a deep breath through clenched teeth. "Sweet Jesu! If you value your life, you will vanish from my sight tonight!"

She had not thought she could still fear him, but the expression in his eyes sent her back to the firelight and Gaston, fetching a silk scarf from the cart to support the weight of his splinted arm.

They had hoped to stay at Souvigny and rest for a few days while Gaston recovered his strength. There was a small *jeu de paume* that had served them as a theater the last time they had passed this way. But the provost of Souvigny met them at the walls of the town and forbade them to enter. Word of the brawl at Moulins had already reached his town, and he was loath to allow such scum (as obviously they were) the freedom of Souvigny's streets, the companionship of its leading citizens.

Exhausted, they pushed on to Montluçon, taking the cheapest inn they could find. They stayed for two weeks, so that Gaston might recuperate, but played only four times, the audiences being scant and poor. Even Pierre, who seemed to be an accomplished pickpocket, complained of the poverty of the folk in Montluçon. In a rage over the lad's stealing, Valentin nearly beat him, but Marc-Antoine, now totally enamored of the boy, would not have it, promising instead to keep a closer watch on Pierre and his larcenous tendencies.

They moved on at last to Bourges, where the company had played before, and were greeted with enough warmth, by townfolk who remembered them, as to dispel the miseries of the last few weeks. They stayed for two and a half weeks, playing almost every afternoon, their days falling into a comfortable pattern. They awoke at nine or ten (though Toinette and Joseph, who were now sharing a bed regularly, slept later, and Hortense, who had spurned both Sébastien and Gaston since the morning near Nevers, arose early and paced the courtyard like a caged tigress), rehearsed for an hour or so, and dined at noon. They played at two, then changed clothes and removed their makeup and strolled about the town until suppertime, supping as often as they could with a petty noble or self-important merchant who was delighted to pay their billet, if only to brag to his friends that he had supped with actors who had seen the world, and actresses whose beauty set a man's heart to fluttering.

As the evening wore on, Marc-Antoine and Pierre would vanish into the night with like-minded companions, and Sébastien, with a great flourish to Hortense, would go off to the local *tripot*, or gambling den, to lose his money as fast as he had earned it. Gaston, still nursing his broken arm, would get drunk and go to sleep, leaving the rest of the company—even a reluctant Valentin—to smile and laugh with their admirers.

Ninon found it a difficult path to tread, keeping her panting suitors at bay while contriving to flatter them and convince them that she found them the most charming gentlemen it had ever been her pleasure to meet. But remembering the fight in Moulins, and the ugly provost in Souvigny, she knew she had no choice. Despite recent royal edicts forbidding bias against actors, they were still considered inferior beings and treated accordingly. Only flattery and agreeableness to the local notables kept them in funds—and out of prison.

Sometimes when the strain of being pleasant became too hard to bear, Ninon would go back to the inn and sit with her sewing. It filled the quiet hours, but it could not fill the longing for Philippe, the pain that had come flooding back as the hard work of the first weeks had lessened, and the heady flush of excitement had worn off. She had given up her love, her heart, for this tawdry existence, and she was beginning to see the real face of the actor's life beneath its pretty mask.

This was her mood by the time they moved on to Auxerre. She no longer tried to be pleasant to Valentin, finding his hatefulness tiring, and the petty concerns and jealousies and *amours* of the company bored her as much as the long hours between performances. Without Philippe, she felt less alive than she had at the convent, when she had still had her hopes and dreams.

She played her roles indifferently at their first performance in Auxerre, and was paid back by the audience with catcalls and a shower of rotten food.

"What the devil were you doing out there this afternoon?" shouted Valentin, as soon as the curtain had closed. "Are you ill that you played like a sleepwalker?"

Colombe smiled like a cat and rubbed her belly, grown enormous by this time. "Do not fret, Valentin. Soon enough I shall be brought to bed with this child. When I have my place back, we can send this creature packing!" She glanced at Ninon, who was still brushing bits of food from her gown. "'Tis remarkable, my dear, how well old cabbages suit you!"

"Madame Guillemot." A young pageboy stood before Ninon. "Monsieur le Duc asks if you will be supping tonight at the Golden Crown? Le Duc de Barre. He would welcome your company."

Ninon hesitated, feeling her heart sink. She had noticed the nobleman in the audience, smiling and winking. A fat old man, with eyes that looked like shiny buttons in a pig's face; he had stared hungrily at her all evening. The thought of being pleasant to him at supper made her stomach turn.

"Madame would be better served staying home and learning how to be an actress," Valentin said sarcastically. Colombe cackled in triumph.

Oh God, Ninon thought, despair clutching at her. If she could only run away. If she could only keep from crying in front of all these vultures who picked at her heart and waited to see her downfall.

"Alas. Madame Guillemot is supping with me tonight. Alone." Chanteclair smiled down at her. "Is it not so, *ma chère?*"

She had never been more grateful for his kindness. They escaped into the soft summer evening and Chanteclair led her to a small inn. Seated at last in a cozy chamber, he sipped his wine and leaned back in his chair. "You must not allow Colombe to make you unhappy," he said. "She is an extraordinarily unpleasant woman and not worth your tears." He laughed at the look of surprise on Ninon's face. "There is not a one of us who finds any merit in her—a bitch she was born, a bitch she will always be!" He took a large chunk of meat pie and shoveled it into his mouth with the end of his knife.

"But you keep her on."

"Indeed, yes. To begin with, she's a fine tragedienne. You have a skill for comedy that she cannot match, but her Miriamne makes grown men weep. And then, she is very beautiful...forgive me."

"I am not consumed with jealousy. You may say it. She *is* beautiful."

"Yes. A strolling company can never have enough beautiful actresses. And she can be charming when she chooses to be."

Ninon smiled knowingly. "And accommodating?"

Chanteclair blushed. "She is...very hard to resist." He refilled his wine cup and laughed. "Unless, of course, one is Marc-Antoine de Ville de La Motte!"

"I like him. The man behind the pompous splendor."

Chanteclair's warm brown eyes searched her face. "You have a good heart, Ninon Guillemot."

"Is he truly nobility?"

"No. He likes to pretend so, despite Colombe's mockery. But he was the son of a shopkeeper, who threw him out because of his 'inclinations.'"

"Alas. How sad for him. But at least he can resist Colombe's charms!"

He shrugged. "As can Valentin."

She shook her head. "Valentin. A man of mystery. And yet he is not...?"

"A *tapette*, as Colombe calls him? An unnatural man? No. Perhaps that is why she dislikes him so. She scorns Marc-Antoine for his ways, but I think she hates Valentin because...you'll pardon me if I speak frankly... because she cannot seduce him, as she has done to the rest of us."

Ninon frowned. "Think you it is a religious vow?"

"Valentin's celibacy? I think not. I have known him to seek out a whore from time to time. And rage for the next two weeks, as though he cursed his own weakness."

"I do not like him or his rages." She picked at her food, then looked reflectively at Chanteclair. "You never get angry, do you?"

"Why should I? Life is a game of chance. What will be, will be."

"*Mon Dieu!*" she laughed. "You are more the gambler than Sébastien! But Valentin…unpleasant man…How did he come to the company? To be its head?"

"It was two years ago, or a little more. Ragotin was ill and wished to retire. I have been an actor most of my years, and glory in it. I should have been a draper like my father, otherwise. But I had no wish to head the company. And then Valentin appeared. He was a natural actor…and a leader of men. Ragotin was delighted to pass the mantle."

"Where did he come from? What was his life?"

Chanteclair shrugged. "*Qui sait?* Who knows?"

"It hardly matters. He is a cruel man. Truly 'heartless.'"

"He is a man in torment."

"What care I? I cannot be concerned with his griefs. I do not like him. I scarcely trust him."

Chanteclair smiled gently. "Or anyone?"

"Why should I?"

"Because you have a good heart, Ninon Guillemot. You are not as hard as you pretend. A good heart." He took her hand gently between his own. "And a broken one?"

She pulled her hand away and busied herself with her food.

"I mind that Valentin called you mistress to a comte," he said gently. "Froissart?" Still she said nothing. "What a strange creature you are. I've watched you change these past weeks. The modest young woman has come alive, *n'est-ce pas?* Have we taught you to laugh?"

She looked at him with grateful eyes. "A little," she whispered.

"Yet always silent when your heart is touched. Will you tell 'Grandmère' someday why your eyes are so sad?"

She blushed, feeling flustered, aware suddenly that they were a man and a woman alone together, sensing his masculinity as she had not before.

He leaned back in his chair, his eyes searching, appraising. "Do you *want* me to pursue you?" he said at last, as though he had read the thought in her mind.

She shook her head. "No. No. And yet…" She took a long draft of wine, feeling foolish, uneasy, insecure. "That is to say…I would not welcome your attentions…anyone's attentions, you understand…I mean no offense to you…and yet…"

A small smile twitched at his lips. "And yet…?"

"The…the women of the company do not want for attention."

"True enough. Though I find Toinette too silly for my taste."

"Am I not desirable?" she burst out, then blushed and turned away.

He began to laugh. "My dear Ninon, there is not a man in the whole company who is not panting for you, myself included. I warrant even Marc-Antoine has entertained an occasional thought!"

"I…I don't understand!"

"You are the loveliest, freshest blossom that this jaded company has seen in many a day. I could love you myself, my sweet, and chase away the sadness from your beautiful eyes. But…"

"But…?"

"But we are forbidden. Because such entreaties would be unwelcome to the melancholy Ninon. Look not so surprised. You said as much yourself, *n'est-ce pas?* And so we have been forbidden."

"Forbidden by whom?"

"By Valentin. The 'heartless.'"

"Mother of God. I don't believe you."

"Whatever you may think, he is not a monster. He did not wish us to add to your grief by importuning you."

"Why should he care? I cannot believe that—"

She was interrupted by a loud pounding on the door. "Chanteclair!" Valentin burst into the room, his face flushed from running. "Come quickly. Hortense, the little fool…"

"*Nom de Dieu!* What is it?"

Valentin stopped to catch his breath. "Do you remember the bailiff Sébastien gambled with?"

"*Mon Dieu!* The one who swore to kill him? Sébastien wasn't fool enough to gamble with him again! Was he?"

"No. He was very discreet. A simple game of *rouge et noir*, an out-of-the-way tavern, a small group of men—what harm? But one of them is the son of the bailiff."

"Sweet Madonna!" exclaimed Ninon. "Does Sébastien know?"

Valentin shook his head. "No. The bailiff is a nobleman of some importance in Auxerre—his son's title is different from his own. But several of the men, leaving the tavern, met Toinette and Hortense, and happened to mention the relationship between son and father." Impatiently Valentin indicated the door. "Pay your bill for supper and come with me as we talk. Ninon as well. We might have need of you."

They hurried out of the inn and followed a road that led to the outskirts of Auxerre. "Where are we going?" asked Chanteclair.

"To save Sébastien, if we can. Hortense is so blinded by anger and malice that she has gone to fetch the bailiff. Toinette could not stop her, and came to tell me. We must get Sébastien out of the tavern." Abruptly Valentin turned off the road onto a small path that wound between dark trees. Before them was an old tavern set on a rise, its peaked roof making it seem all the higher.

They hurried into the common room, ignoring the few carousers who sat about with beakers of ale drinking one another's health, and raced up the long staircase. The first room was empty. In the second room they found only two men, Sébastien and the bailiff's son, who, having sent the rest of the players home as losers, were congratulating each other on their good fortune and pocketing their winnings.

"Monsieur," Valentin said quickly. "Your father is on his way here."

The young man shrugged. "And so?"

Valentin pointed a finger at Sébastien, his voice tense with anger. "My good young sir, did you know that this is the man he has sworn to kill, if ever he found him at cards?"

Sébastien's face went white. "My God! The bailiff's son?"

"Forgive me," the young man stammered. "I...I did not know!"

"Get out!" barked Valentin. "Get you home as fast as ever you can!"

"Too late!" cried Chanteclair, who had been listening at the door.

Sébastien ran to the window and opened the casement. He looked down and groaned. "It's too high. If either of us goes out this way, there will be broken bones."

"If you stay," muttered Valentin, "there will be broken heads."

Below, they could hear Hortense's voice, fawning over the bailiff. "Come this way, monsieur, if you will. You shall not be disappointed, I promise you."

"Humph!" he growled, moving slowly into the common room with the aid of a large, gnarled cane. "You say my son is here? And with that rogue?" He put his hand on the banister and winced in pain. "Damn this gout! I'll kill the plaguey rascal!"

"Oh, no, monsieur," purred Hortense. "Why stain your hands with the blood of one so lowly? A sound thrashing with your cane will teach the devil a lesson."

"Yes. Yes. Magot! Saint-Jacques!" he called to his men who were waiting in obedience at the door. "Come! Follow me." With a great deal of grumbling and groaning, he made his way up the stairs, followed by Hortense and his two men-at-arms. "Damned thief! Filthy mountebank! I shall make him wish he had not been born!" At the top of the stairs he lifted his cane and pointed to the door. "Open it," he ordered his men, "and be prepared to arrest the knave as I direct!"

Valentin looked up from the table where he was sitting, his eyes wide with surprise. He nodded politely to the bailiff and slapped a card down on the table in front of Chanteclair. "Welcome, monsieur," he drawled. "Will you join my friend and me for a hand or two of *piquet?*"

"By my faith!" roared the bailiff, looking at Hortense. "What is this?"

"The other room, monsieur! Try the other room." There was an edge of panic in Hortense's voice.

The bailiff clumped across the room and threw open the door to the chamber beyond. Ninon, sitting on the young man's lap, gave a little gasp and took his hand off her bosom. The bailiff harrumphed loudly. "*Nom de Dieu!* I had not meant...charming young thing...forgive my intrusion." He glowered at Hortense.

"Your pardon, my lord," she said weakly. "It would seem I was misinformed."

"By my faith, young woman, I do not enjoy being pulled from my hearth of a night to go chasing phantoms! You tell me I shall find a gambling villain. I find only my son engaged in an *amour.*" He glanced about the sparsely furnished room. "I do not see the rascal here. Now, if you don't mind, I shall go back to my hearth!" He turned to his son, nodding his approval. "I shall see you at home, sirrah, when you have—ahem—concluded your business."

"No," pouted Ninon, jumping up from the young man's lap. "You may go home now. You are a charming fellow, but if you must be followed about by your father, I shall have nothing more to do with you."

The young man protested halfheartedly, then followed his father down the stairs and out of the tavern. Bewildered, Hortense stared at the three of them, her quizzical frown going from Valentin to Ninon to Chanteclair. Without a word the two men rushed to the window and hauled up Sébastien, who had been hanging desperately to the sill on the outside of the tavern. He scrambled into the room, breathing heavily and rubbing his sore arms. "I could not have lasted another moment," he gasped. Hortense smiled uneasily at him. Ignoring her, he looked at Valentin. The two men nodded politely to each other, then Valentin took Ninon by the arm and ushered her out of the room. Chanteclair followed, closing the door behind him and leaning against the doorframe. Valentin stared out the window at the dark night.

There was the noise of brief scuffling from the room beyond, then the sharp sound of flesh striking flesh, followed by a shriek from Hortense. There was another slap, and again Hortense cried out. Horrified, Ninon turned to the door. Chanteclair grinned, but barred her way. She crossed to Valentin at the window. "How can you let him?" she cried, her voice shaking with outrage.

"Leave them alone," he growled. "He is her husband."

It took her a moment to recover from her surprise. "Why should that matter?" she said at last.

"She endangered his life. And put the whole company at risk." He paused for a moment to listen to the sounds from the other room, which had continued unabated: each time a sharp smack followed by a yelp or shriek from Hortense. "And all for malice. By God, had he not done it, I'd have done it myself!"

She sneered. "Do you take pleasure in playing the brute? What if she had been a man?"

"I should have drubbed him soundly with these two fists."

She curled her lip, a look of contempt on her face.

"Dammit!" he burst out. "There are ten people in this company. And I am responsible for their lives! That man was the bailiff—the justice in this town. He might have found cause to clap the lot of us in prison! And all for Hortense's malice." His eyes narrowed threateningly. "Make no mistake about it, my charming Ninon. If ever you willfully endanger this troupe, I shall not hesitate to fold back your skirts and turn your pretty little bottom as pink as a field of clover!"

She swallowed hard to still her trembling, seeing clearly by his eyes that it was no idle threat; then she took a deep breath and faced him defiantly. "And who punishes *you* when you are reckless and foolish?"

Caught off guard, he flinched as though she had struck him, and turned away to the window. "God," he said, his voice an agonized croak. Taken aback by his sudden change of mood, she reached out and put her hand on his sleeve, sensing his pain in the tone of his voice, the droop of his shoulders. He shook off her fingers and turned, the actor's mask in position, the sardonic smile pasted on. He laughed mockingly. "And then Chanteclair and Gaston have been known to break a few chairs over my head!"

They played well the first week in Auxerre. Ninon, heartened by Chanteclair, recaptured some of her old zest on the stage, and Valentin— perhaps to atone for his coldheartedness in the matter of Hortense—

was almost kind. Hortense seemed more ashamed than angry at what had happened, going out of her way to defer to Sébastien when there was a bit of stage business that they disputed. For his part, Sébastien announced that he had decided to swear off gambling for a while, which pleased his wife. Until, with twinkling eyes, he added that, in any event, his hand was still too sore to deal the cards, at which point Hortense cursed at him and flounced away.

But the second week, the weather turned stiflingly hot. They played with sweat running down their faces and streaking their makeup, with the smell of hot bodies packed into the small theater. The audiences grew restless, and booed and hissed every presentation, until the company felt it could do nothing right. Changing their usual arrangements, they performed at night, but it was scarcely cooler, and the smoke and the stink of the extra tallow candles that were necessary only added to their discomfort.

The night of their last performance, Colombe suddenly dropped her book and candle and clutched at her belly in terror. By the time the play was over she was moaning and begging to be carried back to her room at the inn. Through the night she thrashed about on her bed—her linens growing quite black from the color she used on her hair—and pleaded for a pillow impregnated with a narcotic; at dawn the midwife was sent for, and the child—a healthy girl—was delivered at eight.

When Ninon, exhausted from the long night's vigil, came out of Colombe's bedchamber and announced the news to the waiting company, the men cheered and congratulated one another on their possible fatherhood.

Colombe having been made more comfortable, the men crooped into her bedchamber to wish her well and view the child. She had contrived to rouge her cheeks and lips and out on fresh linen, and Hortense had combed her hair. She received them like a queen.

"You may all kiss me," she said. Each man in his turn sent over her to kiss her lips; Marc-Antoine, captivated by the tiny babe that lay on the pillow beside her, beamed in approval and kissed Colombe sweetly on the cheek.

"What of you, Pierre," she said archly to Marc-Antoine's protégé. "Will you not give me a kiss?"

Marc-Antoine looked distressed. "No…Colombe…he is just a lad…don't…"

She sneered. "I shall not corrupt him…any more than you have done!" She held out her arms seductively. "Come, Pierre."

Marc-Antoine's face was twisted with anguish as Pierre hesitantly leaned down to kiss Colombe. She smiled at the boy; then, darting a malicious glance at Marc-Antoine, she took Pierre's hand and placed it on her breast. He turned around and looked at Marc-Antoine, defiance written in his set jaw and eyes that were strangely old; then he turned back to Colombe and kissed her as hard as he could.

Chanteclair muttered under his breath and covered his eyes, ashamed to be witness to such cruelty.

Colombe smiled smugly, clearly enjoying her day. "Now, Val. You're the only one who hasn't kissed me!"

Valentin shrugged. "Since I'm not one of your legion of lovers, I can scarcely claim the child as mine. Why should I kiss you?"

"Dear sweet Val. You are always so *very* charming. But the closest I've ever come to Marc-Antoine was at the supper table, and *he* kissed me! Perhaps you're afraid, sweetling!"

He stared at her, his face a mask of indifference, then sat on the edge of the bed and let his lips touch hers for one brief instant. In that moment she grabbed his black hair and pulled his mouth back down to hers, straining against him with all the passion in her. He struggled and broke away, jumping up from the bed to storm to the door.

"Damn you!" she shrieked to his retreating back. "Cursed eunuch! You shall not be my child's godfather!"

In the end, it was decided that Hortense should stand godmother to the child, and, by a process of elimination, Marc-Antoine the godfather, since a possible sire could not have the honor, and Colombe would have nothing to do with Valentin. They managed to find a curé who was willing to get permission of the bishop to have the baptism take place in the local church. "Child of musicians," the certificate read, and it cost them a great deal of money, particularly to the bishop, who harbored suspicions about these vagabonds who had no true home. Marc-Antoine beamed with pride at his godchild (Marie-Anne, Colombe had named her), filled with a sense of responsibility and tenderness, a side of his personality that no one had seen before.

At supper that night, Ninon announced that she would leave the company as soon as Colombe could return to the stage.

"You cannot think to go," growled Valentin. "There is room for both of you in the troupe. You're the best soubrette we have had! Colombe shall return to the inamorata roles. But you cannot think to go!"

"What will you do if you leave us?" asked Chanteclair gently.

She shook her head. "I shall find something…a new life…"

"You have a life here," said Marc-Antoine. "Stay."

She hesitated, seeing the resentful look on Colombe's face, then nodded in agreement. After all, why not? What else was there for her to do? She had a place here, and the company (except Colombe) wanted her; she would be a fool to go. She herself held no quarrel with Colombe; with a little effort they might be friends. She nodded again.

They signed an official contract with her that very night, making her a full shareholder in the company for the term of a year; then they celebrated the baptism and Ninon's staying by getting very drunk.

A week later, on a sultry afternoon, Ninon heard Marie-Anne crying and rushed into Colombe's chamber to tend the child. Cooing softly, she picked up the baby, and turned to see Colombe in the *ruelle*—the alcove to one side of the bed—lacing herself into a tight bodice.

"Your child wants her dinner, I think," Ninon said gently.

Colombe smoothed her gown, admiring her slim shape in a mirror on the wall. "Let the brat wait. If we were not leaving Auxerre next week, I should put her out to nurse."

"If you cared so little, why did you carry her?"

Colombe shrugged. "By the time I knew of her in my womb, it was too late to do anything, unless I wished to put my own life at risk. You do not like me," she said, as Ninon turned away from her, rocking the baby in her arms. "No matter. I shall give you less cause in the weeks to come."

"I bear you no ill will, Colombe."

Colombe's voice was hard and ugly. "But I do not like you. I give you fair warning. I shall win back all the parts that Valentin gave to you. And when he writes a new play, it will be for *me*. To carry me to Paris in triumph!"

"We shall see what we shall see," Ninon said mildly.

"Little fool! Do you think you can stop me by capturing Val's fancy?"

"*Nom de Dieu!* Why should I want such a thing?"

Colombe's voice had begun to rise shrilly. "I am not blind! I see how you look at him, your eyes lusting for him, your body trembling for his touch!"

Ninon fell back in stunned silence, clutching the child to her bosom.

"Look not so amazed, you slut," Colombe spat. "I am not fooled. Your face gives you away. You want him as much as I do! But you haven't a chance."

"Nor has any one of us!" snapped Ninon, her patience stretched thin.

Colombe smiled slyly. "No one has ever really tried. Not even me. I waited for him to make his overtures. But now, willy-nilly, I intend to have him. And you, you wretched creature, you will do naught save stand by in helpless fury—and envy me!"

Chapter Seven

Ninon pushed at the curls on her forehead, smoothing them away from her damp skin. *Mon Dieu*, but it was hot! And her ankle had begun to bother her again. They had left Auxerre on foot, there being not a single horse to be had. Somewhere between here and Troyes, God willing, there might be horses to rent. Colombe, taking her ease in the wagon with her baby, had complained the whole morning about the heat and discomfort, until there was not a player plodding along on foot who would not cheerfully have strangled her.

Ninon sighed and looked at the road ahead. It stretched into the distance, bare and unshaded under the hot sun, then rose sharply to a steep hill. It had rained all last night, and here and there were still puddles, their vapors adding to the steamy day. She looked about at her fellow strollers, their faces tight with varying degrees of misery. Gaston's broken arm was healing well, but it was clear from the way he supported it with his other hand, massaging it from time to time, that the humid day had made it ache. Hortense had eaten well in Auxerre; now the added flesh on her already generous body made her puff as she walked. She had tucked her skirt and petticoat into her waistband so that they reached only to her knees, and rolled her cotton stockings down around her ankles, but still she stopped now and again to fan her bare legs with her skirt hem.

Marc-Antoine looked the most woebegone, though his griefs, Ninon knew, were more of the heart than of the flesh. Pierre, less and less the innocent lad he had seemed at first, had stayed out all night, returning to the inn at dawn as the rain had stopped. Marc-Antoine had chided him gently, but in the end had given him a new pair of boots he had bought for himself. And still the boy marched along, sulky and disagreeable, defying all of Marc-Antoine's efforts to cheer him.

Ninon sighed again, feeling her ankle begin to throb. She had twisted it some leagues back, just past Saint Florentin. God willing, they would stop to rest soon, but she did not want to ask Valentin. He had mocked her in the morning, calling her soft, pampered—because she had insisted on wearing a hat to protect her fair complexion. Damn the man! Must everything be a challenge to him?

"Why do you limp?" he growled, coming up beside her.

"I do not limp."

"And I say you do! Have you hurt your foot?"

"'Tis nothing. I turned my ankle a little. That's all."

"Sweet Jesu!" he cursed. "And kept silent! Well, you shall ride in the wagon."

"So you may make sport of me? Thank you, no."

His eyes glowed like black coals. "Shall you ride willingly? Or unwillingly?" He stepped to the moving wagon and pulled down a length of rope. "Well?" He pointed to the new chair, perched atop several large trunks. "You shall ride enthroned."

She wavered, seeing the look in his eyes. She had no wish to be trussed to the chair. "Very well," she conceded. "But only until we pass that stretch of steep road." He nodded and went forward to have Chanteclair stop the team.

With the help of the men, Ninon mounted the wagon and seated herself on the new throne. Colombe, reclining with her infant, smiled unpleasantly. They set out once again, climbing the slope until they had reached the summit of the hill. Ninon found it a chancy ride; the path had become quite rutted and the chair bobbled and rattled on its perch. The embankment dropped sharply away on one side of the road. It gave her a feeling of vertigo just to look down from her height at the jumble of soft shale and boulders that fell away to a small stream far below. But at least her ankle would have a rest for a little while.

Up ahead was a large puddle. Unwilling to wade through it or get themselves splashed, the men stepped back from the wagon and whistled the oxen through, meaning to skirt the water when the wagon had passed. But the puddle camouflaged a treacherous rut; without warning the oxen stumbled, and one of the animals fell to its knees. The wagon tipped crazily before its front wheels lurched into the rut, spilling out Ninon and the throne and tumbling them down the side of the mountain. Her hat flew off and spun away to the stream. She felt herself rolling, head over heels, then sliding on the soft stones, until at last she came to rest on a clump of soft grass. Her body ached all over, and her left leg, from thigh to ankle, felt as though it were on fire. Valentin scrambled down the steep incline, his eyes dark with concern as he bent over her.

"I'm fine," she gasped. "Truly. Let me rest a little. Only see to Colombe and Marie-Anne!"

In the tilted wagon, Colombe, buried under boxes and rolls of scenery, was screaming like a madwoman; beside her the baby wailed in misery. At Valentin's reassuring wave, the rest of the company, concerned at first with Ninon, turned their attention to Colombe and the precariously balanced wagon. If they were not careful, Colombe and the child and the wagon and all their worldly goods would soon follow Ninon down the side of the hill. Carefully they unpacked the wagon and lifted out Colombe and Marie-Anne, while Chanteclair waded into the puddle up to his knees and tried to ease the oxen out of the rut. Unable to do much because of his arm, Gaston moved down to the stream to mourn his new throne, now splintered beyond repair.

Valentin knelt beside Ninon. "Can you walk, or have you twisted your ankle further?"

What was it about the man's tone of voice that always angered her? "I shall be fine," she snapped. "I do not need your help." She wiggled her foot in the air. "You see, I can move it."

"Let me see." Roughly he grabbed her leg, his long fingers probing the bones at her ankle. His hand on her shin burned like a searing flame through the fabric of her skirt and stocking. She clenched her teeth tightly to keep from crying out. "What is it?" he barked.

"Nothing."

He stared at her for a long moment, then tossed back her skirt to her garter. "*Merde!*" he swore, seeing the drops of blood on her torn stocking. Despite her cries of protest, he pushed up the skirt to her thigh, then tore off her garter and pulled down her stocking, revealing the tortured flesh, scraped and bleeding from the long slide through the shale. He frowned. "What manner of woman *are* you?"

"Leave me in peace! I keep my own counsel."

"No, damn you! Not when you're a member of this company, you don't! Where else are you hurt?"

"Nowhere else. Just my leg," she lied, dropping her eyes to avoid his glance.

"By God, if need be I'll strip you naked to find out! Where else?"

She sighed in resignation. "I think I wrenched my back and shoulder. That's all. I swear it."

"Show me."

Reluctantly she loosed the drawstring on her chemise and turned away from him. He pulled the garment down in the back and examined her carefully, his fingers pressing gently on the muscles, and moving quickly to another spot each time she flinched.

"There are no scratches," he said at last, "but I'll wager you'll be stiff and sore for many a day. Come." He lifted her easily in his arms and carried her up the hill. "Hortense will have clean linens for that leg."

By the time the wagon had been unloaded, the animals and cart pulled free of the rut, and the goods returned to their places, night was beginning to fall. They saw nothing ahead but more treacherous mountains; it would be madness to travel in the dark. By the last light they made their way down into the valley, and were delighted to find the ruins of an old farmhouse, parts of the roof caved in, but the soft dirt floor smooth and dry enough to sleep on. Because it was still so hot, they built a small fire only to see by, while they supped on cold meat pastries and fresh water from the stream that flowed nearby. As the moon rose, its clear light shining through the broken roof and dappling the earth with patches of silver, the last embers of the fire died. Stretched out on their cloaks, the members of the Peerless Theatre Company rubbed their eyes and yawned and fell asleep one by one.

Only Ninon tossed and turned for hours, suffocating from the heat, aching in every muscle. Her leg did not trouble her too much: Hortense had bound it carefully, smoothing on a salve that drew the sting from the raw flesh. But her shoulder and back throbbed, making rest impossible. She sat up at last, seeing the sleeping bodies on either side of her, and rubbed at her neck to ease the tightness. A nightingale sang in the soft night air. She imagined it to be two or three by now; if she was lucky, she might manage to sleep for a few hours.

There was a sudden movement beside her. Startled, she nearly cried out. Valentin, bending over her, put a silencing finger to his lips. Gathering her in his arms, he carried her out of the farmhouse and down to the bank of the stream, where a large tree bent its branches to the water. He set her down on the grass, then sat down beside her, his back against the trunk of the tree. A small breeze blew across the water and fanned her face, soothing her burning cheeks. How sweet the air was, after the sweltering farmhouse.

Without warning, Valentin reached out and pulled her to him, twisting her around and burying her face against his hard chest. She grunted in surprise and tried to struggle out of his arms, her fists pushing at his breast. "Keep still!" he hissed. His hands moved across her back, strong and sure, finding the knots in her muscles, massaging the ache away with fingers that pressed deep, touching the pain and soothing it all at the same time. She moaned in pleasure and relaxed against him, trusting herself to his sure hands. She felt herself begin to drift into the sleep that had eluded her for hours, her eyes heavy, body floating—every nerve focused on the warmth of his fingers, the gentleness of his touch.

"Oh," she murmured, her voice muffled against him. "I thought I should never sleep tonight!"

His voice rumbled in his chest beneath her head. "If you had stayed at Marival, you would be in a soft bed now, instead of sleeping on the ground."

She moved against him, melting under his hands, her thoughts beginning to wander. "I have had my share of griefs. I slept on a hard floor many a night—and was grateful for it."

"What? You?"

She laughed sleepily. "You and Colombe and the others—how spoiled you are. I could tell you a tale or two." She drew in a ragged breath, half-transported in her sleepy state to a long-ago time, a terrible time. "...Of fingers that bleed from the cold...and still the wood must be chopped...and hunger that twists at your bowels, filling the days with despair...the nights with torment...and a beating whenever it suited Baugin...Oh, how my bones would ache!"

"Baugin?"

"My stepfather," she sighed.

"*Mon Dieu,*" he said softly, the soothing fingers stilled for a moment. He held her more tightly against his breast, then continued the rhythmic massaging of her back. "But surely not at Marival...?"

"No." Her voice was high and sweet and faraway, like that of a little child on the edge of sleep. "No, not at Marival...ah, your hands...how good that feels...not at Marival..." She was drifting now, teetering on the brink of oblivion.

"But how did you escape your torments?"

"Philippe," she whispered. "Philippe. He saved me. I think I should have died else...I shall love him...forever...Philippe..." With a soft sigh, she nestled closer in his arms and found oblivion.

She woke at dawn to the chirping of birds in the tree high above her. She was lying cradled in Valentin's arms. He slept, his back still against the tree trunk, his head drooped forward to his chest. She lay quietly, unwilling to disturb him, unwilling (if she admitted it to herself) to move from the comforting warmth of his arms. She lay quietly and examined his face.

It was strange, seeing him thus, his features soft with sleep, the angry lines smoothed away by the forgetfulness of slumber. She had thought him a man in his thirties, his hard face carved by time; now she was not so sure. Philippe—her beloved Philippe—was only twenty-nine. It seemed to her that Valentin might even be younger. He was really extraordinarily handsome, seen thus objectively without the intrusion of his abrasive manner. His jaw was long and square, the cleft in his chin a sensual delight, seeming to invite the touch of exploring fingers. She found herself wondering what Philippe's chin would be like, clean-shaven. His eyelashes, sweeping the sun-browned cheekbones, were black and curled, almost too beautiful for a man. His nose was long and straight and flared at the nostrils. The face of an actor. The face of a proud stallion.

And his mouth. Wide and firm, set in a stubborn line even in sleep. But his lips were soft. How pleasant it would be, she thought idly, to be kissed by those soft lips. *Mon Dieu!* What was she thinking of? Colombe had spoken of it: the way she looked at Valentin, wanting him. Sweet Madonna, could it be so?

She frowned and examined his sleeping face more closely. Perhaps it was so after all, and Colombe, in her jealousy, had seen it. Certain it was that she did not like the man; just as certainly she found him attractive, his physical presence disturbing her in an odd way. Perhaps she had misjudged him. He had been kind last night, kind and gentle. And his face in repose was so sad, so vulnerable.

And his mouth. She sighed softly. She did not like him, of course. Still…it would be nice to be kissed by that mouth, to feel a shiver down her spine as his lips took hers. She suddenly remembered his kiss in the stable at Marival. She had not let herself think of it, all these weeks, but now…Without her willing it, her heart began to pound wildly, her bosom heaving. She must be mad…she must be mad…

He opened his eyes and looked down at her. Deep brown eyes, almost black. Soft and melting, as innocent and trusting as the dawn. Was that the part of him she had sensed last night, when she had poured out her heart to him, telling him things she had shared with no one, not even Philippe? She felt an unexpected surge of tenderness.

His eyes searched her face. "Did you sleep well?" The voice was soft with concern, but his gaze focused on her full lips.

"Yes. I thank you." She smiled gently. Perhaps he *would* kiss her.

She could almost see the grating drop before his eyes. Iron bars. To keep her out. To keep himself safe. "Well, I did not," he growled, pushing her off his lap.

She struggled to sit upright. "I wonder you trouble yourself on my behalf!"

"The company has need of you. Of what value is a leading lady who cannot move upon the stage?"

She shook her head, unwilling to take his cruelty at face value. "Come now," she chided. "Does your own kindness shame you, that you must feign a cold heart?"

He laughed harshly, his devil's face mocking her. "Are you such a fool you cannot see what is real and true? We are *all* selfish, we men, however much we hide it. Your pardon. Excluding, of course, your... stepfather, was it? An honest man, no doubt. He wasted no effort on pretense, I should guess."

She put her hand to her mouth, feeling the hot flush of humiliation, silently cursing her candor of last night.

"But we are all selfish," he repeated. "We do what we do—in seeming kindness—for our own selfish reasons. And hope that a woman like you will credit the kindness and be blind to the selfishness."

"Not *all* men!"

"Ah, yes. I forget what a romantic idiot you are in the matter of Froissart. With you, a man need not even study the art of seduction. You said he rescued you. What in God's name do you think he rescued you *for?* The gift of your virginal body, I would guess, from what I heard that day at Marival!"

"May you rot in Hell," she said bitterly, jumping to her feet. "You poison the very air I must breathe." She turned toward the farmhouse, trying not to limp, though her leg throbbed with pain. Would she never learn to hide her heart from a man, to trust no one with her dreams and secrets? Despite her anger, she felt herself fighting back tears as she made her painful way to the farmhouse door. Chanteclair was there, his sympathetic eyes going from her face to Valentin—still sitting under the tree—then back again.

"He's a fool," he said gently.

"No." She sniffled and rubbed her fingers across her eyes, brushing away the tears. "I'm the fool. To seek a spark of warmth where there is none!"

"Are you coming to supper, Colombe?" Valentin poked his head in at the changing-room door. "Gaston says The Cock serves a fine roast turkey."

About to pin up her black hair, Colombe put down her comb and turned to Valentin. "Have they all gone on, then?" she asked.

"Indeed, yes. Will you join us?"

"Come and help me first. My hair is tangled woefully, and I cannot reach the spot." She handed him the comb, sat down on a small bench, and presented her back.

"Sweet Jesu, but this is not my art," he said, reluctantly pulling the comb through her long tresses.

"But it is not difficult, is it?" Her voice was playful.

He laughed. "No. It is not difficult. Nor is it very tangled!"

"Don't stop. Is it such a terrible thing to indulge me for a little?"

"'Tis beautiful hair," he conceded, wielding the comb with gentle hands.

"Was I good this afternoon?"

"You were *sans pareil*, without equal," he said. "The good citizens of Bouilly will not soon again see a Queen Esther of such heroic dimensions."

She sniffed. "It was too good a representation for such a wretched town."

"Consider it a rehearsal for Troyes. God willing, we can stay a month there. Or more."

She took the comb from him and piled her curls on top of her head, twisting about to smile archly at him. "Are you sorry you gave Esther back to me?"

"Why should I be? You play tragedy superbly."

"That foolish jade, Ninon! Her Esther was an abomination!"

"Her Esther was good," he growled. "Not as good as yours, but good! And her comedy eclipses yours every time she is on the stage!"

"Oh, Valentin," she said quickly. "Please to forgive me. 'Tis only my way. Actresses are always jealous of one another, though they be sisters off the stage—even as Ninon and I are. You are right. She plays farce very well indeed." She shook her hair free again and stood up, taking him by the hands. "But I have been practicing a little dance for one of the musical interludes. Sébastien said he would play the music for me. Mayhap instead I shall ask Ninon—the dear lass is so skilled with a guitar. Would that please you?"

He smiled. "Anything that cements the friendship of my two leading ladies pleases me. There is no joy in listening to cats fight!"

"Poor Valentin! How we women try you! But let me show you the dance that I have been rehearsing." She pulled out an elbow chair and pushed him into it. "Sit you here." When he was comfortably settled in the chair, she began to dance slowly around him, humming softly in accompaniment. It was a tantalizing dance, and she did it well, swaying in front of him, her long black hair loose and flowing. He leaned back and smiled, his eyes raking her lithe form.

She was wearing only her chemise and petticoat. Now, still keeping time to her own music, she loosed her petticoat and stepped out of it, then lowered the neckline of her chemise to the tips of her breasts.

Valentin frowned. "Colombe…"

"*Hist!* The dance is not finished!" She turned away from him and pulled her chemise off her shoulders, sliding it seductively down the length of her body and over her generous hips to fall at the floor. She pivoted slowly, taking her own pleasure in a body she knew was ripe and firm, showing no ravages of its recent childbearing.

"Name of God, Colombe," he said. "Stop."

"Don't you like my dance?" she whispered. She put her hands over her head and began to sing again, her body writhing sensuously before him. "It was meant for you alone."

"Sweet Jesu…" he choked, half-rising from his chair.

"No!" She threw herself to her knees before him, pushing him back onto the chair. Twining her bare arms about his waist, she began to kiss his thighs, his belly, his loins. "I love you!" she cried.

"This is madness," he said, struggling to loose her arms.

She looked up at him with tormented eyes. "Am I too old? Too plain?"

"No. Colombe…I beg you…"

She began to weep. "I would die for you. From the first moment you came to the company…I would not sleep with Ragotin after you came. I could not bear it. And I waited for you, and hoped and prayed…Oh, Valentin…I cannot live without you any longer…" Sobbing, she buried her face in his lap, her shoulders shaking in misery.

"Mother of God," he said, touching her head tenderly. "Don't do this, Colombe. I beg you. I am not the man for you."

"Why? *Why?*" She lifted her tearstained face to search his, seeing only pity where she longed to find passion. With a shriek she leaped to her feet and swung at him with a tight-clenched fist. "Damn you! Filthy dung-heap! Pox-ridden excuse for a man! You impotent bastard…"

He held her off as best he could, but his silence seemed only to inflame her fury, and she went for him again and again, her nails like claws, her voice harsh and ugly, spewing foul curses.

Standing outside the open door, Ninon clapped a hand over her mouth, feeling that she would vomit. She had not meant to intrude; she had returned to the changing room only to fetch a lace fichu. Silently she turned and hurried back down the stairs to the door of the *jeu de paume*. She could not bear to witness Colombe's degradation. No woman, not even Colombe, deserved to be humiliated thus. She was a beautiful woman, with a beautiful body, lush and full. What was the matter with Valentin? His pity was aroused, that was plain.

But not his manhood. What was the matter with him?

She glanced up at the evening sky. The moon would set early tonight. With a sigh, she hurried down the street to the sign of The Cock and the warm cheerfulness of her comrades.

She found a small group gathered for supper. Gaston was already beginning his third glass of wine, and Sébastien and Hortense, the only other players sitting around the table, had begun their nightly quarrel, this time disputing the merits of turkey over pigeon. If Sébastien did not storm off in anger and find a game of *rouge et noir*, they would eventually end up in bed together. Ninon found it amusing, the way their passion survived their quarrels, though it created difficulties for her. She never knew when Hortense—with whom she was accustomed to sharing a bed when they traveled—would suddenly announce that the arrangements had been changed for the evening, sending Ninon off to crowd in with Toinette and Colombe. (If Toinette was not sleeping with Joseph!) And if Hortense decided to spend the night in Sébastien's bed, Ninon was left alone in the large bed, forced to share it with a stranger if the inn had last-minute female guests. All in all, Ninon preferred it if the various couplings took place in the daytime, or in a secluded barn or hayrick.

From what she could gather, this seemed to be where Joseph and Toinette were this evening, off in some cozy spot enjoying each other's company. Marc-Antoine and his lad were, as usual, seeking more exotic companionship, and Chanteclair had gone on ahead to Troyes to arrange for their performances and to see if he could manage a commission or two among the gentry.

Ninon took her place at the table, picking at the food when it was brought, still disturbed by the ugly scene she had witnessed. She would have welcomed Chanteclair and his counsel tonight.

The door opened and Valentin strode in, mumbling a greeting before sitting down to eat. There was a long scratch on his cheek; he kept it turned away from his fellows as much as possible, his darting eyes almost defying any one of them to pass a remark.

But Gaston, well into his cups, would not be deterred. "Upon my word, Valentin," he sniggered, "she must have been a tiger!"

Valentin gave him a withering look, but said nothing.

"For my part," said Sébastien, "I should welcome a few scratches like that. 'Tis a sign to the world that a man's a lusty lover, to bear such a trophy!"

"Indeed?" said Hortense. "I must remember that the next time I am vexed with you!"

"Then remember Auxerre as well, my love. If you scratch me in passion, I will be delighted. But if you attack me in anger, I shall answer in kind—and with a little extra for good measure! I wonder I do not dust your backside more often, madame, to keep your disposition sweet!"

"Plague take you," she snapped. "You get no more than you deserve, with your gambling and whoring and…"

"Is it possible to eat supper without listening to you two?" Valentin said wearily. He cut a slice from the roast turkey on the table, placing it on a slab of bread and spreading it generously with mustard.

Gaston chuckled. "Gave you an appetite, eh? Your wench?"

"Once for all…" began Valentin, then stopped as Colombe sailed into the room, chin held high and proud. She sat down at the end of the table, ignoring Valentin, and immediately began to eat. He lowered his eyes to his plate, hoping to avoid a scene.

They were all silent for some time, each with his own thoughts, anxious to be done, and quit of one another for the night. Gaston poured himself another cup of wine. "Look, Colombe," he cackled finally, unable to let the subject rest. "Have you seen Valentin's badge of honor? Some wench has put her mark upon Sanscoeur at last!"

"Don't be a drunken fool, Gaston," she sneered. Her eyes, filled with hatred, bored into Valentin's bent head. "No doubt he passed a sharp branch. Valentin would not run afoul of a woman. By my faith, that great looby would run *away* from a woman as soon as look at her! Is it not so, sweetling?"

He shrugged and applied himself to his food.

Colombe smiled. "You know, most men come into the world with three things—their wits, their honor, their shittlecock. It would seem that Dame Nature has shortchanged Valentin."

Ninon held her breath, half-expecting the explosion. She was astonished at Valentin's forbearance in the face of Colombe's malice and insults.

"Come, Val," said Colombe, "was it a branch that marred your pretty face?"

Ninon saw the challenge in her eyes, saw Valentin glance at Colombe and read it there as well. How reckless of Colombe, she thought, to give him the opportunity to speak up and humiliate her further. A misogynist like that would scarcely spare her feelings.

Valentin stood up from the table and went to the fireplace, taking down a pipe and filling and lighting it. He turned at last, his eyes sweeping Colombe with gentle understanding. "Yes, Colombe," he said quietly. "It was a branch."

Colombe opened her mouth to reply, thought better of it, and kept silent. Quickly she finished her supper and rose from the table. "Gaston, will you see me to the inn?" Without waiting for his answer, she opened the door. There on the threshold stood Marc-Antoine, looking haggard, his face drawn, the flesh seeming almost to sag in misery on his corpulent body. "La! Valentin!" she said brightly. "Your fellow *tapette* awaits you! Dear, sweet Marc-Antoine. Are you weary at last of children? You must seek your warmth of Valentin tonight."

"Be still, Colombe," said Ninon, hurrying forward to Marc-Antoine. She put a soft hand on his arm. "Come and sit down. Have a cup of wine. Have you supped?"

He pulled a handkerchief from his sleeve and sniffed delicately at it, the old Marc-Antoine returned for a moment. "Exquisitely. We frequent only the finest places. But I shall condescend to take some wine." He smiled sadly, the brave mask vanishing. "And a little cheer."

"You look like the devil, *mon ami*," said Valentin gently.

Marc-Antoine rubbed his eyes. "The devil has fewer burdens."

"Why do you not give him up?"

"Yes. 'Tis reasonable." Marc-Antoine laughed softly. "But what was it Pascal said? 'The heart has its reasons, that reason knows not of.' I need fifteen crowns." At Valentin's quizzical look he shrugged his shoulders. "He…has a fondness for fine things."

Colombe's shrill voice cut like a knife. "Fifteen crowns? He sells his body dear, doesn't he? Can you not find a cheaper whore?" Marc-Antoine winced.

Valentin shot Colombe an angry look, then fumbled in his pocket and drew out some coins, pressing them into Marc-Antoine's hand. "Here. You can pay me back in Troyes. Or whenever you can."

Marc-Antoine nodded in gratitude and shuffled to the door; then, turning, he struck a pose of bravado and thumped grandly at his chest. "Like brave Aeneas," he intoned dramatically, "I go where duty summons me!"

Colombe snickered. "You useless *tapette*. Run to your whore Pierre. Buy his love. And if he does not wear out your poor prickle, you can pay back Valentin in services!" She laughed in malicious pleasure as Marc-Antoine reddened and fled into the night.

Without a word, Valentin stalked to the table. Picking up a pitcher of wine, he dumped its contents onto Colombe's head. She shrieked hysterically, surveying her ruined gown, sobbing and cursing him all in the same breath. At last Sébastien and Hortense, taking pity on her, led her back to the inn. "Here," said Valentin to Gaston, slapping a purse of coins on the table, "tell the tavernkeeper I'll pay for the extra wine." He turned to Ninon. "Are you returning to the inn? I'll walk along with you."

"I can find my way."

"Nonsense. The night is dark. And the inn is far."

"Very well." They set out together in silence. Ninon found her thoughts whirling in confusion. What manner of man was this, striding so purposefully beside her in the dark night? A paradox. Capable of cruelty, she knew—his words and actions had hurt her many a time. But how to explain the tenderness? He might have mocked Colombe for her confession of love; he *should* have mocked Colombe—it was in his nature to despise a woman's love. Yet, he had spared her feelings.

Still, he might have done much more. He might have kissed her, petted her, eased her love-torn heart, without returning her love. If he were capable of it. Yet, he was unfailingly kind to Marc-Antoine. *Ah Dieu!* Ninon's brain teemed. Despite Chanteclair's assurances, *could* he be what Colombe accused him of? And why should she care?

They had reached their lodgings. From behind the candlelit windows of the inn, they could hear Colombe's voice, still raised in shrill protest. Valentin mounted the stile set into the stone fence that surrounded the inn, and stepped down to the other side.

"Give me your hand," he said. "'Tis dark."

She slipped her fingers into his and climbed the stile. But the top step was worn, the wood rubbed smooth from numberless crossings; her foot slid out beneath her and she pitched headlong into his arms. He held her tightly for a moment, steadying her against his chest, before setting her gently on her feet. She murmured her thanks and continued on to the inn. But her heart raced within her breast and she trembled. He could not be unmanly when the feel of his arms around her gave her a thrill that took her breath away! And if he was, what manner of woman was she?

What folly to torment herself thus! Why should she care about him one way or another? Sweet Madonna, why should she care?

• • •

"Well, Chanteclair, what think you?" Ninon pirouetted about in the large changing room, doing a little step in front of Chanteclair. Her left leg, from toe to hip, was covered with a tight stocking in a brilliant shade of orange; her right leg was similarly clad in pink. Her modesty was preserved only by short, full breeches of gold brocade that just reached to her hips: the colorful trunk hose were joined only at the waist. The short doublet she wore was also of gold brocade, with an orange capelet; the pageboy's cap, into which her hair had been tucked, was crowned with a pink feather.

Chanteclair smoothed a last bit of white lead onto his face, picked up a black crayon, and outlined his lips. He put down his mirror and surveyed Ninon. "Only a fool would take you for a lad!"

"But how the audience enjoys being fooled."

"Yes. I'm glad Valentin decided we should play *The Generous Lover*. 'Tis a good role for you."

She laughed. "Because of my wit?"

He leered, his eyes caressing her slender legs, long and shapely in their hose. "Yes. Certainly. Your…wit!" He put a little rouge on a fingertip and dabbed it on his lower lip. He glanced up again from his mirror. "Ah, Val. What think you of Ninon in her new costume?"

Valentin allowed his eyes to flick quickly over Ninon's body before coming to rest on her face. He grunted a halfhearted approval. "Do you know your part?"

"I forget at my peril that you are the author."

"And most particular," he snapped.

Damn him and his disagreeable ways, she thought. She smiled coyly. "But do you think my legs are fine enough for trunk hose?"

"They'll do."

"No, no. You must look carefully. What think you of my knees? My calves? My thighs? Surely my thighs are too thin."

"I said they'll do!" he growled.

"But in the back as well? Wait. Let me turn about for you. There now." She smiled and pivoted again to him, seeing the fury in his eyes, the way his jaw had begun to work. "Perhaps I need padding under my trunk hose. Give me your hand. Here. Just here. You see?" Her eyes were wide with innocence as she placed his hand on the inner edge of her thigh.

He withdrew his fingers as though her touch burned him. "Only know your lines," he said through clenched teeth. "You can play the whore *after* the performance is done!" He turned on his heel and strode away.

Chanteclair burst into laughter. "*Mon Dieu!* If you teased *me* that way, I should have you bedded in a trice!"

She shrugged. "I do it for a game. I know how he hates it. He behaves as though every woman—by virtue of her womanliness—is an evil seductress. What sport it is to play the part and watch him writhe!"

Chanteclair finished his makeup, put on a large and oversized hat, and stood up. "I wonder how the house is today?"

They had been in Troyes for several weeks now. The theater was a large one, and equipped with the most up-to-date machinery, which had allowed them to expand their repertoire. They had made a success almost every night. The audiences had begun to thin out now, but only because it would soon be time for the grape harvest, and the local *vignerons* and vineyard-owning nobility had less time for the theater. As soon as the grapes were in, and the wine fermenting merrily in its vats, they could look forward to renewed acclaim, and audiences eager to spend their money. For the next few weeks they would play only two or three days a week.

"I wonder if Colombe's vicomte is here today," said Ninon.

"Has he missed a performance since we arrived?"

"I wish he wouldn't sit upon the stage. He is vexingly rude, forever talking with his fellows and whispering to Colombe."

Chanteclair eyed Ninon appreciatively. "Take care you do not stand too near him today. I vow, in those trunk hose…" He reached out his hand to Ninon's rump. She shrieked and turned to him, eyes wide with surprise. He grinned. "You see what I mean? 'Tis a temptation to a man!"

They descended to the stage where the rest of the company were already assembled. Marc-Antoine, who was to play a Moorish prince, had darkened his face with burnt cork; Colombe, as the queen of Spain, had already begun to pace majestically about, taking on her character with each step. Ninon was always astonished at how a woman who could convey such royalty onstage could be so coarse and low when the curtain closed. Valentin, who, with Chanteclair, was to do the comic passages in what was basically a romance, had also whitened his face, but with flour. Each time Chanteclair slapped him in the course of the play it would send up little puffs of white powder, which always convulsed the spectators.

They took their places. Pierre, to be useful, had condescended to part the curtains, which he did with a flourish. Ninon groaned inwardly. There, facing them, his chair set squarely in the center of the stage, was the vicomte who had been Colombe's persistent suitor since they had arrived in Troyes. He was an ugly little man, with a misshapen back, which Colombe never failed to mock when she spoke of him to the company. It did not, however, keep her from accepting gifts from him or allowing him to take her to supper after each performance. Now she smiled charmingly and blew him a kiss before reciting her first line. The vicomte waved back and moved his chair closer to the actors, earning the catcalls of the spectators in the pit whose line of vision he blocked. He had brought several of his friends with him to share the stage, and he spent much of the first scene loudly inviting his comrades to admire the beauty and grace of his mistress.

The company was used to such barbarity, of course. It was almost the sign of a gentleman to see how much chaos he could cause in the theater, without actually interrupting the performance. If he could carry on an *amour* or make an assignation at the same time, all the better. By the time the second act had begun, one of the other gentlemen onstage had taken to whistling loudly each time Ninon appeared in her trunk hose. She was grateful for Chanteclair's warning, managing to keep her distance from the fop.

Colombe's vicomte had begun to signal to her, making little movements in the air with his hands. From far back on the stage she frowned, not following his meaning. His hand blocking a side of his mouth, he whispered to her, his hissing drowned out by Marc-Antoine's speech. Still uncomprehending, Colombe smiled thinly and moved closer to him, earning Valentin's scowl. Again the vicomte whispered. Ninon answered Marc-Antoine, moving forward, as the play required, to take his cloak.

The vicomte tried again, his voice louder now. One of his friends chuckled.

"'Kind master, good and true, your page salutes you,'" said Ninon, kneeling before Marc-Antoine.

"'Nay, rise, sirrah,'" said Marc-Antoine, "'for I...'" He was interrupted once more by the vicomte, whose voice still did not carry much beyond Ninon.

Colombe's face was frozen in a smile. "What did you say?" she hissed through her teeth, trying to keep her lips from moving.

Ninon had had enough. She marched to Colombe and planted herself before her, hands on hips. "Monsieur le Vicomte would make his applications to you," she said loudly. "He beseeches you to spend the next two weeks as his guest at his château. Will you reward his presumption by saying yes?"

Colombe fell back a step. "But...but...Marie-Anne..."

Ninon turned to the vicomte. "She has a child. May the infant accompany her?"

"Most willingly."

"Is the godfather agreed?" demanded Ninon.

Marc-Antoine suppressed a giggle. "The godfather is agreed."

"Good! Now…" With an elaborate bow Ninon knelt before Marc-Antoine. "'Kind master, good and true…'" she began again, while the house burst into applause and complimented the vicomte on his choice, Colombe on her good fortune, and the pageboy on his matchmaking.

When, at the end of the play, Ninon revealed her femininity, loosing her long curls to the astonished cries of "She's a woman!" by the other characters (although of course the spectators had known it all along), there was not a man in the audience who would not have fallen at the feet of the adorable and witty Madame Guillemot. She had half a dozen invitations to supper, all of which she promised to weigh as she changed her clothes.

She put on her blue gown and tied her lace fichu about her shoulders, then turned to the door. Valentin was there.

"You were very clever today."

"I thought you might be angry. It was your play, after all. And the lines were…extempore, to say the least!"

He smiled. "To say the least! But we shall be quit of Colombe's company for two weeks, except on days we play!"

She returned his smile. "A fitting exchange, *n'est-ce pas*? A ruined scene for two weeks of peace!"

"Indeed." His eyes were warm on her. "Will you come to supper?"

"Alas. I have at least five suitors to placate tonight."

"Of course," he said, suddenly cold. "I had forgot." His eyes dropped to her bosom. "Is your gown low enough to suit you?"

How dare he. "No," she said brazenly, pulling off her fichu and tugging at the bodice of the dress until her breasts rose above the neckline in enticing curves.

His mouth twitched in contempt. "Are you expecting Philippe for supper? Or have you become as undiscriminating as Colombe?"

"My God," she sneered. "Is that jealousy I hear? From *you*? You're like a one-legged man who envies all those who can run!" Pushing past him, she hurried down the stairs and into the soft twilight.

• • •

"Sweet Madonna, 'tis too hot to play today!" Ninon waded out of the stream and sat down on the grassy bank, drying her feet and slipping them, stockingless, into her shoes. She fanned her face with lazy fingers. Even stripped down to her coolest chemise and a single petticoat, she found the September morning oppressive. They had rented a sprawling cottage, well furnished, on the outskirts of Troyes. But even surrounded by trees and the cool stream near which they took their meals, they could not escape the heat.

"We have no choice," said Valentin. "The theater is contracted for, and Chanteclair has posted the handbills. And Gaston has already hired the scenemen to work the machinery." He rolled back the full sleeves of his linen shirt and stretched out on the grass, munching an apple from the early dinner spread out on a cloth beside the stream. He glanced toward the water, where Joseph and Toinette frolicked in happy, naked abandon, then back to Ninon, who had not bothered to pull her petticoat down over her bare legs. "It did not take you long to learn our ways," he said sourly. "Though you will have to go some to better our Colombe. I hear her vicomte gave her fifty livres last week!"

"A hundred," mumbled Gaston, drowsing beneath a nearby tree, its leaves tinged with the first colors of autumn. He burped in contentment and let his empty tankard drop from his fingers. "But at least he doesn't come to the theater anymore."

"A hundred! Fancy that." Valentin's voice dripped with sarcasm. "How much have they offered you, Ninon, those panting fools who buzz around you?"

"Go to the devil."

He sat up and grinned at her. "Enough to make you forget your Philippe? Your broken heart?"

"*If* my heart is broken, it would not take money to heal it!"

He clutched at his breast dramatically. "Ah yes! Tenderness. Kindness. Sensibility."

She looked up to where Chanteclair was just emerging from the house. "Friendship," she said, and ran to meet him. "Good morrow," she said, throwing her arms around him and kissing him warmly on the cheek. "You've slept late. Come and have some dinner." She put his arm about her waist as they walked down to the stream together.

Chanteclair sat on the grass while Ninon fussed over him, plying him with food and wine, playing the coquette. Valentin, gnawing on his apple core, watched in silence, his brows knit together in an angry frown. At last Chanteclair sighed and pushed away his plate. Valentin stood up and tossed the remains of his apple into the shallows of the stream.

"It did not go well," he said, his voice rumbling in his chest, "when we played *Dom Japhet* Tuesday last. I liked not the *lazzo* when I threw you down. It was clumsy. You did not fall easily. Shall we rehearse it again?"

Chanteclair clutched at his belly. "Not now! I have just eaten."

"As have I." Valentin's eyes burned like black coals. "Now!"

Chanteclair shrugged and stood up. The two men pretended to hail each other, shook hands, and then, as Chanteclair started to turn away, Valentin grabbed him by the elbow and flipped him to the ground. Chanteclair grunted loudly and sat up. "Have a care, *mon ami!* You near broke my back!"

"Shall we try it again?" growled Valentin.

"If you must." Again they grasped each other's hands, but this time, as Chanteclair began to turn away, he swiveled back, lifted Valentin over his head, and tossed him into the stream. "Shall we try it *that* way, *mon ami?*" he laughed.

Crowing with laughter, the players gathered about Valentin as he thrashed in the water and tried to stand up. Ninon giggled and threw her arms about Chanteclair's neck. To her surprise, he crushed her in his embrace, his mouth hard on hers, his arms holding her fast. When at last he lifted his head, she gasped to see the passion in his eyes. "You may torment him as you wish," he said softly, "but don't use me as your instrument! First...well, I think you can guess the why. And then, he is my friend."

She felt her face go red with shame. "Forgive me. You have a right to be angry."

He laughed, the old Chanteclair returning. "Valentin needed cooling off. But you're a good actress. I *did* think, just for a moment there..." He smiled regretfully and turned to the stream. "Give me your hand, Val."

Valentin scrambled out of the water, shaking his long black hair like a spaniel. He pulled off his shoes and stockings, and stripped off his shirt, wringing it over the stream. Though he shook Chanteclair's hand in friendship, it was clear that the drenching had put him in a foul mood. He found cause to criticize Toinette for her last two performances, and even barked at Marc-Antoine for a line he had forgotten a week ago. He strode angrily about on the grass, barefoot, half-naked, his wet breeches clinging to him. In spite of herself, Ninon had to admire his body, hard-muscled and sleek, the thatch of black hair tight-matted on his broad chest.

"Can we talk of something else besides performances?" said Gaston at last. "'Tis too hot to roast old mistakes."

"The matter of names," said Chanteclair. "Before I have the next handbills printed. Toinette has decided she is to be *la Gitane*, the Gypsy."

"With that blond hair?" laughed Marc-Antoine.

Toinette pouted. "I like the name."

"But your name is charming as it is," said Sébastien. "Antoinette Vivoin. Antoinette Vivoin." He rolled it on his tongue, smiling warmly at Toinette, until Hortense rapped him on the ear.

"Your name will be *Merde*," Hortense puffed, "if you don't put your eyes back in your head!"

Toinette sighed. "Very well. Do not change my name."

"And what of you, Ninon? Have you thought of a different name?"

She shook her head. "No. I had forgot. Still…"

Valentin stood up and stretched, and grinned down at her, his eyes glittering with malice. "You could call yourself *la Charolles*, for Burgundy."

"I was born in Champagne," she snapped.

"But your heart is in Burgundy, *n'est-ce pas?*" he drawled. "With your…*dommage!*…I keep forgetting his name. You know, the one who called you 'little bird'."

She jumped to her feet, glaring at him. "Perhaps I should call myself Madame Dangereuse! For you had best beware!"

He smiled mockingly, the devil incarnate. "Will you fly into *my* nest, little bird?"

"Damn you!" she shrieked, hating him, hating his seductive body that seemed to promise a masculinity that was clearly lacking. "Chanteclair is the Crowing Rooster. I wonder you do not call yourself *le Chapon*, the Capon, sexless and impotent!"

With a roar, he leaped at her, his head held low like a charging bull. He caught her around the waist and tossed her over one shoulder, marching purposefully in the direction of the house. Head downward, she squirmed and wiggled, losing her shoes in the process, and cursed him with every name she could think of. Carrying her into one of the downstairs bedchambers, he kicked the door closed and set her down roughly.

"Now," he said, breathing hard, "you demand proofs of manhood? You shall have them!" Swiftly he stepped out of his breeches and stood naked before her. She gulped and fell back a step, seeing his power, his virility, his swollen member poised and waiting. He laughed softly. "You see, I have the necessaries, lest you doubted. Have you the necessaries?"

"I curse you forever," she whispered.

"Come now. Don't be shy. Isn't this what you've wanted? Prancing around like a mare in heat, shaking your pretty little rump at me, your breasts falling out of your gowns! Show me your legs *now*. Or do you only play the tease when it's safe?"

"Damn you!" she cursed, feeling more anger than fear, and swung at him with all her might. He ducked her fist and grabbed for her petticoat, tearing it from her in one swift movement. She clawed at his hands as he reached for her chemise, raking raw paths across his forearms. With a wrench that sent the button spinning across the floor, he pulled apart the neckline of her chemise and pushed the garment down to her waist. She broke away and started to run, but he caught her and grabbed her from behind, slamming her naked back up against his chest. His hands slid around her waist to cup her heaving breasts.

His voice hissed in her ear. "Did he touch you like this, your Philippe?"

"Damn you, let me go!" She drew in a deep, gasping breath. "You're just trying to frighten me."

He laughed. "Maybe I am."

She smiled to herself. It *had* been a bluff. "Then let me go. Please, Valentin. Let me go."

His hands were suddenly soft on her breasts, fondling, caressing. "Do you want me to?" he whispered, kissing the back of her neck.

She sagged against him for a moment, feeling her knees go weak at his touch. I must be mad, she thought. "Damn your poxy hide!" she shrilled, and turned in his arms to scratch at him, then drew in her breath sharply at the expression on his face. She looked down at herself—naked save for the last bit of her chemise that still clung about her hips—then glanced back at him. If he had meant only to frighten her, his desire had carried him away long since. His eyes were dark and smoldering, filled with a hunger that made her tremble. "Oh God, no," she whispered, and turned to flee, her anger dissolving in a wave of panic that swept over her. She had barely taken two steps before her ruined chemise—slipping down to her calves—tripped her; she fell forward onto her hands and knees.

Bending over her, Valentin scooped her up with one hand, his arm about her waist, and tossed her onto the bed, ripping away the shreds of her chemise. She scrambled to get away from him, but he grabbed her arm and leg and flipped her over onto her back. He pinned both her arms above her head with one hand; the other hand pressed against her bucking thighs. She gasped as his lips touched her breast, his gentle kiss sending tremors through her body; when his mouth moved downward, she sucked in her abdomen, transfixed by the throbbing, the wild tingling, that followed the path of his mouth. His lips traveled up again to her bosom, pressing and insistent, his strong teeth nibbling at her breasts, her soft neck, her earlobes; there was no pain, just a thrilling sensation, a feeling that every inch of her skin was alive to his roving mouth. By the time he moved upward to kiss her lips, she was trembling violently, her heart thudding within her breast. He still held her hands above her head, but it was no longer necessary—she had gone limp beneath him.

He raised his head, his black eyes sweeping her bosom, and smiled grimly. She followed his glance in horror to see that her own flesh had indicted her: her nipples were rosy and hard, betraying by their eager points what she would deny to herself. "If you would have me stop, say it now," he challenged. She had no will to refuse. Even her silence betrayed her. He laughed softly; then his insolent mouth closed in triumph over her own.

He released her hands and moved on top of her; the feel of his body, strong and overpowering, the rough hairs of his chest scratching her breasts, his hard shaft pressing insistently on her thighs, nearly drove her mad. She could feel herself growing moist and eager for him. She clutched at his shoulders, her fingers kneading the firm smoothness of his flesh, and let her knees fall wide. Waiting, inviting. And when he entered her, penetrating easily, silkily, she felt only a momentary twinge—like the first shock of an icy stream on a hot day, before the senses surrender to pleasure. She was filled, surrounded with warmth, the soft glide of his manhood against the very core of her sending delicious spasms through her body. When he increased the intensity of his thrust, driving harder and deeper, she seemed to lose all sense of time, her head spinning crazily, her body floating somewhere in a world without end, a world of sensation she had never known before, a world of shooting stars behind her closed eyes. She heard a voice cry out in exquisite pleasure; as the stars faded and Valentin collapsed against her, she knew the voice had been her own.

Valentin sighed and rolled away from her. Exhausted, they lay on their backs, side by side, eyes closed. Ninon breathed deeply, trying to still her racing heart, feeling reality return. It was hot. She lifted a heavy hand and wiped the sweat from her face. Beyond the high windows, the birds still sang.

And then Toinette laughed. Just outside the door. A muffled laugh, followed by the sounds of whispering. Oh God! thought Ninon. They were listening. All of them. If they had heard nothing else, they had heard her passionate cry of surrender. Damn Valentin! Damn him! Damn him! With an angry groan she pulled the coverlet about her and turned away from him, dry-eyed, burning with humiliation, with the knowledge of her own weakness.

She stayed that way, curled up in a knot within the coverlet, eyes shut tight, until she had heard him dress again and leave the room, closing the door softly behind him. Then she pushed back the coverlet and got out of bed, surveying her torn clothing and wondering if she could get to her own bedchamber without further loss of her pride. She turned back to the bed and nearly cursed aloud. There was blood on the sheet. She would have to find a way, before she went off to the theater this afternoon, to take it down to the stream and wash out the telltale spots.

If there was anything worse than having Valentin think she was a whore, it was having him know for a certainty that she had been a virgin.

Chapter Eight

"By all that's holy, Hortense, I cannot walk in this!" hissed Ninon, standing up with some difficulty in a sea-green costume that clung tightly to her hips and legs, ending in a sweeping fishtail that hid the opening through which her feet emerged. "You see? It binds my ankles so tightly that I can do no more than hop!"

They were all in the large tiring-room of the theater at Troyes. Colombe, who had come in late from the vicomte's château, hurriedly hooked up her bodice and sat down before a mirror to comb her hair. She smiled sourly at Ninon. "It was not too tight when Toinette wore it. Valentin!" she called. "What is to be done with this fat sow who cannot move?"

Several male heads appeared above the large screen that separated the women's dressing area from the men's. "Walk," said Valentin, frowning at Ninon.

"I *can't!*" she said. "Look." She minced about in a small circle, barely able to keep from toppling. The men came around the screen and eyed her reflectively. She could have kissed every one of them—and Hortense and Toinette, too—in gratitude. Not a word had been said, not an eyebrow raised, over what had happened this morning; only Chanteclair seemed embarrassed, and Valentin was more sullen than usual, if that was possible.

Sébastien knelt at her feet. "We could cut a bit of the fabric, I suppose."

"And ruin the costume?" growled Valentin. "No."

"Wait a moment," said Sébastien. "She doesn't walk in it. She only sits on the rock. And when the wizard changes her into a princess, there's plenty of time for her to return to the tiring-room. Let her be carried in the mermaid costume."

Toinette giggled. "Let Valentin do it! He's so strong and good at it." Ninon blushed furiously as several of the men tried to hide their smiles.

"Is there a joke that I have missed?" asked Colombe.

"I'm not in the scene," Chanteclair said quietly. "I can place Ninon on the rock and then return her here for the transformation."

"But that is such a bother," said Ninon, leaning over to tug at the fabric around her ankles. "Perhaps…"

"Don't you want to be carried?" Toinette, twittering like a bird, was unwilling to let the joke die.

"What *is* this about?" demanded Colombe.

"Shut your mouth, Toinette!" snapped Marc-Antoine, his sympathetic eyes on Ninon.

Colombe drew herself up like a queen. "You lousy whoreson, I'm talking to Toinette. Go and play with your little boy!"

Marc-Antoine bowed elaborately. "Fair Colombe. I think, upon reflection, that I should like to tell you myself. It will give me great pleasure." He took Colombe by the elbow and steered her to a corner of the room, whispering in her ear while she clutched at her bosom and turned pale. She marched to Valentin and slapped him as hard as she could.

He inclined his head in a little bow and turned to Ninon. "I shall carry you to the rock. Chanteclair can carry you back."

"If you must," she said coldly.

He smiled mockingly, his black eyes sweeping the curves of her body, his cheek still glowing red from the marks of Colombe's fingers. "I must."

He waited until the rest had left the tiring-room, pretending to adjust his costume, recombing his long purple wizard's wig. Then he strode over to where Ninon sat waiting, and leaned down. "Put your arms around my neck."

She gulped, imprisoned by those dark eyes, powerless to refuse. Almost against her will, her arms encircled his neck, feeling the strong muscles beneath her fingers. He swept her into his arms and lifted her from her chair, holding her close, his lips perilously near to hers. She held her breath, remembering again the feel of his body this morning, the taste of his kisses.

And then he began to laugh, his eyes glinting wickedly. "Does it not gall you," he said softly, "to know there are things over which you have no control?"

"May you be damned!" she said.

His eyes flickered with sudden pain. "Long since," he said bitterly. "Long since." He turned and carried her to the door of the tiring-room, his body grown cold and rigid.

They descended to the stage, where there was a great flurry of activity. With all the machines and equipment at their disposal here in Troyes, they had attempted more and more elaborate productions, knowing how audiences loved to be dazzled by special effects. Today they were to do a magical piece with Valentin as a wizard who brings on storms and performs all kinds of magic, including transforming the mermaid Ninon into an alluring princess, to make mischief with the lovers until all comes right in the end. The scenemen who had been hired for the day were busy putting the painted waves in ranks upon the stage, each row controlled by a different lever; as the levers were moved independently, the waves would seem to roll. A large whale had been placed over an opening beneath the stage, where a stream of hot air from a fire, controlled by a worker below, would blow the paper streamers that simulated the whale's emissions.

Gaston was hard at work setting up the cloud machine upon which Valentin would descend to the stage, seeing to the strength of the chains, the worthiness of the pulleys. Behind the painted clouds were more than a dozen candles, each backed by a piece of mirror for reflection, and fronted with small bottles filled with a green liquid. The clouds themselves were pierced so the lights would shine through; as Valentin descended from the heavens, he would seem to be surrounded by a green halo.

Even Marc-Antoine's pageboy, Pierre, had been put to work. He was to be the thunder in the storm scene. Behind the back-curtains a ladder had been set up, against which leaned a long wooden trough with shallow ridges in it. At the proper moment, Pierre would climb the ladder with half a dozen cannon balls (borrowed from the local militia) and roll them down the trough. The lightning was even more ingenious. A plank had been cut in two along a jagged line. Behind it, another plank carried a row of candles backed by tinsel for added reflection. When the lightning was needed, two scenemen would quickly separate the jagged plank, then rejoin it. If the theater was dark enough, the effect would be realistic.

The first act went well. The storm raged, the wizard descended from his cloud, and the mermaid vanished in a flash of gunpowder and a puff of smoke. Ninon, carried quickly to the tiring-room by Chanteclair, wriggled out of her mermaid's garb and put on her princess costume, an exotic thing of tinsel and gold braid that Gaston had dredged up from the bottom of one of the trunks. When she hurried back to the stage to appear in a sudden blinding light, the audience applauded wildly, captivated by the effects, the costumes, the beauty of the actress.

But as the act ended and they went forward to take their bows, the boy Pierre, anxious to recover a stray cannon ball, ran in front of Sébastien and almost tripped him. Sébastien cursed under his breath and cuffed the boy's ear. Marc-Antoine could hardly contain his rage until their bows were done and they retreated backstage.

"You will not strike Pierre again," he said, his jowls quivering.

"I'll beat more than his ears if he gets in my way again," said Sébastien. "I still say the imp stole a crown from me last week."

Marc-Antoine drew himself up. "I shall not listen to such slander." He put a protective arm around Pierre, who managed to look hurt.

"Name of God," growled Valentin. "'Tis time for your musical interlude. Get you both before the audience."

"No," said Marc-Antoine sulkily. "I shall not sing with him."

"Sweet Jesu!" Valentin put his hand to his head. "Then sing separately. But sing!"

"I shall go first." Sébastien picked up his theorbo and went out to sing. His offering, delivered in a silverly tenor, earned him loud applause, which seemed only to add to Marc-Antoine's petulance. When it was Marc-Antoine's turn, he glared at Sébastien before going forth; then he began to sing, accompanying himself on his guitar.

"Do you hear what he is doing?" Sébastien was quivering with rage. "That's my song. *My* song! What shall I sing next if he steals my song?"

Valentin groaned. He turned to Gaston, still busy with the scenery. "As soon as the magic grotto is in place, we shall go on." He frowned as Marc-Antoine finished his song and bowed off to applause. "Name of God, Marc-Antoine, will you make peace with Sébastien?"

Marc-Antoine sniffed. "I shall not ever sing with him again," he said waspishly, "unless he asks Pierre's forgiveness!"

Valentin cast his eyes heavenward. "God save me from lovers," he muttered. Adjusting his wizard's cloak, he moved quickly to stand in the grotto.

There were no mishaps during the second act, although Pierre skulked about backstage eyeing Sébastien with malevolence.

They were well into the third act when Ninon found her eyes beginning to water. She looked about the stage and caught Valentin's worried glance. He too had noticed something. The smoke. Even with the added candles and the gunpowder they had used, there seemed to be a great deal of smoke onstage. In the middle of her speech, Colombe stopped and let out a muffled squeak, her eyes darting to the back-curtain. A tiny finger of smoke curled out from the bottom of it, and one of the scenemen whispered the dreaded word. *Fire.*

Novice though she was, Ninon knew the audience must not learn of the disaster, lest they panic. She smiled brightly to Colombe. "And so, madame...?" she prompted. Colombe was unable to go on, standing transfixed as she watched the scenemen's frantic efforts in the wings. They hurriedly fetched buckets of sand to throw on the flames that had begun to curl at the sides of the back-cloth, out of view of the spectators. It was useless to depend on Colombe. Ninon turned to Valentin and the other characters on stage. "I feel sure that madame wished to say..." she began, praying she could remember enough of Colombe's speech. She stumbled through it at last, sighing in relief as Sébastien picked up his lines and answered.

But what were they to do about the smoke? It was growing thicker—despite the scenemen's success in putting out the fire—and the audience was beginning to murmur uneasily. Valentin raised his arms dramatically. "Do you see what have wrought?" he intoned. "A magic fog that will envelop you all and drive away your cares!"

"Yes!" said Ninon. "Behold the fog, how it swirls and mists about us."

Sébastien nodded in agreement, and even Toinette managed to improvise a line about the fog. The spectators relaxed and leaned back on their benches. There was even a smattering of applause for the novel stage effect, and whisperings about the cleverness of a troupe that could so naturally simulate fog. They managed to get through the rest of the play quickly, taking one brief bow before turning their attention to the ruined back-cloths, for more than one had caught fire. Several were destroyed beyond repair, and new ones would have to be bought and painted afresh; the rest could be salvaged with a little patching and repainting. And Sébastien's theorbo was charred and blackened.

"How the devil did this happen?" Valentin angrily tore off his purple wig and slammed it to the stage.

"Your pardon, monsieur," said one of the scenemen. "I thought I saw the lad...he had a candle..."

Valentin let out a roar and turned on Pierre, who backed up in terror and tried to hide behind Marc-Antoine. In a moment he had the boy by the scruff of the neck, the small body bent over his outstretched knee. "Gaston, hand me that stick!" he bellowed.

"No!" Marc-Antoine's face was twisted in distress. He looked for pity to his comrades, who shuffled their feet and turned away.

Sweet Madonna, thought Ninon, are they all afraid of Sanscoeur? "You shall not," she said boldly, "until we hear the boy tell of it! Let him go!"

They glared at each other for long moments, then Valentin released the boy, who immediately threw himself on his knees and began to weep. "I…I didn't mean…I was playing with the candle…I never thought… Please…Madame…don't let him beat me!"

"I believe the lad, Valentin."

"Well, I do not. He has been naught but trouble since the day he came."

Ninon glanced at Marc-Antoine's unhappy face, then turned back to Valentin. "Does your mistrust of the world include children as well? You remind me of a man I knew…one Baugin by name. You remember I spoke of him once, *n'est-ce pas?*"

Valentin winced at that. "Take the little devil away, Marc-Antoine, and see that he keeps out of mischief henceforth!"

Marc-Antoine grasped Ninon's hand and pressed her fingers to his lips. "You are truly a princess, *ma chère.*"

She smiled and sighed. A tired princess. Exhausted from the strains of the day. She climbed wearily out of her costume, then sat at supper picking at her food, aware that Valentin eyed her strangely from the other end of the table, but too tired to care. And when they walked back from the tavern to their rented house in the woods, she stayed apart from them, wanting nothing so much as solitude. She prayed that Hortense was sleeping in Sébastien's bed tonight.

She placed the single candle on the table by the bed and turned down the bedding, stripping off her gown and petticoats and laying them across a chair. She removed her shoes and stockings and set them neatly down. Then she unpinned her hair and shook the curls free, running her fingers through the ringlets. It did not feel so hot tonight; her chemise did not cling damply to her body as it had done for days. God willing, it would be cooler on the morrow. The door opened behind her and closed softly.

"Hortense," she said, turning around. "I…" She shook her head. Valentin leaned against the door, his eyes glinting in the light of the candle. "No," she whispered. "No…no…You shall not…"

He reached for her and swept her into his arms, crushing her mouth with his, while she struggled fiercely against him, more fiercely against the ache, the need for him that filled her. With a cry, she pushed him away and leaned against the wall, gasping for breath.

"Why do you fight me?" He stripped off his shirt and moved, bare-chested, to stand before her, his hands reaching for the drawstring of her chemise. "I could break you in half, if I chose." He loosed the neckline and slipped the garment down over her hips to the floor, then curved his hands around her breasts, his gentle fingers teasing them to hard points. She drew a sharp breath, feeling her body begin to tremble.

With a last effort at reason, at common sense, she wrenched away from the hands that threatened to vanquish her resolve. Drawing back, she slapped his face as hard as she could, and was pleased to see that her blow had drawn blood.

He felt for the cut on his lips with the tip of his tongue, then laughed softly and held out his bare arms; she saw the long red marks of her nails that had dug deep. "Scratches this morning, blows tonight," he said. "And still your eyes shine with passion. 'Tis your pride that rebels, not your body."

"Damn you!" she shrieked. She reached for her shoes and flung them at him, narrowly missing his head.

"Damn *you*," he growled, angry now. "Let us have no more of pride!" His long arms shot out, grabbing her by the hair and pulling her savagely toward him. He bent her back on his arm, his mouth grinding on hers, his kiss hot and demanding. She felt her insides turn to liquid fire; her breasts strained eagerly against his bare chest. It was as though what happened between their two bodies had no part of her heart, her mind. There was only the hunger that took away all reason. She threw her arms around his neck, clutching fiercely at him, returning his kisses with all the passion in her, until kisses were no longer enough.

Like one in a dream, she pulled him to the bed and sat down, her hands working at the fly buttons of his breeches, her impatience beyond containing. He slipped out of his breeches and leaned over to kiss her, his hands stroking her breasts; but she pushed aside his fingers and pulled him down to the bed with her, needing to feel again the thrill that had stirred her before. It was all unreal, a dream. She leaned back on the pillow and closed her eyes, feeling his strong hands parting her thighs, his muscular body lowering to hers. Then she gasped as he thrust into her, a sharp, hard thrust that dispelled the dream. Her eyes flew open, seeing the handsome face above her, tense with passion. That hateful man. And she was letting him do this to her! I must be losing my reason, she thought.

Marshaling all her strength, she waited until his driving thrusts had slackened, then she pushed against him with all her might. "Get off me, pig!" she spat.

He leaned back on his heels, panting. "By God, Ninon, I've beaten women for less than that!"

She flinched at the fury in his eyes and tried to scramble away, making for the far side of the bed, but he grabbed her from behind, holding her tightly about the waist. "Let me go! What are you doing?" she squealed.

"You damned tease!" he growled. He jerked her roughly to her hands and knees, then knelt behind her; his strong hands about her waist kept her from turning or sitting up. When she started to protest, he pushed her face down into the pillow, one hand pressing between her shoulder blades. She wriggled in desperation, her fists pounding the bed in helpless panic, convinced that he would beat her, now that he had her in this vulnerable position. "Don't worry," he said grimly, as though reading her mind. "You're just going to finish what you started."

He mounted her from behind; when he entered her she cried aloud, the exquisiteness of the sensation sending shock waves through her body. He slammed into her again and again, while her hips writhed against him and she clutched at the pillow, gasping in ecstasy. Her every muscle strained to enclose him, envelop him, until his thrusts were met by shuddering spasms of her own. He drew a harsh breath through his teeth and relaxed, then withdrew and rolled away from her. Drained, her passion spent, she let her hips sink to the bed and, still quivering violently, waited for him to leave. Instead, he pulled up the sheet, reached out with his hand, and snuffed the candle.

Oh, God, she thought, burying her face in the pillow, he means to spend the night. She lay there trembling, unable to think clearly, her whole body tingling and alive from the sensations he had aroused. She hated him. No. Perhaps she hated herself, her betraying body. Or perhaps it was only her pride, as he had said. She sighed, still feeling his mouth on hers, his possession of her body. Her pride had lost the battle *this* night! She sighed again. He was breathing deeply beside her. The sleep of the just? she thought bitterly. He stirred in his sleep, his hand reaching out to rest on her bare hip. In spite of all that had happened, it felt strangely comforting. With another sigh, she moved closer to him, pulling his limp arm around her waist, and drifted off to sleep.

She woke to the first twittering of the birds. The room was dim: sunrise was still an hour or two away. She breathed deeply and rolled over onto her back. Valentin was leaning on one elbow, smiling down at her.

"Good morrow," he said softly.

"You're a villain."

He laughed. "Nonetheless, this villain intends to kiss you."

I defy you, she thought grimly. This time she would remember her pride! She kept her lips tight-clamped as he bent over her, yielding nothing to his soft mouth. He looked at her quizzically, one black eyebrow arched in surprise, then tried again. She held her mouth, her body, rigid, denying him—and herself.

"My God, what a stubborn creature you are! I wonder the hairs on Philippe's head did not turn gray, loving you!" He began almost idly to run his finger across her breast, circling the rosy tip, then moved on to stroke her flat belly. She steeled herself against his touch, the hands that roused her beyond endurance. His fingers drifted down to her thighs, gliding up and down on the smooth flesh, but moving ever more inexorably to the soft grotto that throbbed now with passion, beyond control of her willing it or no. When he touched her there, probing gently, she felt her body catch fire. When he stopped, she wanted to cry. He leaned over her, frowning. "Well?" he said. She expected triumph in his voice, that he had revealed her weakness to her once again; instead she was surprised to hear the edge of fear, as though he was afraid that she would reject him, as she had tried to do before.

His eyes bored into her, waiting for an answer. Surrendering her pride at last, she pulled his mouth down to hers, tasting the pleasures of his soft kisses. He made love to her gently, holding her in his arms, loving her with a tenderness that was as sweet and satisfying as had been the hot passions of the night before.

When at last his body had stilled, she held tightly to him, unwilling to let him go, enjoying the feel of him within her, the deep contentment that filled her. She sighed and closed her eyes again.

He kissed her softly. "Sweet Jesu, that mouth…" he nipped at her lower lip, "…that pouting mouth…Your words can be hard and cruel, but that fragile rose of a mouth…*Mon Dieu!* I knew I would have it someday."

Her eyes flew open, flashing with sudden anger. "You arrogant… Oh!" She pushed him off her and tried to sit up, but he pressed her down again, pinning her hands beside her head. "Let me go!" she hissed. "I knew you could not forbear from crowing your triumph! You arrogant dog!"

"What arrogance? You knew it too! From the very first. Flesh speaks to flesh, and pays reason no mind. From the very first—in the stable. Your thoughts were on your precious Philippe, but it was not anger— nor Philippe—that made you tremble when I kissed you."

She was near tears, burning with humiliation, struggling helplessly against him. "You villain, you animal…I despise you…arrogant, disagreeable, hateful…"

"Yes, I know," he said quietly. "And *I* have learned—to my sorrow—that a woman is Satan's creature, not to be trusted or believed, not to…" He sighed heavily. "But my body hungers for yours, despite everything." He kissed her rigid lips, then deepened his kiss until she relented, her mouth responding to his. "Why deny Nature her power over us?" He smiled and kissed her again. "If it's any comfort to you, I envied Philippe his privileges from the moment I first saw you in the stable."

He sat up in bed and glanced around the room, which was beginning now to grow light. "Come. What say you to a swim before the others get up?"

She nodded. Quickly they threw on their clothes and hurried to the stream, shedding their garments once again to plunge into the water. Ninon found herself laughing like a child, her senses alive with the crystal water, the pink dawn rising over a distant hill, the contentment of her body. At last, exhausted, they scrambled out of the stream. Valentin pulled on his breeches and lay down on a patch of grass; Ninon, too lazy even to dress, lay across his chest and draped her chemise over her naked body.

"Today is our last performance," he said, "and then we move on."

"I shall be sorry to leave Troyes."

"There's always another town," he said. "You said that once yourself."

"Where shall we go?"

"South, I should guess. Gaston will not be coming with us."

"I did not know!"

"He did not wish the others to know until we set out tomorrow. But he has cousins…family…just beyond Troyes. He designs to spend his remaining years there, and they are willing to take him in."

"But wherefore?" she asked.

"He is no longer young. And then, his arm troubles him greatly. It has not healed well from the break."

"Alas. I shall miss him."

"As shall I." He fell silent for a moment, then sat up, pushing her gently from him. "There is something we must speak of now."

She slipped her chemise over her head and sat close to him, her hand on his. "So solemn? Well?"

"I…that is…'tis the matter of where we shall sleep in the next town…and the next." He reddened slightly. "I…I had forgot what pleasure a woman's body could bring."

She looked down at a patch of grass. "Even a woman who loves another?"

"More especially a woman who loves another. Your heart is given to Philippe. I have no heart to give. We are well matched. But we find pleasure in each other. I shall not pretend—though, forgive me, I think your dear Philippe did—that I want more from you than the enjoyment of your body. But I challenge you to tell me that Philippe could rouse your senses more than I have. Shall we share a bed henceforth?"

"I…I know not. Who can say…tomorrow, the next day…can we not wait to see what will be?"

His brow darkened. "No. I dislike feeling that I am the brute, raping you each time I invade your bed. If your mind is not as willing as your body, tell me, and I'll sleep alone, and bother you no more. But if you are agreed, I don't expect to be teased—or denied when it suits your fancy. And no false pride. I will not have you play the violated maiden, cursing me while your body welcomes mine! Those are my terms. Are you agreed?"

She hesitated. How different he was from Philippe, negotiating his terms like a general, with no attempt to play the cajoling lover. There would be no soft romance if she shared his bed—true enough. She was not fool enough to think that he had lost his hatred of women. But she had little trust in men. And he was not promising her love, only the pleasures of his bed. Considerable pleasures, she had to admit. Flesh speaks to flesh, he had said. With no thought to reason. It was so. She had wanted him all along, she knew that now; best to be honest with herself and admit she still wanted him.

"Agreed," she said at last, then held up a warning finger. "But in return, I expect to see you smile from time to time. Take another role besides that of disagreeable tyrant. Agreed?"

He stared at her in amazement, his face softening. "There are times, Ninon Guillemot, when I think I shall rue the day you came into my life!"

She poked his bare chest with her forefinger. "*Agreed?*"

He smiled and pulled her mouth to his. "Agreed," he said, and kissed her.

"Whore!" Colombe glared at Ninon, her mouth set in a hard line. They were standing on the stage with Marc-Antoine, waiting for Gaston, the Prologue, to finish his speech and open the curtain. It was the first word Colombe had spoken to Ninon all day. She had watched with envious eyes as Valentin had stayed close to Ninon in the tiring-room, smiling far more than was his wont, putting a casual hand about the girl's waist. She cursed herself, her misshapen vicomte who had kept her away from Valentin these past two weeks. But for the ugly little hunchback, she might have been the one to break Val's stubborn celibacy and earn a place in his bed.

Marc-Antoine cackled with delight. "You must call her *foolish* whore, Colombe. For poor Ninon will not expect to find half a dozen crowns on *her* pillow in the morning!"

"Pox-ridden *tapette*," she hissed. "Small wonder your family threw you out!"

"Stop it! Both of you!" Ninon's eyes flashed.

"And you, you slut!" Colombe's voice was sharp with malevolence. "Stealing Val from me. You shall pay, I promise you!"

"Then steal him back, if you want him," said Ninon coldly. "If you can. But I trust you do not mean to exact your revenge upon the stage. You are too soft of body to risk it. I have spent a deal of my life chopping wood and spading gardens and plucking pigeons. I should find it a simple matter to pluck those mock-ebony curls from your head!"

Colombe's jaw dropped open in astonishment, while Marc-Antoine doubled up with laughter. Ninon turned away from them both and composed herself for the performance, confident that Colombe's basic cowardice would keep her from retaliating.

They played a pastoral first, a romantic piece that ended with an unexpected kiss that Valentin delivered to Ninon upon the stage, much to the delight of the spectators. By the time they began to play their second presentation of the afternoon, an improvised farce in the Italian fashion, the whole company had caught fire from Valentin's lighthearted manner, playing with a zest and a humor that kept the audience crowing with laughter.

Ninon and Joseph, perched on tall ladders behind two set pieces of scenery that represented houses with upstairs windows, leaned out and called to Valentin below. He staggered drunkenly about on the stage, falling into one wall and then another, torn between the two "women"— for Joseph, in a yellow wig, and heavily rouged, pretended to be a female, squeaking out his lines in falsetto. All the while Valentin precariously balanced a tray of tarts on one hand, promising them first to Ninon and then to the "lady" Joseph. Chanteclair, the knave, did a cartwheel onto the stage and announced to the audience (slyly twirling the mustaches on his mask) that he would soon make short work of the tarts for himself. He offered his services to Valentin, and climbed upon his shoulders to be carried unsteadily from one window to the other, pretending to pass on to the women each tart as it was handed up to him, but actually eating it himself. The scene ended with the outraged Valentin trying to dislodge Chanteclair from his perch on his shoulders, while Ninon and Joseph, deprived of their tarts, pelted the shaky two-man tower with puffs of cotton. Filled with high spirits, the actors were laughing so hard themselves that they could scarcely continue with the play.

At the end, when they had taken their final bows, Valentin, as the company's Orator, stepped before the curtain to fulfill his function. He called for silence and addressed the audience, thanking the good people of Troyes for their attention and trade during all the many weeks that the company had been in their fair city. The Peerless Theatre Company, he announced, would be moving on, but he designed the kind folk to remember them fondly, and promised that when they should return—several months hence—it would be with even more delightful presentations. It was both a skillful farewell (to ensure their being able to leave the city with no difficulties from tradesmen or government officials) and a teaser to guarantee an enthusiastic welcome when they should return.

In a jolly mood, they trooped off to their favorite tavern for a farewell supper, Colombe flouncing along with her twisted vicomte in tow, as if to show Valentin that his affairs did not concern her. Valentin, brimming with good cheer, took the opportunity of every dim doorway along their route to pull Ninon aside and kiss her.

By the time they entered the common room of the tavern, Chanteclair was already there, drinking at the large table with a man they had not seen before in Troyes. A shortish man in his mid-thirties, with a head rather too large for his body, he was handsome in an earthy way, his features both coarse and fine. Wide-spaced, small eyes, a prominent nose that flared at the nostrils, thick lips in a broad mouth—altogether unremarkable features, until the man spoke and the face came alive, the deep creases in his leathery skin serving as exclamation points to his words. His hair and eyes were jet black, as was his small, trim mustache.

"Messieurs...mesdames...Valentin..." began Chanteclair, rising from his chair, "I should like you to meet a traveler on his way north to Rouen. Monsieur Jean-Baptiste Poquelin. Monsieur Valentin Sanscoeur, the head of our company."

Valentin beamed and held out a hand to the stranger. "Monsieur Molière," he said, calling the man by the name under which he appeared upon the stage. "'Tis a great honor."

"No…no." Molière rose, bowing to the ladies and motioning the company to be seated. "We are all fellow players. No more, no less." He nodded as the introductions were made all around, then sat down again and poured himself another cup of wine, smiling graciously to Colombe, who had abandoned her vicomte to sit next to him.

"Fellow players! *Mon Dieu*." Colombe giggled coquettishly. "Is there an actor in all of France who has not heard of you and your illustrious company? Your reputation—the work you have done in Lyon and the Languedoc—reaches even the small villages and *jeux de paume* in which our humble company plays!"

He laughed dryly. "My dear young woman, we have been on the road for twelve years now, building that reputation. If an actor has not learned his craft by then, he should give it up and seek another trade."

"You make so little of it," simpered Colombe.

Molière raised a sardonic eyebrow. "Little? Hardly. I spent half of 'forty-four in prison for debt, because of this calling." He indicated his lined, tough skin, his hand making a dramatic gesture almost automatically. "My face is an old man's face from all the years of paint—and grimacing to be seen by the *paradis*. It is scarcely a little matter." He sighed. "It becomes a wearying life."

Valentin had been quietly ordering supper for the company and their guest. Now he dismissed the servants and turned to Molière. "What brings you to Troyes? We had heard you were south, in Lyon."

"Alas. Life is a cruel trickster, always ready with the unexpected cream tart for the face! I had thought our future was ensured. We have been, for some four years, under the protection of Monsieur de Conti. It was a fine life. A fat pension, coaches and men-at-arms at our beck as we traveled back and forth from Lyon to Pézenas—we played there for several seasons when the Estates of Languedoc were in session. As well as privately for Conti, of course. Our handbills read 'The actors of Monsieur le Prince de Conti's Company.' But…" Molière sighed.

"But…?" prompted Chanteclair, helping himself to a roasted pigeon.

"Who would have thought a Bourbon prince, a man of dissolute tastes, would become a *religieux?* Conti has taken up the cause of Jansenism and the Port-Royal nuns. Not only has he renounced our company and withdrawn his support, but he has condemned our profession as ungodly and immoral. At the last session of the Languedoc *Parlement* in Béziers we were forced to toady to the delegates just to obtain permission to play."

Valentin laughed ruefully. "And we bemoan the lack of a patron."

"But you are very good. I saw you this afternoon. Very good indeed!"

"You see, Valentin?" said Colombe, viciously spearing a bit of meat with the tip of her knife.

Sanscoeur ignored her. "What shall you do now, Monsieur Molière?"

"Madeleine and I…that is to say, Madame Béjart, who has a fine head for business…" he smiled at Ninon, "and a crown of copper hair that flames almost as much as yours, Madame Guillemot…though, alas, no longer your fresh youth…Ahem. Where was I? A charming distraction. Ah yes. Madeleine and I have begun to think it is time to mount an assault on Paris. She is staying on at Nîmes for a spell to conclude a legal matter. The rest of the company travels with me to Rouen. We can rehearse, survey the Paris scene, make the necessary arrangements, play just enough so that word of our talent will reach the proper ears at court. And I have had some success with a few plays I penned. If the Muse favors me, I can prepare a new one for our Paris debut."

Valentin pushed his plate away and leaned back in his chair, smiling. "I could wish that you would publish those you have written already. I heard only good reports of your *Dépit Amoureux* when you played it last year at Pézenas. I would dearly love to have access to the book for this company!"

"Don't be a fool! Your company does the finest *commedia al improviso* I have seen in many a year! You need no book to win acclaim! I wonder you do not try Paris yourselves."

"We are not ready," Valentin said brusquely.

"Ah, but I think…"

"Really, Valentin, why are you so stubborn?" pouted Colombe.

"No!" Valentin's voice was harsh and ugly. There was a moment of uncomfortable silence; then Molière turned smoothly to Colombe and offered her a sweetmeat from the platter before them.

"You played the pastoral superbly, Madame Linard," he said to her. She smiled coyly. "Think you so? Valentin says I am an even better tragedienne. Is it not so, Val?"

"True enough."

"If…Monsieur Molière, you will not think me forward…but…if you have need of another actress in your company…I should be more than willing…*I* do not fear Paris, as does Monsieur Sanscoeur!"

Molière cleared his throat. "Ah, madame. There are, even now, three adorable actresses in our company—my dear Madeleine, Madame du Parc, and Madame de Brie. I have had…you'll pardon me…a fondness for each of the fair creatures. My life can be most difficult when they choose to berate me, singly or *ensemble!* I scarce think I could manage another, particularly one as beautiful and charming as you, my dear Madame Linard."

It was both a compliment and a rebuff, but Colombe beamed, hearing only the flattery. Marc-Antoine, with more malice, twinkled knowingly at Ninon.

"*Mon Dieu*, Jean-Baptiste. If we are to get an early start in the morning, you had best come away!" An enormously fat man stood in the doorway, beckoning to Molière.

Molière laughed. "Come in, René. Who is with you?"

The man moved aside, allowing two other men to crowd into the room. "Béjart and Reynolds. Come away, Jean-Baptiste. The women will not sleep until they know you are safe abed."

Molière smiled ruefully at his friends and stood up. "Are they tender sisters? Or jealous minxes? But let me at least acquaint you with this fine band of strollers before we go. Joseph Béjart," he said, indicating the smallest of his three companions. "Brother to Madeleine. René Berthelot," a nod to the fat man, "or Gros-René, as he is known for obvious reasons, who acts under the name of du Parc and is married to one of our charming actresses. This one…" He clapped his hand to the shoulder of the third man, a blond giant who stood half a head taller than Valentin, "is not, strictly speaking, a member of our company, but he has played with us since we traveled up from Languedoc, having no other means of support. James Reynolds, late of the Phoenix Theatre of Drury Lane in London, until that Puritan devil Cromwell closed the English playhouses and burned them to the ground."

There was the business of handshakes and introductions of the Peerless Theatre troupe; then Valentin called for another round of drinks.

"Tell me, Monsieur Reynolds," he said at last to the Englishman, when they had settled down a bit, "is there no theater in England at all?"

"Certainly no public theater," said Reynolds, his French only slightly tinged with the accents of his native land. "I have heard there are still some plays performed privately…and in secret. But I am no longer welcome in my homeland, having declared early for the martyred king, God rest his soul. I was in your beautiful capital of Paris for a time with His Majesty Charles the Second—alas in exile!—and his brother James, Duke of York. Your gracious King Louis was most hospitable to my noble sovereign and his brother."

"They are, after all, first cousins," said Chanteclair dryly. He frowned at Reynolds in disapproval. The man was altogether too unctuous for his taste.

"Yes. To be sure." Reynolds smiled at Chanteclair, a radiant smile that was as false as it was expansive. "But your King Louis is fond of the theater, upon my word! I have suggested to Monsieur Molière," he nodded condescendingly to Poquelin, "that he make an effort to catch the eye of the king, or his brother the Duc d'Orléans. They would be worthy patrons, you may be sure!"

"The king himself takes part in court spectacles, is it not so?" asked Ninon.

Reynolds allowed his bold gaze to linger on her bosom for a moment before he answered. "Yes. I remember…some three years agone…as attendant to my lord the Duke of York, I took part in a court ballet that Louis presented. *Les Noces de Pelée Thétis*…'The Wedding of Peleus and Thetis,' as we would call it…Your king appeared as Apollo. He seemed taken with the conceit of himself as the sun god." There was an edge of disapproval in Reynolds's voice.

"Yes," said Molière. If he had heard the innuendo, he ignored it. "I remember in 'fifty-three the king appeared in *The Ballet of the Night* as the Sun, bringing life and light to the world."

"May it be so," Gaston muttered piously, and crossed himself.

"And York?" asked Valentin. "What did he represent in Louis's ballet?"

Reynolds laughed. "He danced as a coral fisher, fishing for a crown! The court was much amused, I can tell you!"

Molière scratched his chin reflectively. "Tell me, Sanscoeur, could you use the services of Monsieur Reynolds? He has shown some reluctance to our Paris expedition, and had considered traveling to Italy. But it occurs to me you might have a use for him."

"No," said Chanteclair.

Valentin shook his head. "Perhaps. Gaston?" He nodded to the older man, waiting for him to speak.

Gaston stood up and allowed his eyes to travel around the table, silently recording his comrades' beloved faces in his memory. He sighed with regret. "Yes," he said at last. "I have decided to retire from this calling. I leave you in the morning." There was a flurry of questions, protests, expressions of disbelief—and Hortense rushed forward to give Gaston a tearful kiss. But after a time the company was reconciled to Gaston's leaving, and Monsieur Molière raised his glass in a toast to an actor who would, at least, have time to seek absolution of the Church and be buried in consecrated ground.

"But the matter of Monsieur Reynolds," said Valentin at last. "Can he do the Pantalone roles?" He smiled sourly at Reynolds, who had long since found a place beside Toinette and was making her giggle and blush with his whispered asides, much to Joseph's annoyance. "We do not need another Lover. If he can play old men, character roles, we might have a place for him."

"I can assure you," said Molière, "James is quite versatile."

"Well then, James," said Valentin. "The company must discuss it, of course, but I feel sure you can find a home with us. Not as a sharer, you understand. Perhaps a quarter of a share…or a salary. We shall discuss it and draw up a contract."

"A moment." Chanteclair leaned forward, his eyes narrowing as they scanned Reynolds. "Might one ask why you do not wish to go to Paris…James?"

Reynolds laughed heartily. "Please! You must call me Jamie, if we are to be friends! It is only that…I blush to tell it, ladies…I made a few enemies while I was in Paris last! An irate husband or two…you understand…'tis a man's nature, after all." It sounded more like a boast than a confession.

"My faith," said Colombe, beginning to see in this handsome young giant a possible conquest. "What a thrilling life you must have led… Jamie. Irate husbands. Fancy that!" She turned to Valentin, the residual of bitterness in her honeyed words. "Tell me, dear Valentin, is that why *you* avoid Paris and the big cities?"

Chapter Nine

"Dammit, Joseph, have a care! You are not driving the king's coach on a hunt at Versailles!" Valentin's harsh voice cut through the morning mists and sent a flock of wild quail whirring up out of the grasses by the side of the road.

Joseph, perched on a plank thrown across the front of the wagon, glanced sullenly at Valentin and pulled on the ropes that controlled the team of oxen, slowing their pace. Valentin reined in his horse and guided it to one side of the narrow road, scowling as the wagon and the rest of the mounted actors passed by.

Seated behind him, her skirts drawn up so that she might ride astride, Ninon shook her head at his stiff back. "Have a little pity on the man," she said gently. "If the wagon truly goes too fast, Colombe will be the first to scream her protest."

"In the name of her child, of course...the hypocritical bitch," growled Valentin.

"What has put you into such a mood today? We were all sorry to part with Gaston this morning. Chanteclair and Marc-Antoine wept. Only you find in it cause for one of your rages."

"It is my way," he snapped. "And Joseph is careless with the team. It is my way."

Her arms had been around his waist. Now she slipped her hands up under his doublet to catch a fold of flesh at his sides. Smiling grimly, she pinched him with all her might. "You promised me you would not rage so. Have you forgot so soon?"

He twisted around in the saddle and looked at her, his eyebrows raised in astonishment and injured pride. "Sweet Jesu, woman, I shall not turn into a *milksop* on your behalf!"

"True," she said dryly. "I know I should consider myself privileged. For you have unbent your stiff pride enough to allow a *woman* to ride with you, *nom de Dieu.*"

"You teasing devil," he murmured, his mouth at last curving into a smile. "You shall be the death of me."

"If I can tease you into laughter sometimes I will be content." She leaned up to his shoulder to receive his awkward kiss.

Grinning, he turned around again and guided his horse back onto the road to pace beside Chanteclair, who rode alone. They moved along in companionable silence for some time, then Chanteclair turned to Valentin. "By the by, I assume you got the letter last night." Valentin nodded and patted the inside pocket of his doublet.

"What letter?" asked Ninon.

"From Monsieur Molière."

"After we left?" asked Ninon, remembering that the women had retired early, leaving the men alone for a last round of drinks. Chanteclair grunted. "But you did not tell me, Valentin," said Ninon, then blushed furiously, remembering how she had waited for him in bed, filled with anticipation. And welcomed him joyously into her arms, opening wide to receive him. There had been no thought of talk, all through the long night, as they had explored each other's bodies, giving and taking back pleasure. "What was the letter?" she said quickly, to hide her embarrassment.

Chanteclair's eyes were bland. If he had divined Ninon's discomfort, he chose to ignore it. "Monsieur Molière was offered a commission before he came to Troyes. A…marquis, I think…was it not, Valentin? Yes. A marquis near Vézelay. Since Molière's troupe was heading north, they could not oblige. Monsieur le Marquis is celebrating the birth of a son, after several daughters. He wishes to present to his wife his compliments and gratitude in the form of balls and fêtes…and plays. Monsieur Molière thinks that the Peerless Theatre Company would be to the marquis's liking in his stead."

"And he gave you a letter?" asked Ninon.

"Yes. An introduction to Monsieur le Marquis, extolling…pray God!…our skills and virtues."

"It would be a fine commission to have," said Valentin. "Seven hundred livres for two performances, with half to be given in advance."

"And tips besides," said Chanteclair, "if we're clever. The marquis is well connected, I hear. If we can include the names of his relations in our prologues…or even in a bit of spoken dialogue or a dedication, he and his family would respond, in coin, to such flattery."

"I like it not," grumbled Valentin.

"You never do. But you know as well as I it must be done—if we are to survive." Valentin swore under his breath. Chanteclair chuckled. "Put as good a face on it as possible, Val. Béjart tells me the marquis has his own theater in his château. That means far less work for us. And scenemen who have done the job before. I should miss Gaston more if we arrived at Vézelay and Joseph and I had to begin our careers as *décorateurs* with such an important commission."

"Joseph is useless today," said Valentin. "Guiding the team as though he were in a trance. I can scarcely fathom why."

"I wonder you have not guessed it, *mon ami*," said Chanteclair. "Look you." He pointed to where Toinette rode with James Reynolds, sitting in front of him on his horse as they moved through patches of sunlight on the road. Chanteclair shook his head. "I do not like that Englishman. There will be mischief ere he is done."

"Yes," agreed Ninon. "See how she giggles and hangs on his every word."

"Name of God!" Valentin exclaimed. "One would think Toinette was a sweet virgin, to listen to you two! She has been wooed before!"

"Yes," said Chanteclair. "By half a dozen country bumpkins and provincial nobles…and the men of this troupe, in the spirit of affection and camaraderie. But never by an accomplished rake. He had no qualms about moving into Joseph's province. And when he's had enough of her, he'll have no qualms about breaking the girl's heart."

"Pah! You make too much of it. Women are no fools when it comes to men. Reynolds should guard his own heart!"

Ninon stiffened at the sudden anger in his voice. After their night of passion, she had almost begun to forget his feelings toward women, had almost convinced herself that with kindness she could change his ways. God save her, she would try not to forget again. "Then show a little compassion for your own sex, at the very least," she said coldly, "and save a crumb of pity for poor Joseph."

Chanteclair glanced from one tight face to another, cleared his throat, and allowed his gaze to stray upward to the bower of trees overhead, their bright green streaked with the crimson and gold of autumn. "Pray God Molière's letter earns us success," he said at last.

"If not," said Valentin, "we have enough money to go on to Nevers. 'Tis four months since we played there. A fine tennis court, good audiences. Ninon's debut and her triumph." He turned his head, glancing back over his shoulder at her. "But this time, Madame Queen, one trusts you will not forget your lines!" He smiled, his good humor returning.

"Ha! Insignificant peasant! This time in Nevers I shall seek out an inn that is worthy of my exalted station as *prima donna*. You, of course, will be expected to sleep in the barn!"

They traveled at a leisurely pace, moving through countryside golden with ripened wheat, or bare fields where the already-harvested grain stood in sheaves—fat sentries along the stone walls and fences. They followed the paths of man-made canals, lined by long avenues of trees and towpaths for the horses, and waved to the boats that passed on their way loaded with produce and hogs and wine, the last shipments to the big cities before the cold of winter made the waterways impassable.

The nights were beginning to turn cool, presaging an early fall. They sought out inns where a column of smoke in the distance indicated a warm fire, and retired early to huddle with their bed partners of the moment. They stopped an itinerant peddler in a small village and bought out his meager stock of flannel shirts and chemises, to be stored away until the first frosty morning.

Marc-Antoine and Sébastien were still cold to each other (chillier than the mist-filled dawnings), and spoke only when they had to, both nursing their grievances—the one for the abuse of his *amour* Pierre, the other for the theft of a song. Colombe's baby had become colicky, and her unhappy wailing disturbed many a night's sleep, defying everyone's best efforts to comfort her, and causing Marc-Antoine much grief and pain at the distress of his godchild.

Reynolds had worked hard to ingratiate himself with the troupe, regaling them in the evenings with jolly stories, flattering the women, deferring to the men. He seemed eager to study and rehearse any role Valentin assigned to him, no matter how lowly, though he was not a very accomplished actor. And he was totally incapable of improvising, having no familiarity whatever with the Italian *commedia*. But he had a good voice, and a fine ear for mimicry, even making a joke of the way the women pronounced his name. "Zhamie," he would laugh, his lips pouting in imitation, "Zhamie!" stressing the soft J of the French. And Toinette would smile, her eyes shining in adoration, and take him off to bed with her. The company found him charming. Except, of course, the poor hapless Joseph. And Ninon and Chanteclair would exchange knowing glances, wondering when the man's mask of *bonhomie* would slip.

Ninon enjoyed the nighttimes most. Valentin, with a great show of yawning and stretching, would excuse himself early, pulling her along with him. He had denied himself the company of a woman for such a very long time; now he brought an exuberance, a joyousness to the bedchamber that Ninon found wonderful and touching. He was boyish and playful on some nights, making her laugh even as he made love to her. Sometimes he would tease her, his hands and lips rousing her body until she writhed in torment and pulled him down to her, her fingers tangled in his hair, her hips thrusting to meet his. At times he would be angry, hot, passionate, taking her with an intensity that left her breathless. And sometimes, his eyes misty and faraway in the light of the dim candle, he would love her gently, until she thought she could see in his face the man he had been, before he donned the name and demeanor of Sanscoeur, the heartless one.

She had not thought a man's body could bring her such pleasure. Would it have been so with Philippe? she wondered, and cursed herself for having denied him.

They arrived at last at the château of the Marquis de Brinon, a sprawling estate just outside Vézelay. They were received warmly, the marquis being delighted to have a strolling troupe for his festivities, particularly one recommended by the celebrated Monsieur Molière. Would they play for him *Roger and Bradamante*? A charming pastoral, perhaps? A farce or two that he would name? If they did not have the books, he himself would provide them—and the scribe to make copies for all the players. They would have eight days to rehearse before the presentations, during which time he invited them to consider themselves guests in his château (though their quarters were little better than the servants'), and to enjoy the dances and balls he had arranged to while away the long evenings. Valentin, still uneasy about the boy Pierre, took the occasion to pull the lad aside, out of Marc-Antoine's hearing, and warn him that if there was any thieving, he would pay for it with his hide, and not even Ninon could save him.

Colombe was in her glory. The marquis had several brothers and cousins who had come to visit; they vied with one another to woo her, bringing her gifts and reciting poetry, praising her beauty to the skies. More wonderful still was the news that the baby boy—whose birth had occasioned all these festivities—was only a little thing, and barely able to deplete the milk of the nurses who had been hired to suckle him. They were happy to feed Marie-Anne when Colombe was too busy to be bothered.

Madame de Brinon had taken a fancy to Valentin. She found a thousand excuses to hurry to their quarters, her hair freshly coiffed, her cheeks rouged. Were the beds quite comfortable? Did Monsieur Sanscoeur require a valet? Would the company—and Monsieur Sanscoeur, of course—join her and her guests at supper in the *grande salle?* After two days of this, Valentin began to smile tightly, his mouth a hard line, his fists clenching and unclenching with the effort at restraint. Like a man besieged by a monster, thought Ninon, feeling a spark of pity for him. He could not bear to be loved. No. He could not bear even to be admired, pursued, or sought by a woman if he saw more in her eyes than just an animal need. God save me, she thought, from ever loving him, else he would destroy me.

She smiled warmly and slipped her arm through his. "A thousand thanks, Madame la Marquise. Val and I…" she contrived to look embarrassed, though she was not sure she could manage a blush, "… that is to say, Monsieur Sanscoeur and I…are quite content with our accommodations. You have been more than generous." A shy laugh. "Too generous. Three coverlets, *mon Dieu!* I found myself turning back my side of the bed last night. It was too much. Did you find it so, Val?" Her eyes were warm and adoring.

The marquise drew herself up stiffly. "If there should be anything further you need, you must speak to a maidservant." She nodded her head and retreated in haste.

Ninon dimpled up at Valentin. "She will not pursue you again, I think. You see how useful I am to you?"

He grinned, his eyes twinkling wickedly. "Even out of bed."

After that, their hostess turned her attentions elsewhere, though Ninon made a point of clinging to Valentin whenever they were in company (just for insurance), earning for herself an unexpected bonus. The male guests at the château reluctantly kept their distance from her, contenting themselves with longing looks and discreet sighs.

Despite the lengthening nights and the leaves that turned color and fell silently, the days became warm, a last dance with summer before the chill north winds should howl. They took to rehearsing out-of-doors in the great park that adjoined the château, practicing their scenes in a secluded garden next to the river Cure, where they might find a degree of privacy from the intruding guests.

When he was not in a scene, Valentin paced about watching Reynolds, assessing his performance, his assimilation into the troupe. "No, Jamie," he said at last. "I care not what you have done before. You must not intone the Alexandrine verses in a singsong voice. Run one verse into another, with a naturalness and flow, so it may seem prose. This stopping at the end of each line, at each caesura, is an old convention, and one that, I trust, is dying out."

"Of course, Valentin. I thank you. I should never have noted it myself. And you are indeed wise. I mark how the verses flow from you so naturally that, having heard them a hundred times before, I am still moved to weep."

Valentin was clearly pleased.

"I thank *you!* Oh, and one other thing…"

"You have only to name it, Val."

"When you move across the stage…in that last scene…you are to wait for Toinette to hand you your sword. Had you forgot?"

"An oversight, Val. *Mea culpa*. Toinette seemed…ahem…ill disposed to hand it to me. But I shall not forget the next time. I promise you."

Valentin's brow darkened. "What do you mean, 'ill disposed'? Toinette? Are you, or are you not, to hand Jamie the sword?"

Toinette looked flustered. "I…that is…I did not think James would take it from me…he looked…oh!" She burst into tears and ran to hide herself behind a small hedge.

"Toinette!" said Valentin, his voice rising.

"Let her go, *mon ami*," said Chanteclair, stepping up to Sanscoeur. "We have been at this for hours. I, for one, am starving! Can you not dispatch Pierre to the château to have them bring us some dinner here in the garden?"

There were murmurs of agreement from the others, and Pierre was soon sent on his way. While Valentin discussed a point of business with Sébastien, Chanteclair spread his cloak upon the ground and made room for Ninon to sit beside him. He frowned. "Did you notice? Toinette called him 'James.' No more the sweet 'Zhamie'?"

"He's a devil. She was in tears this morning. He was very charming, I understand, but he was through with her. I know not what he said, but it must have been a skillful plot he wove. She believes that she is to blame."

"Damn! And how is Joseph to fight him? Were I Valentin, with his height and skills, I would hesitate to challenge that giant, Reynolds."

Ninon shook her head. "On what grounds can he be challenged? He didn't rape the girl, force her against her will. She'll get no sympathy from the others. What was it Valentin said? She has been wooed before." She indicated Joseph, who had seated himself on a bench with Marc-Antoine, and was now engaged in a lively conversation, though his eyes strayed repeatedly to where Toinette still wept. "Sweet Madonna! I'd like to take him by the collar and march him over to dry Toinette's tears!"

Chanteclair laughed. "I thought, with Valentin as a lover, you had learned more about a man's pride than that! Give poor Joseph a few days to pull himself together. In his present angry state, he would be less than gentle to Toinette."

Ninon eyed him curiously. It was the first time he had spoken openly of her and Valentin. She felt a momentary pang of guilt. "What could be keeping our dinner?" she said quickly.

He looked at her, his soft brown eyes tinged with regret. "Of course I mind," he said softly, answering the question she had not the courage to ask. "But we have a long road before us. Many days, many plays, many towns. *Qui sait?* Who knows?"

She put her hand on his. "Will you take it for an insult if I say that I am grateful to have you as a friend?"

He stirred uncomfortably, then looked up to watch the three serving maids who were coming across the grass, bearing large platters of food. "*Mon Dieu*, but that blond's a handsome wench." He rose to his feet. "You must forgive me, sweet Ninon, if I leave your company."

"Will you abandon me?" she asked with mock indignation.

"If I can't have you, I must find my pleasures where I may! Get that great oaf Valentin to dine with you. He is...*Merde!*" he swore.

"What is it?"

Chanteclair inclined his head in the direction of a small grove of trees into which Reynolds was just vanishing, a large plate of food in one hand, a smiling Hortense clinging to the other. "If it's the last thing I do," he muttered, "I'll see that lecher paid in full for his mischief!"

Brinon gave a ball that night. The actors, dressed in the gayest clothes they could dredge up from their trunks, made up in enthusiasm and beauty what they lacked in style and richness. The women were glorious. Even the normally plain Hortense managed to sparkle, her eyes shining each time Jamie bent down to whisper in her ear. Joseph and Sébastien and Chanteclair were fine-looking men, in the full bloom of manhood, and with all the grace acquired from years on the stage; Jamie and Valentin were quite the tallest and handsomest men in the room. Marc-Antoine cut a flamboyant figure; he had elected to dress in a costume from the days of King Henry IV. It was a felicitous choice. The padded doublet tended to disguise his rather ample girth, while the tight trunk-hose accented legs that were surprisingly well turned for one of his size. He wore a starched lace ruff about his neck and a braid-encrusted hat on his head, a small round headpiece that resembled nothing so much as a butter pot set upside down. A small cape was set dashingly across one shoulder, and a gilt ceremonial sword hung at his side.

He was far better-looking, thought Ninon, than half the nobility in the *galerie*, many of whom had adopted the latest fashion, the one that Philippe had favored—wide, ribbon-swagged petticoat breeches and high-heeled shoes. It had looked foppish, even on her beloved Philippe, she thought, turning to admire Valentin beside her. His doublet was simple and unadorned, reaching just to his waist, with long, narrowish sleeves cuffed back. His cambric shirt was full, but not cut in so exaggerated a manner that it ballooned foolishly out from under his doublet at waist and cuffs. His wrist and neck lace was restrained, a simple scallop on plain linen bands. His knee-length breeches, though trimmed with a row of ribbon loops at the bottom, were cut straight, not extravagantly gathered and full. And his shoes were low-heeled, square-toed—sturdy and sensible. Ninon was struck by the contrast between him and the nobles in the room. He was natural and masculine. No heavy perfume, no mincing walk, no effeminate airs. It was the way she preferred to remember Philippe. Not as he had been that last night at Marival, the artificial dandy, but as the soldier, the hero, the Philippe who had come riding up to Baugin's inn on that long-ago spring evening.

She took pleasure in dancing with Valentin at the ball. He moved gracefully, guiding her about the floor through the patterns of the various dances—*courantes* and *sarabandes* and *gigues*. It excited her just to be in his arms. He seemed to share her mood, refusing to give her up to any man who offered to partner her, only reluctantly allowing her a stately *pavane* with their host, the Marquis de Brinon. If she didn't know Valentin better, she thought ruefully, she would almost think he was jealous.

He left her only once in the course of the evening. Hortense had been completely monopolized by Jamie. To retaliate, Sébastien had gotten quite drunk and gone off with some of the gentlemen to gamble in a private room; losing heavily, he had become rowdy and truculent. Only Valentin's intercession saved him from a horsewhipping at the hands of the vicomte he had insulted, for the gentleman refused to lower himself by dueling with a vagabond. With many apologies for their drunken comrade (which seemed to appease the vicomte as well as the Marquis de Brinon), the actors bundled Sébastien off to his room.

They danced until well past midnight. By the time they made their way to their chambers, Ninon was intoxicated—with the wine, with the joy of dancing, with the feeling of Valentin's strong arms about her waist.

She pulled off her red velvet gown with impatient hands, breathing a sigh of relief to be released from the boned and confining bodice, and left her clothes in a heap upon the floor. Stripped naked, she danced about the room while Valentin sat on the bed to remove his shoes and stockings, watching her with amusement. In a leisurely manner he untied his falling band—the separate lace-trimmed collar—and pulled off his cuffs, carefully putting them away in their own pasteboard bandbox so they would not crease. He stood up and shrugged out of his doublet, brushing away a few bits of lint before folding the garment across the back of a chair.

"Sweet Madonna!" exclaimed Ninon at last. "I shall go mad waiting for you!" She leaped at him, propelling him onto his back on the bed, where she straddled him with her knees. She tugged at his shirt, pulling it free from his breeches and pushing it up toward his neck. He laughed and lifted his arms, attempting, in his awkward position, to pull the garment over his head. He had managed to get it halfway off, his face and arms tangled in the folds of fabric, when she attacked again, the sight of his brawny (and vulnerable!) torso too great a temptation. She curled her fingers in the matted hair on his chest, her nails scratching teasingly, then bent down and brushed her lips against his bare flesh until he twitched in agony, struggling against the confining fabric that still held him prisoner.

"You devil," he gasped, his voice muffled by the folds of his shirt. "You damned vixen!"

She giggled, surprised by her own boldness, and moved lower on his body, that she might work on his fly buttons; releasing the last one, she plunged her hand down the front of his breeches and clutched his burning manhood. He let out a howl and tore his shirt in his anxiety to be rid of it. Freed of the garment at last, he lay beneath her gasping, his eyes smoldering with passion—and delight at her unexpected brazenness.

"Well then, you impudent Amazon," he panted, "you vanquisher of men—must I tear my breeches as well?"

She shrugged—noblesse oblige—and moved off him, but the moment he had removed his breeches she was at him again, pushing him onto his back. She leaned over him to kiss him hard upon the mouth, her breasts rubbing against his chest, her tentative tongue reaching out to seek his. When she couldn't bear the anticipation another moment, she straddled him again, lowering herself onto his hard shaft. She closed her eyes and let her head fall back, barely able to breathe for the exquisite sensations that filled her as she moved up and down on him. Then she squealed in surprise; with a sudden wrench he had pushed her from him and flipped her over onto her back. In command now, he plunged into her again and again, his thrusts deep and hard. She felt herself soaring, a dizzying flight to some unknown and exotic sphere where nothing existed save the throbbing within her, the roaring in her ears. She cried out and, with a draining spasm, fell to earth again.

After a few moments, he laughed softly, his lips against her cheek. "'Tis one thing to win a skirmish or two, my sweet warrior. But I wasn't about to let you win the whole battle!"

He was still sleeping when the crowing rooster woke her. She leaned up on one elbow and watched him, the gentle rise and fall of his broad chest, the way a wisp of black hair trailed boyishly across his forehead. His face was sweet, innocent, young. It always seemed to be so: in sleep, with his demons laid to rest, he was another person. He stirred and opened his eyes, gazing at her silently for several minutes. "Ninon," he murmured at last, reaching up a lazy finger to stroke her cheek. He yawned and blinked, then smiled at her. "What were you thinking of just then?"

Tenderly she brushed the bit of hair off his forehead. "That I don't know how old you are. That you look like a lad when you're sleeping, waiting for your first lover to awaken you with her magic kiss." She cursed herself the moment the words were spoken. She saw his face age, harden with anger and bitterness, even as she watched. It was as though the sign on her, that read "Ninon," had changed abruptly to "Woman."

"I'm twenty-seven," he said sharply. "Old enough to know that one woman's kiss is as good as another's." He sat up in bed. "Fetch me a shirt from my trunk. Thanks to your high spirits last night—or was it merely intoxication?—I've ruined my best shirt."

"I'll mend it," she snapped, feeling anger in spite of herself. "There, at least, is something a woman can do that won't frighten you away! And fetch your own shirt!" She flounced out of bed and retrieved her velvet gown from the floor, tossing it carelessly into her trunk and pulling out her everyday gray gown. Ignoring him, she dressed quickly and swept out to the large sitting room that adjoined the bedchambers of the actors, and where now the maids were busy setting out breakfast.

Chanteclair was already there, standing at the table, stealing a few kisses from his blond serving wench and nibbling at a crust of meat pie—one hunger being as easily satisfied as another. He greeted Ninon and indicated a chair. When they both were seated, he poured out some wine, warm and spicy and sweetened with honey.

"To you," he said, raising his cup.

She returned his salute, smiling tightly. "To Valentin's demons."

He frowned. "Has he brought you grief?"

She laughed. "Grief? Good God, no! Had I stayed a moment longer in that room this morning, I should have crowned him with the chamber pot!"

"If ever you do, I should like to see it."

She helped herself to an apple tart. "Have you seen Sébastien this morning?" He nodded. "How is he?"

"Like a man who wishes he had died last night, I suspect. There is nothing worse than a swollen head after too much wine. Except perhaps a gnawing conscience. He has gone to beg forgiveness of Monsieur le Vicomte."

"And Hortense?"

Chanteclair shook his head. "She spent the night in Reynolds's room."

"And should consider herself fortunate!" Valentin strode up to the table and helped himself to a pigeon wing.

Chanteclair poured another cup of wine. "Good morning, Val. Wherefore fortunate?"

"Hortense is a plain woman. Jamie could take any bed he wanted in this château—from milady's *apartement* to the cottage of the lowliest milkmaid. Yet he chose Hortense."

"Sweet Madonna!" exclaimed Ninon. "Do you consider his attentions benign?"

"I consider him to be acting in his own best interests—as do we all. And then...I should not be surprised if Hortense...and Toinette, too, for that matter...led him on."

"Why should they want to do that?" asked Chanteclair.

Valentin shrugged. "The excitement of a new lover...the zest of making an old lover jealous...a woman likes these things."

"Oh!" Ninon was beside herself. "Why is it women are always the villains? What women have you known to skew your thinking so?"

"Such righteous anger," said Valentin, leaning back in his chair. "But what would you say to your Philippe, were he to appear at this very moment and ask you about *me?*"

She stood up, her eyes blazing. "I should tell him that I was a fool!" Turning to the table, she picked up a large bowl of porridge and dumped it over his head, storming from the room while Chanteclair collapsed in laughter.

He sulked for the next several days, unable to let go his stubborn pride. Taking pity on him at last, Ninon apologized and mended his torn shirt—though it was still an uneasy peace that prevailed between them. She wasn't quite sure whether it had been the incident with the porridge bowl—or her aggressiveness in bed the night before—that had made a stranger of him again, treating her with suspicion, his eyes guarded and full of mistrust. He found reasons to avoid her when they retired; night after night she lay huddled in her corner of the bed, aching for his touch, afraid to drive him further away by reaching out for him.

By day, she threw herself into the long rehearsals, glad to work until she was exhausted—while Valentin barked at the company even more than usual. And not without reason. Hortense, still sharing Jamie's bed, was as giddy and scatterbrained as a country maid, and could barely remember her parts. Sébastien, seldom completely sober, tried to sabotage Jamie, playing havoc with his lines, his entrances, his stage business. Jamie was still determinedly cheerful, but since half the company had cause already to dislike or despise him, much of his goodwill was tiresome and wasted. It seemed not to deter him. Indeed, Ninon had begun to think that, despite his cleverness with women, he was not in some ways particularly bright. He seemed unaware of the damage he caused, the animosity of the players. Or perhaps he was merely indifferent.

By late afternoon the day before their performance, Valentin was moderately satisfied. They had rehearsed in Monsieur de Brinon's theater, a small but splendidly appointed stage set at one end of a long *galerie*. Ninon, who was to appear as Bradamante, the warrior maiden, in the tragedy, paraded about in her new costume to the general approval of the company. De Brinon's armorer had fashioned a shiny tin helmet and breastplate for her, the latter item form-fitting and designed to show the graceful swell of her bosom. Underneath it she wore a pleated tunic that reached just to her knees; her flesh-colored tights accented the shapeliness of her legs.

"You need another plume or two for your helmet," commented Valentin.

"But what a feast for a man's eyes!" said Reynolds. He smiled blandly and turned to Valentin, but not before Ninon had caught a flicker of lust in his face. "There will scarcely be a gentleman among the spectators who would not go to battle for *this* Bradamante!"

Sweet Madonna, thought Ninon, turning about to study Hortense more closely, seeing the pinched features, the downcast eyes. Had that villain Jamie tired of her so soon? She prayed that his sudden interest in *her* was not the overture to a full-scale assault—Valentin would kill him for such boldness.

She changed into her gown and strolled out into the park, seeking solitude, feeling alone and lonely, as she often did these days. She found a quiet spot where a bank of chamomile covered a shallow rise, and threw herself down upon the ground to gaze up at the clear sky, streaked now with the pink of twilight. Idly she plucked a bit of the aromatic plant, crushing the leaves between her fingers and inhaling their fragrance. She sighed. How had her life managed to get to this? Her hopes and dreams drifting ever further away, her heart withering, while her body—her damned betraying body!—yearned constantly for the touch of a man she did not even like. She closed her eyes and sighed again. And yet she would die if he continued to avoid her. In some strange way she had come to need the warmth of his flesh, the feel of his body on hers. Only at those moments was the loneliness dispelled.

She gasped at the sudden pressure of firm lips on her mouth, the weight of a strong body covering hers, arms that circled her where she lay. Then she relaxed to enjoy his kiss, grateful to have him back again. *Mon Dieu!* This was not Val's mouth! Her eyes flew open and she wrenched her lips away from his.

"Damn you, James!" she panted. "Get off me!"

He laughed and held her writhing body more tightly. "By Saint George, I knew you'd be a tiger!"

"I'll tear your eyes out!" she hissed.

"You'll try, I hope! There's nothing I like better than subduing a spirited wench."

"And what of Valentin? He'll kill you!"

"If you prefer me to him—and you will, my sweet, I promise you—what can he say? You shall tell him you have chosen me!"

She gasped in astonishment. Seldom had she known such a swaggering rogue. Small wonder he had been indifferent to the grief he brought to Sébastien and Joseph. He wanted their women. He took them, confident that they could not resist him as a lover. "I should choose the devil first. Let me go."

"The devil would not do to you what *I* shall." He smiled slyly and bent to her ear, whispering obscene suggestions.

"Oh-h-h!" She wriggled and pushed against him, beginning to feel an edge of panic. He was a good deal stronger even than Valentin, and half a head taller—and they were in a remote part of the park.

"God's death," he said, "but I never saw a prettier pair of legs than yours. Made me want to see what they look like with the fleshings off! I always say a woman's legs are only good to look at—and to spread wide, of course."

"Pox take you," she cursed. "If I could, these legs would kick your English backside all the way to the Channel!"

He roared at that, one hand reaching to pull up her skirts. She twisted and turned in desperation, feeling suffocated by his weight, knowing that she couldn't fight him much longer. She let her body relax beneath him.

"Do you want to kiss me again?" she asked. "Then do so."

He almost looked disappointed with her capitulation. "So quickly?"

"If you don't get off me soon, I shall swoon of your weight. I am not Bradamante the warrior maiden. Take what you will."

He smiled in pleasure and pressed his lips to hers. She held her mouth and body rigid, open eyes staring at him coldly. He lifted his head, surprised. "But…wherefore…"

"I give myself to you," she said mockingly. "But when you're through, you'll swear by Heaven above that you have had more pleasure from fondling yourself! And I shall make it known to the entire company that you are the most incompetent lover it was ever my misfortune to endure!"

He frowned and moved off her, sitting back on his heels. "You wouldn't!" he growled.

"If you quit my side this instant, and never bother me more, I shall say nothing. Now begone!"

Grumbling, he stood up and moved quickly away in the direction of the château. Ninon sighed in relief and sat up, smoothing down her tousled skirts. Thanks be to God he was so easily bluffed. With his size and strength, he could have taken her—willy-nilly—and damn the consequences! If he had had the wit, he would have realized that half the company could not think more ill of him than they already did. She looked up. Just beyond the chamomile bank, half-hidden by a row of trees, Valentin was moving toward her. "Sweet Madonna!" she burst out, jumping up to brush off her skirts. "You might have played the chivalrous knight and pulled the lout off me!"

His eyes were veiled, filled with the old mistrust, the old hatred. "I thought you were enjoying yourself. You seemed to welcome his kiss. And he must have had cause to think you would receive him willingly."

"You blind fool! Didn't you see how I struggled to get him off me?" She fought back her angry tears.

He laughed, a mocking smile on his face. "I thought perhaps your efforts were only to dupe me. You're a good actress. But...if what you say is so..." he frowned, "the rogue goes tomorrow!"

"No! We need him in the company."

"And you need him? Is he more like your Philippe...with his yellow hair and his charming ways? And what was his kiss like? Does he look at you as though you were a woman...not just a whore?"

"If I thought I was your whore, I would expect to be paid!" she spat.

"Ah yes! We had an...arrangement! I satisfy myself, and pleasure you while you think of your Philippe."

"To the devil with you!" she cursed, swirling away from him.

"Ninon! Wait!" He grabbed her and pulled her to him, his mouth possessing hers, his hands tight on her shoulders.

Panting, she pushed him away, still angry at his suspicions, unwilling to be reconciled. It was useless to try to convince him of her innocence. And what did it matter anyway? "You must trust me," she said, her jaw set in a stubborn line, "even with temptation in my path...or not at all!" She saw his eyes waver, the pain and doubt sweep across his face. "My God," she said softly. "What hell have you devised for yourself?"

He closed his eyes, as though he could not bear to have her probing his soul, and pulled her back into his arms, holding her silently, drawing strength from her fragile figure. "Come to me," he said gruffly.

He was too proud to beg, too proud to ask her forgiveness. She knew that. She would have to bend. She looked up at him, her eyes twinkling wickedly. "I think it will cost you a crown today!" She smiled and held out her hand, glad to see his answering smile.

By the time they returned to the sitting room, most of the players had supped and gone their ways. Colombe was with her admirers. Sébastien had retired to his bedchamber and the solitary comforts of a beaker of wine, while Hortense mourned the loss of Jamie and her pride in the *cabinet* that adjoined. Reconciled at last, Joseph and Toinette were dancing in the *grande salle* where Marc-Antoine, calling on a little-used talent, was regaling the assembled guests with sleight-of-hand and other tricks and magic. Only Chanteclair lingered at supper, waiting for his blond serving maid to finish her chores. Jamie, downing the last of his wine, rose from the table as Ninon and Valentin entered.

"We missed you at supper, Val," he said warmly, looking past Ninon to focus on Sanscoeur.

"Good evening, James," said Valentin. "We have been walking in the park."

Reynolds looked uneasy, his glance going from one to the other. "Hm. Yes. A fine night for a walk. You'll excuse me. A charming miss…daughter to the baron…I design to make her acquaintance…and Monsieur de Brinon has promised to introduce us." He hurried to the door and vanished.

"James?" said Chanteclair. "Did I hear you call him 'James'? What has happened to our fine comrade 'Jamie'?"

"Plague take him, the lecherous bastard," growled Valentin.

"*Mon Dieu!*" Chanteclair's eyes flew to Ninon. "You don't mean…!"

"If we didn't need him in the plays, I'd kill him!"

"Hush!" said Ninon. "There was no harm done to me. Let it be. There was no harm done."

"Tell that to the other women," said Chanteclair bitterly. "And to Joseph and Sébastien! Well, there will be a reckoning." He looked up to where his *amoureux* stood beckoning him from the doorway. "But for the nonce…" He hurried to the waiting maid, giving her an exuberant pinch on the bottom before bustling her off to his chamber.

Ninon and Valentin laughed, then turned their attention to their food. They ate quickly, eyes only for each other, and retired to bed. They made love passionately, swept by wild hungers, and fell asleep at last, exhausted, in each other's arms.

They were the first to breakfast in the morning, smiling warmly at each other across the table. Ninon found herself blushing at the intensity of Valentin's gaze.

"You must not look at me that way," she said at last.

"Why not?"

"*Dieu du ciel!* Valentin, the world will think us wicked and immoral!"

He laughed at that. "And so we are! But at least we don't pretend to piety, as others do." He hesitated, looking almost embarrassed, and fished in the pocket of his breeches. "I…I had bought you a little bauble some days ago. I had meant to present it after the performance tonight, but…" He held out a small package to her, his eyes cast down, unable to look at her.

It was too intimate a moment for him to endure. She could only save him by making a joke. "But you preferred my performance of *last* night?" she said lightly, and was pleased to see the relief that washed over his face. She opened the packet, exclaiming in delight at the earrings within, crafted of polished coral beads, a treasure from the New World that was more valued than diamonds in fashionable society. She jumped up from her chair and hurried around to kiss him ardently, touched by his unexpected show of kindness.

"Grandmère" cackled behind them. "Shall I go away, children, and return when you have quite finished your silly business?"

"Chanteclair, you ass," said Valentin good-naturedly, "sit you down and eat your breakfast."

Chanteclair reached for a slab of bread, his face wreathed in a great smile. "In truth, I am famished!"

"Too much toil with your blond last night?"

"Valentin!" chided Ninon, returning to her seat.

Chanteclair took a long swig of wine. "No. As a matter of fact I… ahem…had another profession besides lover last night!"

"It must have brought you much satisfaction. I can scarce remember your grinning like such a great looby this early in the morning."

"Indeed it did! Great satisfaction."

"Well? Must we play 'Questions and Commands' with you? Or will you tell of your own free will?"

"If I must." Chanteclair sighed, though the look on his face made it clear he would not have been stilled by Armageddon. "To begin, I should explain to Ninon about Sébastien. He was, before he joined our band of strollers, an operator, a mountebank, a sometime player who made his living by selling nostrums and cures, illustrating the evils of disease with little playlets that he and Hortense performed. He was a successful operator, I am given to believe, until the wife of a fusilier to the intendant of Limousin Province—thinking that if one draft of his potion would make her beautiful then two would make her irresistible—nearly died."

"Great heaven," murmured Ninon.

"Yes. Be that as it may, Sébastien has kept his trunk of remedies, as against his possible falling-out with our company."

"What has this to do with your idiotic smile this morning?" Valentin said impatiently. "Did you find an aphrodisiac among his nostrums?"

"*Au contraire*, my friend. You might say I…that is, we— Joseph, Sébastien, and I—found a few lust quenchers amongst his miraculous cures."

"And what was your other profession? Panderer?"

Chanteclair thought about it for a moment. "Doctor…and actor."

"All three of you?"

"All three of us. Fortunately, our sweet 'Zhamie' has no knowledge of the Italian theater. We played that old chestnut *The Clever Doctor* by Bartoli."

"Good God! When?"

"At dawn."

"Sweet Jesu! 'Tis like pulling teeth! Tell your story before I beat it out of you!"

"Well then…know you that Jamie, unable to lure the baron's daughter into bed last night, was temporarily without a beneficiary of his rather excessive charms. He drank heavily and went to sleep betimes, managing only to get as far as removing his doublet and shoes and stockings. It must have been on to two or three in the morning that Joseph and I, happening at the same time to weary of our labors, came out here to the sitting room for a little wine to quench our heat." Chanteclair leaned back in his chair and scratched his chin. "It seems rather odd that Sébastien, who had spent a solitary evening, was here satisfying the same thirst, but that's neither here nor there. One thing led to another—self-righteousness thrives and flowers in the middle of the night—and our plan was hatched. Sébastien fetched out various medicines and pills and cures from his trunk, and we set to work."

"Playing *The Clever Doctor*."

"Yes. But first it was necessary to create the malady. Sébastien has a most remarkable ointment which, when put on the skin, presently begins to raise little welts that grow anon to large, itching welts! Thanks to Jamie's overindulgence at the punchbowl, he did not feel the gentle brush strokes, and we were able to paint every bit of flesh that was not covered—face and neck, hands and feet, his stockingless legs, and even a large patch of chest where his shirt had fallen open. We waited until the itching had begun to disturb his sleep, and then we raised the curtain."

Valentin began to laugh. "What was the list in the play? *La gale*—scabies, *la téigne*—ringworm…I've forgotten the rest."

"No matter. We began with *la gale*. Poor Jamie awoke itching, to find the three of us shaking our heads in despair over his spotted body. We did the whole scene, just as it is written. *Mon Dieu*, what a gullible fool he is! We moved on to *la téigne*, then *rougeole*, measles, and finally *vérole*, the pox! We quite convinced him if one disease did not kill him, the others would. When at last he was babbling in terror, we held out a crumb of hope. He must put himself in our hands, and trust to our knowledge of these matters. If treated in time, the maladies might be driven out. In order to keep him from contaminating the rest of the household, we told him, we proposed to effect his cure in the great park, near the river. We hurried him thence, by the light of the dawn, which revealed to him the size and extent of his welts, and only increased his willingness to trust us."

Ninon smothered a giggle. "I'm not sure I want to hear the whole story."

"Oh, but you must! It gets better. We began with an ingestion of mercury. Even *he* knew it's an honest cure for the pox. He sweated violently, flushed, turned pale, and then began to vomit. While this is adoing, we are consulting."

"Sweet Jesu," gasped Valentin. "Act two."

"Yes. The scene that begins: 'I fear the man is near to bursting!' And the good doctor fetches his clyster."

"You didn't!" said Ninon.

"Indeed we did. We bent him over a fallen log, pulled down his breeches, and administered to his inward parts. When the poor devil had been thoroughly purged at both ends, we stripped him naked and threw him into the river, claiming still to see lingering traces of the disease. The river, we said, would leach out the poisons. We kept him there until he was blue from the cold, and then hauled him out, shivering. By this time the effects of the ointment were beginning to wear off."

"Then you were not able to play act three."

"Oh yes. There were still enough spots remaining to finish the play. We must drive out the last of the evil humors, we said, and rouse his sluggish blood. We went on a hunt for lime trees—assuring him in all solemnity that lime twigs were the only effective remedy—thrashed him soundly with bundles of the branches, and pronounced him cured. For which he could not express enough gratitude!"

"Oh, you villains," said Ninon, hardly able to control her laughter.

"Yes," said Chanteclair grimly. "And never was a man more deserving of such villainy." He stretched and yawned, putting down his empty cup. "And now, if you'll forgive me...I have not slept all night. I trust you will not rehearse today, Val."

"Only a little, perhaps, before our performance. Monsieur de Brinon has asked us to begin at eight of the clock. He has, I think, planned on illuminations and a light repast at midnight." Valentin laughed. "And I doubt if Jamie will wish to rehearse."

"Well, then, I'm off to find my rest, joining my medical colleagues, who are already sleeping soundly." Chanteclair nodded in satisfaction and left them.

He had barely gone out one door when Reynolds tottered in through another, moving unsteadily to the table. He sank down into a chair and, hands shaking, poured out a bit of milk into a small bowl, lifting it to his lips and sipping tentatively at the liquid. He gulped once or twice, seeming to assess its progress to his stomach, then looked up and smiled thinly at them.

"Jamie," said Ninon, her voice soft with sympathy, "you look ghastly."

"I'm a fortunate man," he said.

"Fortunate? Wherefore?"

He had the face of a martyr. "I was near to death last night, but thanks be to God…" He crossed himself piously.

"Yes?"

"I am free of the terrible diseases that assailed me."

Valentin laughed sharply. "One hopes that the only disease you ever suffered from has been cured."

Reynolds drew himself up. "I like not your tone, sir! What disease is that? I am in no mood for joking. I have endured purges and beatings to be free of my maladies. What disease do you speak of?"

Valentin stood up and held out his hand to Ninon, guiding her to the door that led to the stairway and the sunny day beyond. "Pernicious lechery, monsieur," he said. "Pernicious lechery." And left a bewildered Reynolds to ponder and doubt.

They performed well that evening. Jamie, in a gray wig, acquitted himself well enough in Gaston's roles, though he was uncharacteristically subdued and humble before the members of the troupe. Hortense, pride in hand, made overtures to Sébastien between the acts, and as they waited in the wings to go on; by the time they had finished *Roger et Bradamante* and were starting the farce, it was clear he would forgive her. Colombe was not at her best. Looking extraordinarily beautiful, she was nonetheless distracted from her parts by her admirers who whispered and waved throughout the evening.

But Ninon, glowing in her armor, had never acted more fervently. There was much weeping and sighing among both the men and the women. And when she appeared as the pert maid in the farce, the spectators were charmed.

At the end, Valentin (though with great reluctance) delivered an epilogue heavily larded with effusive tributes to Monsieur and Madame de Brinon and their son and heir, managing to mention every distinguished branch of their family tree. Chanteclair, who had written the shameless flummery, grinned at Ninon in satisfaction as the Marquis de Brinon stepped up upon the stage and presented Valentin with a fat purse for a tip. He returned Valentin's compliments and praised the company's skill, inviting them to join him and his guests for supper and the illuminations as soon as they had changed out of their costumes and removed their makeup.

Ninon had only to slip into her velvet gown and pat at her curls; Valentin, with half a pound of white lead on his face (and a purse of coins to be counted with Chanteclair), urged her to go on to the *grande salle*, where he would join her. Hurrying along the passageway, she was surprised when the Marquis de Brinon stepped out of the shadows.

"Madame Guillemot," he said.

She curtsied. "Monsieur le Marquis."

He cleared his throat. "I did not wish to offend Madame Linard and the others by telling you before the whole company how charming you were, how sparkling your performance."

"That was kind of you. We actresses...alas!...are jealous creatures."

"I cannot believe that *you* are jealous. But then, you have no need to be. When you are upon the stage, you eclipse all the rest! Your beauty sets my heart to pounding in my breast, and I am transported."

"Monsieur!" She laughed brightly. "I have not been so flattered in many an age. You will quite turn my head!"

"I'm not a young gallant at the Louvre Palace," he burst out, "wooing a silly courtesan with words! I desire you!"

She fell back a step, hand to her bosom. What could she possibly say to him? She had had admirers before: she had managed to flatter them and stay out of their beds at the same time. But never one so blunt in his words, never one whose disfavor at this moment could mean their ruin. She decided that honesty was the best defense.

"I'm touched and moved beyond measure," she said gently. "But you would not want me. My heart is long since given." Oh, Philippe. Dearest Philippe.

He frowned, his glance wavering in indecision. He could force the girl, he knew. Seduce her with his wealth. A hollow seduction. His shoulders sagged in disappointment. "He is a fortunate young man, your Monsieur Valentin."

"No. *You* are fortunate. You have a lovely wife who has presented you with a son, and you have a home, a title, a place where you belong. You need not be a gypsy, wandering about the countryside, searching for tranquillity and ease. You have it here."

"Take this," he said. He reached for her hand and slipped a gold and ruby bracelet over her slim wrist.

"Sweet Madonna, I cannot!"

"Please. 'Tis not a bribe, a payment for expected favors. 'Tis a gift, merely, for a charming young woman who touched my heart for a little." He smiled as she reluctantly returned the bracelet to her wrist. "Will you dance with me tonight?"

"No." Her voice was tender with pity. "When I've gone, you'll laugh at your foolish infatuation, and smile at your dear wife—and wonder what you ever saw in that silly actress."

He lifted her fingers and kissed her hand. "You should have been born to nobility. Wear my bracelet, at least." Smiling, he offered her his arm and escorted her up a broad staircase to the *grande salle*. It glittered with the glow of a thousand candles, their flickering light dancing on fine crystal goblets and silver platters piled high with all manner of delectable foods and exotic dishes. The assembled guests fell to with a will, and none more so than the actors, who knew that they would not soon again encounter such a feast on the hard road they traveled. Smiling with delight, Ninon pointed to one dish and then another, urging Valentin to try the artichokes, Marc-Antoine to compare this wine to that, Chanteclair to sample the spit-roasted songbirds and sugar cakes.

All hugs and kisses and tender sighs, Sébastien and Hortense came late to the party, and spent more time holding hands than eating. But by Hortense's reluctance to sit down all evening, Ninon suspected she had paid for her temporary infidelity with more than just remorse.

At last Monsieur de Brinon announced that—if his guests would be so kind as to follow him into the park—there would be illuminations and fireworks that had been brought straight from Paris to celebrate this happy event. The garden was like a wonderland. Small candles set in the grass lined the gravel paths that wound in among the trees, and every pond was afloat with lights set into wooden holders carved to resemble water lilies. The trees themselves were hung with candle-filled paper lanterns of orange and yellow and green, so the groves seemed like magical orchards of exotic fruit. Beyond a large reflecting pool, Catherine wheels had been set up, giant pinwheels that spun wildly, their spiral arms shooting off streamers of fire, the whole dazzling display mirrored in the still water. With a great explosion, the sky was filled with rockets of all colors, bursting like giant blossoms against the velvet of the night.

Ninon gasped with delight and clutched Valentin's arm, smiling up at him. By the light of the fireworks, she could see the crease in his brow.

"By the by," he said, when there was a lull in the rocket bursts, "I meant to ask you. Where did you get the bracelet?"

"From Monsieur de Brinon."

"You will please to give it back."

"Indeed I shall not."

His hand tightened on her elbow. Without a word he steered her away from the guests to a small stand of trees at some distance from the fireworks.

"You're hurting my arm, Valentin. Let me go!" Angrily she shook free of his grasp.

"You will give back the bracelet!"

"Damn you! And I say I shall not!"

"You're an obstinate woman! Must I take it from you and return it myself?"

"And you're a pigheaded fool! Firstly, it would be madness to insult Monsieur le Marquis. His kindness could turn to malevolence anytime he chose, and we would be grateful to leave here with just the clothes on our backs. I wonder you have survived this long if you cannot tell the difference between us and the nobility. They have every right, and we have none! Sweet Madonna, I could tell you stories…" She sighed, remembering the rise and fall of her own and her mother's fortunes, dependent on the whims of the aristocracy. "And then, we can sell the bracelet as soon as we leave here. With winter coming on, there will be hard times for us. Money is scarce, people are reluctant to go out-of-doors—even to see a play—and if the winter snows trap us in one village, how shall we live? Oh, Valentin, how can you be so blind?"

"I like it not," he growled. "That man fawning over you while you smile at him! I wanted to break his head when he danced with you the other night."

"Why such a to-do? There have been other admirers who fawned. I have smiled falsely many a time, and will do so again—aye, and dance too, if I must."

"But no one has given you a gift ere now." His eyes glittered in the light of a rocket. "Did you prefer his gift to mine?"

"Don't be an ass, Valentin."

"Have you promised him favors for his gift?"

"I cannot believe what I am hearing!"

"*Have* you?" His hands gripped her tightly, fingers digging into the soft flesh of her shoulders.

"Would you care to guard the door of our bedchamber tonight, to see that he does not enter?"

"I know what I'd like to do! I'd like to beat you to keep you from dancing from man to man! First Jamie, and now the marquis!"

She drew herself up coldly. "I don't remember that fidelity was part of our agreement! I agreed to share your bed. I did not give you sole claim to me."

"Whore!"

"So be it!" she spat. "You think it every moment! Then say it aloud if you wish. If it helps you to feel superior to a woman, say it and be damned!" She broke free of his hands and turned toward the château. Then she stopped and looked at him over her shoulder, her voice heavy with malice. "You had best stay on your side of the bed tonight. And do not sleep too soundly, lest you miss this whore's goings and comings in the night!" She tossed her curls in anger and strode away into the darkness, while behind her the sky exploded with brilliant color.

In the morning he was haggard, his dark eyes ringed with darker circles. Ninon felt a pang of guilt. He had obviously believed her. Not that she had completely set aside her anger. But she had used him cruelly, more so than he deserved, tormenting him with his own demons, his own doubts, when she might have put his fears to rest with a few words. She resolved to do him a kindness, to ease the sting of her spite.

It was a sunny morning, mild for the end of September; she set out upon the road to Vézelay, some three leagues distant. Valentin had been promising himself some plain collars and cuffs to wear with the flannel shirts they had bought from the peddlar. But he complained constantly of the bother of separate pieces that must forever be tied on, particularly with an everyday shirt. Ninon proposed to seek out the finest linen draper and lace seller in Vézelay. She would buy some holland cloth for neckbands and wristbands, and attach them directly to the shirts, then edge them with lace and frost them with her most delicate embroidery. And when it was done, he might find it difficult to thank her, but he would know, at least, that she meant it for a peace offering.

Vézelay was a small town set against a hill. She found suitable holland at her first stop; then, at the draper's direction, she climbed the hill—the narrow cobbled streets crowded with children and carts and pilgrims—to find the lace seller. Emerging with her small packages, she hesitated, then followed the street to the crest of the hill and the splendid church that sprawled at its summit: Sainte-Madeleine, with its relics of the Magdalen, the mecca of Christian pilgrims for five hundred years.

Ninon untied the light kerchief that she wore about her shoulders and draped it over her head, then passed through the open doors to the narthex—the entrance hall—with its three arched portals leading into the church proper. She looked up. The main portal was crowned with a magnificent carving of Christ enthroned, surrounded by his Apostles. Around this central scene were grouped strange and exotic people, the lame and the leprous, heathens and disbelievers, sinners and knaves—all those to whom the Gospels were to be carried for their salvation. She sighed heavily. Was there, among these tortured and unsaved souls, an actor or two?

Feeling like an infidel, she crossed herself quickly and passed through to the nave. The church was bright and airy, its high vaulted ceiling illumined by a series of arched windows along the length of both aisles. It was an old church, older than the one at Reims, where Ninon had so often prayed in that last year before her mother had died. Reims had been tall and majestic, with pointed arches and stone tracery and stained-glass windows; Sainte-Madeleine had heavy, rounded arches of alternating pink and gray stone, and a simplicity and serenity that reached out to Ninon's troubled heart. She sank to her knees on the stone floor, her hands clasped together. Would *le bon Dieu* hear the prayers of an outcast? It was fitting that she should pray in the church of the Magdalen, the redeemed whore. Perhaps there was more forgiveness in the Magdalen's church.

She looked up. Across the aisle was a woman with two children. Her face was shiny and scrubbed, and her neat white apron and starched cap were spotless. A fine bourgeois housewife. A woman of respectability. Sweet Madonna, thought Ninon, her heart tearing at her. She should have stayed at Marival, married Mathieu Couteau, and raised his children. There was no happiness in this world, not since the days of her father and Bellefleur, but at least she would have had a home, repute, stability. All the things that were denied her now. She bowed her head, feeling the scalding tears on her cheeks, the sweet memories of her lost childhood filling her thoughts.

She spent the afternoon sewing the collars and cuffs onto the shirts, seated at the window that overlooked the courtyard of de Brinon's château. Valentin had joined her after dinner, pulling out pen and ink to work on a play he was adapting from an old Spanish novella. Peace had been declared with a few rueful smiles and searching looks, and now they worked in companionable silence, each with his own thoughts. Occasionally Valentin would stretch and rise from his chair, coming to look over Ninon's shoulder and admire her skill with the needle.

"You sew a fine seam," he said.

"Thank you. 'Tis not so remarkable. Every woman knows how to sew."

"But not like that. You must have had a skillful teacher."

"My mother," she said, then turned away, unwilling to share more with him. She looked out the window, pretending to take an interest in the doings outside. The Marquis de Brinon was putting one of his daughters up on a pony, giving her reassurances as he handed her the reins. Ninon sighed, her heart still heavy from her thoughts of the morning. He would teach his newborn son to ride someday, and his son would teach *his* son, and on into an unbroken future. But the Peerless Theatre Company would play tonight and be gone tomorrow, moving on to the next town, and the next—a band of gypsies with no home. The scene in the courtyard misted as her eyes filled with tears. She let her sewing fall into her lap.

"What would he be doing now?" Valentin asked gently.

She looked down at her hands. "He always liked to gather the children around him after dinner and tell stories of his exploits on the battlefield."

"Philippe?"

"What?" She looked up, bewildered, her eyes sparkling with tears.

"I said…Philippe?"

She frowned. Philippe? Her father? Which one had she seen in her mind's eye, laughing as she begged him to tell just one more story? She looked away. She had said too much, revealed too much already. Valentin was an intruder.

"Put up your sewing," he said. He lifted the shirt from her lax fingers and set it on the table, then pulled her to her feet. He undressed her gently, his hands tender and careful, and carried her to the bed. She watched as he pulled off his own clothes, admiring the beauty of his body, but feeling strangely unmoved. There was too much pain in her heart today. He lowered himself to the bed and kissed her softly; she tried desperately to respond to him, needing the oblivion of hot passion. It was no use. She felt like a coiled spring about to snap.

He sat up and looked at her, his eyes warm with understanding. Without a word he pulled her over onto her stomach and began to massage her back, his fingers easing the tense muscles.

"People who love are fools," he said. "'Tis better not to love." His hands found the tight knot at the back of her neck, working at it until she felt the spring unwinding. "Yet I cannot but admire your folly. You love Philippe truly, for all the grief it brings you. Forgive me if I think he is not worthy of your love."

"Why should you care?" she said, her words muffled by the pillow. "You are Sanscoeur, the heartless one."

"Even a man with no heart can feel pity when love becomes a torment."

That was why he had been so kind to Colombe, she thought. What a strange man. She sighed. His strong hands had begun to roam more freely over her body, caressing her shoulders and arms, the backs of her legs, the smooth roundness of her buttocks. She twitched, feeling her senses stirring, the hot desire rising within her. When he prodded her gently, she rolled over onto her back, welcoming his love-making, the sweet comfort of his kisses. He had never been so tender to her, his mouth warm and undemanding, his body rousing her to a gentle climax that drained away the griefs and bitterness of the morning.

Even after his body had stilled, he held her tightly, his arms about her, soft fingers pushing back the copper curls from her forehead. "Sleep for a little," he murmured. "There's time enough before the performance tonight."

She moaned softly and burrowed more deeply into his arms, vaguely aware (before sleep overtook her) of his firm flesh, the pleasant, masculine smell of his body. She drifted off and dreamed of her father at Bellefleur, the children wide-eyed around him as he told the tales of his battle service.

Chapter Ten

"Dammit, Ninon, I don't know why you cannot remember the lines!"

Ninon glared at Valentin, who was pacing like a tiger about the bedchamber of the inn, and threw herself off the bed where she had been sitting with Toinette and Hortense. "It's cold in here," she grumbled, stalking to the fireplace and holding out her hands to its warmth.

"'Tis colder outside—but the play must be learned before tomorrow's presentation!"

Ninon sighed. She was tired. They had spent the last month traveling between Vézelay and Nevers, playing in the small towns along the way. She was exhausted from the pace—always on the move, always a new theater to set up, another rowdy audience, another official to bribe.

And the cold. The weather had turned sharply, with a steady drizzle day and night that made her bones ache. No matter how quickly she hurried from the theater, her clothes always seemed damp, her shoes cold and wet. The weather had kept the audiences at home, the theaters relatively empty save for the local cavaliers who came more to socialize—flirt with the women, mock the players—than to see a performance. Business was slow, the actors' supply of reserve money dwindling. That, and the weather, had made the whole company quarrelsome. Their nightly meetings for supper and sociability—in her and Val's bedchamber—had become battlegrounds for them all.

"I'm sorry, Val," said Ninon, rubbing a hand over her eyes. "The cold makes me sleepy."

He put his arm around her. "Sit here by the fire, then. Sébastien, pour another cup of wine for Ninon."

"Yes, Sébastien!" Hortense's voice was sharp. "Show how kind you are to the ladies. Tell me, is Ninon as charming as that baggage you were making sweet eyes at during the performance this afternoon?"

"You might as well be civil, Hortense," Sébastien said coldly. "I don't intend to go out on such a foul night, even for *rouge et noir.* Though I'd much prefer a game of cards, I'll settle for you."

Ninon shook her head as Hortense shrieked in outrage and stormed off to her bedchamber. She was becoming as indifferent as were the others to the constant bickering of Sébastien and Hortense. Once she had feared that their passion could not survive the quarrels; now she was beginning to suspect that they quarreled with each other to whet their passion. Indeed, the nights when they shouted most loudly—their voices rising in shrill acrimony—invariably led to mornings with smiles and tender kisses.

Marc-Antoine looked up from the table. "Don't go out, Pierre," he said.

The boy turned from the door, his face an ugly sneer, and gestured obscenely at Marc-Antoine.

"I implore you," said Marc-Antoine.

"Let the little devil go," Sébastien said kindly. "He is not worth your grief."

Marc-Antoine drew himself up proudly. "Please be so good as to keep your own counsel, Monsieur Duvet."

"*Dieu du ciel!*" exclaimed Chanteclair. "Are you two still quarreling?"

"I'm willing to make my peace," said Sébastien. "I'm tired of singing alone. What say you?"

Marc-Antoine looked anxiously about the room. While they had been talking, Pierre had quietly slipped away. Marc-Antoine struggled to hide his dismay. "Plague take you, you shittlehead," he said with a sniff. "There is no forgiveness in my heart."

Colombe turned from the window, where she had been sitting quietly with Jamie. "You pitiful wretch. You spleenish old woman," she said to Marc-Antoine. "Stop making your foolish noises and go and see if your godchild is hungry. If she is, feed her a bit of porridge—the bratling has quite sucked me dry."

Not that Colombe cared, thought Ninon, her anger rising within her. She and Jamie had become lovers this past month—two selfish, unpleasant people, and never better matched. It would be a miracle if Marie-Anne did not die, Colombe was so neglectful. As for Jamie, he played his parts with ill grace, collected the money due him, and spoke openly of his desire to be quit of the company as soon as he had enough gold to take him to Italy.

Valentin turned to Chanteclair. "Will you take the provost to supper tomorrow?"

Chanteclair nodded. "But I think we would be better served in the matter of our permits were you to take the provost's wife to supper. She is the real power in this village, I am given to understand. Her father was a *maréchal* of France. And she finds you attractive. She made a point of conveying her desires to her maidservant, who informed our innkeeper, who in turn informed the serving wench who has been warming my bed this week."

"Ah, ah, ah!" laughed Ninon, pinching Valentin's cheek. "Were you making sweet eyes at *her* this afternoon?"

"'Tis scarcely a joking matter," growled Valentin. "What's to be done?"

"Oh!" Ninon cast her eyes heavenward. "I'll tell you what's to be done, you great sour-face! You shall take her to supper. If you only eat two courses, and gobble your food quickly, you should be able to remain pleasant. About a quarter of an hour is his limit for charm, wouldn't you say, Chanteclair?"

"Indeed. I often think…" Chanteclair stopped and looked up. The boy Pierre was standing in the doorway, rain dripping from his hat and doublet. "Back so soon?"

"Where's Marc-Antoine?"

"With Colombe's baby."

Valentin scowled at the boy. "Don't tell me there's a spark of pity in that twisted soul of yours."

Pierre shrugged. "He didn't give me enough money." Turning on his heel, he went to find Marc-Antoine.

Valentin sighed. "There is more evil done in this world in the name of love." He poured himself another glass of wine. "Now, what am I to do about the provost's wife?"

"I thought we were agreed," said Chanteclair. "You will sup with her, flatter her. You might even manage a kiss or two."

Ninon giggled. "And *I* won't be jealous…as you are of me."

"Once for all," he said, his voice rumbling with anger, "I am *not* jealous!"

"What about the charming chevalier at Guérigny? The one you nearly brained?"

Chanteclair chuckled. "True enough. And the alderman…the one with the red beard…the one you sat up half the night cursing?"

Valentin puffed with annoyance and folded his arms across his chest. "If I find it a source of disgust that Ninon manages to attract every beetle-headed, crack-brained whoreson of a knave who ever drew breath, 'tis not the same as jealousy! I swear the jade sparkles upon the stage just to lure them on!"

Chanteclair twinkled at Ninon. "The jade grows more beautiful with each passing day."

"Thank you, monsieur." She suppressed a smile.

"I see you two will have your sport at my expense," grumbled Valentin.

"Only to coax a smile from you," said Ninon, kissing him on the cheek. She was growing quite used to his ways, learning to ignore the gruff manner that he used for protection, to twit him out of it if she could. And to shun the black humors she could not reach. She would never have believed how comforting it was to sleep with him. Even when he was asleep, his arm reached out to hold her, to pull her close. Then it was that the dark did not seem so lonely, nor the future—without her beloved Philippe—so bleak and empty.

They sat quietly for an hour or so, while the rain fell steadily outside and the fire crackled on the hearth. Toinette, Joseph, and Sébastien reclined on the bed and told stories. Jamie and Colombe, sitting by the window, could not keep their hands off each other, and their soft whisperings were punctuated now and again by a little squeal of pleasure from Colombe as Jamie's fingers found a vulnerable spot. Her chair pulled close to the warmth of the fire, Ninon practiced her lines with the help of Chanteclair and Val.

There was a noise at the door. "Name of God!" Ninon looked up in horror to see Marc-Antoine standing there. He was drenched to the skin, his face and clothing oozing with thick mud that blended with the blood from a gaping cut on his cheek. His eye was half swollen shut, and his jaw was puffy and blue with bruises. He staggered across the room and fell into a chair as the players rushed to him.

"I'll go for a surgeon," said Joseph, throwing a cloak about his shoulders.

"Get him out of his wet things and bring him to the bed," said Ninon.

"Carefully...carefully..." gasped Marc-Antoine, clutching at his ribs. He winced in pain as they stripped off his doublet, and had to be fortified with a glass of wine before they could remove his shirt. His fleshy torso was covered with bruises and red welts, and the fingers of one hand were mangled and bloody.

"Good God, man, what happened?" Valentin picked up Marc-Antoine like a baby and carried him to the bed, depositing him gently against the pillows.

Marc-Antoine closed his eyes and leaned back, his face twisted with pain. "Pierre."

"That rascally whoreson! I'll kill him!"

Marc-Antoine sighed and opened his eyes, smiling thinly at Ninon, who, basin and sponge in hand, was attempting to clean the blood and filth from his face. "No, Val. He's long gone."

"But what happened?"

"When I was with Marie-Anne…he came to ask for more money. I took him to our room…showed him I had nothing left. He said he was leaving me. He wrapped up his own things, then took most of mine as well." Marc-Antoine blinked back his tears, venturing a note of bravado in his voice. "He even took my fine hat. The one with the plumes. He fancies it will make an actor of him when he joins a new company."

Colombe laughed in mockery. "It never made an actor of you, you *cabotin*—you ham actor! Useless as an actor, useless as a man, and now… by the devil's shittlecock, you cannot even keep your *tapette* lover!"

Sébastien reached her before Valentin did, his hand lashing out to strike her to the ground. He whirled to Jamie. "Take that stupid slut out of here before I kill her!"

Jamie hesitated, weighing the possibility of defending Colombe's honor, then shrugged. She wasn't worth taking on the whole roomful of men. He helped her to her feet and led her away sobbing.

Sébastien crossed to the bed and held out a tentative hand to Marc-Antoine, his eyes questioning.

Marc-Antoine brushed away a tear. "I have missed our duets, my friend," he choked, and clasped the proffered hand.

"But how did this happen?" asked Valentin. "We heard no sound from your room."

Marc-Antoine laughed sadly. "Was ever a greater fool than I? Colombe was right. I *am* useless. I had not the sense to be grateful that he was gone, but must go running out into the rain to beg him to return. He acquitted himself well with his fists…" He gasped in pain and clutched at his side. "His shoes did even better work."

Toinette began to weep openly, sniffling and wiping at her face. "I'll see if the landlord has stronger spirits to drink," she said.

"What can be keeping the surgeon?" Chanteclair peered out the window at the black night.

Valentin pounded his fist on the table. "I want to go after the bastard!"

Marc-Antoine shook his head. "No. He will be hiding in the village until we go. He has friends here. I know not who, but they will protect him."

Sébastien looked at Val. "Why can't we go to the provost and have him search the village until Pierre is found?"

"Because we are nothing in the eyes of the law," said Ninon simply. "It's not as though a nobleman had been robbed and assaulted."

"Indeed," said Chanteclair, turning from the window. "I am minded of an actress I knew once. Her husband had been killed in a brawl. They knew who did the murder. At the inquest, the coroner asked if she would have him issue a warrant to take up the murderer. She wished to see justice done, of course, but she had not enough money to prosecute the case, so she declined to have the coroner issue his warrant." He looked up in relief as the door opened. "At last. Here's the surgeon."

It took several hours for the surgeon's work to be done. He stitched up the cut on Marc-Antoine's face, bound up his ribs, several of which seemed broken, and bled him at the site of the more serious bruises, to relieve the pressure. One hand had been stomped on, but, although there were cuts on the knuckles, no bones were broken. He gave Marc-Antoine a narcotic to make him sleep, collected his fee from the grateful players, and went his way.

It was decided that Marc-Antoine should not be moved from the room. Valentin would sleep with him, and a cot was brought in for Ninon. Between the two of them, he would be constantly tended, lest he take a fever from his wounds.

Ninon sighed. "You sleep first, Valentin," she said. "I'll sit and watch him."

"No. I'm not tired."

"Nor am I." She sat down on Val's lap, resting her head on his shoulder. "Poor Marc-Antoine."

He laughed ruefully. "You were the one who trusted that little devil."

"I didn't trust him. I trust no one. But Marc-Antoine loved him. Foolishly, to be sure, but…"

"The poets who write of the joy of love have never known love." He stared with desolate eyes into the fire, his face ravaged by some terrible grief.

Ninon exhausted herself during the following week, tending to Marc-Antoine, and Colombe's baby as well, since Marc-Antoine had long since taken on the chore of nursemaid. Hortense helped, but Toinette was useless, unable to watch Marc-Antoine's pain or hear Marie-Anne cry.

At last Marc-Antoine was well enough to return to his own room, and Ninon and Val could share their bed again. Ninon felt a certain anxiety as the company bade them good night and left them alone.

Valentin had been strangely moody all week, watching her with Marc-Antoine, with the baby. At first she had blamed his strangeness on their enforced celibacy—but now she was not so sure.

He was a thoughtful lover this night, determined—it seemed—to bring her to climax long before he himself was satisfied. And at the very moment of his own satisfaction, he withdrew, spilling his seed harmlessly on the bed between her legs. She thought at first it might have been an accident, and said nothing. But the following night he made love to her in the same way, concerned with her pleasure before his own. This time, suspecting his design, she was ready for him. She waited until his thrusts became hard and rapid, and she knew he would withdraw in a moment.

"No!" she cried, wrapping her legs around him so he could not break away.

He gasped in surprise, unable to hold back; his body shuddered again and again with the force of his passion, and then was stilled. "Damn you!" he panted at last. "Why did you do that?"

"Why did you do what you did last night? And would have again, had I not prevented it."

"I had my reasons."

"No! 'Twas not part of our agreement that you should deny yourself."

"And if something should happen?"

"What will be, will be. You are late coming to the thought, Monsieur Heartless. A pang of conscience, mayhap?"

He sat up and glared at her. "Only a sudden awareness of my own folly."

"I shall inform you if there is anything you must know," she said sharply.

"So be it!" He pulled her to him and crushed her mouth with his, and this time when he made love to her there was no holding back.

Afterward, nestled in the crook of his arm while he slept soundly, she fought back her tears. He had not even considered the possibility of a child until he had watched her with Marie-Anne. And then the thought had obviously been so abhorrent to him that he was willing to diminish his own pleasure to avoid that eventuality. The child as accomplice of hated woman. She was glad now she had not told him what she had known for a week now. Best to wait until her belly had grown to a size she could not deny to him. The child would not be born until the beginning of summer, by her reckoning. There would be time enough to tell him, and face his displeasure and rage.

She slept poorly, angry with him, with her own cowardice in keeping silent, with the thoughts that churned in her brain. Somewhere along the way she had lost the path of her life, the orderly dreams of her childhood. Even in the dark days with Baugin she had kept her own vision of the future—the Prince Charming, the home, the family, the love. Now she was a leaf adrift, wondering where the current would take her.

At first light she slipped out of bed and dressed quietly, wrapping a warm shawl about her shoulders. The day was crisp and cold, the grass behind the inn white with light frost. She hauled up a bucket of water from the well and washed her face, drying herself quickly with her petticoat. Taking the dipper from its hook, she ladled out a bit of the water to drink, then emptied the rest of the bucket onto the grass and lowered it back into the well. In the stableyard a horse nickered. She sat on the edge of the well, gazing into its depths as though she would find answers there.

There was a crackling laugh behind her. "'Tis not a wishing well, you silly child!" said "Grandmère's" voice.

She smiled without turning. "I shouldn't know what to wish for, if it were, Grandmère."

"You might wish for a little less pride and unpleasantness from Valentin, n'est-ce pas?"

"Indeed. He has not lost his dislike of womankind. It's very hard to stay with him sometimes."

"But you are not womankind—you're Ninon!"

She turned to him, her face twisted with dismay. "It would be nice to know, sometimes, if he *liked* Ninon!"

"Are you happy?" he said in his own voice, the brown eyes warm with concern.

"Dear Chanteclair," she said, pressing his fingers with her own. "I stopped asking for happiness when I was still a child." She smiled ruefully. "But…he's a comfort, in his way."

"As are you to him."

"No. Say rather 'convenience.' I'm his unpaid whore, that's all."

"If it was convenience he had wanted, he could have found it long since with Colombe. Or any of the dozens of women who sighed for him. And you see his moods. He is not nearly so morose as he was."

"Ha! A man who has denied himself for…what was it? Two years?"

"Two and a half, with only an occasional woman."

"Well then. A man like that…why shouldn't his mood be brighter now?"

Chanteclair shook his head. "You did not see him when he came to the company. For a time I feared he would do himself harm. I think you have reached a part of him no one else has."

She frowned. What did she care? She had her own griefs. She didn't want to know, didn't want to care about that difficult man. They had an agreement. Bed partners. Damn the man, that's all he was to her—she wished to be no more than that to him. She stirred uncomfortably, disliking Chanteclair's searching gaze, then laughed, her voice harsh and brittle in the still morning air. "I saved a kitten from drowning once. And Pierre from a beating. It seems to be in my nature to succor the needy. If I become a saint, will Valentin be my first miracle? My first Lazarus, raised from the dead?" She turned to the inn, leaving a surprised Chanteclair to shake his head in disbelief.

November the eleventh was Saint Martin's Day. One of the patron saints of France, he had been the bishop of Tours more than a thousand years before. One of his legends had it that, bothered by a goose, he had killed it and had it cooked for his dinner. He had choked on it and died, and it had become the custom throughout the land to eat goose as a sacrifice to Saint Martin each year on his day. For peasants who had not seen meat on their tables for months, it was a day of gorging, of feasting until they could not eat another mouthful. They might starve by January or February if the winter was severe and they had not enough money or foodstuffs to see them through to spring planting, but they took their pleasures where they might, trusting in the will of God. And if the Church sanctioned a feast for Saint Martin, they were willing to mortgage their futures.

The rich bourgeoisie and the nobility saw Saint Martin's fête as an occasion for rejoicing, before the abstemious weeks of Advent ushered in the season of the Christ child. There was much gaiety, visits between old friends, reunions of distant relatives.

And the merrymaking was never better than in the cities. The Peerless Theatre Company, remembering the hospitality and friendliness of Bourges in the summertime, determined to spend the weeks before and after Saint Martin's Day in that fine old city. After their stay, they would move on to Cosnes by way of Sancerre; Joseph had an uncle at Cosnes who would be willing to be their host during Advent, which was celebrated like another Lent. There were too many fast days and days of abstinence during Advent for them to have much success as players, but at least they would not be paying for their own board until after Christmas.

Bourges was an ancient city, partly surrounded by a thick wall surmounted with imposing towers, the whole enclosing a city of meandering streets that led to a magnificent cathedral. Larger, they said, even than the great Notre Dame de Paris.

They reached their inn as night was falling. *La Grasse Nourrice*, The Fat Nurse, was attested to by the carving over the main door, a robust woman with large, naked breasts. They had stayed there before and found the food good and the beds clean; they looked forward to dining on a fat goose on Saint Martin's Day.

But the inn was very crowded because of the influx of visitors to the town; only Valentin and Ninon were able to share their usual room. For the rest, the women were in one room with Marie-Anne, and the five men, distributed among two beds and a small cot, had another room. Colombe, having grown quite attached to Jamie, complained bitterly, but there was nothing to be done. The rest of the inn had been usurped by two noblemen, a marquis and a duc, half a dozen of their men-at-arms, and two servants.

The troupe quickly obtained the necessary permits and contracted for the theater for several weeks, playing on the best days, Tuesdays, Fridays, and Sundays. It was a large and airy building, with a roomy *parterre* and a double gallery; if they could fill it at every performance, they would have fat purses to see them through the lean months. Even the weather was in their favor, a sudden warm spell so typical for November that the people called it "Saint Martin's Summer."

Their audiences were boisterous but friendly. There was not an afternoon that a score of rendezvous were not arranged among the spectators—a few harmless flirtations, a surreptitious meeting or two. And one day the actors were treated to a cat fight, with shrieks and pulling of hair and torn gowns, as two women in the second gallery fought over the same seat. The actors were encouraged to come down from the stage after each performance to mingle with the audience in the pit and the galleries. Ninon was not sure which she preferred. The men in the crowded pit—soldiers, bourgeoisie, lesser nobility—were more unruly, but treated the actresses with a certain deferential respect; the haughty gentlemen in the galleries were not as apt to pinch a bottom in the jostling throng, but Ninon found their suggestions and invitations—clothed in flowery language—to be lewd and offensive.

After a particularly coarse remark from a fat cavalier in the gallery, she had had enough. She pushed her way to the staircase that would lead her down to the edge of the *parterre* and thence to the stage. She would wait in the changing room until the house had cleared a little. She had barely started down the staircase, however, when her way was blocked by an extravagantly dressed nobleman, all ribbons and laces, from the frill of lace on his sugarloaf hat, to the ribbon loops and *cocardes* that trimmed the sides and hems of his full breeches, to the lace boot hose that spilled out over the tops of his bucket boots.

"Upon my word," he said, sniffing delicately at the silver filigree ball that hung at his waist. These musk balls were much in favor because of the everpresent danger of plague; filled with myrrh, cloves, cinnamon, and other essences, they were thought to ward off disease, or, at the very least, the smell of one's fellows. "Upon my word," he said again, "if you are not the sweetest morsel I have beheld all day! I saw you upon the stage and thought your beauty was paint." His eyes lingered at her full bosom. "Is the rest of you as genuine as your face?"

"I am as honest as God will allow, monsieur. May I pass?"

He took another step toward her. "'Tis a toll gate, I fear. You cannot pass without paying the tariff."

"Which is…?"

"A kiss, mayhap. A caress of your white bosom. Your soft hand upon the fount of my power."

"You ask much, monsieur." Ninon glanced quickly about the theater, hoping to find a champion among her male comrades who might come to her aid. Valentin was surrounded by fawning women who clutched at his sleeves and gazed adoringly into his dark eyes. Chanteclair had found a pretty young noblewoman in the upper gallery, and was talking with great animation while she blushed and giggled and hid her face with her fan. Joseph seemed deep in conversation with an elderly gentleman, and the rest of the men were not to be found. She glanced behind her. Already the top of the staircase was crowded with coxcombs and rake-hells; it would be more dangerous to run that gauntlet than to try to reach the bottom of the stairs. She dimpled winningly at her tormentor. "Will a smile satisfy you, monsieur?"

"No," he said, and took another step up toward her.

She took a deep breath. There was no sense in fencing with this dandified rogue. He meant to take what he could. She drew herself up, playing the queen, and extended her hand. "I give you leave to kiss my fingertips. Anything more and I shall scream and accuse you of all manner of foul and unnatural behavior. I suspect that there are at least a dozen gallants here who would willingly defend me."

"*Ma foi!*" He burst into laughter. "But you're a devilish wench! Very well. I'll be content with my kiss." He brought her fingers to his lips. "Are you staying in Bourges?"

"Yes."

"May I take you to supper?"

"Not tonight, alas."

"Tomorrow?" he asked. She shrugged her shoulders in helpless indecision (a trick she had found handy with her admirers—they could not accuse her of refusing, but they could not claim that she had agreed either). "Where are you staying?" he asked.

She hesitated. "*Hôtel de la Grasse Nourrice,*" she said at last.

"But so am I! I knew there were actors as guests, but the only woman I saw was the plain one."

Ninon smiled. "And you are one of the gentlemen who have taken the best rooms? The ones the maids say sleep all day and whore all night?"

"You have a cruel tongue," he said, laughing. He swept off his fancy hat and bowed elaborately to her. "René, Marquis de Garouffière. Your humble servant."

She curtsied as well as she was able on the narrow staircase. "Madame Ninon Guillemot. Now, if you please, monsieur, may I pass?"

He stepped aside. "We shall meet again, *ma belle,* at The Fat Nurse. I promise you that. In the dark of night, perhaps."

"Take care, monsieur. I sleep with a sturdy weapon in the bed next to me."

"And what is that, madame?"

She smiled sweetly. "My husband." She swept past him and hurried to find Valentin, if only to warn him that he must call her wife so long as Monsieur de Garouffière stayed at the inn.

"No, no, Joseph, you are still too awkward. I have seen you dance the *galop* with more grace." Valentin tucked his tin sword under his arm and rolled up his sleeves, then turned again to Joseph. "Now. *En garde.* And remember to move lightly as we fence."

Joseph squinted up at the morning sun, then moved around on the grass so the sun would be shining in Valentin's eyes. "I shall never be as good as you, Val," he grumbled.

Sébastien laughed. "You're not supposed to kill him, *mon Dieu!* Just so you look well matched upon the stage."

Ninon looked up from her sewing and giggled. They were all assembled in the garden of the inn. All except Chanteclair, who was busy in pursuit of the young lady he had met at the theater some days before. Ninon was mending a bit of Valentin's costume before the day's performance. "Yes, Joseph. Don't kill him," she said. "I would not be widowed so soon!"

There was general laughter at this, all the company (save the dour Valentin, of course) having found Ninon's deception of Monsieur de Garouffière a source of merriment. As for the marquis—despite Ninon's supposed wedded state, he had stalked her with such persistence since their first meeting that it was all she could do to keep Valentin from flying into a rage and attacking the man.

While Valentin went on with his fencing lesson, and the other actors rehearsed their lines and business, Ninon bent again to her sewing. She would be glad to leave Bourges. They had feasted well on Saint Martin's Day, and the visitors to the town were beginning to disperse; there was no reason to remain much longer. And the sooner she could get away from Garouffière, the happier she would be. She did not like feeling uneasy each time she was alone in a room or the garden of the inn. He was a lecherous man. A dangerous man. She looked up from her work. The Marquis de Garouffière was coming out of the inn toward them, sniffing daintily at a lace handkerchief.

"Upon my word," he said, addressing himself to Valentin. "You fence as well. I had seen you upon the stage, monsieur. I thought you were only good for attracting the sighs of the women—and marrying the prettiest of the lot."

Valentin parried Joseph's thrust, then turned to Garouffière and bowed. "No. As you can see, we must also be adept at turning aside the treacherous attack."

"And defending what is yours?"

"If need be."

"But this is just a boy," said Garouffière, indicating Joseph with an airy wave of his fingers. "Can you draw your sword against a man?"

"If there is a man to be found," snapped Valentin.

Garouffière stiffened, then allowed his mouth to curve upward in an ugly smile. "Come. What say you, monsieur, to a match? The training of a gentleman as against the training of an actor, a wandering rogue."

"It would be my pleasure."

"Not with that stage sword, of course. I prefer the heft of a true rapier."

"I am agreeable."

Ninon motioned Sébastien to her side. "*Nom de Dieu!*" she whispered. "Stop them!"

"I cannot! Valentin is set upon his course. And they mean only to test each other's skills."

Ninon bit her lip in dismay. She was not so sure. And if they were serious, nothing good could come of it. Valentin wounded—or worse. Or Garouffière wounded, and the whole company thrown into prison. Nervously she pressed her hands together as the two men saluted each other and began.

The marquis attacked first. Valentin turned aside his passes with ease, his rapier point deflecting a thrust that was aimed for his breast. He feinted once or twice, to gauge Garouffière's reflexes, then leaped forward, his blade flashing. Taken by surprise, the marquis fell back a step, then closed with him, their blades crossing together up to the quillons. Valentin smiled. It would not be too difficult to disarm this popinjay. He prepared to disengage. At that moment Garouffière lifted his knee and thrust it into Valentin's groin.

Ninon gasped as Valentin doubled up in pain, and forced herself to stay where she was. She could not shame him by interfering.

"Come, gentlemen!" Sébastien tried to laugh. "This is a trial of fencing skills. No more."

Valentin straightened up, struggling to recover himself. He took a deep breath and wiped the sweat from his face. His eyes were burning. "Let it be what it is," he growled. "With no pretense. Monsieur?" His jaw set in anger, he attacked Garouffière, who sought to defend himself against a blade that seemed to be everywhere at once. In less than a minute, the marquis's rapier was sent flying, and he found himself with his back to a tree and Valentin's point against his throat.

Valentin smiled and bowed, lowering his rapier to the man's groin. "I could return the favor, you know. If I thought there was anything there to skewer. Will you agree you were outmatched by this rogue?"

"Pox take you. I'll see you hang!"

"For shame, René! You lost the match fairly."

They turned to see the speaker, a tall man who lolled in the doorway of the inn. It was clear by the fineness of his clothes that he was a gentleman, but with none of the flamboyance and gaudy show of Garouffière. He moved easily across the lawn and bowed to Valentin.

"You must forgive my hot-headed friend, monsieur. He forgets himself. And you are a superb fencer. One can see it in a moment. I have the honor, I believe, of addressing Monsieur Sanscoeur of the Peerless Theatre?"

"Indeed, monsieur. And you?"

"Your fellow guest at *La Grasse Nourrice*. I regret we have not met until now. But..." he shrugged, "my business has kept me elsewhere. I am Charles, Duc de Boisrobert." He turned to Garouffière. "Now, René, I suggest you shake Monsieur Sanscoeur's hand and make your peace with him."

The marquis frowned. "But..."

Cold blue eyes bored into Garouffière. "I will not have this fine company as an enemy because of your excessive pride."

Garouffière nodded in agreement. "So be it," he said, and held out his hand to Valentin.

"Now," said Boisrobert, "I should like to meet your company, Monsieur Sanscoeur. I saw you upon the stage the other day and found your performance as a troupe to be quite remarkable. Seldom can a company boast so many fine actors and beauteous actresses."

Introductions were made all around, and the duc was unfailingly courteous to each of the players, recalling a clever *lazzo* Sébastien had done, complimenting Colombe on her playing of the tragic heroine, and envying Valentin for the freshness and beauty of his wife, Ninon.

Recalling the hour, Valentin cut short the pleasantries, so that the company might go in to dinner before the afternoon's performance. He slipped his arm about Ninon's waist (to the consternation of Garouffière, who was still having difficulty hiding his animosity), and prepared to join the others.

"A moment," said Boisrobert. "The innkeeper tells me you are off for Sancerre the day after tomorrow. My company and I travel in that direction. I have armed men with me. They are fine protection from brigands and highwaymen. Would you permit us to accompany you?"

"That is most kind of you. You have business in Sancerre?"

"Yes. Garouffière and I are to do a bit of hunting. What say you?"

Valentin hesitated. "We have a heavy wagon, a team of oxen. And we ride double. We can only slow your own journey. Thank you, Monsieur le Duc, but..."

"You cannot think to refuse me. We're in no hurry." Boisrobert laughed. "I rather suspect our host would not welcome our company too soon. And I myself look forward to a verse or two, well declaimed, as we ride along. Well?"

Valentin nodded in agreement and ushered Ninon into the inn. "I like it not," he muttered when they were alone in the vestibule. "That treacherous Garouffière…"

"I agree," said Ninon. "But what are we to do? We can scarcely insult Boisrobert by refusing. And it *will* be safer, with his men-at-arms." She grinned up at him, her eyes twinkling mischievously. "Is it that you have just now realized that I must remain your wife so long as we are in Garouffière's company?"

"You devil," he said. "If ever I had entertained thoughts of marriage, I…" He looked up. A young man in livery stood before them. "Are you seeking the duc?" he asked.

The servant tugged at the curl on his forehead. "No, monsieur. I seek a lady." He looked down at the letter in his hand. "Mademoiselle… Guillemot," he read.

"I am she," said Ninon, taking the letter as he offered it. Valentin peered over her shoulder. Her hand began to shake when she examined the seal. The Froissart crest. Philippe. She clutched the letter to her bosom, unable to think.

"Is an answer expected?" Valentin growled to the lackey.

"No, monsieur."

"Then be off with you." Valentin threw him a coin and watched, his face creased in a frown, as Ninon tore open the letter. She read it through, her expression inscrutable, then folded it carefully and tucked it into her bodice.

"If we don't have dinner soon," she said, "we shan't be able to eat before the performance." She swept past him into the common room of the inn, where the other players were already putting away a huge meal.

She was surprised that she was capable of eating, that her appetite was not impaired—nor her skills upon the stage. She acted superbly, though she seemed to watch herself from afar, as in a dream. And when they returned to the inn for supper she was hungry again, and ate, and talked, and laughed—as though she were still alive.

She urged Valentin to go to bed without her. She was not tired, she said, and would come along later. She sat in the common room, huddled close to the fire, and pulled out Philippe's letter. Boisrobert's servants snored on nearby benches, and the men-at-arms, bedded down on straw in the corner of the room, turned and prodded one another in their sleep. One of them stood up for a moment, looking challengingly at her before moving quickly to a cabinet where the maid had left a half-larded piece of beef. He wrapped it in a napkin and tucked it into the breast of his doublet, then returned to his straw bed beside his fellows. She shrugged her shoulders and turned away from him. She had known what it was to be hungry. What did she care if he stole? She unfolded Philippe's letter.

My dearest Ninon,

You cannot imagine the grief I suffered when I discovered you were gone. I heaped curses upon you, and sent my men out to search for you. I dreamed of dragging you back, of reviling you for the misery you had caused me, of bending you to my will, whether you would or no. I confess it now to you, my love, with shame in my heart. You had hurt my pride. You had thwarted my lustful passions. And it *was* lust. Forgive me, my sweet. It was desire I felt, that night in the summerhouse.

Then you were gone. I found myself recalling your sweetness, the habit you had of looking up at me as you read aloud to the boys, your shy silences. Oh, little bird. I knew then that I loved you with a love I had not thought ever to feel. My days were filled with longing, to have you by my side, to tell you of my love, to open my heart to you.

At last my men came and told me they had learned of your whereabouts. They said you were a great actress upon the stage. I near flew to your side at that moment. My horse was saddled. My heart beat in expectation.

But I could not come to you, for I knew in that moment that I could bring you naught but grief. Henriette will never relinquish the marriage. I could offer you only my heart and my love. It is not enough for you, my dearest Ninon. And Henriette's malice would turn it to dust.

And so I release you. Find a man who will love you, little bird. Who will marry you, and give you children, and the life you deserve.

I wish you well. May God protect you.

Forever,

Philippe

She threw the letter into the fire and watched it burn, and with it the last of her dreams. She crept quietly into her room, grateful that Valentin was asleep. She blew out the single candle he had left, and curled up on her side of the bed.

And then the tears began. Great sobs that she muffled in her pillow, while her body shook with grief and she clutched her arms to her breast to still her tremors. She choked and gasped, swallowing the sounds of her misery. Valentin would never know. No one would ever know. That her life was over, her heart was dead.

They set out the following morning for Sancerre, in the company of Monsieur le Duc de Boisrobert and his party. There was no love lost between Valentin and Garouffière, of course, but the marquis made an effort to be courteous, if not pleasant. They stayed at a country inn the first night. On the second night, arriving at Angillon, a large town some ten leagues from Sancerre, they were persuaded by the town council to stay for a few days and present a play or two. It seemed foolish to refuse: the town was willing to guarantee a large sum of money. The players urged Boisrobert to continue his journey without them, which he would willingly have done, had not one of his manservants taken a sudden fever which necessitated a stopover in the town. As they had in Bourges, they shared the inn at Angillon.

Ninon sighed and finished the last of her supper wine. They would be leaving in the morning. Their presentation had gone well, and they had been amply paid, but the performance had taken place in a barn, under the most primitive conditions, and the whole company was exhausted and fretful. They ate largely in silence, sitting around the table in the women's chamber. Hortense ate hardly at all, preferring to lose herself in the wine and mutter darkly about Sébastien. He had gone directly from the performance to the local *tripot*, whether to gamble or to whore she knew not; but she cursed him soundly for both weaknesses.

"Valentin. Name of God. I can scarce believe it!" A gasping Sébastien stood at the door, his clothes askew, as though he had dressed hurriedly.

Hortense looked up from her wine. "Did the slut throw you out so early?"

"I have no time for quarrels. All of you. Listen to what I heard." Sébastien threw himself in a chair and poured some wine, while the rest of the company gathered around the table.

"What is it?"

"To begin, I was with a whore tonight." He held up a warning hand. "Hortense, hold your tongue. In the course of things, she began to tell me of a certain gentleman she had entertained last night. He was very drunk…and very talkative. It did not take me long to realize she spoke of Garouffière."

"That traitorous devil," muttered Valentin.

Sébastien laughed bitterly. "*Au contraire.* Hardly a traitor. A loyal subject to the king. And one of Cardinal Mazarin's spies!"

"*Mon Dieu!*"

"And Boisrobert?"

"The same. In truth, he is Garouffière's superior."

"Why are they here?"

Sébastien sighed. "They are searching for plotters against the crown. There are still some nobles who secretly long for the return of the Fronde movement, and would do anything to remove that despicable Italian cardinal from the side of the king."

"Why should that concern us?" asked Valentin.

"Because it is presumed that a strolling company, going from town to town, has ample opportunity to serve as a conduit for messages and plots."

"But how foolish!" said Ninon.

Sébastien shook his head. "According to Garouffière, a letter was passed at Bourges. From a known traitor."

Joseph had gone white. "That's why Boisrobert and his men are traveling with us. Why Garouffière made his peace with Val!"

"Well, we have nothing to fear," said Hortense.

"We do," Joseph groaned. "*I* was given a letter…at Bourges. I was well paid. The nobleman said it was a love letter."

"Sweet Jesu, why didn't you tell us?" said Valentin.

"It hardly seemed worth your notice."

Ninon frowned at Sébastien. "But if they know that Joseph has the letter, why don't they arrest him? And the lord at Bourges?"

"They are waiting for the letter to be delivered. They suspect a nobleman in Sancerre, but they want to be sure. And have the letter for evidence. Then they intend to arrest the lords from Bourges *and* Sancerre…and the Peerless Theatre Company! The whore, of course, didn't know I was an actor when she told me all this."

Marc-Antoine breathed a sigh of relief. "Then the difficulty is no more. Destroy the letter, Joseph."

"I cannot. I passed it on to a messenger only this evening."

"Oh, God! Where is he?"

"Somewhere in the town, resting. I know not where. I only know he leaves for Sancerre before dawn tomorrow."

"'Tis a simple matter, then," said Chanteclair. "We shall waylay the messenger and steal the letter."

"Wait," said Sébastien. "According to Garouffière, they mean to bribe the messenger, to see that the noble who receives the letter does not destroy it."

"And even if they did not bribe him," said Valentin, "Boisrobert would know who attacked him. Our guilt would be verified in his eyes."

"There must be another way."

"I like it not," said Jamie nervously. "I don't fancy spending my days in a French prison!"

Chanteclair laughed in mockery. "Why is it always so, that the larger the man, the greater his capacity for cowardice?"

"*Nom de Dieu*," said Valentin, as Jamie rose in his chair, his face twisted with anger. "This is no time for a quarrel! We must do something, and do it tonight, else we are all doomed!"

"Can one of us not seduce the messenger?" asked Colombe.

"Where? Joseph doesn't know where he is staying. He would have to be seduced on the road to Sancerre."

"But that's ridiculous! The man would hardly tarry in the woods with an important letter to deliver!"

Ninon had been sitting quietly, deep in thought. Now she looked up at Joseph. "Tell me, what did the letter look like?"

"An ordinary letter. Folded twice. And with a seal."

"Crested?"

"No. Plain."

Ninon nodded in satisfaction. "Easy enough to duplicate. Where did he put it?"

"In a pouch slung diagonally across his chest."

"He could not lose it by accident, then. Hortense," Ninon put a gentle hand on the woman's arm, "forgive me if I ask this of you. I know that Sébastien was an operator. But...I have seen at fairs, many a time... the mountebank's lady was not only a fine actress but a pickpocket as well. Forgive me if I err, but..."

Hortense blushed. "'Tis an art not unknown to me."

"How fast could you exchange letters if I could get him off his horse in the woods?"

"One embrace and the job would be done."

"Good!"

"But how do you propose to do it?" said Valentin.

"Look you. Boisrobert will not leave tomorrow until we do, *n'est-ce pas?*"

"True enough. He has kept close since Bourges. Probably since the day the letter passed to Joseph. I suspect his man never was ill. Merely a ruse to stay here until *we* were ready to continue our journey."

"I agree," said Ninon. "He would then notice if most of the company were missing, particularly the men. But if it's only Hortense and me…"

"What do you intend?"

"In the morning, take breakfast with Boisrobert and Garouffière. Linger over your food. Tell stories, play cards, whatever you must. If they ask, you can say that Hortense and I are asleep."

"And where will you be?"

"Hortense and I will be performing. At dawn."

Chanteclair laughed shortly. "You cannot mean to play *The Clever Doctor*, as we did with Jamie?"

There was a low growl from Reynolds. Ninon put a quieting hand on his shoulder. "Hush, Jamie, 'tis long forgotten. No. We shall not play the doctor tomorrow. But what of *Scévole?*"

"*Scévole?*" Valentin frowned. It was not a well-known play, having been published only recently. It dealt with a Roman hero, Gaius Mucius Scaevola, who, when captured by the enemy, had shown his disdain of torture by thrusting his right hand into a fire and keeping it there until it was consumed. He had, by this brave deed, won peace for Rome, and the nickname Scaevola—"Left-handed."

"Yes. *Scévole*," said Ninon. Quickly she outlined her plan, while the company listened in rapt attention.

"I like it not," said Valentin. "'Tis too dangerous. Gaston always handled those appurtenances. That's one of the reasons I haven't wanted to play *Scévole* since he left."

"Can you think of a better plan? If not, put what we need on a horse tonight, while I compose a letter for the nobleman in Sancerre. Hortense and I shall ride out at midnight and wait on the road for the messenger."

Valentin nodded a reluctant agreement and turned to the players, his dark eyes lingering on Colombe and Reynolds. "Our lives and safety depend on the silence of everyone. Do you understand?"

Jamie stirred uneasily. "God's death! Don't look at me! I have no love for the lot of you, but…"

Chanteclair laughed, his voice filled with contempt. "But to save your skin, you'd cut out your own tongue!"

• • •

Henri Targon fastened the fly buttons on his breeches, scratched at a stray flea under his shirt, and remounted his horse. He should never have had so much ale for breakfast. At this rate, he would have to stop every few leagues to relieve himself. And it was important to get the letter to Monsieur le Comte de St. Gregoire as soon as possible. Targon pushed aside the pouch slung across his shoulder to pat at the sack of coins under his doublet. He was a rich man. And would be richer before the day was through!

And safer, God knows! All those years in the service of St. Gregoire, delivering and collecting letters. Riding to this town and the other, to meet with men he never knew, but recognized only by the blue book of poetry they read in whatever inn or rendezvous had been arranged. All those years. And, until that Duc de Boisrobert had told him, he never knew he was helping to betray his king. It made a man's blood boil! Boisrobert might have arrested him, hanged him, even. Instead, Targon had fifty crowns in his pocket, with fifty more to be delivered when Boisrobert came for the letter.

It would be a simple matter. St. Gregoire always received the messages in his *cabinet*, read them carefully, and cast them into the fire. If he was seated in a chair, as was his wont, he would crumple up the letter and ask Targon to burn it for him. There would be no difficulty in taking an old letter from St. Gregoire's library before he went in to the *cabinet*. He would burn the old letter and save the new for Boisrobert. And devil take St. Gregoire for trying to make a traitor of him!

Targon shivered. The damp mists rising in the woods shrouded the ground with a thick blanket that obscured the horse's hooves, and the first light of dawn, streaking through the trees, only made the fog appear more dense. He slowed his horse so the animal would not stumble on unseen rocks, then froze in the saddle as a loud wailing sound came out of the mist. He reached for the knife in his belt and inched his mount forward, prepared to battle—or bolt—as need be.

The road veered sharply. Just beyond the bend, he saw a small bonfire in the middle of the path; in front of it squatted a creature who appeared to be a woman. Her yellow hair was tangled wildly about her face, and she was covered in filthy rags. She rocked back and forth on her haunches, moaning and crying and pulling at her hair.

Targon frowned. It could be a trap. Brigands had been known to use a decoy. And he had an important letter to deliver. And fifty crowns to safeguard. Whatever happened, he would not get down off his horse. He gathered the reins more tightly in his fist and glared down at the woman.

"Get out of the road, hag!" he growled.

She turned and looked at him wildly, one arm thrown up as if to shield herself from a blow. "You cannot harm me, devil!" she shrilled. "I defy you!"

"I mean you no harm! Get out of my way."

She pointed an accusing finger. "You think I'll tell you where he has gone! Never, you villain. Never!"

"*Merde!*" he swore. "Will you get your stupid backside out of the road, woman?"

Her voice rose to a shriek. "You cannot threaten me. I defy you and your tortures! Look! See you!" Jumping to her feet, she thrust her hand into the bonfire. He watched in horror as the flesh charred and the blood oozed from the raw wounds and sizzled as it hit the flames. She began to scream, a horrible sound that pierced his ears—but still she kept her hand in the fire.

"My God!" he choked, and leaped from his horse to pull her away from the flames. At that very moment another hag emerged from the mists and threw her arms around him, sobbing with grief.

"Leave her be, good sir! I beg you! She is mad. My sister is mad! She will do you harm. She has killed ere now. Get you on your horse and begone! I shall tend her. Begone! Begone!"

Targon needed no more persuasion. In a minute he was in the saddle; in another minute, the sound of his horse's hooves had been swallowed up by the mists.

"Thanks be to God!" said Ninon, pulling the artificial arm from her hand and blowing on her fingers. "That was becoming very hot! Did you get the letter?"

Hortense laughed and held up her trophy. "Do you want to read it?"

"Not I! If it contains treason, it is better we not know it. Throw it on the flames." When the letter had been consumed, they stamped out the fire and scattered the ashes, then pulled off their wigs and rags and changed into their own clothes. By the time they returned to the inn, emerging into the common room with much yawning and stretching, breakfast was over.

"Slug-a-bed!" Valentin laughed, getting up from the table where he had been playing cards with Boisrobert. "I thought we would have to leave without you!" He put his arms around her and kissed her.

She buried her face in his neck. "We left the horse at the end of the lane," she whispered. "Joseph can fetch it when he gets the others." She turned and curtsied politely to the noblemen. "Good morrow, messieurs!

Have you left us any breakfast? I cannot speak for Hortense, but as for myself I am famished! Valentin, my sweet, I had the strangest dream!"

They set out at last with Boisrobert's party, reaching the outskirts of Sancerre early in the afternoon. There was a crossroads. Boisrobert pointed to one fork. "Our…hunting is in this direction."

Valentin urged his horse to the other road. "Then we leave you here. This is the road to Sancerre."

"Alas," said the duc. "We are not to be parted as yet. You will notice that my men have drawn their pistols. I assure you, my fine companions, this is not a joke. I am empowered, by the authority given to me by the cardinal, to hold you as possible traitors to the crown."

"You're mad!" said Valentin. "On what proofs?"

"The proofs will not be long in coming. You will please to follow me. All of you." He turned to one of his men-at-arms. "Arsène. You are to guard the strollers' wagon while we pay a visit to our friend, Monsieur le Comte. The actress," he indicated Colombe, "and her infant may stay here. Oh, and one more thing, Arsène. Search their belongings for political pamphlets. Mazarin has a particular interest in seeing that the *nouvellistes*—those journalists of the clandestine press—are eradicated."

Garouffière smiled at Valentin. "I pray Arsène finds something, monsieur. It would bring me great joy to see you imprisoned, flogged, exiled. And your charming wife would need protection to save her from the same fate."

"We are loyal subjects of His Majesty," Ninon said coldly. "We have nothing to fear."

They rode in silence for the better part of an hour, the actors guarded by Boisrobert's men, the noblemen following behind. When they reached a fine château nestled among the trees, the duc demanded to see Monsieur le Comte de St. Gregoire. The men-at-arms prodded the strollers up a marble staircase to the wide *galerie* where St. Gregoire received them all.

"Will you explain the meaning of this, messieurs?" said St. Gregoire. "I scarcely think this is a friendly visit."

Boisrobert eyed him coldly. "You will please to send for Henri Targon."

The comte shrugged and clapped his hands, summoning a footman who was dispatched to find Targon.

"While we wait, monsieur," said Boisrobert, "I should like to ask a question or two. In the king's name. Take care you do not add perjury to your other crimes. Now. You received a message this morning?"

St. Gregoire hesitated. "I…yes. It was a private letter. I destroyed it."

"Sweet Jesu!" said Valentin angrily. "What has all this to do with us? You have carried us out of our way, searched our belongings, insulted us…and for what? That you may ask this man here about a letter?"

Henri Targon stood in the doorway. If his father could see him now, he thought. Upholding the king, playing a major part in the downfall of traitors! He raised an arm dramatically and pointed to Joseph. "A letter which *that* man, messieurs, gave me only yesterday!"

"My God, Joseph, is this so?" demanded Valentin.

Joseph began to blubber. "I know not what was in the letter. It was sealed! A man gave it me…in Bourges…he accosted me in the theater… said that if I went to a certain tavern in Angillon…and sat with a book he gave me…a messenger would pick up the letter. He gave me two crowns. That's all I know. I swear it, my lord!"

Garouffière sneered. "Your pretended innocence will not save you…nor your fellow conspirators!"

"We are here for justice, René," said Boisrobert, "not vengeance. If these men are guilty, the courts will decide." He turned to Targon. "Do you have the letter?"

"I do, monsieur."

St. Gregoire looked startled. "What? Henri? Did I not give you the letter to burn? Have you been in my employ all these years to betray me?"

"I do not serve traitors," said Targon, drawing himself up with righteous anger. "I serve my king! The letter, monsieur." He handed a crumpled piece of paper to Boisrobert.

"I swear we are loyal!" cried Joseph.

"We shall see." Boisrobert unfolded the letter and smoothed it out. "'I pray this message reaches you in time,'" he began, reading aloud. "'We cannot see each other again. It becomes too dangerous.'"

"It has always been too dangerous to plot against the king," said Garouffière, obviously enjoying the expressions of fear on the faces of the actors.

Boisrobert threw him an angry glance. "May I continue with the letter? 'We shall have to find other means of communicating. I do not trust your messenger. And my…husband…grows suspicious. But oh, my dearest love…'" Boisrobert looked up in consternation. "What the devil is this?"

"Go on with the letter," said Garouffière.

"I…I cannot! The damned thing is filled with sighs…and kisses… and protestations of undying love…"

"And how is it signed?"

Boisrobert looked pained. "'Your sweet turtledove.'"

Chanteclair began to chuckle. "For shame, Joseph. To be the instrument for an illicit romance!"

St. Gregoire indicated the door, his mouth set in a hard line. "I trust, Monsieur le Duc, that you will not besmirch the lady's honor further by demanding to know her name. As for you, Targon, you are quit of my service!"

"Wait!" said Garouffière, unwilling to lose his quarry. "Is there any possibility the letter was replaced with another?"

Targon shook his head. "Certainly not, monsieur! I rode straight from Angillon to Monsieur le Comte. And the letter never left my person." He frowned, as though he was remembering something.

"*Mon Dieu!*" said Ninon brightly. "The man thought he was on the king's business! You cannot think to accuse him of carelessness. Not on the *king's* business! Is it not so, Monsieur Targon?"

Targon put the nagging thought behind him. "Indeed, madame, indeed."

"Now," Valentin said coldly, "if you will allow us to proceed on our way…?"

"With my apologies, monsieur," said Boisrobert. "I cannot think how we could have erred so greatly, René."

"I can," said Ninon, turning to Garouffière, her blue eyes like ice. "It was all because of a kiss you could not have!"

Chapter Eleven

January was bitterly cold, with a north wind that howled and piled the snow in drifts against the doorways and windowsills. They stayed in country inns, huddled around the fireplace, and counted out their meager coins, eating less grandly so they might stay an extra day, an extra week. When there seemed to be a break in the weather, they rented a few horses and moved on to the next town, playing in drafty barns and old theaters for as long as they could attract audiences.

Jamie spoke longingly of Italy and its sunshine, and Colombe cursed Valentin for not having followed Monsieur Molière to Paris, and fame and fortune. Only the frequent appearances of "Grandmère" raised the spirits of the company when the evenings were cold and the wolves bayed loudly beyond the tavern windows.

Marie-Anne began to cough and cry fitfully through the cold nights. Colombe swore she would give up the brat for foster care as soon as they had played in a village that paid well and she could afford a nurse.

"Damn the lot of you," she said one night, when Marc-Antoine had gone off for the fourth time to look in on the child. "You, Sébastien! Chanteclair...Joseph. You're all responsible. She might be your child. I cannot see why you won't pay to have her boarded out. The lot of you!"

"Your mother's heart touches me," said Valentin. "She might be Gaston's as well!"

Colombe sneered. "That impotent old fool?"

Chanteclair looked at her with disgust. "But if that 'impotent old fool' were here, I have no doubt you would ask him for money as well."

"Plague take you! I..." Colombe looked up at the doorway. "Marc-Antoine, you shittlebrain! What ails you?" Marc-Antoine stood on the threshold, his large body shaking uncontrollably, a torrent of tears pouring down his cheeks.

"Sweet Madonna," whispered Ninon, leaping to her feet. "Marie-Anne?"

"She…she was so still…I thought she was s-s-sleeping…it was only a bit of a fever…such a little thing…" He sank to the floor, sobbing, as Ninon rushed to put her arms around him and Hortense went off to look at the child. Valentin poured a large cup of wine and brought it to the prostrate Marc-Antoine.

Hortense returned to the room white-faced. She nodded. "'Tis true. The babe is dead."

Colombe began to wail and beat at her breast, accusing them all of caring more for Marc-Antoine's feelings than her own. "Am I not the mother?" she shrieked. "And without a crown to bury the poor thing!" She swung around the room, pointing accusingly at the men. "You would not give a sol when your child was alive! Now you shall pay to bury her! Damn you all!" She refused to be comforted until they had reached into their pockets to find what money they could spare for poor Marie-Anne; only then did she allow Jamie to lead her, sobbing, to her room.

In the morning, she was gone. With Jamie, her trunks and boxes of clothing, and Valentin's sword. And the money they had given her for Marie-Anne. Still distraught, Marc-Antoine sold his only pair of boots to pay the local curé for the child's funeral rites and burial in consecrated ground.

"Good riddance to the bitch," Valentin said bitterly. "She'll drag Jamie to Paris with her, I have no doubt."

"Aye," said Chanteclair. "Until she finds someone better. Or richer."

Toinette shook her yellow curls. "But Jamie can't go to Paris!"

"Wherefore not?"

"Well…he told me it was not his fault, of course. But…he quarreled…an angry husband, he said. A madman."

"Alas! Poor Jamie," said Chanteclair with mock sympathy.

"What happened?"

"I'm sure he was not to blame. He's such a gentle man."

"Good God, Toinette!" said Hortense in exasperation. "After all this time, you can still speak well of the knave?"

"What happened to the angry husband?" asked Valentin.

"Jamie killed him. It was a fair fight, he said. A fair fight!"

Chanteclair began to laugh. "No wonder Jamie was so fearful of Boisrobert, and arrest! Poor Colombe. The final irony. If she stays with Jamie, she'll find herself in Italy, and farther away from Paris than ever!"

• • •

Late in January they played at Montargis, north of Bourges, on the road to Paris. As usual, Valentin grumbled about being so close to the capital, but Chanteclair, who had gone ahead to arrange their performance, was strangely elated. Ninon found him copying love poems from a book—which he was at great pains to hide from her. And at their first performance at Montargis she thought she saw, in the gallery of the *jeu de paume*, the young noblewoman he had spoken to in the theater at Bourges.

They performed with some difficulty. To begin with, they were now reduced to eight players—Val, Joseph, Sébastien, Marc-Antoine, and Chanteclair, and the three women, Ninon, Hortense, and Toinette. They were forced to eliminate a few plays from their repertoire, and double up on one or two parts in others, changing back and forth from one character's costume to another. And they had not the money to hire competent scenemen, but contented themselves with vagrants who were only too happy to lend a hand for a crown or two.

The *jeu de paume* at Montargis was old and in need of repair. The platform stage they built wobbled slightly on the warped floor, and the room was dim and badly vented. The more oil lamps and candles they needed for illumination, the more smoky became the stage, and the more unbearable the stench of the tallow. They eased it somewhat by using aromatic oils in the lamps, but by the end of each performance the company was gasping for fresh air, their eyes red and watery. They played mostly farces and pastorals. Though the audiences were more sophisticated this close to Paris, they found that laughter was all that kept everyone's mind from the numbing cold.

It was a dim afternoon, the sky overcast and dull. They were playing the tart scene, with Ninon and Joseph on their ladders behind the upstairs windows. Valentin, staggering drunkenly below, was playing more broadly than usual, exaggerating his movements so he could be seen despite the heavy smoke. Pretending to stumble, he fell against the wall of Ninon's "house"; the painted set piece, badly propped by an inexperienced sceneman, began to sway dangerously on the lopsided stage. Ninon felt it pushing against the ladder, and attempted to scramble down from her perch, while Valentin cried a warning below. But it was too late. With a crash, the scenery toppled backward, sending Ninon and the ladder flying to the stage. Stunned, she lay there for a moment, then smiled reassuringly to Valentin. She was just struggling to her feet when a searing pain tore through her. She felt as though her insides had given way. Dropping to her knees, she was horrified to see a great gout of blood staining her skirts, as waves of pain and nausea swept her. Her body shook all over and her teeth began to chatter, while she fought to keep the blackness from engulfing her. An ashen-faced Valentin shouted for the curtain to be closed, then wrapped her in a cloak and sped with her to the inn while Sébastien hurried to find a doctor or midwife.

He's glad, she thought, seeing Valentin's scowling face through the mists. He's glad. He would not have welcomed the child. *Ah Dieu!* Was she always to be a fool, letting her heart trust and hope, only to be brought to despair? Despite herself, she had begun to care about him, had begun already to love the child that had been in her womb. Would she never learn? All was ashes. She lay back on the pillow as Valentin bent over her, and let herself drift into unconsciousness. It felt like death—freezing her brain, numbing her heart.

"Her name is Dorothé. She's seventeen." Chanteclair unrolled a back-cloth at the rear of the stage and indicated the painted scene to Valentin. "Do you want the castle of Jerusalem for tomorrow?"

"No. The paint is beginning to crack. Let's have the streets of Seville instead. Does Dorothé have another name?"

"Des Loches."

Valentin whistled through his teeth. "Nobility?"

Chanteclair smiled ruefully. "'Tis my misfortune."

"And you met her in Bourges."

"Yes. She was visiting a cousin for Saint Martin's Fête."

"And here in Montargis?"

"She has an aunt. But she has gone home now. Her father's estates are near to Nemours."

"And you love her, I suppose," said Valentin.

"I had not thought it was possible. But…yes."

"And so we have been dragged across half of France while you pursued your heart. Does she love you?"

"I think so. She has given me…proofs of her affection."

"In bed?"

"Damn you, no! She is a woman of great virtue. But I think she loves me. Despite the difference in our stations. I hope to see her again at Nemours. I know you don't like to be near to Paris…but I had thought, in the spring…"

"We shall speak of it when spring comes," said Valentin, frowning.

Chanteclair laughed shortly. "What do you fear from Paris and the cities? Do you hide from a crime? A dead man, as Jamie did?" He had meant it as a joke, but the look on Valentin's face gave him pause. Quickly he turned and rolled up the back-cloth. "At any rate, we cannot travel until Ninon is stronger."

"True enough." Valentin moved a chair on the stage, slamming it down angrily. "Damn the minx! It makes my blood boil to think she did not tell me of the child! I can only guess she said nothing because it was Froissart's. At least she seems to be taking the loss well."

Chanteclair shook his head. "Either you are blind, or you know little about her heart. 'Tis not natural, the way she has behaved these past weeks. Good God, man, she has not wept! Not a tear, not a drop. Even that cold bitch Colombe grieved a little at the loss of her child! I have not seen Ninon so sad-eyed and silent since first she came to us at Marival."

Valentin rubbed at his eyes. "I *must* be a fool. I thought perhaps she did not care."

"And she insists on leaving her sickbed and playing tomorrow?"

"And rehearsing today. But I have sent a chair to bring her here."

In a while, the rest of the players began to drift into the *jeu de paume*, Ninon at the last, seated in a wicker chair that was attached to two long poles and carried by four men. She looked pale and drawn, still suffering the effects of the fever that had racked her after the miscarriage. She nodded to the others and they began the rehearsal. Though she knew her lines well, she played listlessly, her voice a soft monotone, her eyes lacking their usual sparkle.

Valentin watched her for a while, scowling, then planted himself before her, arms crossed against his chest. "Do you think to earn our sympathy by playing in so dispirited a fashion?"

She gasped as though he had struck her across the face. "Go to the devil," she breathed.

"Sweet Jesu," he sneered. "Women suffer miscarriages every day of the week! Is it in their natures to need pity?"

"Valentin, I must protest!" cried Marc-Antoine, rushing forward to put his arm around Ninon.

Sanscoeur pushed him roughly away. "Leave the foolish jade alone! She will have you running her errands next, if she can. There's not a trick that's unknown to a woman!"

Ninon turned away from him, feeling her facade, her carefully constructed wall, beginning to crumble. "I shall not rehearse today," she said unsteadily.

"And when you make a fool of yourself upon the stage tomorrow, will you beg the audience to forgive your woman's weakness? *Mon Dieu!* I shall have Joseph put on a gown and play your role! He cannot do it better, but at least he will not be dead upon the stage!"

She fled at that, seeking the sanctuary of the changing room. Valentin's face was like stone; at the sound of muffled sobbing, he sagged against the chair, drained. He turned to Chanteclair. "Is that what was needed, my friend?"

"Fool! Do you want her to hate you? Go to her!"

He took the stairs two at a time, finding Ninon huddled on the floor in a corner of the room, her knees drawn up to her chest. He knelt beside her and pulled her into his embrace, holding her tightly as her body shook with grief and her tears drenched his shoulder. "Forgive me," he said gently. "I could think of no other way." Murmuring soothingly, he held her until she could cry no more. Then he wiped the tears from her face and gathered her into his arms, carrying her back to their room at the inn. He sat at the table with her, called for wine, and urged her to drink. His fingers played absently with his glass; he stirred in his chair, feeling awkward and foolish.

"Ninon…I…I have been thinking much of late…I have no wish to beget a bastard. A child without a father is a sorry thing." He laughed bitterly. "Half a person. Like the wraiths we represent upon the stage. If… if you conceive again, you must tell me at once, and we shall be married."

"For the sake of the child?"

"Yes."

Ninon bit her lip and looked at him. Why not marry him, if it should come to that? He had not been dishonest about their relationship when first they had embarked on it; he was not dishonest now. For the sake of the child. That was all. She herself knew the griefs of a bastard birth—she would have married Mathieu Couteau to prevent the same thing. And in spite of Valentin's gruff manner, there was a gentleness in him. However clumsily, he had made her cry on purpose, to ease the pain that had numbed her since the loss of the baby. Why not marry him, indeed? She would hold her heart more tightly, that was all, so life—and Valentin—could not hurt her.

"Well?" he said, then scowled as the servant girl came into the room. "We need no more wine," he growled.

"No, monsieur. But a letter came for you this morning…" She held out the missive.

"Damn!" he cried. "Burn it!"

"But, monsieur…"

"Burn it, I say! And any other letter that might come for me!" She curtsied quickly and then fled. Valentin turned back to Ninon, his eyes like black coals. "Well?" he said again.

She hesitated, seeing the anger, the flash of hatred that glinted in his eyes.

"Before you agree to a marriage," he said, "I would expect you to put aside all thoughts of your Philippe forevermore. I should not like to think that he could snap his fingers whenever he chose, and have you as his mistress. I may be a fool. I shall not be a cuckold. Nor would I welcome seeing him in your eyes."

What was she thinking of? There it was, writ clear across his face. The old hatred. The old mistrust. He offered her nothing, save a name for a child that might be; he demanded all. Not only faithfulness and virtue, but an undivided heart. His alone. To be spurned and treated with contempt if he wished—but his alone. "It is best we not speak of marriage," she said coldly. "I cannot promise I would not leave you if Philippe needed me."

"Then I withdraw the offer."

"I give you leave to do so."

"So long as we understand each other."

She sighed, feeling suddenly exhausted. "We always did," she said. She stood up. "I am too weary to play tomorrow. You shall have to do without me." She moved slowly to the bed and lay down, welcoming the sleep that followed.

"The armorer is down that street, Val." Hortense licked the pastry cream from her fingers and pointed to a narrow lane. "The *pâtissier* says he is the finest in all of Montargis."

Valentin nodded. "If he has a sword to suit me, it should not take all that long."

Hortense smacked her lips, savoring the last of the confection. "May *le bon Dieu* bless the good people of Montargis, and their esteem for the theater! I have not had an extra crown for a sweet in months."

"Nor I for a new rapier, plague take Jamie and his thievery! Have you more errands before we return to the others at the inn?"

"Toinette wanted a new petticoat, and Ninon's shoes need a cobbler."

Valentin frowned. "Show me." He turned over the pair of shoes that Hortense handed him, swearing under his breath at the large holes, the cracked leather. "Has she no other pair?" Hortense shook her head. "Damn!" he muttered. "These can't be mended properly. Why doesn't she buy new?"

"She spent her money on a warm cloak instead."

He shook out a handful of coins from a small pouch and counted them carefully. "I can buy her a new pair...But she is so distant of late, so strange. I scarce think she would accept them from me."

"'Tis her birthday next week. Didn't you know? She'll be nineteen. You can give the shoes as a gift. But what will you do for a sword?"

He laughed ruefully. "I promise I shall kill no one this month! And if we play Sens at Carnival time, I shall have the means for several rapiers."

Hortense put a soft hand on his arm. "You must not mind Ninon's strangeness. She grieves for the child, that's all. And 'tis a good thing. Her mood will pass in time." She looked at him quizzically. "But I wonder *you* do not grieve."

"Sweet Jesu, why should I? I feel pity for Ninon, of course. But for aught I know, the child was begot by her lover in Marival."

"Oh, you fool! What lover?"

"Why...Monsieur le Comte...or...there was a bumpkin she was to marry...I..."

"Oh-h-h!" Hortense was beside herself. "How can you hate women when you know so little about them? Have you never had a virgin before?"

"A *virgin?*"

"That day in Troyes...before the performance...she was at the stream, washing her bloody sheets."

"*Mon Dieu,*" he whispered, and turned away, making for the row of shops at the far end of the street. They managed to persuade the cobbler to fix Ninon's shoes as well as he could, and bought a new pair for her as well, using the old for a measurement.

Valentin was silent on the long walk back to their inn, his cloak bundled to his ears, his shoulders hunched up against the cold day. It was beginning to snow. In the communal bedchamber the troupe was gathered around the fireplace, roasting chestnuts and drinking hot wine, an unaccustomed treat after the months of scrimping.

Only Ninon sat alone, in a large elbow chair drawn up to the window, her shoeless feet tucked under her for warmth. She was sewing, embroidering a handkerchief, the flowers of spring blooming under her skillful hands. She started as the needle pricked her finger, then frowned and dabbed at the drop of blood on the snowy linen.

Watching her from across the room, Valentin cursed his own stupidity. A virgin. He had never thought, never dreamed…It had pleased him to think her no better than a whore, to think there were no chaste women in all of God's earth. He had mocked Philippe to her, deriding his clumsy wooing, his selfish desires. But Philippe, whatever his hungers, had not violated her. That was why she had left Marival—because she *was* virtuous. Valentin should have realized it. A whore would have stayed.

He sighed, watching her as she worked, silhouetted against the window and the soft fall of snow beyond. She was as pure as that snow, with her solemn face and sad eyes, as fragile and lovely as the flowers she embroidered. And he had stained that purity. Like the drop of blood on the linen. Once spilled, it could not be taken back.

She had called him a brute once. God forgive him, it was so. He had taken what he wanted—first by force, and then with a seductive reasoning that was more false than even that which Jamie had used. He had wanted her. And so he had beguiled her willing body, ignoring her feelings, ignoring the bitter tears she wept into her pillow for a man she loved, ignoring all save his own need.

And he had brought her nothing but grief. The child had been his. And the accident. His the clumsiness in crashing into the scenery. And his the stupid thrift. If he had not been so eager to save a crown or two, that dangerous stage and scenery might have been secured by a proper carpenter.

Well, he had done enough mischief. He would visit no more grief upon her. She deserved better in life. There would be no more miscarriages to break her heart. And no more the thoughtless lover to remind her what she had lost with Philippe.

They would be traveling on in a few days. At the new inn he would move in with Chanteclair and Marc-Antoine. They had slept three to a bed before; they could do it again.

But he would no longer bear the burden of Ninon's grief on his conscience. He had too much to atone for already in this world.

"Think of it this way, Val. We can now consider ourselves true mountebanks." Chanteclair smiled ruefully as he helped the workmen arrange the rows of long benches.

"Have a care," growled Valentin, as the large platform stage was placed over the benches—hence the name "mountebank," from the

Italian *monta in banco*. He looked around at the open marketplace of Sens, his handsome features twisted in distaste. "To think we must play in the open air, like common *forains*, crude actors of the fairs!"

"Why trouble ourselves? 'Tis Carnival," said Sébastien. "We can make a deal of money wherever we play."

"But we had been promised to share the theater with the local company. Was it not agreed, Chanteclair? And the fee paid?"

"Indeed. With all rights to use music and spectacle. And permission to act any type of play we chose, with the exception of tragedy. Their leading actor, I am given to understand, fancies himself another Montfleury, of the Théâtre de Bourgogne in Paris."

"Then why have they rescinded the rights at the last moment? Forced us out into the streets?"

"Jealousy, I suppose. They have heard of our success in Montargis, no doubt."

"Plague take them all!" Valentin fell to cursing, kicking savagely at a bench with his foot.

Watching with the other women, Ninon sighed. She had had enough. "Unless you need me, Valentin, I shall wander a bit in the marketplace."

He glared at her, his eyes like cold steel. "Only be sure you know your lines."

She shrugged and turned on her heel, making for the booths and trestle tables that were being set up for the month-long season of Carnival before Lent and Easter. She could not even talk to him. He was the Valentin of old—angry, impatient, impossible. But now it seemed as though the anger was meant for her alone. His passion had run its course, and now his hatred of her seemed deeper than his hatred for womankind in general.

She paused at a booth and admired the carved trinkets and boxes displayed there. Moving on, she considered the purchase of a bit of lace, and sniffed at a vial of perfume. A runny-nosed urchin with a stack of handbills pressed one into her fingers. It was an advertisement for a new drink that was beginning to find favor, particularly in England. It "brightens the spirits," said the handbill, "and makes the heart gladsome." It claimed to be a fine cure for sore eyes, dropsy, gout, and scurvy, neither laxative nor restringent. There was even a picture of a smiling man drinking this new potion, which had been brought to England from Turkey. It was called coffee.

Ninon smiled sadly. Could this wonder of a drink cure *her* malady? For she still craved him, with waves of desire that swept over her each time he touched her, even upon the stage. He had lit a flame within her body—it would take time to quench the hungry spark.

And she could not talk to Chanteclair about it. How could she explain what she herself did not understand? That a man who could not touch her heart could rule her flesh, make her ache with longing. Besides, Chanteclair was not himself anymore. Lovesick and distracted, he burned with a desire that had yet to be fulfilled, contenting himself with long, impassioned letters to his Dorothé.

She sighed. Welladay! This had not been what she had expected as an actress. But perhaps it was in the very nature of the life, the impermanence of place, of emotions. Wasn't Joseph sleeping with the innkeeper's sister, and Toinette earning a few extra livres on her back as Colombe had done? And neither of them seemed to mind that they now slept apart.

The life of an actor. It was over with Valentin. Cold and dead. Best to forget the feel of his mouth, the warmth of his body. It was over.

They played the next afternoon in the open fair, earning such success that their rivals, who held the acting monopoly in Sens, were filled with rage. They could not forbid the Peerless Theatre Company to act in the town, particularly if the local officials had already issued the permits, but they had the right to control what was played. The very next morning the company of Sens obtained an injunction prohibiting dialogues, tirades, monologues, songs—in short, every form of spoken business upon the stage.

Undaunted, Valentin had scrolls of explanatory verses printed up; unfurled from the wings and back-cloth, they explained to the audience the plot and action as the strollers acted out their plays in mime. It was a technique being tried only here and there in France, to thwart the monopolistic local companies, but the spectators were enchanted with the novelty of it. The Peerless Theatre Company played *The Imaginary Cuckold* in silence, and although the scene with the box was difficult to convey without words, the fight in the kitchen, with slapstick and plates, was almost more successful than when they had put words to it.

Valentin was elated, and swore henceforth that the scene should be played in mime. The acting company of Sens, finding themselves outwitted and outacted by the Peerless troupe, agreed to share their theater during Carnival, giving them alternate days, and secretly hoped that they would draw patrons who were expecting to see the much-acclaimed Peerless group.

By the time Carnival was drawing to a close, Valentin's troupe had earned a great deal of money. Marc-Antoine had bought himself a new pair of boots, and a hat more flamboyant than the one Pierre had stolen; Valentin had found a fine rapier of Toledo steel. And Sébastien discovered he had more money than even he could gamble away. They moved to the finest inn in Sens, a large, thatch-roofed building set on the edge of the town, nestled up against the remains of the Roman walls that had been built when Sens had been one of the largest cities in ancient Gaul.

It was a bright night. Ninon sat up in bed, the light of the full moon streaming through her small casement window. A small window, a small room…a small bed. Now that she slept alone, she did not need a large chamber; her room was just under the eaves. A cozy room. She would have thought she could sleep easily in such a room, but night after night she tossed and turned on her straw pallet, her insides curdling with desire and torment, until she dreaded the loneliness of her bed. And now with the moon…she would never sleep this night.

She got out of bed and slipped into her shoes. Her new shoes, a gift from Valentin. The last kind thing he had done before…She could not even curse him. He had been characteristically honest and direct. I don't wish a bastard, he had said. You don't want a marriage, child or no. 'Tis best that we end our arrangement. And then he had not been able to resist the bit of malice, his mouth twisted with sarcasm.

"I dislike thinking that I might have kept you from dreams of your Philippe every moment of the day. I give you back to him…little bird."

She sighed and wrapped herself in her warm cloak. It must be on to midnight, she thought. She tiptoed across the room and made her way down the stairs of the inn. It was very still, save for the sound of snoring behind one closed door. The courtyard of the inn was bathed in light, the large hay wagon filled with threads of silver. The ancient, moss-covered wall cast a black shadow that stretched across one side of the yard. She breathed deeply. It was warm for March, the air filled with the rich scent of thawing earth. Time to plant peas and cabbages. Tomorrow was Shrove Monday; they would not play. Perhaps she would offer to help the innkeeper's wife with the planting. She had forgotten the joy of a garden, watching the first seedlings appear, glorying in the fruits of one's own labor.

But she was an actress, a homeless wanderer now. Someone else would enjoy her plantings. She gulped back a tear, then jumped at a sudden noise in the shadows.

"Who's there?" she whispered.

A figure emerged from the darkness. "'Tis I, Chanteclair. Is that you, Ninon?"

"Yes. I…I could not sleep."

"And you came to seek solace of the moon."

She bowed her head, feeling overcome. He took her by the hand and led her to a small bench, urging her to sit beside him.

"Poor Ninon," he said. "We should have named you Madame Tristesse, for those sad eyes."

"Don't," she choked. "You must not pity me. I had forgot what it was like to be lonely…that's all. Even with a rogue like Valentin, I could forget." She sniffed and wiped her eyes. "Am I not a fool?"

He brought her fingers to his lips and kissed them gently. "There was a time I could have loved you, Ninon Guillemot, had you let me. But now…" He laughed in irony. "'Tis like a clumsily acted play. You enter upon the stage, alone at last. And I have just made my exit with another player. Or will do so shortly."

"How fortunate is your Dorothé."

"I pray we are not both doomed by this love." In the shadow of the Roman wall a horse snorted. "I had thought…well, perhaps I'm glad after all that you could not sleep. Another quarter of an hour, and I should have been gone."

"Gone? Gone where?"

"You will not need me. Lent begins in three days, and we cannot play much after that. And if all goes well, I could return after Easter."

"But where do you go?"

"To Nemours. To be near Dorothé. To see her."

"And then what?"

"I shall pay court to her. Try to persuade her father to let us marry."

"But he's a nobleman! If he's a man with any ambition for his family, he will refuse your suit. What else could he do?"

"Then we shall elope. Dorothé is a woman of such modesty and virtue, I could not take her without the Church's blessing."

"Oh, my dear Chanteclair, you speak madness!"

"No. If her father is a man of honor, he might let the marriage stand, rather than see his daughter's reputation besmirched."

"And if he will not?"

He laughed softly. "I scarce can believe it. That divine creature that I love so, that angel who should dwell in a silver palace all her days, has sworn to me that she will take another name and join me as a stroller!"

"I called you a gambler once. 'Tis true."

"But I gamble for such a great prize. Now you must not tell Valentin and the rest until morning."

"Indeed," she said bitterly. "Valentin does not believe in love."

"Valentin *does* believe in love. It is only for himself that he refuses it. If I were an ordinary man, going to an ordinary lover, he would wish me Godspeed. But I am an actor, and Dorothé is a noblewoman, and he would call me fool. And so you must not tell him tonight."

She began to weep. She had no shame with Chanteclair, no need to hide her heart from his gentleness and goodness. "Oh, Chanteclair, I shall miss you so. You have been friend, brother...so much to me that I had never known before."

He brushed a curl from her face, caressing the cheek that glowed like velvet in the moonlight. "I used to watch you sleep. Did you know that? When we spent the night along the side of the road, or in some deserted barn. I would watch you sleep and wish that you were mine. But I knew then what I know now. I can never be more to you than friend and brother."

"Oh, God..." She felt as though her heart would break.

"So then!" he said brightly. "Dry your tears and bid your brother *au revoir*, and I shall be on my way. And another thing. You might persuade the company to add the Nemours road to the itinerary. If you can manage to get there in a month or two, you shall find me the happiest man in the world...or the most despairing."

"What shall we do if we need 'Grandmère'?"

He cackled softly. "You silly goose," he said in a high falsetto. "You must teach Marc-Antoine to play the role!"

He stood up quickly and whistled to his horse, which moved out of the shadows toward them. He mounted easily and waved her a last farewell, then guided the horse to the breach in the Roman wall.

"Wait!" she said. She scrambled onto the wall, climbing across the broken boulders until she was even with him. She tugged at his sleeve so that he leaned over in the saddle, then she put her hand behind his neck and pulled his mouth to hers. She kissed him with warmth, glad to feel an answering warmth on her lips, devoid of passion. "Thank you for your gift," she said.

"What gift? Alas, I learned too late it was your birthday last month! What gift?"

"The gift of laughter," she whispered, and waved him into the black night.

Chapter Twelve

"The sky was pink tonight. It will be a fine day tomorrow." Chanteclair crossed the small room, ducking under a low beam, and placed his candle on a table near the bed. He moved quickly to the window, his footsteps rustling over the fresh sweet reeds strewn on the oak floor. He leaned out between the mullions for a moment, seeing the first star, then closed the casement against the chill of the April night. "The landlord said my horse will be saddled by half after seven." He turned to the young woman who still paused at the threshold, holding her mantle tightly about her shoulders. "Dorothé. Love," he said gently. "Do you want to return to your father's house?"

She looked up, surprised. "Oh no, Jean. Never! He's a man with no heart, no soul. I'm not sorry to leave. How could I not despise him when he said...oh, such terrible things about you."

Chanteclair laughed softly. "That I am an actor? That I am a vagabond? All that is true."

She shook her head, her elfin face solemn in the dim light. "No. That you were less a man than that villain LaPierre he wanted me to marry."

"LaPierre has money."

"LaPierre has influence," she said with contempt. "He is a member of that corrupt and voluptuous circle of courtiers who shame the nobility of France with their ways. But my father hoped to better himself through LaPierre."

"By selling you in marriage."

"'Tis done every day." She shuddered. "Yet my flesh crawls to think of the man. His first wife died. They said it was a fever. But I have heard," Dorothé crossed herself quickly, "she took her own life because she could no longer bear his depravity."

"And still you hesitate at the door."

234

"No longer." She smiled and stepped into the room, closing the door softly behind her. "A foolish thought that troubles me no more."

He crossed to her, the old inn floor creaking beneath his boots. "Will you tell me your foolish thought?"

"Soon enough."

He took her face between his hands, his fingers caressing the pink roundness of her cheeks. "My God, how I love you." He kissed her gently, pushed back the hood of her cloak, and stroked the pale brown curls at her temples. Then, overcome, he swept her into his embrace and held her close while his mouth tasted the sweetness of hers, and her lips parted to yield all to him. He stepped back at last, and turned away from her, unbuckling his sword and placing it across a bench. "I have spoken to the priest in Vauvert," he said, his voice hoarse with passion kept in check. "He was pleased to agree to marry us tomorrow. Now that Easter is past, the pious but generous frauds who thronged his church will not be seen so often. He must again depend on his bishop for that bit of *clairet* to wash down his austere bread. The fat purse I gave him has bought his compliance—and his discretion."

"What did you tell him?"

"He thinks we're both aristocrats, eloping because your family has had a serious reversal and is too ashamed of its fall to come begging to my family."

She giggled. "What a tale."

"Thanks be to God for my training as an actor. I can play a noble—*mon Dieu*, I have played kings!—and I can tell a story with great sincerity."

She frowned. "But will the marriage be legal if you give a false name?"

"Don't fret. I used my own name, Jean la Couronne. I only added a 'de.' I didn't even take a title. I called myself Chevalier de la Couronne. *Morbleu!* My mother would take a fit if she knew!" He took off his doublet, then knelt and peered under the bed. "Good. There's a truckle bed here." He stood up and smiled. "I feared I should have to be content with the hard floor."

"No." Her voice was soft and low. "I have thought about it and made my decision. I want you to be my husband tonight. I give myself to you tonight."

"Dorothé. My sweet love. Dearest flower of purity. I cannot let you do this. I can wait."

"I beg you, Jean."

He laughed lightly, trying to make a joke of it. "What would the sisters at the convent say? You must not destroy their faith in you!"

"Don't you want me?"

He groaned in agony and turned his face away. "I have done many wicked things in my life, but I cannot bear the thought of defiling you, my chaste Dorothé. I know it's contrary to all your teachings."

She knelt at his feet, throwing her arms around his legs. "Listen to me," she said. "I can make my own peace with God. When my mother died, I could not bear to stay with my father, to be witness to his corrupt ways, and those of his friends at court. *There* was evil to affront God's teachings. And so I stayed at the convent to live and study. To learn that happiness is to be taken where you find it." Her voice caught on a sob. "I found my happiness with you, Jean. I shall be your wife tomorrow. God will forgive me if, in my great joy and happiness, I cannot wait to be your lover."

He lifted her to her feet, filled with the wonder of the love he had found, and kissed her mouth and closed eyes, tasting the salt of her tears. He untied her mantle and let it fall to the floor, then unhooked the bodice of her gown.

"No," she said shyly, "let me do it." While he watched, his eyes worshipping her, she pulled off her bodice and skirt and petticoats, and laid them neatly on the bench next to his sword and doublet. Blushing a little, she lifted her chemise and unfastened her garters, then removed her shoes and stockings, and came and stood before him, her slim fingers playing nervously with the drawstring of her chemise. "Let me be a good little wife and help you off with your boots." She led him to the bed and made him sit, pulling off his boots and stockings; then she undid the button of his shirt so he might slip it over his head. Nervously she put her hands on the firm flesh of his chest and shoulders. "I...I never felt a man's body before. 'Tis a wondrous thing."

He laughed softly, afraid to trust the stability of his own voice. He felt like a virgin himself, trembling before this wondrous creature who had stolen his heart so completely and given him back a love he had never known before.

"You must tell me what I am to do next," she said, standing before him. "The sisters were not very helpful on these matters."

He pulled her to him, burying his face in her bosom, too overcome with emotion to speak. He held her tightly for a moment, then undid her chemise and pushed it down over her hips to the floor. He slipped out of his breeches and moved over on the bed, patting the sheet next to him.

She hesitated, then climbed in beside him. "I feel so foolish, so helpless. You must tell me how I am to lie—on my back, like this? Shall I touch you? Shall I..."

"Hush, hush," he whispered. "'Tis not a performance upon a stage, with the proper movements. Only let me love you. You have naught to do but take my love. I shall do the rest." He kissed her tense mouth, then began to laugh. "You may kiss me in return, if you wish, and put your arms about my neck if you are so inclined. 'Tis an improvised performance." He stroked the soft curves of her young body, feeling her tremble and quiver under his gentle caresses, then bent his mouth to her breast and teased her nipple with his tongue. She gasped in wonder, her flesh burning with his touch, her senses reeling with the strange waves that rippled through her body. At last he parted her thighs and moved on top of her, his hands sliding under her hips to bring her closer to his throbbing manhood. He felt the tenseness of her body, the sudden tightness of her muscles at the unfamiliar feeling. He started to enter her, then stopped, seeing the look on her face by the light of the dim candle. "I'm hurting you!"

"No, my love. No."

"I'm the actor, not you," he said dryly, and moved off her.

She bit her lip in dismay. "I have disappointed you."

"My foolish, sweet Dorothé. You have nothing to reproach yourself. 'Tis I who was clumsy. We shall begin again." He kissed her gently, his mouth soft on hers, his hands caressing her face and neck, until he felt her begin to relax under his tender ministrations. He deepened his kiss, his tongue exploring the corners of her mouth, the edge of her teeth. She sighed and slipped her arms about his neck, her fingers tangled in his long curls. He let his hand stray to her bosom, fondling her firm young orbs, feeling her strain against him with awakening passion. His hand moved lower, stroking the inner flesh of her thighs, gradually separating her legs as he caressed her. It seemed a natural progression. His fingers were on her thigh, then gently rubbing the guardians of her maidenhead, then slipped within her, moving in a rhythm that made her twitch with ecstasy and moan softly. When he withdrew his hand and mounted her, she let her legs fall wide in anticipation, no longer fearing the unknown. He pushed gently, feeling still a bit of resistance. "Forgive me, my love," he whispered, and plunged hard, cringing to hear her momentary gasp of pain.

"No," she breathed, her arms going around his waist to hold him close. "'Twas only a moment's grief. And oh! how sweet to feel you in me."

"Dorothé!" He deepened his thrusts, seeing the pleasure on her face, losing himself in the pleasure of her sweet body, until his own body exploded in a great drenching rush, and he collapsed against her.

She began to weep then, her overcharged heart unable to contain the emotions that shook her. "My love," she sobbed over and over, as he folded her tenderly in his embrace. "My love. My husband."

When she awoke, the room was gray with first light. Chanteclair, in his breeches, was standing at the window peering through the leaded panes. She sat up in bed. "What time is it?"

"Nearly dawn. I thought I heard a noise." He turned and smiled at her.

She dimpled prettily. "'Tis very early. Hours and hours before breakfast!"

He laughed and crossed to the bed, sitting beside her. "Brazen hussy, will you have me out of my breeches at every opportunity after we are married?"

"If I can!" She pulled his mouth down to hers, purring in contentment as he wrapped his arms about her and returned her kisses.

There was a noise on the stairs outside, and the door crashed open. Chanteclair leaped from the bed and reached for his sword, but two burly ruffians were there first, kicking away his hand from the blade and grabbing him savagely by the arms. He struggled and cursed them, until one of them dealt him a blow to the side of the head that almost rendered him unconscious. He sagged between their restraining arms, dimly aware that Dorothé had screamed, that two men stood before him. He shook the mists from his eyes and looked up.

"You villain!" The elder of the two men slapped him sharply across the face. "Would you rob me of my daughter? Did I not say you could not have her?"

Chanteclair nodded his head in mock politeness, his lip curled with contempt. "Monsieur le Baron des Loches. I had not thought to see you again." He jerked his chin in the direction of the other man, a tall nobleman with cruel eyes, who glared at him and slapped the side of his boot with his riding whip. "And this gallows-bird?"

"Monsieur le Vicomte de LaPierre, the injured bridegroom that was to be."

"Monsieur." Chanteclair's voice oozed charm. "If you will but tell these men to release me, and permit me to regain my weapon, we can settle our differences."

"Insolent cur! I don't do battle with scum!"

238

Dorothé, crouched on the bed, the sheets pulled around her naked body, found her voice. "No, you coward! You hire cutthroats to do your filthy work!"

"Hold your tongue, saucy miss!" Des Loches whirled on his daughter. "Monsieur de LaPierre is a man of great importance! He was willing to take you as his bride, despite your willful ways. You foolish jade! Had you wanted that vagabond, that useless stroller, you might have had him as a lover after your marriage to Monsieur le Vicomte!"

Dorothé gasped in horror. "*Mon Dieu!* Father! Would you have your daughter a married whore?"

"I should never have allowed you so many years in that convent. You speak like a bourgeois schoolgirl!" He smiled obsequiously at LaPierre. "Is she not a foolish child?"

"Indeed." The Vicomte crossed to the bed and laid his hand on Dorothé's bare shoulder. Chanteclair growled and struggled against the hands that held him. LaPierre smiled, his fingers playing with a curl at the girl's temple. "I have always found that many lovers make a woman more interesting in bed. More...adventuresome, *n'est-ce pas?* I should have allowed you to seek your pleasures where you might, my dear." His face darkened. "But now...you have run away...injured my pride. Still, you're a pretty little thing..."

"My good Vicomte," said des Loches effusively, "can I take your tone to mean that...despite the insult this unworthy chit has done to your honor...I might dare to hope—?"

"That a marriage can still take place?" LaPierre shrugged. "I might be persuaded to accept her, when my pride has been salved." He smiled patronizingly as des Loches sighed with relief, then he turned to Chanteclair, still straining against his captors. "But as for you, *actor,*" he spat the word, "you have cost me a deal of time and money to recover my bride. You shall pay for it!"

"I have committed no crime. I have dared to love a woman another man desired. If that were a crime, half the men of France would hang."

"True enough. 'Tis no crime. Though I could have you killed and no one would care—the law favors my class over yours. But I shall be merciful. My men will release you after we have gone. However..." his mouth curved in an evil smile, "before they do, they will see to it that you are incapable of debauching a woman ever again!"

"Father!" Dorothé shrieked. "You cannot allow this!"

Des Loches shrugged. "Whatever Monsieur le Vicomte wishes, I shall not stand in his way."

"But I carry Jean's child," she said. "Doesn't that make a difference?"

Des Loches frowned at LaPierre, clearly upset. "What's to be done? If she carries his child...she can swear it in holy church...before a court of law...Can I forbid her marriage to him then? And risk the shame of society, the dishonor to the family name?"

LaPierre began to laugh softly and pointed to the bed, indicating with his riding-crop the bloodstains on the white sheet. "If a seed was planted, it was only last night. But if I take the minx now...here...who can say, in a nine-month, that the child is not mine?"

"Damn you!" Chanteclair was beside himself, fighting to get loose.

"Mother of God," sobbed Dorothé. "Would you abandon me, Father?"

Des Loches scowled at her, his eyes cold. "Wretched child. You have disgraced me, beyond all redeeming. Only the generosity of Monsieur le Vicomte—agreeing to marry you despite your wickedness—will save our house from shame and ruin!" He turned to LaPierre. "She is yours, to do with as you wish. I shall wait below." With a last look of scorn for his daughter, he left the room.

The vicomte smiled, clearly enjoying Chanteclair's anguish. "Hold the rogue," he said to his men. "I want him to watch." His eyes swept Dorothé, cowering on her knees behind the sheets. "This is only a taste, my love, of what's to come."

She drew herself up proudly, stilling her trembling mouth. "You shall find no pleasure if you rape me, monsieur. I shall curse you to your face." She looked at Chanteclair, her eyes warm with tenderness and longing. "I have known the love of a true man. How can you harm me? I shall curse you with my every breath."

"Insolent baggage!" he cried. "Will you defy your husband that is to be? Well, then, the battle is joined." Savagely he ripped the sheet from her shaking fingers; he raised his riding crop above his head, poised over her naked body. "You'll start married life, my sweet, with a few stripes on your pretty-skin!"

Chanteclair let out a roar and tore himself free from the two men. Before they could stop him, he had snatched up his rapier and plunged it between LaPierre's shoulder blades. The vicomte gasped, sighed, and fell on his face across the bed. Chanteclair felt a blow to the back of his head, and then another. He stumbled to his knees, feeling the rain of fists and boots on his ribs and head, pounding him to the floor.

The last thing he remembered, before blackness closed in on him, was Dorothé's tearful face, and her white breast spotted with LaPierre's blood.

"Name of God, Valentin," said Sébastien, keeping pace with the other man's long strides. "Stop tormenting yourself. We shall be in Nemours in another two or three weeks. Time enough to discover how goes Chanteclair's suit."

"I like it not. Easter is long past, and we have had but one letter. If only I had been able to stop him from going. I could strangle Ninon for not telling me!"

"She meant well. And it was Chanteclair's wish."

"What a fool! She thought his mad scheme brave and sweet. She's a simple-minded romantic who still dreams of true love and noble heroes."

Sébastien laughed. "*Eh bien!* She did not find one in you! Is that why she left your bed?"

Valentin whirled to him, his eyes like black coals. "She left my bed because *I* wished it!"

Sébastien opened the back door of the theater and began climbing the stairs to the changing room. "Then tell me, my friend," he said softly, "why you are so out of temper since she has been sleeping without you. Were I in your shoes, I should beat the wench soundly and take her to bed. Put a stop to her willful ways."

"Mayhap I don't want her," growled Valentin.

"Mayhap you lie. Or, rather, you *wish* to lie…with her!"

"For the sake of our friendship," said Valentin, pushing open the changing room door, "hold your tongue. Save your wit for the stage."

About to step out of her skirts, Ninon looked up as they entered. "Ah, Valentin," she said, her eyes wide with mock innocence, "today you wear your half-angry mask. What an improvement over yesterday's scowl!"

"Your tongue grows sharper with each passing day," he said. "'Tis remarkable how quickly a woman can transform into a shrew."

She shrugged in indifference and stepped out of her skirts, then unhooked the bodice of her gown. "I see no reason to be pleasant," she said.

"Ah yes. With your gallant Chanteclair gone, there is no one to cosset you, make you think you are a fine lady in a château."

"Chanteclair was a gentleman."

He smiled, one eyebrow arched in mockery. "*I* am a gentleman. When I find a lady who's worth the effort!"

"Plague take you," she hissed, and swung at him. He clutched at her wrist, his hand wrapping about hers. They glared at each other for long moments, then he released her, as though her very touch burned him.

"If 'Sylvie' misses her cue this afternoon," he said through clenched teeth, "I swear I shall stop the performance and rebuke you before the whole audience!"

"*Mon Dieu!*" said Hortense, poking at Valentin's sleeve. "Go away and get into your costume. I vow you two put Sébastien and me to shame!"

Ninon whirled away from them and pulled off the rest of her outer garments, stripping down to her chemise. She felt like the strings of a lute, stretched to the breaking point. She could not eat, she could not sleep. She hated him. She wanted him. Oh, God, she thought, how long could they go on this way, rubbing each other raw? He hated her, that was clear. He had taken her into his bed, into his heart (as much as he would allow), and now he was reproaching himself for his weakness, making her pay for his brief lapse.

She looked up. Two elegant noblemen had strolled into the changing room; after a pause to survey the three actresses, they ambled up to Ninon. She smiled falsely. It was common for the young idlers to come and watch the women change into their costumes. There was very little that could be done about it. If a cavalier was treated rudely in the changing room, he might be disposed to hiss and boo the actress when she appeared upon the stage, thereby turning the whole audience against her. It meant being pelted with candle ends, fruit pits, and orange skins, and sometimes being driven off the stage entirely. Quickly Ninon reached for the shimmering gauze gown she was to wear as "Sylvie," ignoring the eyes that swept over her brief chemise and seemed to strip the garment from her.

"Oh. Wait a moment. Upon my word. Let me look at you, goddess, just as you are!" One of the noblemen leered at her, lifting an eyeglass to one eye. A silly fop, she thought, from the blond curly wig he wore to the ribbon bows on his high-heeled shoes.

"For shame, monsieur," she chided. "Have a little respect for my modesty!" She slipped the gown over her head, then presented her back to him. "But you may lace up my bodice for me!" Grinning, he complied, his hands lingering on her waist.

His companion, a short cavalier with a tall hat, grumbled at Ninon's choice and went off to seek solace with Toinette, who was only too glad to let him fondle her breast for the price of a supper after the performance. Ninon sat down and proceeded to change her stockings, while her suitor crouched before her, admiring her ankles and hoping for a glance up the front of her skirt.

She smiled uncomfortably at his scrutiny and slipped into her shoes. "Chéroy is a charming village," she said, by way of making conversation. She straightened her hair and placed a crown of silk flowers on her curls.

"I find it so," he said, sniffing at his lace handkerchief. "Will you take supper with me?"

She contrived to look helpless. "I cannot think now, when my head is filled with my parts."

"Pox take me, but I should like to fill you with *my* parts!"

"You wicked sir!" She stood up, smoothing her skirts. "Do you live here in Chéroy?"

He shook his head. "No. Merely visiting. I come from Dijon."

Valentin strode over to them, in the costume of a court jester, his face white with paint. "Your pardon, monsieur," he said coldly. "While I hate to disturb your traffic with this jade, I must tell you the play begins in a moment. Please be so kind as to find your seat out front."

"But the lady has not answered my question. Will you sup with me, my charming flower?"

"The company sups together, monsieur," said Valentin, indicating the door.

"Wait!" Ninon put a hand on the gentleman's beribboned sleeve. He came from Dijon. It was months since she had received Philippe's letter. She longed to know if he was well, if he was happy. And this man came from Dijon. Surely he must know Philippe. She smiled coyly. "Where shall we meet, monsieur?"

He beamed in pleasure. "The Sign of the Brown Cow."

"Till then," she said, and pushed him gently through the door to the theater.

Valentin eyed her with contempt. "You're getting more like Colombe every day."

"'Tis none of your concern. I don't belong to you." She laughed sharply. "I'm only surprised you no longer call me whore. Is it that you've changed your opinion of me? Or that my whoredom is so confirmed in your mind that it's no longer worthy of your notice?"

"Don't take supper with that coxcomb."

"Go to the devil."

They played the pastoral in a state of war, Valentin taking every opportunity to criticize her performance each time they were backstage, Ninon deliberately confusing her lines so he missed his cues and appeared a clumsy fool on the stage. They managed to get through it at last, receiving much applause in spite of everything. They hurried to the changing room while the scenemen put out new wings and a back-cloth that represented a village street on one side, and a kitchen on the other. Several chairs and benches were set in place, as well as a kitchen table laid with saucepans and pots and the breakaway plates. They were playing *The Imaginary Cuckold*, or *The Jealous Vicomte*, as the day's farce.

Ninon put on her gray skirt and sleeveless jerkin, pulling down the neckline of her chemise to an immodest level, and shook free her chignon, letting her copper curls run riot. She ignored Valentin, who glared at her from across the changing room as he savagely wiped the paint from his face and replaced it with his comic half-mask with its sharply pointed false nose. Of shaped leather, it covered most of his face—forehead, temples, cheeks. Only his mouth and chin were uncovered to allow him to be heard clearly.

She hesitated, unwilling to speak to him even to discuss the business of the stage, then crossed the room to where he stood buckling on a sword harness and slipping his slapstick into it. "Shall we play the kitchen scene in mime? As we did in Sens?"

"I think so," he said coldly. "The lines are useless in any event, when the audience is laughing." His lip curled in an ugly smile. "But since we improvise anyway, I give you leave to insert in the first scene a brazen speech or two, directed to your gallant, your supper partner. Or would you prefer me to speak up and play the procurer, and arrange his entertainment for *after* supper?"

"My God!" she breathed with contempt. "You're as jealous as the cuckolded vicomte in the play. But you gave up your right to dictate to me months ago—if indeed you *ever* had the right! I do as I choose! And if I choose to dance naked before that man, I shall do so! Now get out of my way."

"You shameless strumpet! Will you warm every bed in Chéroy?"

"Where was your concern for my shame when I warmed *your* bed?" she asked, and was glad to see him flinch.

Then he shrugged. "I had no more scruples on that score than had your Philippe. At least I took you in a bed. I would not have deflowered you in a barn, on a pile of hay—as he seemed willing to do." He laughed cruelly at the look of surprise on her face. "Yes. I knew you were a virgin. Did you think I didn't?"

It was too much. She turned on her heel and stormed from the changing room, gnashing her teeth in fury. Damn him! Damn him! All the times he had called her whore—when he had known, from that first day, that she had never had a man before him.

They played the first act of *The Imaginary Cuckold* with the proper degree of animosity, hurling lines and insults back and forth like daggers. Sébastien, watching from the wings, shook his head and wondered how they would manage the reconciliation of the lovers in the third act. The first act ended with the scene where Valentin asked for the box. They had rehearsed the movements—she pretending to give him a box on the ear—a thousand times. But Ninon was still seething from his words. She made as if to strike him with her right hand, as usual; as he ducked away and howled, she slapped him as hard as she could with her left. His eyes, behind the mask, widened in shocked surprise. They played the scene out with Ninon's mock assault (Valentin carefully avoiding another genuine blow) and left the stage to much laughter and applause.

But the moment they were out of sight of the audience, Valentin whipped off his mask and whirled to her. "I warn you, Ninon!" he said through clenched teeth.

She tossed her head and moved away from him, going to stand behind the back-cloth that represented the kitchen. She smiled sweetly at Joseph, who was already waiting there, and refused to look at Valentin. When Sébastien and Marc-Antoine had finished the duet they were singing, Ninon waited for the applause to die down, then stepped through the slash in the canvas that represented the door. In silence she fussed with the plates and saucepans on the table, then clasped her hands together in delight as Joseph, her hopeful suitor, entered the kitchen. They played their amorous scene in mime, with many kisses, and pinches on the rump—Joseph all the while indicating, with lewd gestures, exactly what he had in mind for his inamorata. It was a scene that never failed to earn the audience's approval; the coarser his suggestive movements, the harder they laughed, adding bawdy comments of their own, which Ninon had long since learned to ignore.

At last, hand to ear, Ninon pretended to hear a noise. Joseph rushed into the wings, while Ninon bent over at the painted window and looked out for her husband, the jealous vicomte of the title. She waited for the noisy but harmless clap of Valentin's slapstick on her rump, her thoughts already on the third act. When they were lovers, they had always kissed at the final scene. And afterward, sleeping apart, they had still managed to hold hands. But this afternoon they were adversaries: she was not sure she could even look at him.

She gasped as the slapstick struck her bottom, a sharp, stinging smack that hurt even through her skirts. She spun around to see Valentin grinning at her, dark eyes glittering wickedly through his half-mask. He had carefully removed from the slapstick the extra lath that rendered it harmless.

Damn him, she thought, and his smug satisfaction! She turned to the table, reaching for the breakaway plates, then hesitated, feeling her anger boiling over—for the smile on his face, for the smack to her rear, for the weeks of aching days and lonely nights. Damn him! Bypassing the plates, she picked up the iron skillet from the table and swung at him with all her might. She hit him on the side of his face and head, the heavy blow catching him unaware and sending him reeling against the table. The plates crashed to the floor, large shards spinning halfway across the stage. Valentin staggered about, clutching at chairs for support, half-senseless from the blow.

The audience was ecstatic. It was surely the best brawl they had seen in months, the degree of realism worthy of their applause. Ninon smiled at Valentin and tripped daintily to the table to lay down the skillet, then moved to the center of the stage, where she might take her bows and receive the plaudits of the wildly cheering spectators. Valentin, partially recovered by now, waited until she had taken her third curtsy, then kicked her smartly in the rear so that she went sprawling. Gasping, she struggled to her knees to see him bearing down on her, the skillet now clutched tightly in his fist. She gulped, aware for the first time how poorly she had used him. His eyes, through their mask, were burning in fury. Her rump was already sore; if he laid hands on her now, he would be merciless in his punishment. Still on her knees, she tried to back away from him, her hands scraping against the bits of broken crockery, her memories flashing back to Baugin and the evil days of her childhood. No, by Heaven! she thought. He would not touch her! He would not beat her before all these people! By God, she would not endure it! As he reached down a sinewy arm to snatch her up, she found a piece of broken plate in her hand; she struck upward, piercing the flesh of his thigh. He howled and jumped back as blood spurted from the wound.

"You madwoman!" he bellowed, as the audience stamped their feet with delight. "You willful trollop!"

She scrambled to her feet, shrieking curses at him. "I shall do as I please! Do you understand? I am not yours! You pig, you villain, you…" She went to kick him, but was restrained by Joseph, who had rushed onto the stage and was shouting for Hortense to close the curtain.

"Let me go!" roared Valentin, as Sébastien and Marc-Antoine clutched wildly at his arms. "Give me a minute, and I'll teach the bratling a lesson she'll not soon forget!"

In the end, with much shouting and cursing, they were led away separately. Beyond the closed curtain, the spectators continued to cheer and clap, hoping for an encore to rival the scene they had just seen performed.

Valentin and Ninon kept to their rooms the following day, and had their meals sent in: Valentin was too injured to show himself, and Ninon burned with shame at her own savage behavior. The day after that, limping heavily, his face painted with white lead, Valentin appeared at the theater to play a pastoral, then returned to his room and shut himself up as before. They did not play for the next two days, being Wednesday and Thursday, the least profitable days to perform. On Thursday evening, the company, with the exception of Valentin, went to a nearby tavern for supper. Ninon ate little, still feeling the eyes of her fellow strollers on her, and excused herself early. She walked through the spring twilight, her thoughts in a turmoil. Chanteclair would scarcely recognize her now. Where was the sweet Ninon who had come from Marival nearly a year ago? The shy, retiring, fearful Ninon, holding in her emotions, afraid to laugh or to cry. It was as though the strollers' life had opened the floodgates of her locked heart, and all the torrent of anger, and passion, and temperament—held so long in check—had come pouring out. She had laughter now, true enough. But she had the dark side of laughter as well—a new awareness of the bitterness and resentment she had kept hidden from herself for so long. And she had done just what she despised Valentin for: turned that bitterness into cruelty against the people closest to her.

She sighed heavily and mounted the stairs to her room, moving quietly down the dark hallway as she passed Valentin's chamber with its half-open door. She heard a soft oath and peered into his dimly lit room, standing far back so that he would not see her. He was sitting in a straight-backed chair near the cold fireplace; by his side was a small table that held a candle, a basin, and clean linens. He was wearing nothing except his shirt, which was drawn well up so that he might minister to his injured thigh. He cursed again, twisting to reach the wound, which extended to the under part of his leg and partly out of his view. He dabbed at it with a sopping sponge, and groaned as the water ran down his leg and dripped onto the floor.

"Plague take the damn thing," he muttered, and threw the sponge across the room. Ninon stepped quietly into the chamber and closed the door, then bit her lip when he looked up at the sound. The entire side of his face was black with bruises, his eye swollen and puffy. Silently she retrieved the sponge and knelt in front of him. She dipped the sponge into the basin of warm water and wrung it out, dabbing gently at the gash in his leg. She dried it carefully with a towel and examined it. The wound had begun to heal around the edges, but the middle was red and corrupt. She frowned. The sisters in the convent, without the means to buy medicines and salves, had devised methods of their own to treat illness and accidents, and they had been effective. She went to the cold fireplace and pulled out a piece of half-burned wood, crumbling the charcoal into a fresh bandage that she could use as a poultice to draw out the poisons from his wound. She wrapped his leg tightly and tied the bandage, then remained kneeling at his feet, too filled with shame and remorse even to look up at him.

He reached down, his hands under her elbows, and pulled her up to stand before him. He smiled as well as he could, and rubbed her bottom gently through her skirts, a movement both apologetic and conciliatory.

"Alas! Your face," she whispered, near tears. "I must have been mad."

"You had provocation," he said dryly. "I was…ahem…somewhat intemperate myself that day."

"I didn't mean to hurt you so badly."

"Thanks be to God I was wearing the mask. You might have broken my nose!"

"*Ah Dieu!*" She sighed unhappily. "I shall get a leech from the apothecary tomorrow to drain the color from the bruises."

He grinned with the side of his mouth, wincing slightly at the pain to his face. "Come now, you needn't do penance! I have been cruel to you many a time, without a shred of remorse. And I fully intended to thrash you, had you not saved yourself by crippling me! So then. Let us declare a truce." He laughed softly and wiped a tear from her cheek. "But we gave them a show for their money, did we not?"

She sniffled and tried to smile, but found she could not. She stroked the side of his face with soft fingers, as though she could cure him with her touch, then bent down and kissed him tenderly, her lips brushing his bruises. But when she would have straightened up, he put his arms around her and pulled her mouth down to his, kissing her softly at first, then deepening his kiss as his ardor grew. She trembled, her lips hungry for his, her body quivering with long-suppressed desire. At last he leaned back in the chair and looked up at her, his questioning eyes seeking an answer in her face.

"Yes. Oh, yes," she breathed.

She still stood before him. Without a word, he pulled off his shirt so that he sat naked, his swollen member attesting to his hunger, his passion. He gathered up her skirts, raising them to her waist; then, his strong hands about her hips, he lifted her and impaled her on his hard shaft. She gasped in pleasure, straddling him, allowing his hands to move her up and down on his body while her fingernails raked his back and she moaned softly. It was over in a few moments of frenzy. With a cry, he shuddered and thrust violently upward, then was still. They stayed thus for a very long time, his head cradled against her breast, her arms holding him fast. She sighed in contentment, feeling at peace with her body for the first time in months.

He stirred at last and lifted her from his lap, then stood up and limped slowly to the bed. "Come," he said, holding out his hand for her. Quickly she shed her clothes and left them in a heap upon the floor, then hurried to join him under the sheets. She had never felt such pleasure with his body before. She could not get enough of him, her hands stroking his strong shoulders, his chest, his flat belly ridged with hard muscles. Her senses caught fire from her own fingertips, the very feel of his smooth flesh exciting her beyond anything she had experienced before. She touched his flaccid member, feeling it grow with passion under her soft caresses.

"You witch," he said hoarsely. "You tantalizing devil." He rolled over and pressed her down upon the pillows, his mouth hot and insistent on hers, until she pushed him away, gasping for air. "No," he said, chuckling softly. "No quarter." And kissed her again.

"Will you defeat me totally, villain?" she asked, when she had managed to catch her breath again.

"Without mercy." Taking one of his pillows, he slipped it under her hips, then lifted her legs and rested them on his shoulders. She closed her eyes and relaxed, feeling wonderfully comfortable and at ease in this position. When he entered her, thrusting slowly, silkily, it only added to her sense of well-being. He seemed content to make love to her gently; she quivered with the exquisiteness of the soft sensations he aroused within her. Or perhaps the injury to his leg made violent passion impracticable. Whatever his reasons, he did not stop until they were both sated, their naked flesh misted with a thin film of sweat. At last he withdrew; she would have curled up on her side of the bed, but he pulled her into his arms, holding her close while he covered them both with the sheet.

He sighed deeply, the pillow of his chest rising and falling beneath her head. "Tomorrow, I shall move my trunk into your room. Are you agreeable?"

"Yes."

"It was a mistake," he said. "We should not have ended our arrangement."

"No." And yet he had. And still she didn't know why. She waited, hoping, feeling estranged from his heart, from the deepest recesses of his soul—as always. And in spite of her resolve to protect herself from him, she felt the pain of his silence like a knife to her vitals. A mistake. Was that all it had been?

He seemed to sense her sudden tenseness. He sat up and peered down at her, his eyes searching her face; then he lay back and held her again. "Ninon," he said at last, his voice so low she had to strain to hear. "I...I didn't know you were a virgin. Not in Troyes, and not afterward."

"But you said...the other day..."

"Cruel words. Meant to hurt you. But untrue, I swear it. I did not know, until Montargis, when you lost the child. I thought it was Philippe's. Then Hortense told me...the sheets..."

She shrugged. "And would it have made a difference to you had you known?"

He sat up again and stared down at her. "Of course!" he said, his voice sharp with surprise. "I would not have touched you again after that first time!"

She suppressed a smile. It never ceased to astonish her: the sudden flashes of youth and innocence in him, for all his tough exterior. As if a virgin was less-hated womankind. Eve before the Fall. She felt a surge of warmth and pity for him. That was why he had stopped sleeping with her. Had she slept with Philippe, it would not have bothered Valentin to take her. A whore. It made it so much simpler for him. Hatred could not be confused by any other emotions. But she had been a virgin...and he burned with guilt. What a poor, tormented wretch he was. Well, she could at least ease some of his torment. "I'm not a whore," she said. "I never shall be. You may rest easy on that score. And put down your jealousies once for all. I have not slept with another man, nor shall I, so long as we share the same bed. Not nobleman, nor soldier, nor coarse lout who calls up to me from the *parterre*. Your jealousy is unfounded... and ugly."

He stirred uncomfortably. "Ninon, I..."

"You may not think so, but some women are capable of fully as much loyalty as a man. I have been fair to you. And honest. I will not be treated as your enemy. I have earned your friendship, at the very least, Valentin."

He turned away. "You shame me to my face," he said hoarsely.

She giggled, her hand going behind his head to turn him back to her. "And oh! 'tis such a very damaged face!"

He gave her a lopsided grin. "I said once you'd be the death of me. I did not think you'd do it bone by bone!" He swept her into his arms and kissed her, then pulled her down to lie with him once again. "At the very least, I *shall* be your friend, Ninon." He hesitated. "And then, perhaps, later…"

"Wait," she said. "One more thing. To put your mind at rest, lest you still have doubts. That…ass of a nobleman. Who was to take me to supper. It was not because I cared for him. Nor was it to make you jealous. He told me he was from Dijon. I had hoped to hear some news of Philippe, that's all. But you were saying…perhaps, later…? What?"

"Nothing. There is nothing more to say."

She frowned, hearing the sudden edge in his voice, and burrowed more deeply in his arms. They lay in silence for some minutes.

"Did you speak with your foolish nobleman?" he said at last. "To ask about Philippe."

"No." She laughed sadly. "Our battle on the stage frightened him away. I shall never know if he had news of Philippe."

She jumped as the door crashed open, and Sébastien stood there, his face white as death. The rest of the company pushed in behind him. They seemed not to notice or care that Ninon was in the bed with Valentin, but crowded around Sanscoeur like children seeking comfort from a parent.

"Valentin!" cried Sébastien. "Travelers in the tavern. Newly come from Nemours. They said an actor has killed a nobleman and is sentenced to hang. God save us—I think it's Chanteclair!"

Chapter Thirteen

Chanteclair gazed out the barred window at the sunny town square. He laughed softly and turned to Ninon and Valentin. "The Rooster crows his last this morning, I fear! Still, I'm glad you came to bid me *adieu*. I only wish I could have seen the rest of the company."

Valentin shook his head. "The townsfolk grow uglier and uglier. LaPierre had much influence—if not friends—here in Nemours. There is talk of banning actors henceforth, and burning down the *jeu de paume*. And that is the least of the threats against strollers and gypsies and vagabonds. The company is safe in the woods outside of town. 'Tis best they remain so."

Chanteclair smiled. "I am grateful, at least, for my 'brother' and 'sister'..." He nodded in their direction. "How much did it cost you to persuade my jailors of that fantasy?"

Valentin shrugged. "Enough. But I told them we all had different fathers. And that you were the black sheep. They did not, of course, believe me, and were delighted to be confirmed once again in their low opinion of actors."

Chanteclair breathed deeply at the window. "It will be a sweet day. A man should not be hanged in May."

"*Merde!*" Valentin swore bitterly, and pounded his fist on the small wooden table in the center of the cell. "Is there no more that we can do?"

"Name of God—stop!" said Ninon, putting a restraining hand on his arm. "We could not pay the judge enough for him to stay the sentence. And there is no escape from this jail, even if we could afford to hire an army of assassins." She choked back a sob and turned away. She had thought there were no more tears left to cry. For a week now she had sobbed in Valentin's arms, each night when they returned to their inn after another fruitless day of seeking someone who would accept a bribe, who would speak up on Chanteclair's behalf.

"Come, sister," said Chanteclair, putting his arm around her, "I will not have your tears. Not on a beautiful day in May." He turned to Valentin. "Have you heard further news of Dorothé?"

"Only that she has fled back to her convent and renounced her father. Why don't you write to her?"

Chanteclair shook his head. "No. We lived our lifetime in the inn near Vauvert. 'Tis enough. I would have her remember that. Not the self-pity I would pour into a letter, despite my best resolve. But I would have you send word to my parents when you can. La Couronne, the draper and his wife in Angoulême—if they yet live. My mother always said I should come to a bad end. I should not like her to be disappointed." He grinned wickedly at Ninon.

"Damn! How can you jest?" cried Valentin. "You fool! You mad fool! Risking all for love…"

"Love is always worth the risk, *mon ami*."

Valentin's mouth twisted in a bitter smile. "Is it?"

Chanteclair's soft brown eyes went from Valentin to Ninon and back again. "There might come a time, my raging friend, when *you* will be forced to risk all for love."

"Then I shall tip my hat and let Love pass me by."

"I would rather die in the spring than have a heart as cold as yours. Forgive me, Valentin…but 'tis my privilege to speak my mind today." He sighed and turned away, looking once again across the town square to the lofty tree where, even now, the hangman, perched on a high ladder, was arranging his rope across a branch. "Have a care, man," he said softly. "It lacks yet an hour to noon." He turned back to Valentin. "There is another matter that concerns me. An actor's foolish vanity, perhaps, but…It was part of my sentence, to have my corpse dismembered, disemboweled, the limbs hung separately after the grisly job was done. I have seen executions of the sort before. The parts have a way of disappearing as mementos. I should not care to have my foot—which trod upon many a stage—sitting on someone's shelf while my corpse danced upon the wind with only one leg. And as for my poor prickle, dried up and useless…God save me from having it carried around the village in some oaf's pocket, to be dragged out and exhibited. 'Ah, yes!' the ladies will say, 'I knew Chanteclair well! There is not a cock-a-doodle left in him!'"

"I have already made the arrangements," Valentin said gruffly. "The hangman will not touch your parts. Nor will the provost's men who guard your body. The provost was very agreeable. He has a mistress to support."

"And what will you do for money when you must eat?" Chanteclair asked gently.

Ninon smiled. "We still eat. We merely walk, instead of riding. Besides, Sébastien can take out his miracle cures and sell them."

Chanteclair laughed. "But will he ever find a dupe as willing as was Jamie? Now that I come to think of it, we could have charged him a fee for his torments!" His eyes turned serious. "Is the curé waiting below, Valentin?"

"No. I must have him sent for. But he has been paid. And handsomely. You have only to make your *amende honorable* to be forgiven your wicked profession."

"Then send for him now, if you will. I fear my confession will take half the afternoon!"

Valentin knocked on the door, which was opened by the guard waiting in the corridor beyond. He stepped out for a moment to talk to the man.

Chanteclair took the opportunity to tilt up Ninon's chin and kiss her tenderly on the cheek. "All is well between you again, *ma petite?*"

"Yes."

"And still, Madame Tristesse, your eyes are sad. And not only for my sake. What will take the sadness away, I wonder?"

"Please..." she choked.

"No. Don't turn away. Will you tell 'Grandmère'...at last?"

"To go home," she whispered. "My heart yearns for home...a place to belong...my own..." She covered her eyes with her hands, unable to go on.

He folded her into his embrace. "But what a foolish wish, my dear Ninon. Home is where lies the heart, the sages say. Not in a place! You must be sure you know where to search. Now dry your tears before Valentin returns. You must take care of him. He needs you."

She sniffled. "But he..."

"Hist! Here he comes." Chanteclair stood back from her and smiled gently as Valentin limped into the room.

"'Tis all arranged, Chanteclair. The priest will be here in a quarter of an hour or so."

"Good. I have one more favor to beg of you. Do not stay to see me hang. It's dangerous for you...and shameful for me."

"Chanteclair...my dear friend..."

"Please. It will not be my best performance. Give me your promise."

"And my hand on it," said Valentin, his voice cracking.

The two men embraced, then Chanteclair grinned. "You promised to tell me all this week why you are limping, and why your face bears the remains of considerable damage. You said it would make me laugh."

"Indeed, yes," said Valentin.

"Well then, my friends, make me laugh until the priest comes, and then be on your way. I swear I shall be laughing still as the hangman tightens his rope."

The sun balanced on the edge of the twilight sky, a brilliant ball of orange. Valentin stopped on the dusty road and rubbed his hand across his eyes. "I'm going back," he said, his voice hard, his jaw set in a stubborn line.

"You must be mad!" said Sébastien. "Wherefore?" He signaled to Joseph, who brought the ox team and wagon to a halt.

"To steal Chanteclair's body and bury it. In consecrated ground, if I can. But, by heaven, he shall be buried!"

"Don't be a fool, Val!" said Hortense.

"'Tis too dangerous," said Marc-Antoine. "You cannot."

"I must! I just remembered what he said." He turned to Ninon, his face twisted in agony. "Do you recall it? When we told you the story of the hanged men in the woods?"

"Sweet Madonna, yes," she said softly, her eyes wide with pain. "He did not want to spend eternity dancing in the wind, he said." She gulped back her tears.

"And he shall not."

"But it will be night before you get back to Nemours. At least midnight."

"All the better. It must be done in the dark."

"Then we'll all go," said Ninon.

"I'm damned if you will," growled Valentin.

"You'll need help!" she snapped. "It cannot be managed alone if the provost's men still guard his body. We can leave the wagon and team in the grove outside of Nemours, as we did before."

"No!" Valentin's eyes narrowed in anger.

"Yes! He was dear to all of us!"

Sanscoeur hesitated, then nodded in agreement. "I have a scheme. Hortense and Marc-Antoine can safeguard the wagon and wait for the rest of us." Quickly he outlined his plan, then held up an admonishing finger. "But if anyone fails to return to the wagon, the rest are not to wait!

Do you understand? When the provost discovers what has happened, his men will be out searching for actors. I would be as far away from Nemours as possible."

It was close to one o'clock before they reached Nemours. The large oak tree stood at the edge of the town square, beyond a row of ancient houses. By the light of the full moon they could see Chanteclair's body hanging from a thick branch and swaying slightly in the spring night. Next to the tree was a small guardhouse before which two fusiliers squatted, playing dice in the glow of a tallow lantern. Every few moments, one of them would take a swig from a bottle that sat on the ground between them, then shake it to assess the amount of liquid cheer still remaining.

Crouched in the shadow of one of the houses, the Peerless Theatre Company did the same. Valentin removed a leather flask from his belt, unstoppered it, and handed it to Ninon and Toinette. The women sipped tentatively at the strong distilled spirits, then passed on the flask to the men, who drank more freely, deliberately allowing the aqua vitae to slop onto their clothes. Silently Valentin pointed to the row of houses, indicating by his movements that the women were to emerge from the shadows as far away from Chanteclair's body as possible. Ninon nodded and stood up, pulling at Toinette's sleeve. Even in the dark, she could feel Toinette trembling in fear. Well, if need be, she would play the scene alone.

The two women moved softly in the gloom, grateful that the square was packed earth, and quiet underfoot; a cobbled way would have revealed them too soon to the soldiers. The moonlight was white on the ground, the line between light and shadow challenging them to cross. Ninon put her arm about Toinette's waist and stepped into a path of silver, giggling loudly as she did so. The fusiliers looked up from their dice.

"Hell's fire," said one, whistling softly through his teeth. "But here's sport for the night!"

Whispering and laughing to each other, Ninon and Toinette crossed the square, seeming not to notice the men.

"Wait a moment, you pretty creatures. You cannot mean to leave us!" The soldiers put aside their game and stood up, moving quickly to stand before the women and block their way.

"If you please, messieurs," said Ninon primly. "Let us pass."

The man laughed in mockery. "Is it a fine lady who does command it?"

"Yes."

"Saucy wench!" He reached out and pinched her on the cheek. "A *lady* does not go abroad in the dead of night!" He sniffed. "Nor reek of drink."

The other soldier had been eyeing Toinette; now he pulled her from Ninon's encircling arm and held her close to his side, his large hand cupping her buttocks through her skirt. "Where are you going, pretty jade?"

Toinette gulped. "H-home," she stammered.

"And where have you been?"

"I...we..."

Ninon put her hands on her hips. "'Tis none of your concern. Now get out of our way!"

The first soldier frowned. "You're a brazen wench, aren't you. Would you talk so bold, I wonder, with your skirts pulled up?" Roughly he grabbed her by the arms and slammed her against his body, his hot mouth seeking hers.

She struggled half-heartedly, intent on watching for Valentin over his shoulder. Toinette had already allowed her soldier to kiss her, turning him away from the tree; now, with both guards distracted, Valentin slipped into the moonlit square, carrying a dummy dressed like Chanteclair. Tossing the mannequin over one shoulder, he leaped for the lowest branch of the tree and swung his leg up, his actor's agility smoothing the difficult ascent. He moved out across the branch that held Chanteclair's body, lowering the dummy on its noose until it was level with the actor's corpse, then fastening the rope securely to the branch. Ninon saw the flash of his knife in the moonlight; with a soft thud, Chanteclair's body dropped to the ground.

Ninon's suitor pushed her away and turned his head slightly, as though he had heard the noise. "Pox take you," she wailed, her voice a sharp whine. "I'm not a common whore. Let me pass!"

He shrugged off his uneasiness and pulled her back into his arms. "You're as common as they come, you doxy!" He laughed, his hand grasping the firm roundness of her breast.

Valentin was now hanging by his hands from the branch. Just as he let go and dropped to the ground, the branch creaked loudly. He froze for a moment, then dragged Chanteclair's body to the shadowy side of the tree.

Ninon threw her arms around the soldier's neck. "I expect to be paid, of course," she said coquettishly. "My sister and I have just come from entertaining an alderman tonight. Very tight-fisted he was...and how's a girl to live?"

This time he could not be distracted. "I'll pay you if you're worth it, whore," he said, disengaging her arms from his neck. "Michel!" He turned to the other fusilier. "I thought I heard a noise."

Michel pinched Toinette on the rump and she shrieked loudly. "'Tis only our dancing actor, who envies us this night's sport."

"No." The first soldier bent to pick up his fusil—his flintlock rifle—and moved toward the tree.

"You lousy shittlebrain," Ninon said with contempt. "Would you abandon me?"

"Only for duty, my sweet. There are those who find it diverting to strip a corpse. And the provost has given us our orders."

Sweet Madonna, thought Ninon. Was there no way to stop him from discovering Chanteclair's body or Valentin? And if he looked closely at the hanging "corpse," they would be undone. "Damn you," she said sharply. "I'm for home. I shall not wait while you tiptoe about in the middle of the night!"

"You poxy whore," he snarled. "I'll have you tonight whether you will or no!" Grabbing her savagely by the wrist, he propelled her toward the other soldier. "Here, Michel," he said. "Hold this jade until I've gone once around the tree." Keeping his weapon at the ready, he moved toward the hanging body. Ninon and Toinette, held fast by Michel, looked at each other in panic.

Just then, Valentin began to sing. A bawdy ballad, in a voice that cracked and wavered drunkenly. He lurched out from the shadow of the tree and bowed elaborately to the fusilier, tripping and stumbling over his own feet.

"You crack-brain!" said the soldier. "What do you there?"

Valentin moved with unsteady steps, all the while easing himself away from the tree and toward Michel and the two women. Watching him carefully, the soldier followed, his ready-charged weapon aimed at Valentin's head. "Why, good sir," said Valentin, his voice a slur, "I came to ask that man if he would drink with me." He jerked his thumb back in the direction of Chanteclair's body. "The scurvy rogue would not even answer!"

"Ah-h-h!" said the fusilier, giving Valentin a cuff on the side of the ear. Plague take the drunken wretch, he thought, keeping him from his doxy! "Be off with you, fool, lest you join yon gallows bird!" He put down his weapon and emptied the last of the wine into his mouth.

"Without a kiss?" muttered Valentin. He stumbled over to Toinette and pulled her from Michel's arms. "No. I don't like this one. Not enough meat on her. Go…get you hence!" He delivered a resounding smack to Toinette's bottom, propelling her away from him. She needed no further encouragement, but vanished into a dark alley between the houses. Valentin turned to Ninon. "*This* is a saucy wench! Come give us a kiss."

"I'll break your head," the fusilier said ominously.

"Pish-tush!" said Ninon, moving into Valentin's arms. "What's the harm in a kiss?" She smiled coyly at the fusilier. "The poor devil has sucked up his tipple tonight! Let me send him home happy, then you and I shall while away the rest of the night." She tried to look bored while Valentin kissed her, managing to show a certain impatience with the lout when he insisted on putting his hand down the front of her bodice.

"Can you see Joseph and Sébastien?" he whispered.

She frowned and pushed away his hand, managing to shake her head slightly.

He turned away from the fusiliers, bending her over his arm while he kissed her again. "They must have taken Chanteclair away by now. Get you out of here as soon as ever you can. Don't wait for me." His voice was soft, but urgent.

"Villain!" she shrilled, swinging at him. "You have taken enough liberties! Find your drunken way home."

He drew himself up proudly, though unsteadily, swaying with the effects of drink. "Madame," he said, "I am no villain. I have a purse of ten crowns...and you are a pleasing wench. If you will accompany me..." He offered her his arm.

"Ten crowns! *Mon Dieu!* For ten crowns you could buy my mother and half her kinswomen! Show me your house, my friend—and the color of your coins—and I am yours."

"Damned if you are!" cried the fusilier. "You're mine!"

"And what of me?" complained Michel. "Thanks to that drunken sot, I've lost my own bit of baggage." He clutched unhappily at his groin. "And never a birding-piece more primed and ready than mine!"

The first fusilier eyed Ninon, his mouth curved in an ugly smile. "That damned whore would have deserted me, gone off with a drunkard. She deserves whatever she gets. But she's woman enough for both of us, eh, Michel? I'll take the first *tour*, while you hold her down. Then I'll do the same for you." He moved menacingly toward Ninon.

Valentin laughed and held up his flask of spirits. "Can we not all share? Give me my turn between the jade's legs, and my flask is yours. What say you? 'Tis good aqua vitae." He held out the liquor as the two fusiliers hesitated. "Come," he said, "to show you I'm a good fellow, I'll hold her down first!"

Michel nodded and reached for the liquor, while the other man began to unbutton his breeches. Valentin grabbed at Ninon, attempted to wrestle her to the ground as she cursed and struggled, though not so loudly that she might wake the other fusiliers in the guardhouse. With a sudden movement, she whirled about in Valentin's arms and pushed him to the ground, then raced for the end of the square and the safety of the narrow streets. Michel let out a roar and threw the flask to the ground, meaning to follow her, but Valentin contrived to rise unsteadily to his feet at that precise moment. Michel, tripping over him, cursed and went crashing to the earth.

"*Merde!*" swore the fusilier, working frantically to re-fasten his fly buttons. "Thanks to you, you drunken pricklouse, we've lost them both!" He reached for Valentin as Michel scrambled to his feet. "You'll wish you had stayed at home with your bottle tonight, rogue!"

Oh, God, thought Ninon, racing through the dark streets to the edge of town. Let him be safe. Let him be safe.

She met Joseph and Sébastien on the road from Nemours, carrying the body of Chanteclair between them as though he were a drunken comrade. She was glad for the hat they had put on his head, and the setting moon, which had plunged the night into blackness. She did not want to see his face.

When they arrived at the wagon, Toinette was already there, tearfully explaining to Marc-Antoine and Hortense how frightened she had been.

They wrapped Chanteclair's body in an old back-cloth for a shroud—it seemed fitting—then laid him tenderly in the bottom of the wagon, and waited for Valentin. After half an hour, Joseph took the oxen by their halters and clucked softly to them, leading them out of the grove toward the road.

"No," said Ninon. "We wait."

"But Valentin said…"

"He will be here. We wait."

"I like it not," said Hortense.

"'Tis foolish, Ninon," said Sébastien. "He knows we move toward Ferrières. 'Tis foolish to wait."

She sighed. "I know. But the whole scheme was mad and foolish. And brave. A fitting tribute to our gallant Chanteclair. Let us be foolish a little longer, and wait."

Toinette giggled nervously. "Valentin will take a fit when he comes!"

"Pray God he comes," said Marc-Antoine. "If he takes a fit, I myself shall rap him soundly on the head!" They all laughed at that, the laughter helping to ease the dread that filled them all. Hortense, always practical, brought out some bread and cheese. They ate, then took turns sleeping while Sébastien paced the road, coming back to the grove every quarter of an hour to shake his head in despair.

"What shall we do, Ninon?" he said at last, pointing to the pink streaks in the eastern sky. "We must be gone. At daylight they will surely discover the mannequin and come looking for us."

"A little longer, Sébastien. Please. A little longer." She walked back to the road with him, fighting the tears that burned behind her eyelids, the grief that threatened to overwhelm her. In a nearby birch tree, a morning lark sang, its sweetness a painful counterpoint to the desolation of her heart. She looked up. The sun, just cresting the hill, blinded her for a moment and she blinked, shielding her eyes from its rays. She blinked again. Silhouetted against the dawn was the figure of Valentin, limping slowly toward them. "Thanks be to God," she whispered, and ran toward him while Sébastien called the rest of the troupe.

Valentin's face was battered and bloody, with cuts on lip and eyebrow, and he seemed to breathe with some difficulty. But he managed a smile as the players gathered around, filled with questions and concerns. He eased himself onto a large rock, clutching at his side as he sat. "Curse all fusiliers," he said. "It cost me a rib or two, I fear. And my last ten crowns to persuade the whoresons to let me go...but 'tis done. You have Chanteclair's body?"

Sébastien nodded. "What took you so long?"

Valentin rubbed a hand across his eyes. "I stopped to rest. I think I must have been asleep for a time." He looked up at the bright sky, seeming aware of the dawn for the first time. "Why are you here?" His voice rumbled ominously. "I told you not to wait! Sébastien...Marc-Antoine...were you mad?"

"We...that is..."

"*Dieu du ciel!* I told you to go on! 'Twas a simple enough matter. I should have met you in Ferrières. Did you take leave of your senses?" He stood up, glaring fiercely at them all; it was clear he meant to rage for the next quarter of an hour.

"*I* bade them wait," Ninon said evenly.

He whirled to her, his eyes blazing. "You did? I ought to wring your neck! *You* did?"

She held her ground. "Yes! I did. Now stop making such a great to-do and come along with me to the stream. I'll clean up your face, and bind your ribs, if they are broken...though I cannot imagine they can be, and still suffer the strain of such noise and wind!" She turned to Joseph and Sébastien. "Get the team ready to travel. And fasten the furniture well. Now that daylight is come, we should take the narrow lanes to Ferrières, and keep well off the highroad until we have left Orléanais Province. Oh. And one more thing. Make a space in the wagon for Valentin to lie down."

"I shall walk like the rest of you," he snarled.

She smiled sweetly. "If need be, I shall have the men tie you into the wagon. Mayhap, after a little rest, you will have recovered your pleasant disposition. Now, come along," she said, as he stared at her, his jaw gaping in astonishment. She turned about and made for the small stream hidden behind a large thicket of gooseberry bushes. "Well?" she demanded. "Are you coming? Or must I take you by the ear like a stubborn schoolboy?"

Valentin glared at Marc-Antoine, who was attempting with some difficulty to hide his smile, and limped off after Ninon. He sat on the stump of a tree, as she indicated, and watched her angrily as she lifted her skirt and pulled off one of her petticoats. "You sharp-tongued virago," he muttered.

"Yes, I know. Take off your shirt."

Painfully he complied, grumbling and cursing as he did so. "To speak thus to me...I shall not have it..."

She moved toward him, frowning, her hands pressing gently against the bruises on his rib cage. "You are a king only upon the stage," she said. "I shall speak to you however it suits me. Does that hurt?"

He grunted and kept still, contenting himself with scowling at her as she tore strips of cloth from her linen petticoat and bound them tightly around his ribs. But when she had wrung out a square of linen in the stream, and had begun to dab gently at the cuts and filth on his face, he found his voice again. Angrily he assailed her for disobeying his orders, cataloging the dangers they now faced, the risks to the company because of her stubbornness.

She scarcely heard him, her heart so filled with gladness at his being alive. The cuts to his face were less serious than she had at first feared—they would leave no scars. His beautiful face. She saw it as though through new eyes—his strong jaw, the deep cleft in his chin, the patrician nose, the arrogant set of his head. She had thought never to see it again, picturing it cold and dead all through the long night.

Let him rage. It could not touch her. She was content to have him back safe. And besides, his rantings were half-bluff. She had learned that much about him in their time together. His protection, his shield against pain. Against feelings that overwhelmed him. He had been angry the day Gaston left; angry in her first weeks with the company—denying his physical need of her; angry at the loss of the child. And now Chanteclair was dead, and he raged like a madman.

"Hush!" she chided at last. "Have done with your ravings!"

"I am to let it go? When you have been willful, stubborn..."

"Will you beat me?" she asked with sarcasm.

"By *le bon Dieu*, I should! You risked the whole company!"

She gazed tenderly down at him. "Foolish man. There is no company without Sanscoeur."

"Pah! Witless sentiment!"

She smoothed the black hair from his forehead. "Sanscoeur is the head, the brain, the soul. We cannot do without him."

He laughed bitterly. "But who will be the heart and the laughter without Chanteclair?"

"Why then, Sanscoeur must take that role as well."

"Damn you! Don't speak like an idiot! Sanscoeur has no heart."

"Yes, I know," she said softly, the tears welling in her eyes.

He stared at her for a moment. Then the mask of pride crumbled and he turned away, his shoulders shaking with grief. She gathered him in her arms, holding his head against her bosom, feeling his burning tears on her flesh. He sobbed out his pain, his arms tight about her waist, while she wept her own tears and murmured his name over and over again.

Chapter Fourteen

On a soft spring evening, the sky streaked with gold, they buried Chanteclair. They found a tiny churchyard set apart from a village on their way. While the women kept watch, the men laid him to rest, smoothing the earth and pressing on fresh sod to hide the place. To keep the country priest from hearing the noise, Marc-Antoine dressed in uncharacteristically somber clothes and presented himself at the church as a penitent sinner. As the curé listened in wide-eyed wonder (till then he had counted the theft of a cow as the wickedest sin), Marc-Antoine confessed all, dredging up every lurid tale of his colorful past. In the end, he bestowed upon the priest a large purse of gold, begging him to have Masses said *in perpetuum* for a departed brother and friend named Chanteclair.

They moved on again, traveling south, playing where they could, sometimes just for food and lodging. They had spent most of their money in the futile attempt to save Chanteclair, and had not the means to hire a theater that would bring a decent day's receipts. They played in old barns, broken-down guild halls, anywhere.

And their performances, by and large, were disastrous, earning them boos and catcalls. They played listlessly. Without horses to carry them about, they were constantly exhausted from their travels. They could not afford to eat well, to sleep comfortably, to linger in a town. Valentin, nursing his ribs, was forced to curtail the physical aspects of his playing, and his voice had not its usual strength. And Hortense began to cough.

By the time June arrived, with sunny skies and flower-filled meadows, she was desperately ill. The physician had come, and prescribed a hippocras for her to drink, but still she tossed and turned on her sickbed, her eyes glazed with fever.

"We should have another doctor!" said Sébastien, pacing the cobbled courtyard of their shabby inn. They had just finished a meager dinner out-of-doors.

Ninon looked at Valentin, her blue eyes clouded with concern. They had spent a week now in this inn, barely able to afford the two rooms they had taken—one for the women, the other for the men. How could they pay for a doctor? They could hardly afford more medicine.

"Do you still have your nostrums and cures from the days when you were an operator, Sébastien? You can play the mountebank again."

"They are mostly dried out by now," he said.

"Why can't we make up new potions?" asked Ninon. "There must be a dozen herbs growing wild in the woods."

Sébastien looked shamefaced. "To speak truth, I was not a very good operator. It was only our singing and dancing that attracted the spectators—not my orations on the miraculous cures. And Hortense always managed to nim a purse or two."

"How much have we left?" asked Joseph.

Valentin took out a small purse. Pushing aside the dinner plates, he spilled its contents out onto the table. "There. 'Tis all we have. It must pay for the rental of the hall tomorrow, and candles to light the stage."

"What of our lodging here?"

Valentin shrugged up his shoulders. "God willing, tomorrow's receipts will cover that."

"If we don't eat," Joseph said bitterly.

"Here," said Toinette. She blushed and reached into her bodice, pulling out a handkerchief that held several coins. "It's all I have. And I earned it…on my own. But if it will help, take it." She giggled. "Besides, the bailiff is taking me to supper tonight. He will be astonished to discover what a fine appetite an actress has! And if I can, I shall hide away a pastry or two, to bring back as a treat for Hortense."

"I spent my last crown this morning," said Marc-Antoine. "To mend my boots." He brightened suddenly. "But the apothecary's shop is dim, and he's an old man. Could we not play a scene and distract him…and steal what we need for Hortense?"

Valentin frowned. "Don't be an ass, Marc-Antoine. It has not come to that yet." He picked up a coin from the table and held it out to Sébastien. "Why don't you try your luck in the local *tripot*? You have done well before."

Sébastien hesitated, then pushed away the money. "I can't," he said, his face twisted in agony. "I never cared before. To win, to lose. It was all the same. But Hortense could die for the want of that one coin if I lost it." He covered his eyes with his hand.

"Never mind," Valentin said softly.

Ninon put a hand on his sleeve. "Val. Let me sell the earrings you gave me."

"No."

"We need the money. When I sold Brinon's bracelet…you remember how much it brought in."

He turned away. "No," he said gruffly. "They were a gift for you."

She pulled him away from the others, into the shade of a tree, and put her arms around his neck. "You dear, foolish man," she murmured. "Will they bring me joy if Hortense dies? And they have brought me joy many a time. Because they were from you. I have them, I have them not. But the giver remains."

His dark eyes searched hers, a light of wonderment dawning on his face. "Ninon, I…"

"Is it to be done then?" Sébastien asked impatiently.

"Yes, of course," said Ninon, turning back to the company. "And I have a few lace handkerchiefs I embroidered. I can sell those as well."

"I shall come with you to the village," said Valentin.

They concluded their transactions quickly, finding a goldsmith to take the earrings in pawn, and a mercer who was delighted to buy the delicate handkerchiefs. They came away with more money than they had hoped to earn; elated, they stopped at the apothecary shop to buy more medicine for Hortense before setting out once again for the inn.

"'Tis a beautiful day," said Ninon, glancing around at the sunny fields that bordered the road. "I feel sure our fortunes will change."

"As do I." Valentin put his arm around her shoulders as they walked. "And if not, I shall set you to work as a seamstress. *Mon Dieu!* Twenty livres for a bit of fluff…I could not believe my ears when the mercer offered it."

She smiled sadly. "Don't set your fortunes on my nimble fingers. My mother was a seamstress. It did not provide for us."

"What was she like?"

"She knew little of happiness. She suffered greatly."

"With your stepfather? As you did?"

Ninon sighed. "No. She suffered more. She had only regrets. I had my dreams then."

"Yes. Your dreams." He withdrew his arm from her shoulder and plucked morosely at an overhanging leaf. "My mother was full of joy and laughter," he said at last.

"Does she yet live?" Ninon looked at him with interest. He had never spoken of his family before.

"No. It must be near to ten years now that she is dead."

"And your father?"

His face was like stone. "It will rain before nightfall." He increased his pace, so she had to skip to keep up with him.

"But it will not rain now," she said. "Give me a moment to catch my breath!"

"Forgive me." He moved under the shade of a large oak and sat on the grass, pulling her down beside him. "I have missed you from my bed. Sébastien is poor company."

She laughed. "At least he stays the night! I never know when Toinette has a rendezvous." She turned to him, her full lips rosy and inviting. "Must we hurry back?"

He cupped her face in his hands and kissed her gently, his fingers caressing her cheeks, her delicate ears.

He frowned, seeing her bare lobes. "Philippe would have covered you in jewels." He rose to his feet. "Hortense will need her medicine. Come." He smiled crookedly, his mouth twisted in bitterness. "Poor Ninon and her lost dreams."

The company was still gathered in the courtyard when they returned. At sight of them, Marc-Antoine rushed to Valentin, his face beaming.

"Val!" he cried. "Thanks be to God. We have a commission!"

"Where? What are the terms?"

Marc-Antoine indicated a man who sat at the table talking with Sébastien. "Let me present you to Monsieur Villebois. And then we can celebrate with the finest wine our flea-bitten landlord can provide. Monsieur Villebois has promised to pay!"

As soon as introductions were made, and they were all sitting around the table enjoying the first wine they had had in weeks, Valentin turned to Villebois. "If you please, monsieur, tell me the terms you propose."

"I am, of course, acting for my master. Monsieur le Comte proposes a fee of two hundred crowns in advance, and two hundred for your performance, as well as the charges for the journey. Monsieur Duvet tells me you are in need of horses. Permit me to present you with a carriage and team."

Valentin raised a quizzical eyebrow. "Your master is extraordinarily generous. Four hundred crowns. *Mon Dieu!* We are used to four hundred livres—a third the amount."

"Monsieur le Comte has heard much of your troupe. And he cannot travel readily. He considers it money well spent to enjoy your representations in his own domain."

"You have not told me where that is," said Valentin.

Sébastien looked uneasy. "I beg you, Val, for Hortense's sake, to put a good face on it."

"Wherefore?" said Valentin, frowning.

"I fear it is very near to Paris."

"Where?"

"Ivry-la-Bataille."

Valentin's face went white. He turned to Villebois; when he spoke, his voice was a harsh croak. "Who is your master?"

"Monsieur Georges d'Ivry, Comte d'Arouet."

"No. By God, no! We shall not take the commission."

"Valentin, are you mad?"

"And wherefore not, monsieur?" asked Villebois.

Valentin took a deep breath, seeming to recover himself. "To begin, our company is woefully reduced in numbers. We have just lost the actor who played the first parts. And then, one of our ladies is ill. I feel sure her husband will wish to stay with her while she recovers. *N'est-ce pas*, Sébastien?"

"Yes, but…"

"You see, Monsieur Villebois, we would be a company of five players. Hardly enough to justify Monsieur d'Arouet's generosity."

"I have no doubt you are skilled enough to take several parts."

"Indeed, yes, Monsieur Villebois!" said Marc-Antoine in his most jovial manner.

"I say no," Valentin said coldly, rising from his chair. "Good day, Monsieur Villebois."

Ninon hurried after him, clutching at his arm. "Have you lost your senses, Val?"

He looked at her, his eyes filled with pain and betrayal. "Will you take the part of the others against me?"

"Sweet Madonna! I take the part of reason! Would you see Hortense die?"

"She will not die. We will fare well enough without Monsieur le Comte."

"But why say no?"

His mouth was set in a stubborn line. "Because I wish it."

"You know that if we put it to the vote, all would agree."

"Would *you*? Would you agree?"

She looked down at her hands, unwilling to see the expression on his face. "Yes. Please, Valentin. 'Tis more than just Hortense. Since…

since Chanteclair, we're a poor excuse for a company. If a new hat will restore Marc-Antoine, enough to eat hearten Joseph, how can you say no? One night, one performance, and we shall be rich enough to snap our fingers in contempt at half a hundred comtes." She laughed gently. "Shall I have Sébastien and Joseph break a chair or two over your head to persuade you?"

"No." His eyes were cold. "Your disloyalty is wound enough. Tell Villebois I am agreed."

They set out the following morning in a fine coach that Villebois had provided. Joseph grumbled at first, but finally agreed to drive the wagon with their goods in exchange for twenty extra crowns. Sébastien, provided with a large enough purse to see to his and Hortense's needs until the company should return, waved them farewell on the dusty summer road. Villebois had tied his horse to the wagon, and rode in the coach with Ninon and Valentin, Toinette and Marc-Antoine.

Ninon frowned at Valentin. He had become a stranger again. But more than that. He looked as Chanteclair had looked on the day he was to hang. A man going to his doom. When they stopped that night at a cozy inn, she saw to it that they would share the same room. After supper, he hurried immediately to bed, as if he would avoid her, but she excused herself from the rest of the company and followed him.

She slid under the sheets and turned to him, wrapping her arm around his waist and kissing his rigid back through his nightshirt. "Such a long time," she murmured.

"Leave me in peace," he muttered. "I'm tired."

"I cannot believe that. When it's been weeks…" She leaned over him, blowing softly in his ear, kissing his neck.

"Leave me alone!"

"No." She was determined to tease him out of his black mood, to ease his tenseness with the act of love. "Don't you remember our agreement? You cannot sulk and deny me when it suits your fancy."

He sat up angrily. "Don't chivy me, Ninon! I'm in no humor for games!"

"You great sour-face. I want no games. I want you."

"Damn you! So be it." He pulled her roughly into his arms, his mouth hard and punishing on hers. While she yet gasped with the cruelty of his kiss, he began to tug at the hemline of her chemise, pulling it up above her waist.

She struggled in his arms, filled with anger and disgust. It was like being violated by a stranger. "Let me go," she said at last. "You *are* too tired."

He laughed in mockery, moving on top of her. "'Tis what you wanted, *n'est-ce pas?* Such a very long time, you said." His knee pressed down on hers, forcing apart her tight-clamped legs. "Did you think you played games with a lad?"

She was beginning to feel panic. He was pushed to the edge of whatever torment obsessed him. He was capable of anything. "Name of God, Valentin," she panted, "not like this!"

"However I want it," he said through clenched teeth. "You think you rule me? You think you have wheedled your way into my heart so you may lead me around like a fool?"

"Let me go!" She pounded on his chest until he grabbed her hands and forced them down onto the bed beside her head. It was no use. She could not fight his strength. He would take her—as if she were some whore in a brothel—and she could never forgive him. It would never be the same again. With a choked sob, she relaxed beneath him. "I should have stayed with Philippe," she said. "He was a man—not a wild-eyed savage."

He froze for a moment, then moved slowly off her and turned away to his side of the bed, pulling the coverlet up to his shoulders. "Let that serve as a warning," he growled. "I belong to no woman!"

With shaking hands she smoothed down her chemise and curled up in her corner of the bed, filling her pillow with burning tears.

After two more days of travel, during which Valentin seemed to sink further and further into himself, staring morosely out the carriage window for hours, or sleeping hunched up in the corner of the carriage, his broad-brimmed hat pulled over his eyes, they arrived at Ivry-la-Bataille. It was a small but charming town, with a dancing fountain in the middle of the town square, and flowers in boxes at every window. At the far end of the square was a large stone wall with an arched gateway, simple and unadorned except for the gilded clock on its face. When their carriage passed through, they found themselves in a wide courtyard bounded on three sides by low buildings, some of which appeared to be stables and workshops and servants' quarters. Directly in front of them was the *corps-de-logis*, the main living quarters of Château d'Ivry. At Villebois's directions, they alighted from the coach. He indicated one of the low buildings.

"Monsieur le Comte thinks you would be comfortable there. You will find servants waiting on your needs. Will you be rested enough to play tonight?"

"The sooner the better," said Valentin.

"Good. Before you repair to your quarters, I should like to present you to Monsieur d'Arouet. He has been waiting for your arrival."

Valentin shook his head. "Not I. Monsieur d'Arouet will see me upon the stage tonight, and not before. You have a honeyed tongue, Ninon. You can persuade a man to anything. Explain to our host that I am too weary. Monsieur Villebois…" Valentin gave a little bow, "convey my regrets to your master." He turned on his heel and made for their quarters.

Ninon bit her lip in consternation, but followed Monsieur Villebois and the others across the cobbled path to the archway in the *corps-de-logis*. Passing through, she nearly gasped aloud. The modest front of the building had not prepared her for the splendors beyond the arch. The château opened up into a large U-shaped building that overlooked a vast and magnificent expanse of gardens and crystal pools spanned by graceful bridges. The château itself reflected centuries of a proud lineage: ancient round towers of golden stone had been joined by later additions of red and black brick in geometric patterns, and carved stone tracery nestled side by side with turrets that had been built for defense. Each succeeding generation, it seemed, had added a wall here, a pavilion there, leaving its mark for posterity. All individual, all different, but somehow combining to make a whole that was utterly charming and timeless, the very stones seeming to sing: This is the realm of Arouet—today, tomorrow, forever.

She had never seen such beauty, such serenity, in one place before.

Villebois led them through a door into a wing of the château. They mounted a circular staircase and passed through a large hallway hung with tapestries, and at last found themselves in a small *cabinet* with brocade-covered walls and gilded furniture. While they waited for Villebois to fetch Monsieur d'Arouet, Ninon glanced out the window, admiring once again the beauty of the gardens. From here she could see—beyond a grove of trees—a small, semicircular garden, like a natural amphitheater, surrounded by statues, that looked out upon a reflecting pool. Not a breeze disturbed the glassy water. Ninon was enchanted. If she had the time, she resolved, she would spend a few tranquil moments there before they left Château d'Ivry. A door opened in the brocaded wall, and Monsieur le Comte entered. He had once been a tall man, that was apparent, but now he walked stooped over, leaning heavily on a cane. His hair was snow white, and his eyes were warm and intelligent in a proud face. He moved to an elbow chair and sat down, nodding as Villebois introduced each of them in turn.

"I welcome you all to Château d'Ivry," he said at last. "You are a small company. Smaller than I had been led to believe. But I have no doubt you are worthy."

"We beg your indulgence, monsieur," said Marc-Antoine with a bow. "We are short by several members, because of illness and misfortune. And Monsieur Sanscoeur begs you to forgive him, but…"

Arouet cut him off with a wave of the fingers. "Yes. Villebois has told me. I trust Sanscoeur will play, however. A company of five I can allow. A company of four cannot be countenanced."

Ninon smiled grimly. "Monsieur Sanscoeur will play. You have our assurances."

"Good. I have no theater in the château. You will play in the *petite galerie*. Villebois will show you the way when you wish to go there. You need not set up your scenery. It seems an unnecessary bother. If you are skilled in your acting, I shall not miss a tree or two. If you are not skilled, all the trees in the world could not hide that fact. My men will see to the proper lighting, as you direct. And a simple stage for you to play upon."

"And what will you have us play, monsieur?"

"I leave that entirely in your hands."

"But, monsieur," Ninon curtsied politely, "would you laugh or weep?"

He turned to her, smiling gently. She had never seen such sadness in a man's eyes. "Does it matter, madame?"

"But…but your guests," she said. "What would they prefer?"

"I have no guests. You play for me. I wish to see you play—I care not *what* you play." He sighed heavily and rose from his chair. "You will excuse an old man. Villebois will see to you."

They spent the afternoon setting up their stage in the *petite galerie*, a charming room with paneled walls and frescoed ceilings. Valentin allowed Joseph and Marc-Antoine to act as *décorateurs*, while he sat in his room and altered several plays to suit the diminished company.

They rehearsed for an hour, then had a bit of bread and cheese as the sun was setting (Villebois had promised a hearty supper after their performance).

Costumed and made up, they trooped through the twilight to the wing of the château that held the *petite galerie*. Valentin had decreed that they should play a pastoral and then a farce. He had covered his face with white lead for the pastoral, and then, at the last moment, had painted a large blue teardrop on one cheek. For Chanteclair, he said, when Ninon questioned him.

He played magnificently, his tirades eloquent, his moments of pathos heartrending. He seemed more real, his emotions more true upon the stage than in those brief interludes when he waited behind the curtain with Ninon. Once she reached for his hand, and was dismayed to see the emptiness in his eyes, as though Valentin had fled, and only the shell, the play's character, remained.

When the pastoral was over, they retired to a small antechamber that adjoined the *galerie*, quickly changing their costumes for the farce. The men wiped off their face paint and replaced it with masks, Valentin adding a wig and small beard to his usual mask, so that his own features were totally obscured.

He played the farce with great animation, adding leaps and handstands to his already robust performance. The company, fired by his vigor, performed their *lazzi* to a turn, and improvised comic speeches and bits, delivering their lines with great wit and crispness. Toinette had never been a sillier inamorata, nor Ninon a more pert and devilish soubrette. Joseph was a sighing lover, filling the hall with his lamentations; Marc-Antoine, as the pompous savant, had foolish advice for everyone. And Valentin's bragging captain had an unexpected element of pity in him, revealing the fragile man behind the bravado.

Through it all, Monsieur d'Arouet sat in a large elbow chair placed in front of the stage. He seemed small and fragile, alone in the center of the room, his hands folded quietly in his lap. He applauded not at all, and smiled seldom. Occasionally he motioned to Villebois, standing along a side wall, and whispered something in his servant's ear, or drank the wine that was brought to him; but otherwise he sat like a statue. Ninon found it disconcerting to play to silence, after the hurly-burly of their audiences. She found herself wondering if he was pleased with their playing; indeed, she had begun to wonder why this strange man had spent so much money to invite them in the first place.

At last the play was over and they took their bows. Arouet applauded politely, then rose to his feet, supporting himself on his cane and straightening his bent back as much as he was able. He cleared his throat. "Permit me to say you are the finest company I have seen in many a year. I am honored to have you in my house. You do your fathers proud… wherever they may be. You are welcome to return at any time. You will be received warmly." He cleared his throat again, as though he had found the words difficult to say, then indicated his servant with a nod of his head. "Villebois will wait on you until you have changed your costumes, then escort you to my *apartements*. I shall be pleased to receive you for supper in

273

my *antichambre*. Mesdames. Messieurs." He bowed slightly in their direction, then moved with great dignity to the door that a footman held for him.

The actors changed quickly, remarking to one another on the success of their playing, the strangeness of Monsieur le Comte, the possibility of playing soon again before such a generous, if not demonstrative, audience. Only Valentin kept apart, combing out his wig, folding his costume with unaccustomed care.

"Come along, Val," said Ninon, when they were all changed. "Monsieur Villebois waits for us."

Valentin looked up and shook his head. "No. I shall return to our rooms."

"But...Monsieur le Comte..."

"Make my excuses."

"Hell's fire, Valentin," Joseph said in astonishment. "Would you miss supper? The kitchen in this place must be a wonder to behold!"

Valentin laughed mirthlessly. "I have not your appetite, Joseph. And I think I can persuade one of the footmen to bring me a bit of supper in my room."

Ninon put her hand on his sleeve. "But why, Valentin?"

"Grant me my own life," he said gruffly, and turned away.

Monsieur d'Arouet's *antichambre* was a large and handsomely appointed room, its ceiling coffered and gilded, its tooled-leather walls hung with paintings. Beyond a partly opened door, Ninon could see his bedchamber, the carved bed swagged with velvet hangings. It was a man's *apartement;* she wondered idly if a woman shared it.

In the center of the room a table had been set up, covered with a fine tapestry. Joseph could hardly keep from gaping at the platters of food laid out: ham and sausages, quail and songbird, bowls of fresh strawberries and cherries, pâtés and fruit tarts and meat pies. And crystal goblets waiting to receive the finest wine, and snowy napkins and silver knives as though they were visiting royalty.

The Comte d'Arouet was already seated at the head of the table when Villebois ushered them in. He nodded graciously but did not rise. "And Monsieur Sanscoeur?" he asked.

Ninon blushed, feeling humiliated for him, for Valentin. "Please to forgive him, Monsieur le Comte. He was overtaken with a weariness."

He sighed. "I understand. But sit you down. I trust the cook's offerings will meet with your approval."

They needed no further encouragement, but applied themselves to the food with gusto. While they ate, Arouet questioned them about the company—where they played, how successful they were, how broad their repertoire. After an hour or so, Toinette, Joseph, and Marc-Antoine were quite giddy from the wine, and even Ninon had begun to feel a bit lightheaded. She rose from the table and went to stand at the window, opening it slightly to catch the night air.

"You played superbly, Madame Guillemot." Arouet was standing at her side. "You must have laughter in your soul."

"Thank you, monsieur. But it does not follow. Monsieur Sanscoeur plays comedy well. Would you not agree? Yet he has forgot how to laugh."

His eyes searched her face. "You grieve for him."

She blinked back her tears. "No matter." She turned to the window. "Château d'Ivry is beautiful."

"And very lonely. It needs a woman."

She stirred uncomfortably. She had not thought him a libertine, expecting more from an actress than her performance upon the stage. But perhaps her concern for Valentin had blinded her. "Such a number of paintings," she said brightly, indicating the walls of the room. "What a fine history you must have!"

"Yes. The family can be traced back to Saint Louis in a direct line, and there are branches that date to the time of Charlemagne. Let me show you the earliest portrait." They made a tour of the room, Arouet pointing out his various ancestors, Ninon exclaiming in wonder at the lineage. Not even her father's family could boast such continuity through the ages.

Yet all the while she was conscious of his eyes upon her. She prayed he would not importune her. She could turn aside a coarse lout, flatter (while refusing) a lecherous noble; but Arouet seemed too dignified for such a tawdry scene. Sweet Madonna, she thought, let him not press me.

"Do you care for him?" he asked suddenly.

"What?"

"Monsieur Sanscoeur. Do you care for him?"

She stared at him. Was this an overture to a full-scale assault? "Yes," she said at last.

"Come into my bedchamber," he said. "There's a portrait you might find of interest."

"Monsieur, I…" she stammered.

"Good God, woman!" he said, his voice hard and angry. "Don't stand there like an idiot. Come along!"

In spite of her own common sense, something in his eyes compelled her. Meekly she followed him into his bedchamber, skirting the wide bed and standing as far from him as she was able without deliberately insulting him. He picked up a candelabrum from a table and crossed to the fireplace. The candles flickered with each halting step he took, leaning heavily on his cane. He lifted the candles high so that she might see the portrait over the mantel.

"*Mon Dieu!*" she gasped, her hand flying to her mouth.

It was a painting of a young woman and two small children. The woman was very beautiful, with a pale, heart-shaped face, black hair, and soft, dark eyes. She might have been Valentin's twin.

"My wife," said Arouet. "My late wife. Painted many years ago, of course."

Ninon's voice trembled. "And the boys...your sons?"

"Yes."

"But they are grown by now, *n'est-ce pas?*"

"My elder son is dead. A fever two winters ago."

Ninon stared at the face of the younger child, dark-haired like his mother, with melting eyes and a deep dimple in his chin. "And the other son?" she asked softly.

"Driven away by my own folly and pride." He laughed bitterly. "Pride is a worthless possession when one has nothing left."

"But what happened?"

"We quarreled...it must be three years agone...over a woman. In a moment of madness that I have regretted ever since, I banished him from my sight, disowned him, cut him out of my heart."

There was a long silence. "Tell him so," she said at last. "If you regret it, tell him so."

He looked at her in despair. "Nicolas is very stubborn and proud. My letters of reconciliation go unanswered. He will not even stand before me face to face. What more am I to do?"

Ninon looked at the painting again. "He seems so sweet."

"He was gentle, like his mother. Even as a man. A gentle and trusting nature."

Ninon felt tears well up in her eyes. "A person who trusts too much drinks deep of the cup of bitterness and anger when that trust is shattered."

"And brings grief to others, I think," he said gently.

She brushed away her tears. "I'm surprised he goes unrecognized."

"He has changed greatly. See you." Arouet pulled a small case from his pocket. Opening it, he showed Ninon a portrait carved in wax *in relievo*: the man depicted had a small, neat beard and flowing mustache.

But the profile was unmistakable—the high forehead, the patrician nose. "Greatly changed. A man may go unrecognized by his friends, if he sets his mind to it."

Ninon smiled sadly, remembering the many quarrels. "And if he travels the byways and avoids the big cities, where will he find those erstwhile friends?" She looked hard at the comte, seeing the grief etched on his face. "Cannot the past be buried?"

"How? He will not even allow me to speak to him. I have my own pride. Let it be, madame. Come. We shall rejoin your companions."

"A moment, monsieur. 'Tis a lovely night. I marked from the window of your *cabinet* this afternoon a beautiful little garden. Like a stage, cut in the greensward, with statues for auditors."

"Yes. It was a favored spot of Nicolas and his brother. They played at actors, declaiming to the wind, performing for the statues—and any footman unlucky enough to be waylaid by two lively lads."

"Is that spot torchlit at night?"

"If I order it so. Why do you ask?"

"On such a sweet night, it seems to me that Monsieur Sanscoeur could be persuaded to take a stroll. To that very garden…if it is lighted. I should reckon we will be there in a little more than a quarter of an hour." She curtsied deeply. "Your servant, monsieur. I thank you for your courtesies and bid you good night."

"I shall have the garden lit, madame. Enjoy your stroll."

She found Valentin lying on the bed, staring up at the ceiling. On a nearby table was his supper, barely touched. He turned his head to look at her as she entered their room, then resumed his inspection of the ceiling beams. She perched on the bed and smiled down at him. "It was a fine evening. Monsieur le Comte is a gracious host." He grunted, but said nothing. "Valentin, come with me out into the park."

"Sweet Jesu, whatever for?"

She bent down and kissed him gently. "Because it is a pretty night. Because I don't wish to walk alone in the dark. Because you are my comrade, and it grieves me to see you so burdened. Come. Let the sweet breezes blow away your gloom."

"I have no place in my heart for cheer tonight."

"Oh, Val. I saw such a beautiful garden from monsieur's window. A little round garden, with statues, and a still pond. Won't you come with me? No one is about."

He sat up and rubbed his hand tiredly across his eyes. "Mayhap a walk is what I need."

She led him out to the park of Château d'Ivry. From ground level, the round garden could not be seen; only the fact that she had seen it from Arouet's window led her to the correct path. There was a crossing of two paths farther on. Ninon stopped, perching on one foot, and pretended to shake a pebble out of her shoe. Valentin, preoccupied with his own thoughts, walked on. She smiled to herself, seeing him take the right path without thinking.

They reached the garden at last. With the lit torches, it was as bright as day, the lanterns flickering on the graceful marble statuary, and twinkling back at themselves in the glassy pond.

"There," said Ninon. "Did I not tell you it was a charming spot?" Valentin said nothing, gazing about as though his eyes saw ghosts and spirits in every shadow. There was a rustle in the line of trees that bordered the garden; Monsieur d'Arouet moved slowly into the firelight. Valentin started violently, and whirled about to flee the garden. In that moment, Ninon slipped her arm through his, and held him fast. "Valentin," she said brightly. "You cannot think to leave without first being presented to our host. Monsieur le Comte d'Arouet, Monsieur Valentin Sanscoeur."

Valentin glared at her, his eyes murderous, then nodded stiffly to Arouet. "Monsieur."

Ninon ignored his look. "Monsieur d'Arouet was telling me the most curious story this evening, Valentin. He had two sons. He quarreled with one—over a woman, I am led to believe—and disowned him."

"A tragic tale," said Valentin, his lip curled in scorn. "How fortunate he still has another son."

"No," said the comte. "My elder son is dead."

Ninon could feel Valentin stiffen beside her. "Dead?" His voice grated in his throat.

"A fever. The winter of 'fifty-six."

Valentin was silent for a very long time. Then he laughed mockingly. "And now you have no sons, Monsieur d'Arouet."

"I would have my younger son back. All I own, my lands and titles, are his should he wish to reclaim them."

"'Tis easy to need the one when you have lost the other."

"Valentin…" Ninon shook her head in reproof.

"You have a cruel tongue, Monsieur Sanscoeur," said Arouet. "But I felt the loss of the one long before the other was taken from me."

Valentin frowned down at Ninon, his face a mask of hatred. "And all for a woman. That was what you said, was it not, Monsieur le

Comte?" He pushed Ninon away and stared up at the night sky, the dark trees beyond the torches. "I knew a man like that once," he said at last, his voice soft and filled with sadness. "A man who destroyed himself because of a woman. Who damned his soul to Hell because of her." He laughed bitterly. "Her name was Angelique. How the Devil must have enjoyed *that* jest! She was his father's mistress, and quite the most beautiful creature he had ever known. He was young. Sweet Jesu, how young he was! Not in years, but in trust. He had played at love, sweet and innocent and artless, but Angelique was different. He longed for her, he burned with a passion that drove him mad. He began to hate his own father for possessing her."

"Why did he stay?" Arouet asked in agony.

"Because he had not the strength to leave. Nature had favored him in every way, then thrown the temptress in his path to make a mockery of all his fine resolves. To show himself to himself as a weakling and a coward." He drew a painful breath. "She came to him one night, at last, all soft and sighing; to his eternal shame and damnation, he took her. And not just that one time. He was mad beyond all reasoning. He believed every honeyed lie she told him. He found it easy to betray his father's trust...my God, he would have killed for her, he was so besotted!"

"And his father learned of it?" Ninon asked softly.

"I think the whore told him. They quarreled—he and his father— and the quarrel led to blows and then to swords. Do you understand? He was young and strong; he had trained for a soldier. But he drew his sword against an old man."

"*Ah Dieu*," whispered Ninon.

"There *was* no God that day. He left his father bleeding and crippled upon the floor, and went off to bed his slut." Valentin groaned. "For a woman. For a sweet-tongued, worthless whore. He was branded with the mark of Cain. Worse than Cain. Cain slew his brother—this man raised his hand against the father who had given him life."

"What happened to Angelique?" asked Arouet.

Valentin laughed bitterly. "Ah, yes, Angelique. Who had invaded his heart, clouded his reason, blinded his eyes. They fled together. The whore stayed only until they learned he had been disowned. He had lost his title, his inheritance, his wealth. My God! He had lost a great deal more—his good name, his self-respect, his honor. Seeing him thus bereft of all she had craved...and with no prospects for a comfortable future... Angelique vanished." He turned to Arouet. "Was that not wise of her? To abandon a fool to his own folly?"

Arouet shook his head. "His father's was the greater folly. For the son was young and headstrong. The quarrel should not have taken place. The father should not have disowned his son."

"No. No. He drew his sword against his own father. God cursed him that day."

Ninon was near tears. "But his father forgives him!"

Valentin whirled to her, his eyes burning. "Damn your meddling!" he cried. "How does a man forgive himself? He drew his sword against his *father!* How does he make his peace with God?"

By swearing never to love again, she thought. By guarding his heart against betraying womankind. She put a gentle hand on his arm. "Valentin…"

He scowled at her, his eyes narrowing in anger. "If you have no more scenes to play tonight, you deceiving bitch…"

"Monsieur Sanscoeur," chided Arouet, "I do protest. Madame Guillemot is a generous woman, with a kind heart. She…"

Valentin laughed mockingly, his mouth twitching. "Do you find her attractive, monsieur? Charming? Would you care to do battle to take her from me?"

Arouet flinched at the cruel thrust. "Monsieur. Your servant," he said at last, bowing to Valentin. With a heavy sigh, he turned about and vanished into the dark trees. Valentin, with one last look of contempt for Ninon, stomped away in the direction of their quarters. She hurried after him, torn between the desire to comfort him, or rage at him for his stubborn pride.

"You fool!" she cried at last, when they had reached the privacy of their bedchamber. "You pigheaded fool!"

"And you? Are you pleased with the scene you played? Did you and he laugh as you planned how I was to be ambushed? Did he give you thirty pieces of silver to arrange the meeting?"

"Oh!" She turned away from him and said no more. In his present mood he would twist her every word, no matter how she tried to reason with him. In silence they stripped down to their nightclothes—chemise and shirt—undressing on opposite sides of the room. Ninon folded her skirts and bodice neatly over the back of a chair and laid down her shoes beside the cold hearth. She hoped he would go to sleep at once. In the morning, God willing, she would be able to talk to him. Deliberately she pulled the pins from her copper curls, taking her time as she shook out the long tresses. She crossed the room, meaning to retrieve her comb from a little table. But Valentin was suddenly standing before her, his eyes burning with intensity by the light of the single candle.

"Get into bed," he growled.

"Sweet Madonna, you cannot want…"

"Get into bed!"

She pursed her lips in angry defiance. "No."

"Damn you!" His hand shot out, slapping her sharply on the side of the face.

She caught her breath at the fierceness of the blow. He was beyond reasoning. She turned to the bed and crawled beneath the sheets. She felt neither fear nor hatred, only helplessness. She could not protect herself from his suffering; she could not keep him from bleeding in pain. Had she not helped Arouet to open the old wounds?

He smashed his palm down on the candle to extinguish it, then got into bed beside her, pulling her roughly into his arms. His mouth was hard on hers, bruising her lips, his hands on her arms cruel and tight. Impatiently he pulled off her chemise and mounted her. He had no thought for her readiness; when he entered her she fought back the urge to cry out in agony. He had never hurt her before—not even that first time—but tonight he took her savagely, as though he wished to punish her. She closed her eyes against the tears that burned: tears of pain, tears of pity for his poor tormented heart. She was grateful for the darkness that hid her misery, her shame.

Tonight she was not Ninon for him. Tonight she was Angelique, atoning for all the griefs of the past.

She awoke with her body aching and sore. He had used her hard through the long night, turning the act of love into an act of vengeance. She had said nothing, letting him have his way; only when he slept had she allowed herself to weep. Now she yawned and stretched gingerly, pushing off the sheet, then opened her eyes. Valentin, fully dressed, was staring down at her. She followed his gaze to the dark bruises on her arms where his hands had gripped her. Hastily she tried to re-cover herself, but he frowned and pulled away the sheet, then sat on the bed beside her. His face was filled with pain and remorse as he reached out a hand and stroked her bare arms.

"You never cried out. Damn you! What makes you play the fool? Is it pride? Stubbornness? That you should keep your own counsel, hold your tongue—even as you suffer?"

"You were not yourself last night. Let it be."

"No. Last night…a thousand nights…a hundred days. What difference? I have been cruel to you, abused you, struck you. Played the brute more times than I care to recall. And still you hold your tongue, and bow your head, and wait for the next blow. Why? *Why?*" He took her by the shoulders and shook her, his tortured eyes seeking answers in her face.

"Name of God, Valentin," she whispered, "let it be."

"What are you," he asked, his voice ragged, "that you hold your pain inside and say nothing? Damn you, what are you?"

"Your mirror," she said simply.

He fled then, leaving her to dress alone and pack her few belongings into her hamper. A small breakfast had been left on a tray; she ate it with complete indifference. The food tasted like ashes in her mouth. When she emerged into the courtyard, the players were already fastening the last bits of baggage into the wagon, and exclaiming in delight at the three horses that had been given them by the Comte d'Arouet.

"Is it not grand, Ninon?" exclaimed Toinette. "The use of a carriage to get here—and now a gift of horses! What a fine gentleman he is."

"And a suit for me!" exclaimed Marc-Antoine, parading about to exhibit his newly acquired doublet and breeches of elegant blue velvet.

Valentin tightened the ropes on the oxen. "I shall be pleased when Monsieur le Comte sees fit to pay us the remainder of our fee and we can be quit of this place." He looked over to where Joseph was admiring a chestnut mare. "Go and find Monsieur Villebois and ask him when we are to be paid."

"Upon the instant, Monsieur Heartless." The Comte d'Arouet moved slowly through the arch of the *corps-de-logis* toward the strollers. Ninon ran to him, letting him lean on her instead of his cane.

"Your eyes are sad this morning, madame," he said softly.

"'Tis my nature."

He sighed. "Have I done a foolish thing?"

"No. I feel sure that, in time…"

"Will you return? I would know how he fares."

"You have my word, Monsieur d'Arouet. If I must move Heaven and Hell, I will see that the Peerless Theatre Company returns to Château d'Ivry."

By this time they had reached the center of the courtyard, where the rest of the players waited. Arouet fumbled in the breast of his doublet and withdrew a large sack of coins, holding it out to Valentin. "Monsieur Sanscoeur."

Valentin bowed and took the proffered money. "We trust you enjoyed our endeavors, monsieur."

"Indeed. You are a fine company. I wonder you do not play in Paris."

Valentin gazed at him steadily. "Mayhap we shall...now."

"I wish you well." Arouet hesitated, then offered his hand to Valentin. Ninon held her breath. Valentin stared at the comte for a long time, then clasped the man's hand in a firm grip.

"*Au revoir*, monsieur," he said gruffly, and turned about to Joseph. "If you wish to ride a horse, I'll take the wagon."

"I'll sit with you," said Ninon.

Valentin shrugged. "As you wish." He pocketed Arouet's money, then swung himself onto the seat of the wagon, holding out his hand for Ninon to scramble up beside him. They moved out slowly through the frontispiece, crossing the village square toward the highroad that led south. Ninon had turned about at the last to wave to Arouet. As their cavalcade took a bend in the road, leaving the town and château of Ivry-la-Bataille behind, she stole a surreptitious look at Valentin. He was staring straight ahead, his face like carved stone. Proud and stubborn to the end. She bit back the angry words that sprang to her lips.

Suddenly he put his hand over hers, and squeezed her fingers in silent acknowledgment. When she looked again at his face, she saw that he had begun to weep.

Sweet Madonna, she thought. Let them be tears of forgiveness. Forgiveness for himself.

Chapter Fifteen

"*Benissimo!*" Valentin threw back his head and laughed, clapping enthusiastically for the young boy who blushed and bowed to the company.

The innkeeper beamed at the players gathered around the supper table. "Did I not tell you my son was a fine juggler?"

"Indeed he is." Valentin fished in his pocket for a coin. "If we return to Pithiviers in a year or two, we will consider taking the lad into our company." He smiled again as the boy puffed with pride and his father clapped him on the shoulder.

Seated across the table from Valentin, Ninon felt her heart swell with joy. These last few weeks, since Ivry-la-Bataille, she had watched him in wonder and delight. The years had seemed to melt from his face, the weight of his remorse and guilt slowly lifting. It was as though the meeting with his father had been a sort of catharsis, releasing him at last from the burden he had carried for so long. He still raged from time to time—he would not be Valentin else—but his troubled heart seemed lighter.

She turned and smiled sweetly at the vicomte sitting beside her. She did not care for him very much—his eyes were cruel despite his gracious manner—but he was brother-in-law to the provost, and a man of some influence in Pithiviers. Besides, he and his wife were their hosts at supper tonight, and had promised to bring their friends to the performance on the morrow. She looked across to where Valentin was entertaining the vicomtesse, surprised to see his pleasant demeanor, the way he bent attentively to the woman so that she dimpled like a coquette and ducked behind her fan. Could it be that he was learning to play the diplomat? And when they rose to leave, the company full of gratitude for their host's many kindnesses, Valentin even managed to kiss the woman's hand.

"Methinks I should be jealous," she said to him with mock seriousness, when they were alone at last in their chamber.

"Of what? She was old and fat and tiresome." He took her in his arms and kissed her.

"Then at long last you have learned Chanteclair's skill at flattery, when it is in the best interests of the company."

"Sweet Jesu," he growled, "I wasn't kind to her to truckle to the beldam!"

"Then why?"

"You yourself spent the evening with her husband. What thought you of the man?"

"Cruel, I think, despite his charm. I should not care to cross him."

"Yes. It was clear from what the poor woman said to me that she is lower to him than his grooms."

She looked at him quizzically. "And that is why you flattered her, kissed her hand?"

He shrugged. "If the poor creature can feel admired for a moment or two—though it be sweet illusion—what's the harm?"

She stared at him in astonishment. There had been a time when a woman's tenderness would ignite his malevolence. "You softling," she teased. "Do you mean to tell me there are times when a woman is worthy of your kindness? The great Monsieur Heartless?"

"Very few times," he said dryly. "As for 'softling,' you saucy wench, I'll give you 'softling'!" He grinned and began to tickle her playfully, stopping only when she begged for mercy and swore that he was still the same sour-faced Valentin he had always been. Still laughing, they fell into bed and made love with lighthearted abandon, finding new joy in each other, as though they had never been lovers before.

"How many peaches are left, Joseph?" Ninon rolled over onto her back and gazed up at the clear blue sky.

"Two."

"No more?"

"I only stole a score. I thought I heard the farmer's dog."

"Here," said Valentin, leaning over Ninon. "Have a bite of mine."

"Mmm." She smacked her lips, savoring the sweet fruit, and closed her eyes. The scent of summer flowers filled the meadow, and the warm sun kissed her cheeks. She could hear the humming of bees as they worked a patch of clover, and a distant thrush sang. She sighed deeply, filled with contentment. The company had never done so well, playing success after success, despite their reduced numbers. They had bought new scenery, new gowns for the women, new boots for the men. They stayed in the finest inns, dined well, satisfied their every wish. Hortense had recovered her health, and Valentin…Valentin…Ninon sighed again. Every day was a joyous revelation, showing her a man she had not known before. A man who was become so dear to her that her heart ached to think of ever parting from him.

If only he would see into her heart. It was the one dark cloud on the clear blue of her horizon. If only she could make him see.

She opened her eyes and sat up, looking about at her comrades sprawled on the greensward. She had known them for little more than a year, but they were the dearest friends she had ever had. There was a sense of community in their little band; where they touched on matters that concerned the whole company, they thought and felt as one. That was why they were here this afternoon, stretched out in a sunny meadow, munching on stolen peaches, instead of in the next town unpacking their belongings. The glorious day had called to them all—there was time for a picnic under the blue sky. They would arrive at their destination after dark, but what did it matter? The day was too sweet to waste in travel. Ninon scanned the sky, idly noting a large white cloud on the horizon.

Sébastien wiped his mouth on his sleeve and tossed his peach pit over his shoulder. "*Nom de Dieu*, Marc-Antoine, share some of that wine!" He drank deeply from the demijohn and handed it on to Joseph. "I forgot to tell you," he said to no one in particular, "when we were in Saint-Benôit I met a merchant just come from Paris. He heard that Monsieur Molière has gained for himself a fine patron—the king's brother, 'Monsieur' Duc d'Orléans. I should not be surprised if Molière played Paris in the near future."

"And came to the king's notice as well," said Joseph.

"We might have done the same," Marc-Antoine said sulkily. "I shall stifle with provincialism!"

"Come now, Marc-Antoine," chided Valentin. "The provinces have put money in your pockets and boots on your feet."

"Ah, but in Paris…a man may live his life however he chooses, without fear of censure and bourgeois morality. I tire of provincial naïveté."

"And the pickings are slim," Toinette said waspishly. "How many Pierres can you find in the provinces?"

"Stupid bitch," said Marc-Antoine, obviously stung by her words. With great dignity he marched to a nearby tree, sat down—his hat pulled low over his eyes—and went to sleep.

Hortense frowned at Sébastien. "Where were you in Saint-Benôit when you met that merchant?"

He sighed. "Must we play this scene again?"

"Damn you!" Her voice was shrill. "The local gambling hall, *n'est-ce pas?*"

"We can afford it."

"Ahhh! You would take your last crown—that was to buy my shroud—and lose it on *rouge et noir!*"

"Don't start with me, Hortense," he said, jumping to his feet. "Val, I shall take a horse and ride on ahead to town. Do you want to stay at the Black Swan?"

"Why not? Their beds are clean, as I recall."

"Then I shall take rooms and await your arrival. If you find me not at the Black Swan," he smiled maliciously at Hortense, "look for me in the *tripot.*" He moved to one of the grazing horses, swung up into the saddle, and disappeared over the crest of a hill.

Concerned as always with his stomach, Joseph reached into the wagon and brought forth a loaf of bread—round and flat like a discus—that they had bought in the last town. "I'd give my soul for a bit of lard or honey at this very moment," he mourned, breaking off a dry crust from the loaf.

"The field is full of clover," said Hortense. "There must be a beehive nearby."

"Indeed, yes." Joseph was all smiles. "Toinette, will you come with me to look?"

"Don't be a fool," said Valentin. "'Tis no simple matter."

Joseph bristled. "My father did it all the time. He would throw sticks at the hive until the bees went away. Toinette, will you come?"

She made a face. "I cannot even think of food while my stomach churns. Go without me."

Ninon glanced at the sky. More clouds had appeared, large white puffs that held an edge of gray. "But do not tarry, Joseph. I like not the look of that sky."

"It will not rain," he said, and strode off to a small grove beyond the meadow.

Hortense had been eyeing Toinette. "Your stomach churns," she said at last. "Have you been taken with a looseness?"

Toinette shook her head. "No. Only that…I know not what it can be…" She gulped and clutched her belly.

Valentin laughed. "Mayhap it is the result of a looseness in your behavior!"

Toinette gasped. "*Mon Dieu!* Do you really suppose…?"

"Come along," said Hortense, slipping her arm through Toinette's. "We have much to speak of." The two women strolled to the edge of a small brook, and soon were talking animatedly to each other, Hortense waving the air with a cautionary finger, Toinette nodding her head in agreement while her yellow curls bobbed up and down.

Ninon looked at Valentin and began to giggle. Under his tree, Marc-Antoine still snored. "I was only just thinking what happy comrades we are," she laughed, "and here we are scattered to the winds like dandelion seeds."

Valentin yawned and stretched. "'Tis too lazy an afternoon to be troubled by the cares of others. I shall sit here and write a play in my head."

"What will be your theme? Will there be a part for me?"

His dark eyes studied her, suddenly serious. "Perhaps. My heroine will be a princess who keeps her heart locked in a tower."

"But surely she is only waiting to be rescued."

"Yes. I think my hero will be strong and noble—and fair."

"Why not dark?"

"Because she prefers a man who is fair."

Ninon frowned. "Is she so simple that she judges a man by the color of his hair?"

"She has no judgment left, for her heart is locked up. Remember?"

"Dark or fair," said Ninon sharply, "how shall he rescue her? He must have obstacles of course, to make the plot more interesting. Give him chains to drag about with him. Chains forged of his own pride!"

"Would you write a comedy, then?" he muttered.

"No. A farce. For the hero is a buffoon."

"And the princess is a fool!"

"Wherefore?" she asked, gazing at him with yearning eyes. "She has her dreams, and her hopes—"

"Foolish dreams," he interrupted angrily. "Empty hopes! Do you think Philippe still remembers you?"

She fought back her tears. "Let us play Oedipus and put aside the writing. You play his blindness exquisitely!" She looked up at the sky, now dark with clouds. "And if that fool Joseph does not return, we shall be drenched long before we reach town." She hurried to the wagon and began to cover their furnishings with the canvas they kept for inclement weather. Damn Valentin and his stubborn pride. She would not let him break her heart.

A sudden howling from the woods snapped her head around. Valentin jumped to his feet and Marc-Antoine started in his sleep. Joseph emerged from the grove of trees, runnning like the wind, a swarm of bees in close pursuit. They caught him a moment before he splashed into the brook; he yelped in pain and swatted furiously at the creatures. Laughing at first, and then filled with sympathy for the hapless Joseph, the players gathered around. By the time they had packed his face and arms with mud to ease the sting, and laid him, groaning, into the bottom of the wagon, the rain had begun.

They arrived at the Black Swan after dark, drenched through, grumbling and angry with the weather, with one another, with their wretched lot that put them—like gypsies—forever upon the road. While the rain beat loudly upon the roof, they ate in silence in Ninon and Valentin's bedchamber, sunk in gloom, shivering still (though they had stripped down to shirts and chemises and hung up their wet clothes), filled with their own private miseries. Ninon sighed and pushed away her plate. Was it only this afternoon that they had seemed so happy?

There was a sudden cackling laugh. They looked up in astonishment at the sound. Valentin stood in the doorway, a shawl about his shoulders, Chanteclair's glasses on his nose. "You foolish children," he said, his voice a high squeak, "is there not enough rain and misery beyond the casements without you bringing it into the room?"

Marc-Antoine grinned in delight. "Grandmère, we have needed your cheer."

"Then why go to Paris, you silly ass? You may find a better troupe, you may find a new lover. But you shall not find warmer friends and companions."

Marc-Antoine looked shamefaced. "True enough."

"As for you, Toinette," "Grandmère" pursed her lips in vexation, "have you not enough charm—after your parade of lovers—to help poor Joseph forget his pain and grief tonight? Your ministrations should be better than any doctor's, *n'est-ce pas?*"

Toinette laughed and blew "Grandmère" a kiss, then led Joseph into her bedchamber.

Hortense shook her head sadly. "You cannot resolve my concerns, Grandmère."

"Wherefore? Because Sébastien gambles? Many a man does as much."

"No. Because gambling is his wife. His mistress."

Valentin laughed sharply and pinched Hortense's cheek. "You goose! Are you blind? Know you that Sébastien would not gamble when you were ill—not even when we urged him to double our capital. He feared to lose the one coin that might save your life."

"*Ah Dieu*," whispered Hortense, turning to Sébastien. "Is it so?"

"Have you so little faith in me?" grumbled Sébastien. He turned to Valentin. "Grandmère, what think you of beating a wife with some regularity?"

Valentin snickered slyly. "I can think of a better reason to tuck up a woman's skirts." He turned to Ninon and smiled, pulling off his glasses. "Now be off, the lot of you," he said in his own voice. "'Grandmère' has business of his own this night." He took Ninon's face between his hands and kissed her softly. "Dearest Ninon, why do you weep?"

"For Chanteclair's legacy," she said, and put her arms around his neck.

He carried her to the bed and made love to her as he had not before, almost reverently, his hands caressing her in adoration, his lips doing honor to her eyes and mouth and bosom. And when at last his body had stilled, he folded her into his embrace, as though he could not bear to be parted from her even while they slept.

The sun was bright in the room when she awoke. She stretched in pleasure, feeling the smoothness of the sheets against her naked body, the contentment of her senses. Valentin was already moving about the chamber, putting on his clothes, but when she stirred he came and sat on the bed beside her.

"I thought you would sleep the day away."

"Would you have minded?"

He stroked back the hair from her forehead. "Yes. For then I could not kiss you." He bent down and put his lips to hers, then smiled, his eyes enveloping her with their warmth. "Beautiful Ninon. I never remember to tell you so. And then I hear some coxcomb flattering you, and I curse my own silent tongue."

"You wicked man," she said tenderly. "How am I to forgive you?"

"Let me atone in some small way." He fingered her earlobes. "Joseph and I must arrange the *jeu de paume* for this afternoon. But it would please me if you would seek out a *bijoutier* and buy a new pair of earrings to replace the ones we sold."

"Valentin…how foolish…I would be as happy with an armful of summer flowers from the meadow. I scarcely need…"

"Please. Buy them for me. And I promise that when Joseph and I have concluded our business, I shall bring you flowers."

She dressed and breakfasted, then hurried down the street to the village square. A tinsmith, spreading out his wares to the morning sun, directed her down a narrow lane to a jeweler's shop; she was delighted to find that the *bijoutier* had among his stock a fine pair of coral earrings. She paid for them quickly, eager to see Valentin again—he must have returned to the inn by now. She could hardly wait to show him her purchase, so like the earrings he had given her. She hummed a merry tune, skipping blithely over her shadow on the cobbled way, and turned into the inn courtyard.

She saw the splendid carriage first, the Froissart crest painted on its door, then Valentin standing like a statue, the summer blossoms forgotten and scattered at his feet. He looked up as she approached, his face a mask, one eyebrow cocked in cynicism. He smiled stiffly, indicating the servant in livery who waited near the coach.

"This is Philippe's man. Come to take you back with him."

"But...you cannot mean..."

The coachman stepped forward. "Mademoiselle Guillemot?" She nodded in silence, too stunned to speak. "I have a letter for you," he went on, fishing in the pocket of his doublet.

She reached for it, her hand shaking, and tore open the seal, conscious of Valentin's burning eyes on her. Philippe's letter was filled with extravagant outpourings of love, vows of undying devotion. He had put aside the differences in their stations, he said, and now waited— his heart surcharged with longing—for her to fly to his side.

"What does he say?" asked Valentin, his voice harsh with contempt. "Is he panting for you? Is he filled with desire? Does he need your love beyond all reason?"

"Name of God, Valentin..." she whispered. Stricken, she turned back to the letter and read it again, seeking a spark of warmth, the anchor upon which to fasten her floundering heart.

"And what of Madame de Froissart?"

"Henriette is dead."

He laughed sardonically. "Why then, little bird, nothing stands in your way. Your dreams have come true at last."

"Val..." It was a cry of agony.

"Go, damn you! Go to your Philippe!"

She stared at him for long moments, seeing his handsome face contorted with anger. She sighed. "Yes," she said quietly. "I must go." She turned to the coachman. "Tend to your horses and have the innkeeper give you something to eat. I shall not be long." She glanced up at the sky. "'Tis almost noon. Have him pack a little dinner for me."

"It will not be necessary," said the coachman. "Monsieur de Froissart has provided me with a purse for your food and lodgings on the journey."

"How solicitous your lover is, little bird," said Valentin. "He has considered your every need."

Dear Heaven, she thought, I shall die. She turned quickly so that he would not see her face, and hurried toward the inn, speaking over her shoulder to the servant. "I shall not take long. My packing…a few things…no more."

"Mind you take only those gowns that belong to you!" Valentin's voice was hard and angry. "We can always find another soubrette to wear your costumes."

She fled to her room, choking back her tears. What a fool she was! She was going to Philippe, and he loved her. What more did she want? Have a little common sense, Ninon, she thought. She opened her large trunk and emptied it of its contents, spilling her clothes out on the bed. She fetched her hamper from a shelf and began to sort her things, replacing the borrowed costumes in the trunk (which belonged to the company), and neatly folding her own skirts and bodices into her hamper. She was rather proud of herself and her newfound composure—it was really the best course of action, to go to Philippe. She worked quickly and efficiently: the tights and spangled gown into the trunk, the petticoat into her hamper. The red velvet gown was hers, but the mermaid costume… the mermaid costume…Her busy hands slowed and she began to tremble, holding the costume to her cheek, remembering the times when she had worn it. Her eyes filled with tears.

She heard a step behind her and brushed at her cheeks. She must not weep.

"He'll break your heart," Valentin said gruffly. "You're a fool."

Resolutely she kept her back to him and said nothing.

"If he loved you, he would have come for you himself."

She shrugged. "I am not so thoroughly the romantic that I expect a panting swain. He's not a schoolboy with his first love."

He sighed heavily. "I suppose it's for the best. He will not rage at you for looking at another man."

"No."

There was a long silence. Then: "I suppose you expect marriage!" he blurted.

"I would want my children to have a father."

He laughed bitterly. "You will be a comtesse and live in a great château. Just like your dreams."

She closed her hamper and fastened it. "Is that so wrong?"

"Dammit, you cannot leave!" She felt her heart leap in her breast.

"Joseph and I have contracted for the *jeu de paume* this afternoon. We cannot play without you."

"Nonsense. You've done it a score of times."

"And tomorrow? And next week?" His voice rose angrily.

She longed to turn around, to see his face. She closed the trunk before her, fingers playing absently with the hasp. "You know as well as I the company is breaking up," she said evenly. "Toinette is carrying a child. I think she means to marry the first fusilier or merchant who will have her. The rest of you will find other strollers. You can cast in your lot with them."

His next words were soft; she strained to hear them.

> *"Take not the roses from my days,*
> *But stay with me and be my Spring.*
> *When on your smile I may not gaze,*
> *Then Winter to my heart doth cling."*

She blinked back her tears, feeling her heart break. She would give him no quarter. "From *The Invisible Mistress*," she said at last.

"Yes. Don Carlos's speech."

"Yes."

His defenses were stripped away. "Don't go," he said hoarsely. "I love you."

She turned at that and threw herself into his arms. "Oh, my dearest love…how could I leave you?"

He kissed her hungrily, then pushed her away, his eyes wide in amazement. "You love me? You love *me?*"

She was laughing and crying all at the same time. "Of course I do!"

"But you love Philippe! You dream of Philippe!"

"Do I?" Her eyes were wistful. "Do you remember sometimes when a perfumed coxcomb would come into the changing room and then leave? And we joked about his presence still being there, like a ghost, because the heavy scent lingered. Only the scent. That's all. I say I love Philippe. I have loved him for years. My heart keeps the memory of love out of habit. I love him. My mouth speaks the words. And yet…just now…hurrying to be with him, I could not call to mind his face before my eyes." She sighed. "We play at sentiment upon the stage—passion and anger and joy. But they are not real. Mayhap my love for Philippe was always an illusion, a trick of my conjurer's heart. From the very first. Gratitude masquerading as love."

"Yet you would have gone to him, had I not shown you my heart."

"Yes."

His eyes were full of pain. "Wherefore?"

"Because…because I'm proud."

"*Mon Dieu!*" He swept her into his arms and held her close. "I should have lost you!"

"Chanteclair said that love is worth the risk. Do you remember?"

"Did you gamble on my taking the risk?"

She shook her head, her eyes filling with tears. "No," she said softly. "I should have gone to Philippe and married him."

"And broken my heart."

"Philippe, at least, would have been happy. He loves me. Though he does not need me."

He laughed. "As I do?" There was a touch of bravado in his voice. The old, guarded Valentin. She looked at him somberly, her clear blue eyes peering beyond the mask. He dropped his gaze, his handsome face awash with self-reproach. "As I do, Ninon. Always."

"Oh, Valentin. My dear love. Only hold me in your arms." She clung to him, filled with wonder and relief and a great joy. Chanteclair had been right. This was her home, locked in Valentin's sweet embrace. She was giving up a comfortable life with Philippe for the wanderings of a gypsy. And without a pang of regret. Philippe had been romance, the romance of her childhood fantasies. Valentin was real—and more dear to her than any dream could ever be.

They played a tragedy that afternoon. *Dido and Aeneas*, with Ninon as the hapless Queen Dido. She had never been better, her impassioned love tirades delivered from the depths of her joyful heart. At the very end, mourning the loss of Aeneas while the flames of her funeral pyre rose around her (one of Gaston's cleverest tricks), she brought the spectators to their feet, cheering and weeping. And when the curtain had dropped, they brought her back again and again to take her bows, tossing flowers upon the stage in homage to her performance. She gathered the blossoms in her arms and retired behind the curtain. She leaned against a wing and smiled at Valentin, her face flushed with success, her eyes shining.

"We should go to Paris," he said. "The Théâtre de Bourgogne would welcome you with open arms."

"If you think so."

He frowned. "Would you grieve to give up this life?"

"You mean for Paris? To give up the life of a stroller?"

"No. To give up the life of an actress."

She looked surprised. "What would you, Valentin?"

"I...have been thinking for some time now...he is an old man... the years have been hard on him. How much longer can he manage the estates alone? And the thought of his loneliness troubles my heart." He looked at her with tenderness. "I want to marry you, Ninon. I want you to bear my children. But how much sweeter if those children have a home—and a grandfather to love them. It would bring great happiness to his fading years."

"Valentin. My love. It would bring me great happiness to see you reconciled."

He laughed gently. "'Tis a very different life than what you have known. Sometimes tiresome. You might miss the excitement of the theater. And aristocracy can be a burden."

"I think I can play the role," she said with a sniff.

He bowed in mockery. "Of course, Queen Dido. I forget. But there is more to the role than commands and noble tirades. You will be the Vicomtesse de Bovier in sooth—the title is mine while my father the comte lives. Not a shadowy Queen Dido upon a stage. Do you think yourself a skillful enough actress to play the part?"

She drew herself up with dignity. "Pish-tush, you great looby! I was born the daughter of a marquis!"

He began to laugh, thinking it a joke, then stopped, seeing the look on her face. "Sweet Jesu, what an astonishing creature you are!" He nodded to the rest of the company, who had begun to gather around and urge them to change their costumes for the next play. "We come. We come." He held out his hand to Ninon, kissing her fingertips and leading her toward the changing room. "Come, my love. Let us play the farce to a fine turn, and then you shall sit by me and relate how my sweet Ninon came to be born the daughter of a marquis!"

Epilogue

1670

The laughing of a child woke her. Ninon stirred and looked over to the other pillow, where Nicolas still slept. The years had been kind to him. His handsome face was unlined, his hair as black as ever—though one or two gray curls had appeared on the ebony thatch that covered his chest. She almost bent over to kiss his lips, then thought better of it. He had ridden like the wind from Versailles to be with her last night. Let him sleep.

She eased herself out of bed, wrapping her naked body with his discarded cloak that lay on the floor. Her eye was caught by the painting of his mother over the mantel, seated with the boy Nicolas and his brother. How much her own two lads were come to resemble their father.

She heard the laughter again. Crossing to the casement, she looked out onto the vast garden; the servant Girard's boy was playing with his dog. The day was sunny, the sky a limpid blue. She felt young and reckless. It was early—her duties would not call her for a while yet. Quickly she donned her clothes and tiptoed out of Nicolas's bedroom to his *antichambre*, motioning for quiet to his *valet de chambre* who waited in attendance.

He tugged politely at his forelock. "Good morning, Madame la Comtesse."

"Good morning, Achille," she murmured. "Monsieur d'Arouet still sleeps. I would not have you disturb him."

"As you will, madame."

She hurried along the passageway and sped down a back staircase to the sunny garden, feeling deliciously wicked and wanton. Her lover was home, the sky was blue, and she was free from her cares and duties for a few moments. Skirts flying, she ran among the trees and danced

296

along the graveled paths, coming at last to the secluded garden with its crystal pool and circle of statues. She breathed deeply of the soft spring morning, catching a whiff of lilacs. She seated herself on a small bench, feeling a contentment and serenity that was mixed of equal portions of sunshine and lilacs and love.

"I knew I should find you here, when Charlotte said you were in the park. Is something troubling you?"

She rose to greet him with a kiss. "Good morrow, Nicolas. Put your mind at rest. It was only that the spring day whispered at the casement and called me out."

"To this spot, of course."

"It holds such fond memories."

His eyes were misty and faraway. "Yes."

With a sweep of her arm, she indicated the statues, silent witnesses to the traffic of the small garden. "Did you know that the children play at actors here?"

He laughed and shook his head. "I knew we should regret ever telling them of our shameful past!"

"By the by, did you see Hortense and Sébastien on your way to Paris?"

"Yes. Their inn prospers, though of course they still quarrel day and night."

"*Mon Dieu.* I thought that Sébastien had given up his gambling."

"For the most part. But now he has taken to letting the rooms go for a pittance when a charming woman asks for lodging. And Hortense is in a rage because a strolling company passed through last month and he would not even present a bill!"

"We should have been grateful for a landlord like that many a time! And Marc-Antoine...had you the opportunity to see him?"

"No. Molière said he was deep in rehearsals for Monsieur Lully's new opera."

"Poor Molière. Do the rumors still persist in Paris?"

"Alas, yes. And he is not well. A morbid cough, I fear."

Ninon clucked her tongue in sympathy. "After all these years. Still the ugly gossip. The taint of incest."

"His wife, Armand, is so much younger...and a Béjart..."

"But to noise it about that she is Madeleine Béjart's daughter...not her sister...Sweet Madonna, 'tis ugly enough. And then to claim that Molière himself sired her when Madeleine was his mistress...I cannot believe such calumny."

He sighed. "I thought when their child was born, and Louis himself stood godfather…"

"The act may have legitimatized the child, and shown the world the esteem the king holds for Molière…but…"

"But it cannot stop the gossip mongers, more's the pity."

"To have all that success," she said, "and still to be tormented…"

"'Tis a chancy life, to be an actor and playwright. Have you forgot? Racine's star is rising…they speak of him in the length and breadth of Paris. And I think that Lully means to see that music and opera take precedence over farce in the king's attentions."

"I was not thinking of Molière's torments as an actor. Only as a man. Armand was an unfortunate choice for a wife. She cuckolds poor Jean-Baptiste and breaks his heart."

Nicolas cocked a mocking eyebrow at her. "We all make mistakes."

She glared at him, hands on hips. "Valentin Sanscoeur!"

He laughed softly. "Now may Heaven protect me. There's the devil to pay when you call me Valentin!"

"Valentin *was* the devil. I thought so the first time I saw you at Marival."

"In Philippe's stable. When I kissed you."

"And took my breath away."

He put his arms around her. "But even the devil was an angel fallen from grace." He kissed her tenderly. "And as for Sanscoeur—Heartless— it was only because my heart was given to you."

She dimpled prettily. "You're filled with compliments this morning! While I have you in this mood I should ask for favors."

"Shameless hussy!" He tweaked her nose. "What do you want?"

"Arnaud. Is there not a title for him? He feels it keenly, that he is only Chevalier d'Arouet while Pierre-Augustin is Vicomte de Bovier."

"I'll speak to the lad. And to Pierre-Augustin. It may be that a little humility from Pierre-Augustin will benefit Arnaud as much as a title of his own." He held her tightly in his arms. "And how else may I serve you?"

She giggled. "You might take me to Versailles. The last time we were at court, I met the most charming duc…"

"Saucy wench!" He pinched her soundly on the bottom. She shrieked and pulled his hair. In a moment they both were on the ground, rolling about and laughing. When she stopped to catch her breath, he kissed her, his mouth possessing hers, his hands stroking her soft shoulders. "Now," he said, looking up at the line of statues that surrounded them, "unless you wish to be ravished in sight of all these witnesses, madame, you will move with all haste to have my breakfast prepared." He stood up and helped her to her feet, holding her hand as they strolled toward the château. "*À propos* Versailles," he said, suddenly serious, "the court is leaving in a week or two for Flanders. To visit the towns that were annexed in Louis's last campaign. Or so the *Gazette* has printed. But the court gossips, always alert to intrigue, suspect another story. If the court were in Flanders, it would put the king's sister-in-law, Henriette d'Angleterre, near to the coast and her brother, Charles II of England. There is some suspicion that negotiations might take place between brother and sister. A treaty between France and England."

"To what end?"

"To destroy the Dutch, I suppose, and drive Spain out of the Netherlands once and for all."

"Will you serve?"

"If I must. Look not so unhappy. 'Tis not likely. Louis prefers to depend on his standing army. He has not forgot the Fronde, and the nobles who rose against him. He'll break the backs of the aristocracy and beggar us all before he's through."

She smiled up at him. "Why then, if we're reduced to poverty, you and I shall gather up the children and take to the road! Can you still play a part, do you suppose?"

"Not on an empty belly, *mon Dieu*. I want my breakfast!"

They were passing through formal gardens with sculpted box hedges interspersed with bright tulips. *Parterres de broderies*, they were called, because they resembled embroidery. Ninon pushed Nicolas ahead of her. "Go in without me," she said. "And have your breakfast. The tulips are so lovely. I must choose a few for my *apartement*." She kissed him warmly and watched him stride toward the château, then bent to the flowers, gathering the blossoms in her arms. She heard Rachel's voice and looked up. The children had run out of the château to greet him. He picked up Arnaud and put him on his broad shoulder, laughing as the boy squealed in delight.

Through the mist of sudden tears she saw Bellefleur, her father, the shadow of memories long forgotten. Echoes of her own childhood laughter. Pretty little Ninon. You shall be a queen, a princess, a great lady.

Her lips still tingled from Nicolas's kiss. Her love and husband. Her Valentin.

"Rest content, *Papa*," she whispered. "I've come home."

Marielle
(The French Maiden Series - Book One)

Armed with only a disguise and her wavering courage, Marielle Saint-Juste goes on a perilous mission to free her brother from unjust captivity. But when she enters the prison of Louis XIII, it isn't her wounded brother she finds, but a mysterious stranger—and her destiny.

In this French dungeon, a love illuminates the darkest shadows in two hearts. Marielle will not only face her deepest fears, but change her life forever.

Lysette
(The French Maiden Series - Book Two)

Lysette, the Marquise de Ferrand, is left penniless after her husband dies. With nowhere else to turn, she ventures across the turbulent French countryside to the safety of her brother's home. But when she meets Andre, Comte du Crillon, her plans change. She cares not that he's married; using her beauty as her weapon, she sets out to seduce him.

But little does she know, there's another man in her midst, waiting for the perfect time to take her for himself. It is in his arms that Lysette is destined to find that true love and sanctuary she seeks.

Delphine
(The French Maiden Series - Book Three)

Unable to deny the attraction that simmers between them, Delphine and Andre fell willingly into one another's arms on their long journey from Canada to France. But after an impassioned night, come morning, the ship has docked, Delphine wakes alone, and Andre has fled.

Scorned, Delphine soon finds herself determined to avenge her broken heart. But a love that will not be denied soon gets in the way of her journey to vengeance.

Gold as the Morning Sun

Seeking to ease her ailing father's mind as his body fails him in his final days, Callie Southgate agrees to marry the mail-order groom sent to her from back east. When she meets her husband, she is timid around the handsome but mysterious man. But when they marry, she finds passion she never knew in his embrace.

Jace Greer, a con-man and bank robber, is given the perfect opportunity to start over when the stagecoach carrying a mail-order groom is ambushed, leaving Callie's future husband dead. Taking on the deceased man's identity as his own, Jace continues to Callie's home in Colorado with the hope of leaving his murderous past behind him.

But as true love blooms between Jace and Callie, secrets Jace tried to keep buried begin to surface, threatening their futures—and their lives.

The Ring

Prudence Allbright believes Lord Jamie's declarations of love—so much so that she vows to follow him to the Colonies. It is onboard the ship that will take her to him that she meets the honorable Dr. Ross Manning, and a flame of passion ignites.

Ross is determined not to defile the memory of his late wife, but night after night he longs to hold Prudence in his arms. When Prudence discovers Jamie has already gone back to England without her, Ross knows he may have only one last chance to claim Prudence as his own. But can love stand against the secrets of Prudence's past?

Summer Darkness, Winter Light

Allegra Baniard is an independent young woman who lives for only one thing—revenge. Her family had been branded traitors and banished from Shropshire. After eight years, she returns incognito to the ancestral home of her once-noble family, vowing to avenge her family. But when she meets Greyston Morgan, the new owner of Baniard Hall, he ignites desires inside of her that burn as hot as her fiery rage.

Caught between her own love and hatred, Allegra must decide whether to destroy Grey, or surrender to the flame of passion between them.

My Lady Gloriana

In this twist on the Pygmalion story, a duke makes a wager that he can bed the uncouth Lady Gloriana. But the bet takes on a life of its own...

The year is 1725. Lady Gloriana Baniard is a beautiful fish out of water. Brought up on the mean streets of London, she is a brash, blunt, obscene force of nature. But thanks to a brief marriage to a disgraced aristocrat, she is forced to live with his noble family and endure the humiliating process of learning to be a lady. Rebelling, she runs away to Yorkshire, where she intends to be a blacksmith, a skill at which she excels. She knows she'll need a manservant to front for her. When John Thorne appears, she hires him, stirred as much by his irresistible attraction as by his strength.

John Haviland, Duke of Thorneleigh, is an arrogant, indolent gambler and womanizer. Having seen Gloriana just once, he yearns to make her his own. When he learns she has run away from her family, he makes a wild bet with his wastrel companions—he will find the lady and bed her. Disguised as a humble servant, he becomes her assistant, learning the blacksmith trade. The clash of wills between these two proud people creates more sparks than a blacksmith's anvil, as Gloriana learns to be a lady, Thorne learns humility—and desire deepens to love.